Novels with Terence Brady:
VICTORIA
VICTORIA AND COMPANY
ROSE'S STORY
YES HONESTLY

Television Drama Series with Terence Brady:
TAKE THREE GIRLS
UPSTAIRS DOWNSTAIRS
THOMAS AND SARAH
NANNY
FOREVER GREEN

Television Comedy Series with Terence Brady:
NO HONESTLY
YES HONESTLY
PIG IN THE MIDDLE
OH MADELINE! (USA)
FATHER MATTHEW'S DAUGHTER

Television Plays with Terence Brady:
MAKING THE PLAY
SUCH A SMALL WORLD
ONE OF THE FAMILY

Films with Terence Brady:
LOVE WITH A PERFECT STRANGER
MAGIC MOMENTS

Stage Plays with Terence Brady:
I WISH I WISH
THE SHELL SEEKERS
(adaptation from the novel by Rosamunde Pilcher)

GOODNIGHT SWEETHEART

Charlotte Bingham

BANTAM BOOKS

LONDON · TORONTO · SYDNEY · AUCKLAND · JOHANNESBURG

TRANSWORLD PUBLISHERS
61–63 Uxbridge Road, London W5 5SA
A Random House Group Company
www.rbooks.co.uk

A BANTAM BOOK: 9780553817812

First published in Great Britain
in 2007 by Bantam Press
a division of Transworld Publishers
Bantam edition published 2008

Addresses for Random House Group Ltd companies outside the UK
can be found at: www.randomhouse.co.uk
The Random House Group Ltd Reg. No. 954009

The Random House Group Ltd supports The Forest Stewardship
Council (FSC), the leading international forest certification organisation.
All our titles that are printed on Greenpeace approved FSC paper carry
the FSC logo. Our paper procurement policy can be found at
www.rbooks.co.uk/environment

Typeset in 11/14pt Palatino by
Kestrel Data, Exeter, Devon.
Printed in UK by
CPI Cox & Wyman, Reading, RG1 8EX.

2 4 6 8 10 9 7 5 3 1

*To the unsung heroines of
the First Aid Nursing Yeomanry
and of
Special Operations Europe
1939–1945*

Prologue

Events of the past so often become more than they truly were, most particularly to those who were not there. Here is placed an assumption, there an undue emphasis – master and servant, mistress and maid, the first insensitive, the second inevitably downtrodden. Often, too, placed in the hands of those that were not there, the past becomes either a place of darkness or a landscape lit only with blazing floodlights, without even a suggestion of dappled shade, or gentle breezes.

Occasionally, a photo album, a love note from a supposed mistress, a card bearing the profound condolences of some patrician writer to the grieving – the writer a duchess, the grieving a former maid – speaks of a different world where friendly formality, not unlike the neat edging of lawns around an abundant border, might have made for a calm, which, in contrast to the present, would seem deceptively serene.

And so it is with the mural painted by Walter Beresford. Visitors to the house can stand before it and perhaps enjoy something of the past of which they were previously unaware, a feeling of ease that springs quite naturally from each personality depicted. It is as if the people painted on the wall are aware that they have each been assigned a role that they must play as best they can. As if, too, they know that what they are, what they are wearing, indeed everything about them, will quite soon be as fascinatingly old-fashioned as the house upon whose wall they are displayed.

To begin with the maids: Trixie and Betty. They are wearing their uniforms not with an air of servitude, but with pride, and if you look closer the expression in their eyes is at quite delightful odds with the strict decorum of their starched uniforms. Young Trixie, cap set on a thick spread of dark curls, seems to be staring out at the painter really quite critically, as if saying, 'Watch where you put those brushes and paints on my nice clean floor, Mr Painter.' And Betty's face, while innocent enough, reflects a firm ambition, the set of the mouth and the look in her eyes marking her out as quite determined on improvement. Neither of these girls is going to stay in service if she can help it. Then there is Trixie's father, Raymond, chauffeur and handyman. He has set his chauffeur's hat under his arm, and his expression is as commanding as any High Court judge. Standing with his favourite motor car behind him, he is wearing old-fashioned chauffeur's clothes, a long dark coat and black breeches tucked into long leather boots. Of course, by sporting this costume he wants you to know that he may be a chauffeur now, but he can also ride, and his father and his grandfather before him were in charge of the horses, long before the invention of the internal combustion engine.

And so to the family, who are not standing together in

a formal group but threaded in and out of their servants, or standing about the garden, or by the river with their dogs and ducks. The painter's intention, it seems, was to make sure that Mr and Mrs Anthony Garland, their twin sons and their two daughters look no more important than their servants. They are all quite simply part of a lively, but passing, scene. So much so that a detached observer could be forgiven for expecting that any minute now all the people depicted will step down from the wall, and very soon they will hear their laughter, listen to their gossip and their chatter, watch them dining, dancing, picnicking, fishing in the river that runs through the grounds, admire their grace and their kindness, perhaps even cry for them . . .

PART ONE

'Will it never begin?'

Chapter One

Caro was aware that she was probably the only person excited about the arrival of the fashionable painter, for this reason perhaps she had spent the greater part of the morning pretending to interest herself in Katherine's ball gowns, while secretly waiting only for the arrival of the artist.

The dress that her elder sister was currently sporting was blue, with immense silver sleeves. Privately, Caro herself did not particularly like it, but Katherine obviously did, perhaps because it showed off her long swanlike neck; and it *was* swanlike. Everyone had always remarked on Katherine's beautiful neck. It was a fact.

'How about these ones?'

Katherine was holding up a pair of black evening gloves with small pearl buttons that did up with a neat little glove hook. She held them against the blue sheen of her ball gown, while tossing back her dark hair, which was almost as black as the long, long gloves.

'Very *femme fatale*, lovey.'

Caro was sitting on the window seat, which overlooked the drive, so she was able to see all the visitors that

15

morning: the postman, twice within an hour, because he had forgotten to bring a parcel; the lady from the village, who came for second-hand clothes to sell for the orphans; the grocer in his van, who stopped at the front of the house, as if to register his presence, before moving slowly off down the back drive towards the tradesmen's entrance.

'Don't say "lovey", Caro. You're too old for that kind of talk, really you are.'

Katherine did not look round at Caro as she told her younger sister off, but rolled her eyes at her own reflection in the dressing mirror. Really, Caro was eighteen; you'd have thought that she would have become more sophisticated by now.

'I know I'm too old, but because I'm the youngest I always feel younger than I really am,' Caro murmured, as usual unable to resist taking up the challenge of her sister's quite open despite. 'Actually I don't just feel yards younger than you, dearest Sis, I also feel horribly plain; but with your looks, you wouldn't know what that feels like, Katherine, would you? Such a burden for you to be a beauty, to never hear people say, "Well, *we* all know who has drawn the long straw as far as *looks* are concerned,"' she added mischievously, while pretending to pull a sad face.

Katherine did not turn to look at Caro, but continued to stare at herself in the mirror. They had both long ago accepted that poor Caro was not, and never would be, a beauty.

'You're perfectly pretty, and you know it,' Katherine stated absently, while not denying that she herself was not merely pretty, but beautiful.

16

'And you're too, too kind, my deah. But I am quite sure, looking as I do, that I shall probably never, ever marry,' Caro went on, pretending to sob uncontrollably, putting her head in her hands, while watching Katherine's reaction through her fingers.

'Oh, you'll marry all right,' Katherine stated absently, paying absolutely no attention to her younger sister's pretend histrionics, not even turning from the mirror in front of which she seemed to have been frozen. 'It's *who* you marry that will be the crux of the matter. You could marry anyone, Caro, but what you want to do is to make sure that you marry *someone*.'

Caro pretended not to hear; she also pretended not to have spotted a pale grey, open-roofed motor car, which was even now pulling up below, outside Chevrons' double front doors.

From her window seat she could see that the car was being driven by a tall man wearing a light suit. He pulled on the brake, but for a moment did not get out of the car, remaining in the driver's seat, possibly drinking in the vision of the beautiful white-painted, delightfully rambling house, the back of which faced on to a wide, fast-flowing river, a part of which could just be seen from the front drive.

Upstairs Katherine remained mesmerised by her dressing mirror.

'It's a very good colour for me, this particular blue,' she murmured. 'David is right; he said it was a very good colour for me.'

At last Katherine moved, but not away from the mirror, merely turning slowly in front of it, black gloves now covering her arms. She held up her hair, seemingly absorbed in her own image.

Caro moved off the window seat just as the man below, having parked the motor car, was taking a straw hat from the back seat. After which he paced the drive, obviously admiring the house, as visitors always did when they first arrived, and for good reason. It was not just the deer under the trees, many of which were white, like the frontage of the house, or the distant sheep on the surrounding hills, it was the *feel* of Chevrons: the calm, the peace, the utter tranquillity of its surroundings.

Chevrons in early summer was idyllic, mystical. It was as if there had never been the Great War, as if not just Time had passed it by, but that time had decided to rest on his laurels there, to let the domestic idyll that was Chevrons seep into his ancient bones, and calm his frenetic hurtle towards his next engagement.

Caro herself always thought the magic of Chevrons lay in the fact that the house was so much off the beaten track that it surprised you when you came across it so suddenly. Perhaps because of this her directions to visitors were invariably the same.

'You toddle along the main road until you are about two miles from Speytesbury, but you must be careful, because if you aren't looking you will whoosh past it; but if you just toddle along quite slowly and pay great attention, suddenly you will find there's a little sign which says, in quite small letters "Private", which is where you must turn off, being careful of the potholes in the road, which are really quite huge, I'm afraid because . . .'

But of course even as she issued instructions to

visitors, Caro was well aware that, careful though they might be to follow her instructions, there would be no inner warning voice to say to them, 'Just wait till you see this.'

This would also have been true for their newly arrived painterly visitor as he had turned off the main highway and bump, bump, bumped down the narrow lane, with its tall bramble hedges, which at this time of year would be full of madly scrambling wild honeysuckle and nesting birds, and rabbits that scuttled out in front of his car, and then disappeared into the thick hedges at a vague, arrogantly slow pace, giving the impression that, as far as they were concerned, all was well with the world. Sometimes a hare could be seen in a nearby meadow, staring with momentary interest at the approaching motor car, before cantering off on far more urgent business than the rabbits, so urgent that it could wait for no one, not even the new king.

The visitor was looking around him with a puzzled expression, as if he was thinking, why did no one warn me about the beauty of this place? For in its way, Chevrons was quite perfect, not just because the house was so pretty, and yet, being only two storeys high, held no pretensions to grandeur, but because it was so well set in its grounds.

Caro's father, Anthony Garland, always said that Chevrons was the kind of house that Englishmen dream of coming home to when they are abroad. Not too grand, not too fussy, not the kind of house that overpowers human beings. It had not been built following a great military victory, or to make a statement of power, it had been built a century and a half before by a young squire as a wedding present for his bride.

Caro always thought that something of their happiness had stayed on in the old house. As a child, on rainy days, she had wandered down the light-filled corridors and up the wide wooden staircase, imagining that she could hear the happy laughter of the first Mr and Mrs John Anthony Garland as they played with their children and their pug dogs, or rode out together into the surrounding country-side, cantering into the far-flung woods where often on a summer's day they would picnic beneath trees that had seen a thousand just such summers.

The portraits of the Garlands down the centuries reflected the line of both humans and pug dogs that had continued without interruption right to the present day. Caro's father and elder brother had both been christened, in the Chevrons tradition, 'John Anthony Garland', which actually was a kind of living hell for young Jag – as the elder twin had inevitably been nicknamed at school – most especially if his father opened one of Jag's bills by mistake. But it was also comforting because it meant that by retaining the same names, the Garlands did not need to remind themselves, or indeed the rest of the world, that after all these years their line had survived, that they had gone on, despite, as Jag, and Francis, his twin, always joked, 'war, pestilence and sheep's feet'.

However, it was largely thanks to judicious husbandry and to the sheep – and their sometimes troublesome feet – that the Garlands had always lived well, if not extravagantly. Certainly they had never been in danger of starving, Chevrons coming as it did with a parcel of land amounting to a little over four hundred acres. Admittedly it was not good land, certainly not land on which to build, for once away from the house and the river, it sloped gently upwards, but it was good heath land, which drained well, the winter rains running down into the river, thus enabling generations of Garlands to keep, and prosper, from their herds of famous Garland sheep.

The kitchens were too busy that day for Trixie Smith to pay any attention to the arrival of the new house guest. Her father, Raymond Smith, chauffeur and handyman to the family, as his father had been before him, was busy polishing his shoes in the boot room, while Trixie and the rest of them were occupied making luncheon for the family.

To the continuing relief of Cook and her attendants, Mr Garland Senior liked only good standard English food. For lunch he liked a thin soup, followed by a pork or meat pie, or something similar, then invariably, most invariably, apple crumble and Cheddar cheese, the whole washed down by light ale served in pewter tankards. His wife, on the other hand, preferred only a hard-boiled egg salad and a glass of water, although she sometimes did eat a little cheese on its own.

When she did, Mr Garland always said, 'Having a little piece of naked, are you, Meriel?' which for some reason they both always found funny.

Trixie had been serving in the dining room now for over a year. She was immensely proud of the fact that she had moved upstairs at a much younger age than any of the other maids. Betty, Trixie's best friend, although two years older and still not used in the dining room, remained resolutely unimpressed by her friend's elevation.

'You have friends at Court, you get a leg up. That's well known, that is. Nothing to do with your quality, everything to do with being Mr Smith the chauffeur's daughter,' she would remark every now and then.

Trixie always made sure to laugh at this. She knew she was pretty and bright, and both she and Betty knew that she had ambitions far beyond the dining room and kitchens at Chevrons.

'Be that as it may, chauffeur's daughter or maid of all work, it means the same to me, because I'm going up, up, up, Betty, and no one, not you, not no one can stop me, you know that?'

At this standard Trixie-type reply Betty would sigh and nod, then sigh again. Unlike Trixie, Betty was from the local orphanage, and appreciated only too well how lucky she was to be employed at all, let alone at a fine house such as Chevrons, and then only because Mrs Garland took such an interest in the orphanage, having been an orphan herself.

'My dear,' she would say to Trixie, whenever Trixie was standing in for Mrs Garland's personal maid on her day off, 'I am only too well aware of how it feels to be poor little Betty, truly I am. It is terrible not to have some sort of family, and to always feel that you are a burden to everyone is truly dispiriting, even when one is only a child, and therefore not of any consequence.'

Trixie would observe a reverential silence at this, knowing that Mrs Garland's poor parents had both been lost in the *Titanic* disaster, and that the little orphaned girl had in consequence been passed from one set of relatives to another in swift succession, until the day when all the legalities had been finalised, and it was revealed that she was an heiress.

This fact being made generally known, all of a sudden, and to Meriel's bewilderment, a great many of the relations who had initially refused the orphaned child board and lodging were suddenly only too eager to open their doors to her.

'What a tremendous relief it was to finally reach my majority and to realise that the choice of a family was my own and no one else's, and then to meet Mr Garland, by the merest chance, in an art gallery where he was buying that painting . . .'

At this point in the story Mrs Garland would always gesture to a watercolour painting above their bedroom chimneypiece, an energetic depiction of waves splashing against mauve-hued rocks.

'That was the very painting that I had wished to buy, but for Mr Garland to give way and to allow me to purchase it in exchange for accompanying him to the theatre, how fortuitous that was, was it not, Trixie?'

Although Trixie had heard this tale many times, she always delighted in the retelling of it, revelling as she did in the same emotions as her mistress, albeit that they were necessarily second-hand.

First of all there was the loneliness of the young heiress valiantly making her way in the big city, a loneliness at which of course, having been brought up in a cottage on the estate at lively Chevrons, Trixie could only guess.

Then there was the spirited refusal to have anything to do with the relatives who had been only too glad to pass her on – that was a delightful moment in the story in which Trixie revelled unashamedly. Then again, for all this to be followed so swiftly by a chance meeting which had resulted in the happiest of marriages to Mr Garland turned it into a lovely story that Mrs Garland herself seemed to relish more and more; as if each time she re-told the story her own astonishment at her subsequent happiness was somehow confirmed by the repetition of the train of events that led up to her becoming mistress of Chevrons, and the mother of four children.

Something of the feeling of contentment that seemed to be so much part of the old house undoubtedly came from the Garlands themselves over the centuries. Their tenure of the estate had proved to be secure, untroubled and, to an outside observer, seemingly unremarkable. This would also appear to be true of the family. Indeed, their history was such that they seemed well content to remain unremarked outside of the county in which they lived, whilst going about their business with the kind of unassuming modesty that always encourages popularity in the English countryside.

Over the years of her marriage, Mrs Garland's reputation as a beauty remained happily undiminished. The result of this meant that she had sat to many famous painters, including the portraitist, Philip de Laszlo, and even now, although some few years past her fortieth birthday, when at a public gathering, her beauty and elegance attracted the kind of appreciative looks that delighted her husband.

Tonight Trixie knew Mrs Garland would be wearing the gown chosen by Mr de Laszlo himself for his last, much-admired portrait of her. She knew this because Miss Berenger, Mrs Garland's personal maid, had arranged the dress and all its accoutrements – underclothes, petticoat, jewels, hair combs – reverentially on the bed in the small dressing room that led off Mrs Garland's bedroom. The dress in the much-admired portrait downstairs was the same cherished dress now lying on the dark red quilt of the bed.

It was of a delicate cerise silk. The upper bodice was made of a contrasting grey gossamer silk, and the under-skirt, showing at least a foot beneath the upper silk, was of a toning oyster-grey colour. Across the overskirt, the underskirt and the bodice was laid yet more gossamer-like silk threaded with gold thread. The whole effect was of lightness and beauty. No one could pass this dress, worn or unworn, without stopping to admire its subtle beauty.

The design of the dress meant that the accompanying jewellery had, of necessity, to be of the simplest: a plain pearl necklace, and diamond and pearl earrings. Brocade shoes that exactly echoed the oyster grey of the under-skirt.

Trixie was always excited by the idea of standing in for Miss Berenger. It was not just a great privilege to help to dress Mrs Garland, it was a great compliment to Trixie that Miss Berenger always chose her over the other, older maids.

'Why me?' Trixie had asked the first time Miss Berenger had summoned her to the inner sanctum of Mrs Garland's dressing room.

Miss, actually Mademoiselle, Berenger, small, thin, and seeming to the rest of the staff to be really quite Frenchified – although actually Belgian – had straightened herself and pulled sharply down on her already elongated cardigan before answering.

'Mrs Garland – she has to have someone bright around her, otherwise socially she suffers from her *nerfs*. If there is to be a change of her clothes-es it must be executed with confidence and intelligence. She cannot be handled as if she is an animal in the field, you know, push, prod, push, prod. *Beside*, you have small, neat fingers, as I, so you will be quick with the buttons and the laces, no?'

And Trixie *was* quick with the buttons and the laces, and she *was* bright and always smiling, as well as determined that she would do everything possible to make Mrs Garland's life better and better.

There were surprises, of course.

Until she stood in for Miss Berenger and had been warned by the older woman, Trixie had always thought that grand ladies such as Mrs Garland were confident, and moved in Society without any degree of what Miss Berenger called '*nerfs*' and what Trixie called 'nerves', but this was just not so. Before a grand ball, Miss Berenger had warned Trixie, Mrs Garland was apt to become uncertain of her choice of gown, or of how to wear her hair, or which necklace to choose. It was necessary to talk to her in a calm and soothing manner, as you would a child.

Tonight was just such a night. The Lord Lieutenant of the County was giving a grand ball, there would be royalty present – not King George or Queen Elizabeth, but some of their princely relatives, who at this time of year, lived, or stayed, at various points in the county.

'Do you really think this old gown will do, Trixie?'

Trixie's eyes travelled from Mrs Garland, seated in front of her dressing-table mirror, to the gown on the bed. Surely this heartbreakingly beautiful creation could not possibly be described as an 'old gown'?

'I know Mr de Laszlo designed it for me, but it was rather a long time ago, Trixie,' Mrs Garland continued. 'And although I have never yet worn it to a ball in the country, nevertheless . . .' Her voice tailed off as if her confidence in Mr de Laszlo's taste had tailed off over the years.

Mrs Garland stood up, went to the side cupboard and took out a discreet decanter, which Trixie knew contained her favourite gin. While she poured some into a glass and drank from it as if it were medicine (which to her it most likely was), Trixie, used to this pre-ball routine, thought quickly.

Now that she looked at it more closely, Trixie could see that the dress *was* a trifle old-fashioned. Not that any beautiful gown ever aged, but this creation did not have all the up-to-date details that she knew Miss Katherine's gown would be flaunting. Nevertheless it was still truly beautiful.

'A thing of beauty is a joy for ever, Mrs Garland, ma'am – at least, that is, as I understand it – and as you have not worn this gown since Mr de Laszlo painted you in it, you will, I am sure, be the belle of the ball, as beautiful as a May morning, just like your painting downstairs. Every eye will go to you, every eye will – will – *dwell* on you.'

Perhaps it was the gin from the decanter, perhaps it was Trixie's carefully chosen words of encouragement – she was proud of remembering that word 'dwell' from her reading – but Mrs Garland returned to her dressing table once more, and they resumed their routine. Trixie dressed her mistress's long dark hair with expert twists and a modest use of the curling tongs on the upswept curls about her pale face, before finally pushing her evening combs firmly into place. The combs, Miss Berenger had taught Trixie, must always be pushed first one way and then the other, so that they glittered discreetly and there was never any danger of them falling out. They both knew that the correct placing must hurt, but whenever Trixie pushed in the combs Mrs Garland's face in the mirror never, ever betrayed even the slightest emotion. She hardly blinked, but more often than not continued to powder her nose with the large powder puff on a stick, which she dipped delicately into a cut-glass bowl filled with her favourite Houbigant face powder.

Trixie had learned to admire so much about Mrs Garland: her beauty, her elegance, her gentle manner, but most of all her ability to hide pain. Once, very early on, when she was with Mrs Garland in her dressing room Trixie had dropped the hot hair tongs into her mistress's lap, and as bad luck would have it, just before Mrs Garland was due to host an important dinner party downstairs.

It was proof of Mrs Garland's quality of character that she had not uttered a sound, even though the tongs had burned right through one of her best silk petticoats. Instead of losing her temper, as she might have been expected to do, she had merely smiled and returned the tongs to Trixie saying, 'Oh dear, Trixie, I'm always doing that!'

Of course they had both known that she was *far* from always doing any such thing, but it was her thoughtfulness, her adamant refusal to admit that her leg had been scorched and her petticoat ruined, that brought about Trixie's understandably unwavering devotion to her mistress. Indeed, she had become so devoted to Meriel Garland that she often felt that, if asked, she would not hesitate to give her life for her. Mrs Garland was a proper lady, not like the jumped-up ladies who sometimes came to dinner at Chevrons. Those pretend people talked in over-loud voices, and went out of their way to be rude to the servants at every possible turn.

No, as everyone at Chevrons knew, Mrs Garland was a lady all right, from the top of her head to the soles of her elegant feet. Because of this she had become the standard bearer, the marker, the person whom, above all others, Trixie wanted to be like.

It might have been a cause of some surprise to those who knew the Garlands socially that, due to the steady decline of sheep farming and the increase in lamb imports, in all her long years of marriage Mrs Garland's dress allowance had never been increased, which meant that Miss Katherine, and soon, Trixie presumed, Miss Caro, had to be dressed from the same allowance as their mother. Trixie was aware that this was the reason that, rather than buy herself something modish for the ball, Mrs Garland had plucked the de Laszlo creation from the back of the wardrobe and had Miss Berenger clean and press it to within an inch of its life, thus saving money, and allowing Miss Katherine to shine in either her brand-new Piguet satin frock, or, failing that, the dark blue Maggy Rouff-designed ball gown, which was undoubtedly quite beautiful.

However, just as Trixie had confidently predicted, once dressed in Mr de Laszlo's original choice of gown, Mrs Garland looked quite as stunning as when she had first sat to the painter.

Trixie stepped back to admire her.

'If you don't mind me saying, Mrs Garland, ma'am, you look just as you do downstairs in the painting that I have always enjoyed dusting, even though it does mean climbing stepladders. You look as young and beautiful as ever, truly you do.'

Meriel laughed. 'You must have Irish blood, Trixie,' she said. 'Either that, or you have kissed the Blarney Stone.'

Trixie shook her head, not bothering to reply, still staring at her beautiful mistress with adoring eyes.

'Every head will turn when you enter the ballroom tonight, Mrs Garland, ma'am,' she murmured, as Meriel walked elegantly ahead of her on to the landing.

As bad luck would have it, at that moment Miss Katherine, too, was emerging from her bedroom, so mother and daughter paused at precisely the same moment, preparing to walk, or sway in the accepted manner, hips slightly forward, down the large staircase to the hall below.

Trixie could have kicked herself for opening the door before looking out for Miss Katherine, for whom she had no love whatsoever. Miss Katherine might be the toast of the county, and Mrs Garland might love her, but such was her sharp tongue and her haughty ways of late, few other people who knew her could, or did, any more.

'Katherine, you look beautiful,' Meriel murmured.

There was a small pause during which the ever-loyal Trixie hoped that Miss Katherine would return the compliment. After all, no one could say that her mistress did *not* look beautiful because it was quite evident to anyone with eyes in their head that she blooming well *did*.

'Thank you, Mummy,' Katherine replied, before waiting for her mother to walk downstairs in front of her.

'What a good choice, the blue, a perfect choice for this evening,' Meriel went on valiantly, even as she knew that hers was a lost cause. Her elder, more beautiful, daughter had changed so much in the past two years. *Her* Katherine seemed to have gone far away, spiritually, if not physically, lost to her parents, although not for good, her mother hoped and prayed.

As her mother preceded her down the stairs, Trixie hovered on the landing above them, waiting to hear what Miss Katherine might say, or if indeed she *did* say anything.

Finally the beautiful lips parted.

'I am surprised, Mummy, truly I am, I am surprised that you are wearing *that* gown. I mean, I really thought you might have gone for something *new* for this evening.'

For a second Meriel looked back at her daughter, the expression on her face one of calm disinterest, before she continued down the stairs, but Trixie knew from the sudden tilt of her mistress's head, the sudden anxious smoothing of the silk of her dress, that Miss Katherine's comment had taken away what little remained of her mistress's confidence, and not even the glass of gin would now help overcome her sense of disquiet. Not that Mrs Garland was shy – she was too unselfish to be shy – but she did lack confidence, particularly when Miss Katherine was around her. The truth was that if someone was always out to find fault with a person it was difficult to put one foot in front of the other without becoming convinced that you were about to trip.

Seconds later Trixie returned to Mrs Garland's dressing room and, going straight to the glass that Mrs Garland had left, she finished up the remaining gin.

'Ooh, caught you!'

Trixie turned to see Caro, who had crept into the room after her.

'Yes you did, you caught me all right.'

Seeing the furious look in Trixie's eyes, Caro pulled a little face.

'What is bugging you this evening then, Trixie Smith?'

'Bugging me is right,' Trixie agreed, beginning to put away all the paraphernalia that had been left about after dressing Mrs Garland.

Caro sat down suddenly and thankfully on her mother's dressing-room bed, but Trixie waved at her indignantly.

'Off that bedcover, please, Miss Caro. That's silk, that is. Off of it, I tell you.'

'No, shan't and won't budge until you tell me what's bugging you – go on, what's bugging you?'

'Miss Katherine, that's what's bugging me,' Trixie muttered, after a short pause. 'Your mother, Mrs

Garland, is looking like something dropped from heaven, though I say it myself, and then what happens? Out comes Miss Katherine, all got up like some sort of Parisian doll—'

'And looking quite beautiful too. Katherine *does* look beautiful this evening, doesn't she, Trixie? Although, if you really want to know I think the sleeves on her dress are a bit much, just a half-inch too tall, but if anyone can carry them off, Katherine certainly can.'

'Oh yes, Miss Katherine *looks* beautiful all right,' Trixie agreed, grimly, 'but *being* beautiful is another thing. Now take Mrs Garland: this evening, she *looks* beautiful and she *is* beautiful, which is more than can be said, saving your presence, of Miss Katherine.'

'I know but you see, Trixie, Katherine is still a *young* beauty, and that's quite difficult, because everywhere she goes people sigh in admiration, and we don't know what that's like, truly we don't, do we?' Caro informed the maid in a kind voice. 'It must be very difficult, so we can't expect her to be nice too, really we can't.'

She said this in such a matter-of-fact voice that Trixie had to laugh.

'You're a one, you are, Miss Caro.'

'You bet I am,' Caro agreed, standing up and, to Trixie's relief, at last smoothing out the wrinkles in the silk bed-cover. 'Now come on, let's get reading before someone finds out where we are . . .'

As they read together, Trixie kept one ear open for the downstairs bell, and Caro, one ear on the departing guests, both girls worried in case someone came up and found them together in Mrs Garland's room.

Caro said, 'I say, this is nice and cosy, isn't it, Trixie? And this story is really exciting, don't you think? It's actually one of my favourites.'

Trixie looked up, at the same time stabbing her finger under a word on the page to keep her place.

'It would be more exciting if you'd stop interrupting, now wouldn't it?'

'Yes, yes, of course, I suppose it might,' Caro agreed, pulling a little face. 'But do admit these little detours add a lot to our sessions.'

Trixie looked down at the words again.

'You've been born with charm, you have, Miss Caro.' She looked up, remembering what Mrs Garland had said to her. 'You've got Irish blood, I expect; kissed the Blarney Stone too, I dare say.'

Caro smiled, and sighed with contentment, if only because the attention was back on herself.

'I say, Trixie, did you know the painter person has arrived?'

'Course I did.'

'He's downstairs now, in the Long Room – "setting up", I think he called it.' A dreamy look came into Caro's eyes. 'I think painting is the most exciting thing in the whole world, don't you, Trixie? Imagine being able to make a whole new excitement out of paints, all that colour at your fingertips; or like this man will be doing, painting for posterity, so that everyone will know how we looked now, in early summer 1939.'

Trixie looked vastly unimpressed by this idea.

'I just hope he puts down the dustsheets I left, that's all,' she said shortly. 'We don't want any nonsense in the

Long Room, not if Miss Katherine's going to have her twenty-first birthday party there.'

'Oh, Katherine's twenty-first birthday's not for ages and ages; anything can happen between now and then. But, you know, the Long Room is going to look so exciting with a great big wall painting with all of us in it. You and me, and Betty, and Miss Berenger, and Mrs Grant, and your father, and my father, and the boys, and even Katherine, if she'll deign to sit for it. Everyone will be in it, which means it will take quite a time, I should have thought.'

Trixie banged her finger back down under the words on the page.

'Come on, Miss Caro, we must get on with the story, because I'll have to go and help downstairs in a second, which is what I'm meant to be doing anyhow.'

Caro sat back and listened to Trixie reading, her finger now moving swiftly under the words on the page in front of her. She hardly needed to use her finger any more, although Caro would be the last to say so because, knowing Trixie as she did, she was certain that pretty soon this would be something that the maid found out for herself. Trixie had always been what Cook would call 'monkey quick', not to mention as sharp as Cook's best knife.

Of course, they both knew that Trixie reading out loud was about Trixie learning to speak properly. It was about leaving Chevrons, getting away from her upbringing, becoming something better than just a maid. In this Caro was at one with her, realising that while Chevrons might be nothing short of a country paradise to its younger daughter, for someone like Trixie it must serve only as a stepping stone to something better.

Caro held up her hand. 'No, Trixie, not "lie-lack"; no, you have to swallow the "lack" and make a sound more like "lake" except – ' she frowned – 'except not like "lake" either.'

'Well, make up your mind, Miss Caro. Either the blooming flower is a "lie-lack" or it's "lie-lake". Which is it?'

Caro frowned, momentarily stumped by the vagaries of correct standard English pronunciation, something that had never really bothered her until Trixie had collared her for their evening sessions.

'It's said more like "lie-luk" – that's it.'

Trixie, as she always did, got the point.

'Ssh!'

Trixie's hearing was so good, she could pick up the slightest sound, particularly that of a creaking stair.

'It's Mrs Hitler.'

They sprang up as one, and within a few seconds Caro was out of the room and passing their housekeeper, Mrs Grant, on the stairs, while Trixie, flushed but, as always, the picture of innocence, was found to be busy tidying Mrs Garland's clothes, the treasured copy of *The Lilac Tree* by Rosalie Gresham, well hidden under Mrs Garland's bed.

Downstairs, Caro passed as swiftly as she could across the hall and into the Long Room. As she closed the first of the two doors that led into it, she could hear more guests arriving and the twins' laughter. She noted the sophisticated chatter of Katherine and her friends as they gathered for drinks before going on to the Lord

Lieutenant's annual ball. Caro knew that David Astley, Katherine's great love, would be among the guests. Soon she would be able to smell cigarettes and imagine the admiring glances that her elder sister, in her ravishing blue and silver dress, would be attracting. In her mind's eye she could see the young men all crowding around her rather than any of the other girls, imagine Katherine stalking from the drawing room, closely followed by her clique of admirers.

'Who are you?'

Caro was so busy closing the door silently that she almost jumped at the sound of the male voice in the long wooden-floored room.

'I am Caro Garland, and goodness, you very nearly gave me a fit,' she said, turning round quickly. 'I mean, I knew you were there but—' She stopped.

She could not remember exactly what the painter had looked like without his hat, but now he *was* without his straw hat she saw that not only was he tall and slim, but also startlingly handsome. His features were not over-regular, so he did not look too pretty-pretty to be masculine. His nose was strong and straight; his mouth attractive, curving upwards at the side as if he smiled a great deal. But the main attraction of his face was undoubtedly his startling eyes. They were large and dark, and the look in them, it seemed to Caro, must surely mirror a passionate soul.

'I'm Walter Beresford. How do you do? I've already met your sister, Katherine.' He stared down at Caro momentarily. 'You don't look at all alike – but you know that.'

'Oh, yes,' Caro agreed cheerfully. 'Katherine is Proud

Beauty, whereas our father always says I am quite the opposite – a tomboy in skirts.'

Walter stretched out his hand and shook Caro's, barely touching it before walking down the room, already caught up in the excitement of creation.

'I was talking to Miss Garland a little earlier about how and where I would like to start, and it seemed to me that the ideal place would be here.' He pointed towards the large empty part of the wall. 'I made sketches last time I was down, and took measurements, but you were all on holiday. Now I have met your sister and your twin brothers, I think I must place them hereabouts, against the backdrop of the house, the water, and the garden. And I would certainly like to paint Proud Beauty in that blue dress she is wearing tonight, with the great silver wings – a bird of paradise indeed.'

He looked at Caro, who was now standing by his side, staring up at the blank wall and frowning as she tried to imagine what he had in mind.

'You're already quite famous, aren't you?' she asked factually, still studying the wall, her head on one side. 'I know I saw something about you in the *Tatler* about six months ago.'

'Did you indeed?'

He glanced at her briefly and without interest; indeed, his look was so vague that Caro immediately felt piqued.

'Yes, I did, I saw something about you in the *Tatler*.'

'Really?'

He was still staring at the wall, not really listening to her, but starting to walk up and down the room, treading

38

on the dustsheets that someone had had the foresight to put down already.

'Yes, I saw all about you in the *Tatler*,' Caro continued, raising her voice slightly. 'I particularly liked the pale turquoises you used for the mural for Bryan McMahon's house in Chelsea. They were very subtle, and not a little mystical, and combined with the unicorns, and so on, it was, I thought, all very Ancient World in feeling.'

If Mr Painter had known Caro at all he might have been alerted by her look of thoroughgoing innocence, but as it was he did not, so he walked straight into the trap.

'A young woman like you should be reading something better than the *Tatler*,' he joked absently, his back to her, as he once more went to work on preparing the surface in front of him.

'Really? Well just as well, for your sake, that I don't read something better, Mr Painter person,' Caro retorted sharply.

It must have been the tone of voice that she used, because at last he turned to look down at her instead of at the wall.

'For my sake? Just as well, did you say?'

'Yes, just as well.'

'Because . . . ?'

'Because it was me who pointed the piece out to Papa, which was why he asked you to Chevrons. Papa only reads accounts, and books on fishing and birds, which are actually his hobby, you see.'

Walter went to reply, and then shook his head and laughed instead, pulling at his forelock as he did so.

'In that case, thank you very much, Miss Garland. Now

I know that it's you I have to thank for the commission, I shall have to show more respect for you, won't I?'

Caro crossed her arms, staring at him with a determined look in her eyes.

'As a matter of fact, *yes*, Mr Painter.'

'And so will it be you then, Miss Garland, from whom I have to take orders?' Walter asked, adopting a rural accent.

'Not orders, no,' Caro retorted. 'But you will have to accept my help.'

He frowned. 'What do you mean by that, exactly?'

'I'll hand up your paints to you, that sort of thing.'

'Oh, you will, will you?'

'Yes, because you're going to need someone to do that, I should have thought.' She pointed to the height of the wall. 'Not only that, but you will need some stepladders, which I will get Betty to bring in for you, now I come to think of it. We can trust Betty.' Before Walter could reply Caro went to the chimneypiece, and tugged at a brass bell pull. 'Betty is the best person to ask things from – either her or Trixie,' she went on factually. 'I am marking your card, you see, because at Chevrons, although we are not grand like some of the houses around here, nevertheless there *is* a way of going on. The servants, you see, they rule *us*, and we have to let them, otherwise we would all be living in one room, with Mamma doing the cooking, which would mean bread and gruel, Papa says.' As Walter stared at her, she went on, 'If, for instance, you should ask Mrs Grant for some stepladders, which if you're doing a mural, you will surely need, I know that she would make quite sure to give you her very wobbly pair, because she will be hoping that you will immediately plunge to your death, or at the very least sustain terrible injuries, and so be forced to return to London to be put in plaster and bandages, never to return.' As Walter stared at her, she added gleefully, 'Mrs Grant doesn't like painters, or anyone else, as a matter of fact. She only really likes people plunging to their death off cliffs, or ladders, as I just said. That's all she reads out to Betty and Trixie – and me, of course – at tea-time: bits in the papers about murder and suicide and that sort of thing. Just now she is very cross with me for getting Papa to ask you down, because she knows you will be here for ever and ever, and that means that she will have to have either Trixie or Betty bring you trays of sandwiches, and cups of coffee. To her, you see, you're not a gifted painter, but just another mouth to feed, just someone making a horrid mess on the Long Room wall.' She produced a key from her skirt pocket with a flourish. 'I should lock the Long Room door at night too, if I was you, Mr Painter, or you might find that she has done a bit of her own decorating on your mural painting, with a pail of whitewash!'

Walter didn't laugh. He stared first at the key and then at Caro.

'Is the housekeeper really like that?'

'Do cats eat mice? Is Hitler beastly? Will there be a war? Life is more than a little interesting at Chevrons, Mr Beresford, and the sooner you find out, the better. Now I'll go and get some *safe* stepladders for you to climb, not wobbly or broken. I will get Smith's ladders; they are the only ones to be trusted.'

'Thank you.'

Walter stared after Caro, frowning, half wanting to turn on his heel and leave Chevrons, which now struck him as going to be a great deal of trouble, what with housekeepers waiting in the wings with buckets of whitewash to wipe out his work, and daughters who couldn't wait to put him in his place.

The real reason that he stayed on at Chevrons was, however, more powerful than any risks hinted at by Caro Garland. The reason he was staying was because he could not wait to paint the beautiful Miss Katherine Garland, of the haughty manner, the dark hair and the stunning figure, with whom, along with the rest of the world it seemed, he had fallen in love at first sight.

Chapter Two

'Katherine!'

'Yes, Daddy?' Katherine was at pains to look at her most innocent.

'Come into my study at once.'

'Yes, Daddy.'

Katherine followed her revered father into his large, book-lined study.

Anthony Garland went behind his desk and sat down. He did not invite Katherine to sit down, he merely leaned back in his chair and stared at her, his face – not unlike that of his elder daughter – looking pensive.

'You've been at it again, Katherine, and I have to be honest with you, I will not, I repeat, will *not* tolerate such behaviour.'

'No, Daddy.'

Katherine looked through her father, thinking only of what David had said to her as dawn broke that morning while Anthony wondered why she was the only one of his children to address him and Meriel as 'Daddy and Mummy'. Not that he minded, not that Meriel minded, but he knew that these subtle differences in his elder daughter meant that she was being influenced by someone outside the family. Doubtless the Astley man addressed *his* parents in such a manner.

'What is it that I will not tolerate, Katherine?'

Katherine hesitated. She had not returned from the ball until well into the small hours, having been enjoying herself far too much with David and his friends, plus she could not bear to miss out on the midnight supper of kedgeree and ham, of smoked salmon and delicious pies of every kind. The food at Haddington was always utterly, but utterly delicious, most especially compared to Chevrons' fare, which was plain to the point of being extraordinarily dull.

'You won't tolerate my bad behaviour?' Katherine volunteered, determined not to give herself away unless, and until, it was absolutely necessary.

'Can you imagine what would happen if this got out, Katherine?'

'No, Papa, I can't.' Katherine said, in an attempt to flatter him.

Anthony felt a small sense of relief at not being addressed in the modern manner, while Katherine found herself thinking hard. Who could have seen her returning as the dawn sky broke into what had seemed like a thousand pieces of pink and grey and white and blue? 'A piece of broken china of a dawn', David had called it. It could only have been that wretched Mrs Grant, whose cottage she had passed on her way to climbing in at the pantry window at half past five in the morning, which was all too probably about the time the housekeeper started to busy herself cooking ahead for her own family.

'You have got to control these unholy activities of yours, Katherine.'

Katherine frowned. She was not quite sure that 'unholy activities' would be a fair way to describe a late return from a ball. However, perhaps her father was becoming puritanical now that another war seemed to be looming so large.

'I can be sympathetic about anything, really almost anything,' Anthony continued, 'except the feeding of fox cubs. Can you imagine what would happen if any of our neighbours got to hear of it?'

Katherine went to say something but realising that if she did she would probably give way to giggles, she merely lowered her eyes and stared at the Persian rug on which she was standing.

'Papa?' she asked, once again returning to her childhood habit of address, having exercised huge control over her desire to collapse with laughter. 'Papa?'

'Yes, Katherine?'

'Do you think – ' she pointed down at the carpet – 'this is why people are always described as being "carpeted", Papa?'

Her father frowned, momentarily distracted, as indeed he was meant to be.

'How do you mean?'

'Do you think it was because one is always standing on a rug or a piece of carpet in front of someone's desk? Do you think that is why one is described as being "carpeted"?'

Her father frowned, then quickly stood up, waylaid, distracted but also immediately fascinated, as his

45

daughter knew he would be, by such a question. He darted towards his bookshelves and, taking down a huge volume, started to thumb through it.

'Yes, you're right,' he announced to Katherine, after a minute or two, while she made sure to keep her expression serious. '"Walk the carpet – to be reprimanded, 1820." Or, in another context,' he held up his hand as if she had been about to interrupt him. 'Or could be "bring on the carpet", which was used to mean the start of a meeting, when carpets covered tables – yes, that was the sign for a meeting to commence.'

'You're so clever, Papa,' Katherine murmured. 'I knew you would know.'

Anthony nodded, already preoccupied with such words as 'carpet knight' and 'carpet dance' and 'carpet road'; also 'carpet slipper', which was nothing to do with beds and nightgowns, but, apparently, actually a naval term.

'A "carpet slipper" was a shell that passed over the ship. Hmm. Well, you live and learn, you surely do. I wonder therefore where carpet slipper relating to footwear comes into the scheme of things; obviously much later, something to do with the Ottomans, perhaps . . . ?'

Katherine left him to his book of etymologies, and slipped quietly and silently from her father's study, her expression becoming grim the second she was in the hall. She had neatly sidestepped having to take the blame for feeding the blasted fox cubs, but that did not mean she herself was not going to carpet wretched Caro. She rolled up her sleeves mentally, and went in search of her.

She found Caro in the Long Room, contentedly sitting

on the bottom step of the ladders being used by Walter Beresford, who was busy with his mural.

Katherine beckoned Caro from the door.

'I'll see you outside!'

Caro shook her head, knowing that as long as she stayed at the bottom of the ladder within the protection of Mr Painter, not even Katherine would dare to *make* her do anything.

'I can't move, Katherine, really I can't. Not when I'm helping Mr Painter here,' she said, straight-faced, assuming a saint-like expression.

Walter stopped in the middle of a stroke, brush in hand, and turned to see Katherine standing below him.

'Good morning, Miss Garland,' he said, using measured tones to counteract the increase in his heartbeat that just the sight of her brought about. 'May we help you?'

Despite her outwardly resolute air Caro was more than grateful that by saying 'we', Mr Painter had taken it upon himself to unite the two of them, that they had become a duo, conversationally at least, in front of Katherine, who now, it seemed, was at pains to be at her most stern.

'Yes, you may help me—'

'Oh, sorry, did *I* forget to say good morning, Miss Garland?' Walter asked, lightly sarcastic.

Katherine coloured a little. 'Oh, yes, sorry. Good *morning*, Mr Beresford. Yes, it *is* a lovely morning, but I must have a word with Caro, if you don't mind, really I must. It is quite urgent.'

'Later perhaps. You might not have noticed, Miss Garland, but at the moment we are in full swing. As a matter of fact, just as well you did come in, because we were debating where might be the best place to put *you.*'

Katherine hesitated. She wanted to haul wretched Caro over the coals about the fox cub feeding, which she knew must be down to Caro *again*, but now that her position in the mural was being discussed she found herself neatly distracted, as her father had been minutes before.

'I would like you to put me, place me rather, somewhere there,' Katherine stated, having studied the outlines on the wall. 'By the water. I love water.'

'Good, then so be it. By the water, and in your blue dress, the one that you were wearing last night, if you will agree?'

'Oh, very well, if you think it's nice enough to be on a wall.'

'When will you be able to sit to me, do you think?'

'Perhaps this afternoon – no, I am going out – no, perhaps tomorrow morning, if that would be congenial?'

Walter did not answer for a few seconds.

'Yes, tomorrow morning would be congenial.' He looked down at Katherine's perfect complexion. 'You are not yet of an age when I would have to diplomatically postpone painting you until after midday.'

'How very reassuring,' Katherine said, shrugging her shoulders lightly.

She quickly left the room, feeling that in some way Walter had got the better of her, and it was only when she was climbing the stairs to her bedroom that she realised that she had forgotten to give dratted Caro a wigging, but since she was now on the landing and she did not want to be late for David and his people, she disappeared into her bedroom to powder her nose. Really, Caro and her fox cubs could wait until tomorrow. What David was planning for them both was much more important.

Downstairs, Caro stared up the ladder towards Walter.

'Is that true? Do you really have to wait to paint older ladies after luncheon?'

'After midday, certainly. They would not thank me for painting them after breakfast, I do assure you. Now tell me,' he glanced down at Caro, 'what was all that about?'

'All what about?'

'You know what I mean: the beckoning finger, the dark expression? Madam your sister was not altogether in a very good mood with you, was she?'

'Oh, you mean what was *that* all about?'

'Yes, what *was* all that about?' Walter murmured, staring up at the wall, while silently marvelling that Katherine Garland looked quite as beautiful in the morning as she had the evening before. She looked as beautiful in her many-buttoned yellow linen two-piece, with its double collar of matching linen and dark velvet – a silk scarf of a startling green paisley tucked into the neck – as she had looked in her great silver-winged blue evening gown.

'I am afraid that was all about Katherine coming in here to read me the riot act,' Caro sighed, mock sadly. 'I am just everyone's dogsbody round here, really a martyr to the inner life of Chevrons.'

Walter glanced down momentarily and laughed.

'What then has the poor martyr to tell me?' he asked, as he leaned forward once more to make a sharper outline on the wall.

49

'I can't tell you. It's a burning secret. I don't suppose, being a painter, you can keep a secret for more than one sitting, can you?'

'To whom have I to tell your dreadful secret, except the wall?' Walter murmured.

'Well, between you, me and the wall, of course, I have been doing something which is absolutely criminal.'

'Really? Shall I have to visit you in prison if you are caught?'

'No, but you might have to go looking for me and find me at the bottom of the lake in the wild garden.'

'Might I know why I shall find you at the bottom of the lake?'

'Yes, but you still mustn't tell anyone, not a soul, because it will be counted against me for the next six centuries.' Caro dropped her voice. 'I have been feeding foxes. Well, not foxes exactly, but fox *cubs*, although they are getting so big and fat now, they are beginning to look more like fox terriers than fox cubs.'

Walter looked down at the head of shining dark brown hair, which was all he could see of Caro at that moment.

'You are a minx, you know. You could be shot by your father's neighbours for doing such a thing.'

'Oh, yes,' Caro agreed gleefully. 'Shot at dawn, and my head hoisted up on a spike at London Bridge.'

'And that would be the least of it.'

'I know, I know, but the cubs were so thin, I had to help them. I hate to see animals, wild or domestic, looking thin and unhappy.'

'I understand, but even so, you must not do any such thing again, you promise?'

50

'I'll try not to, but I can't promise.'

'In that case *I* will only *try* to promise not to tell any-one.'

There was a long silence as Walter's point finally sank in.

'Oh, very well.'

'Good. Now move your body, Miss Caro Garland, and let Mr Painter down from his height. I need some per-spective, and not only that, I need some fresh air too.'

They stood outside the long windows, enjoying the fresh air, and as they did so a car, being driven rather too fast, drew up in front of the house. Because they were on the back terrace they themselves would not necessarily be noticed through the tall, iron gates that separated the terrace from the front of the house, but they could see, so inevitably they watched with interest as the occupant stepped out.

'That's the Astley man, as my father calls him – David Astley,' Caro said in a low voice, as Walter tried not to notice how Katherine Garland came galloping towards him, and how he, in his turn, put a guiding and, what seemed to Walter, a definitely possessive arm around her as he opened the door of his car.

'Are they engaged, your sister and this David Astley?' Walter drew on his cigarette, frowning.

'Sort of, not really. Well, yes, if you really want to know. As far as they are concerned, yes, they are engaged, but as far as my father is concerned, no, they are not at all engaged, and never will be.'

'Why not?'

Caro looked embarrassed. 'According to my father,

David doesn't quite fit the bill,' she admitted after a pause. 'My father, you know, is somewhat of a liberal, not a Liberal as in politics – I mean he's not a sort of Lloyd George or anything – but he is, well, all the Garlands are just countrymen, I suppose you would call us. As my father says, we are the kind of people who believe in looking after our little bit of England, while at the same time hoping to goodness everyone else will do the same. Work is our rent for life, my father believes, and my mother too, although she is more bohemian. She had an uncle who lived in Camden Hill and painted, and another uncle who was a poet, but died young.'

'As all poets must.'

'Yes, exactly. So that's why my father believes that David does not fit the bill, despite being the son of a neighbour and very good-looking. All that blond wavy hair, and the blue, blue eyes and so on does make him so very fascinating to girls, but it is Katherine whom he is besotted with, and has been since they were quite small, apparently.'

Walter turned about, and they strolled down the garden towards the view, which was of gently sloping hills and the slim line of a river making a vaguely green-silver line through the fields. He threw away his cigarette and, after a minute or so, put a brotherly hand on one of Caro's shoulders.

'Tell me more,' he ordered.

For the first few yards, with Walter's hand on her shoulder, Caro felt vaguely unsettled, but then, realising it was a compliment to their already easy friendship, she relaxed. Her father had always done the same thing when they walked along, talking, always talking, his hand on her shoulder.

'I don't know whether I *should* tell you any more,' she admitted.

'If I am painting you all, I need to know a little about you. Not too much, of course, but a little is helpful,' Walter stated.

Caro continued walking, stopping once or twice to pluck a piece of thick-stemmed grass, which she bit into, savouring the sweet fresh, familiar taste of early summer. After a while she handed Walter a nice piece, and they ambled along, once more separated, during which time Caro found to her surprise that she now missed his hand on her shoulder.

'I suppose you have to know a little about us,' Caro conceded, after a judicious pause.

'You can't paint people you know nothing about, at least not a great many people in one piece, I need to know something in order to assess the weight I give to each character's association with the house.'

Caro frowned. 'I expect that's just painterly tosh,' she told him after another pause. 'I expect you're just like the rest of us, a demon for gossip and innuendo.'

'You don't want me depicting cardboard cutouts, leaving posterity to believe the occupants of Chevrons were characterless, do you?'

Caro realised that there had to be at least some truth in what Walter had just said.

'Well, I dare say you will realise what a potpourri of people we are soon enough,' she reasoned. 'So there is not much use in my pretending that we are all plaster

53

saints, when in all honesty we are rather far from being so.'

'You are human beings, diverse, complex, fascinating, finally unfathomable.'

'It's not that Katherine and David's relationship is exactly a secret,' she admitted. 'It's just that it's rather embarrassing.'

'I am a painter, Miss Garland; I am not easily embarrassed.'

'I didn't mean that sort of embarrassing. Not life-class embarrassing, no, I meant embarrassing from a relative's point of view. After all, Katherine *is* my sister, but she's so unlike anyone else in the family now that she and David have taken up with each other. I mean, we have all known David and his brothers since we were born, but David too – *particularly* David – has changed so much in these last years, he's become the sort of person none of us can really like, yet Katherine adores him, can't see anything wrong with him, can't seem to mind or care that he has changed.'

'Now I really do have to know what is wrong with this Astley man. Come on, confess. You're jealous of your sister. You want this Greek god for yourself.'

Caro's colour deepened. 'No, of course I don't want him,' she snapped. 'I could never ever even *like*, let alone be in *love* with a Blackshirt.'

Walter stopped, removed the grass stalk from his mouth and threw it behind him.

'He's a . . . *Blackshirt*?'

Caro nodded, turning away, and she too threw away her grass stalk, treading on it with her foot as if it was a stub of a cigarette, before continuing to walk towards the view.

'Yes, David is as black as your hat, blacker than black. Well, your hat isn't black, but his shirt certainly is. Yes, he is a convinced Nazi, and as fascist as anything you could wish for. So embarrassing to say it, to have to admit it, but he is a Blackshirt.'

'You are teasing me, of course?'

'Don't you think I wish I *was* teasing you?' Caro asked sadly. 'Gracious heavens, we've all loved David for ever, and now this has happened: him falling in line with these beastly Mosley people, and going on rallies, and then taking Katherine down with him. It's breaking my parents' hearts, although they don't say so. That's why I thought it would be a good idea to have you here doing a mural, if you really want to know. I hoped that it would be a cheerful thing for them to see happening, take their minds off the Astley man and his bad influence over Katherine.'

There was a long pause as they continued walking.

'Well, yes, I do wish you were teasing me, but how sad for you and your family. Such a beautiful young woman to have her soul corrupted by something or someone so wrong-headed.'

'Yes. The truth is that Katherine was just like us, a real Garland from head to toe, until she fell for David after he came back from abroad. Then she seemed to change overnight because, we have all had to suppose, she must have become convinced by him. He spent a great deal of time in Germany and Austria, and I think someone there influenced him, and now it seems he has influenced *her*.

My mother says love changes people; and of course the fact that Katherine is so in love with David makes it even harder for my poor father to step in and try and convince her that her opinions are so misjudged as to be well . . . ludicrous.'

'This is truly a tragedy, most especially for a family such as yours.'

'Yes, and happily the twins and I can only *imagine* how difficult it is for my parents. We know they *do* suffer, although they would be the last to admit it. They don't want to estrange her – or him, for that matter. My father feels that to do so will only drive them closer, so he and my mother just have to carry on with the show, all the while hoping that Katherine will finally see sense, which I actually don't think she will, not for an instant.'

'Don't look sad.'

'It is sad. If you really want to know, she has told me many times that she is convinced that fascism is the only way to make the world a better place, and that she and David are all for getting rid of everyone they think harms this country. They say they are patriots – well, at least that is what they pretend – but to me that is just an excuse to drive everyone they don't like out of England. I have tried to argue with her. I mean, I keep saying, what happens if they get a leader who wants to get rid of people with red hair? Or a new leader is elected, say someone who hates people who are over six foot, or who have big noses or small feet? And then yet another leader comes along who hates people who are musical, or have brown eyes?'

'That would be me out, for a start,' Walter agreed,

sighing over-dramatically, before glancing down at Caro's small feet. 'And you too, Miss Garland, for I can see your feet are really quite small.' He paused. 'Could someone else perhaps persuade Miss Katherine Garland of the wrongness of her opinions, do you think?'

'No, I don't think so. At least . . .' Caro glanced up at him and then, having seen the look in Walter's large brown eyes, she turned away. She had seen that look in other men's eyes, other men who had fallen for her sister, only to have their hearts not so much broken as wrecked. 'Well,' she finished finally, feeling sorry for Walter for the first time, 'I suppose someone else could *try*.'

Walter brightened, because he dearly loved a challenge, but as his expression lightened, Caro's grew despondent. It was no use trying to explain to people, particularly male people, about Katherine. They all thought that because she was so beautiful on the outside, she must be beautiful on the inside too, but the truth was that nowadays she just wasn't. She was not only capable of pulling the wings off butterflies, given half a chance Caro was sure that Katherine would pull the blossoms off peach trees, or the fur out of a dog. She had become horrid beyond measure.

David kissed Katherine goodbye, not the way he would have liked to have kissed her, but the way the other members of the Party, some of whom were still standing around the drive, would like him to kiss Katherine, a quick peck on the cheek. Happily Katherine knew this, for they planned their every move together before, during and after every meeting of the Party.

Katherine smiled, remembering how they had kissed the night before in the Orangery at Chevrons – which was when she had come across the vixen and her cubs enjoying the scraps that Caro had left for them. David had looked handsome then, but now, as always after a meeting, he was looking most especially so; so handsome, in fact, that she knew that everyone at the meeting had been unable to pay proper attention to what he was saying, feasting their eyes instead on the looks of the ravishing young man standing before them on the rostrum.

'The meeting went well, didn't it, darling?' she said, a little over-brightly, because the mere handful of hours' sleep that she had managed that day were at last beginning to make themselves felt.

'Very well,' David agreed. He smiled, his handsome features, with their particular look of lazy charm, giving way to a brilliance of expression that Katherine always imagined was an echo of the faces of heroes of long ago.

'The Führer would be proud of you,' one of the older ladies at the meeting told him as she came up to shake his hand.

'He certainly would,' agreed another. 'He would be proud of you, and so would everyone in the Party. If they could they would be here cheering, and not in exile in France.'

'We will have Edward VIII as crowned king one day,' Katherine murmured.

'Of course we will. Mark my words, his brother will be proved to be powerless over our movement, as will everyone in this country who does not agree with us,' the respectably dressed older woman went on, before making a vaguely fascist salute and stalking off towards her car.

David stared after her, a thoughtful expression on his face.

'Without women like Mrs Billington and Mrs Raven the Party would be foundering.'

'It most certainly would,' Katherine agreed loyally, before she was forced to turn away and stifle a yawn.

'I will see you tonight, perhaps?'

'Not tonight, no. My father is giving a dinner for the newly arrived painter person.' She shrugged as David regarded her with a jealously protective look in his eyes. 'Nothing to do with me, I assure you. It was Caro who persuaded Daddy to hire Walter Beresford to do a mural in the Long Room.' Katherine looked helpless. 'I ask you, as if we have not enough on our minds with all this talk of war. Cook is already planning to leave to go to a factory where she can earn yards more money.'

'*We* will prevail before there is a war. Lord Halifax is on our side. He will not oppose the Führer and his Nazi Party, as some in the government want us to do.'

'I know that, David, you know that; if only we could persuade other people of the same.'

'We shall. One way or another, we shall.'

All this was overheard by people returning to their cars, with whom Katherine and David made sure to shake hands.

'We need more funds, truly we do, David. I have a bequest coming to me soon. I shall use it to help the Party.'

'And I too shall use whatever I can lay my hands on to help the cause.'

They smiled and shook hands with yet more of the Party members and officials, before climbing into David's car and driving off towards Chevrons.

'Goodbye, darling. See you tomorrow night at the Orangery, perhaps? It's safest for us to meet there.'

They kissed, and kissed, and kissed some more.

'It's so difficult to be parted.' David let go of her, most reluctantly.

'It certainly is,' Katherine said, feeling a little faint, as she always did after David had kissed her.

'But soon we shall not be parted any more.'

'You've heard something?'

'Yes.' The expression in David's eyes was sombre. 'We have to leave England, and sooner than we think. I have heard if things go against us we will be rounded up and imprisoned.'

Katherine nodded. Everyone knew that since spring of the previous year, the Anschluss, the Führer's invasion of Austria, had changed a great many things, and British people had at last come round to the idea that war could, after all, despite what Mr Chamberlain might say, be inevitable.

'I am due to hear from our people in Victoria. I'll let you know tomorrow night. It might all happen rather quicker than we imagined.'

Katherine's heart sank. She loved David deeply, but it was only now, after two years attending Party meetings, that the enormity of what she was doing was becoming a reality. She would have to leave home and follow David, no matter what. She might never see Chevrons again.

She reined in the sudden despair that was threatening to cloud her patriotism. They believed in England, in England's future; they must do their duty. Besides, it was too late to turn back now. They were beginning to go from an easy canter to a full gallop, about to face the biggest fence of them all, and they both knew it. They also knew that on the other side lay, not the sweet green grass of her father's meadows, but exile.

Following an enjoyable dinner with the family, Walter resumed working. A small interruption came when Caro brought him in a glass of whisky, and teased him that he had shot back to the Long Room because he was afraid of Mrs Grant and her bucket of whitewash; but the truth was that he had to prepare a great deal before the Proud Beauty, as Caro called her sister, came to sit to him, which she did, shortly after ten o'clock the following morning.

'You're late and you're not wearing the blue ball gown,' Walter said, speaking from the top step of his ladder.

Katherine looked up at him, and slowly raised a haughty eyebrow.

'I thought black would be more appropriate, given the present situation in Europe, everyone determined to misunderstand each other.'

Walter stared down at her, trying to read the expression in the young woman's beautiful blue eyes.

'Black is very smart, and of course, fashionable,' he agreed tersely, turning back to the wall while sighing inwardly, because the blue gown showed off the blue of her eyes, and he liked the great sweep of the sleeves. 'Black, I

61

must admit, does show up your necklace and earrings to a great degree.'

'How do you want me to sit to you?'

'I don't want you to sit to me,' he said firmly, at which Katherine gave a sharp glance up only to be rewarded with the back of his head. 'I want you to stand. You don't mind standing, do you, Miss Garland?' he finished.

'Why should I mind? I didn't commission you.'

Walter glanced at her as she pointedly tapped at her watch, before giving him a look that he immediately took to mean 'if it was up to me I wouldn't have commissioned you at all.'

Walter turned back to the Long Room wall, *his* wall, as he had already started to think of it.

'I am placing you walking beside the water here, as you said you wished,' he told her, pointing to the place with his paintbrush.

'Why beside? Surely you should have me walking *on* the water.'

Walter laughed.

'Why do you laugh? It's not funny. I meant it,' Katherine murmured, before turning her attention to straightening her skirt.

Walter turned back to the wall. Just for a second what her younger sister might have called 'the old Katherine' had seemed to be there – humorous, intelligent, even kind – but seconds later the look was gone, to be replaced by the cold, detached expression that he assumed was the new Katherine Garland, of the black dress and the even blacker views.

He began to sketch her figure and her dress in total silence, looking from her to the wall and back again. Minutes went by, and more minutes, and still he said nothing, until finally he stopped.

'It's no good, Miss Garland. I can't paint you, really I can't. The black gown, it's quite wrong for the composition, and most particularly in a bucolic setting. If you want to be by the water, as you stated, you will have to wear the blue dress.'

Katherine's mouth set in a mulish fashion. 'This is the dress I want to wear.'

'Yes, but unfortunately it is not the dress in which I want to paint you.'

'Why not?'

'I'm afraid, as I said, it is wrong for the painting, and besides, it doesn't inspire me. If you wish to be included in the mural I must insist you wear the blue dress.'

There was a long silence, broken at last.

'You can't force me to change. It is just not fair to force someone to wear something that they feel is wrong for them.'

Walter gave her a cool look. 'I agree with you. It is quite unfair to *force* anyone to do anything. I am quite against anyone *forcing* anyone. That is why certain political ideals are so wrong, don't you think?'

There was another long silence.

'At Chevrons we make it a rule never to talk politics with our guests,' Katherine finally stated, giving the painter's back a haughty look, which was naturally wasted on him.

He turned at this. 'Mmm, very wise, really, very wise

indeed, but the fact remains, Miss Garland, if you want to be in my painting, you will please go and change into the blue gown with the silver winged sleeves.'

Katherine drew in a sharp breath, and then she finally laughed, at the same time colouring, which caught at Walter's heart because it made her look yards younger, and endearingly vulnerable.

'Oh dear, I think you must win this one, Mr Beresford.'

'I hope so, Miss Garland.'

Katherine disappeared back up to her bedroom to change, finally emerging in her blue gown with the silver sleeves like great swan's wings, and looking more than ever like something dropped from heaven.

Walter studied her up and down, before walking round her.

'Much better,' he said, his tone not serious, but grave, as well it might be, because he knew with each glance from her to the wall, and from the wall to her, that he was becoming more and more fascinated by this tall, dark-haired, blue-eyed beauty.

He walked back again, and then took another turn around her.

'No gloves,' he said commandingly. 'You can put those aside, if you would, please. What I want you to do is to raise your arms a little, like so.'

Katherine started to laugh.

'You look rather good like that!'

Walter took no notice. 'Come on, come on,' he said, not smiling.

Katherine raised her arms.

'Good, that's better. Now we can begin.'

He picked up his palette and brushes, and climbed his ladder.

'The look in your eyes is becoming increasingly sad over these last sittings, were you aware of that?' Walter remarked some days later. 'I shall not ask you why, although there must be a reason.'

Katherine's expression became wry.

'Oh, don't you worry. That's just put on for you, Mr Painter,' she stated with sudden assumed gaiety. 'You should never smile for posterity – always look grave, full of thought, or else they will see you for the lightweight that you are!'

But Walter did not believe her because it was not just the look in her eyes that was sad. Katherine Garland's whole aura, in contrast to her beautiful gown and her breathtaking looks, had become tense and dark. It was as if she had just been told the day the world would end, or perhaps as if she had just been told the day *her* world would end.

'I wonder if you could do me a favour, Mr Painter?' she asked, quick to change the subject. 'I wonder if you would paint something on my finger? It's only very small, but if you could paint it where an engagement ring would be, if I had one, if I was engaged, I mean . . .'

'Very well. What is it?'

When she told him, Walter laughed. 'A ladybird – oh, very rural, and no trouble. Besides, I love them; they intrigue me.'

Katherine smiled. 'Yes, they are intriguing, aren't

they?' she agreed, and the expression in her eyes became oblique. 'Somehow not quite what they seem.'

A week later found Caro going to lunch with Robyn Harding. She put on a checked jacket with a large collar, and a wide matching skirt. It was a two-piece that Katherine had handed down to her, and which, slightly altered, the hem shortened and so on, she was pleased to think now fitted her without a trace of a hand-me-down look to it. At least she hoped it had none of that altered look that could come about when something was second-hand; but at any rate, to make quite sure, she had teamed it with a new silk blouse, because Robyn Harding was nothing if not chic. Older than Caro, she might more probably have been Katherine's friend, but Caro and she had more in common, sharing interests as they did in books and paintings, something for which, as it happened, Robyn's family, the Hardings, were not exactly famous.

Caro wandered into the back pantry where every key was carefully hung with a little gold notice above it, where all the bells for all the rooms were placed, their names also placed above them. Caro loved the decorative order of it all, which meant that, as always, she stared up at each name 'Mrs Garland's dressing room', 'Maids' recreation room', and so on, before beginning to search for the keys to Katherine's Fraser Nash six-cylinder BMW, with its fold-back blue roof.

'Can I help you, Miss Caro?'

Smith had appeared from nowhere, as he always seemed to when Caro wanted to go for a drive.

'Oh, yes, Smith, as a matter of fact you can, I'm looking for the keys to Miss Katherine's car.'

'You're not going to drive her, are you, Miss Caro?'

'As a matter of fact I am, Smith. Miss Katherine has graciously given her permission for me to do so, while she's sitting to Mr Beresford. Meanwhile I'm off to have lunch with Miss Harding at Brookefield.'

'I'll accompany you while you drive, Miss Caro. Rather that than you drive on your own,' Smith told her, as she wandered on ahead of him.

'Oh, don't worry, Smith, I shall drive quite slowly.'

In answer to this Smith himself breathed in and out quite slowly – so slowly and not a little noisily that, as Caro took the keys for the Fraser Nash, she was compelled to turn to look at him.

'As I remember it, we did end up in the ditch the last time we went to lunch with Miss Robyn, did we not, Miss Caro? And that was with me in the motor beside you.'

'Did we, Smith?' Caro was careful to assume her most innocent expression. 'Goodness, so we did. You were very good; you said nothing to my sister. I was grateful. But the car survived all right, didn't she? I mean, no dints or anything?'

'No dints, no, Miss Caro, but you, if you remember, were somewhat the worse for wear afterwards.'

'A few bumps and bruises, nothing to write home to Mother about, Smith. Anyway, serve me right for driving too close to the ditch. I'll be more careful this time. Promise.'

She put out a small gloved hand for the keys, and Smith, with every show of reluctance, but having given yet another heavy sigh, this time accompanied by eyes raised to heaven, reluctantly placed them in her out-stretched hand.

'*Try* not to drive so fast, Miss Caro.'

'Of course I will try, but it is difficult, Smith. It is more *Blue Angel*'s fault than mine. You know how it is: one puts one's foot down and you can almost hear her shouting, "Hurray for the open road." She is such a beautiful car. But I promise I will be careful of her. Anyway, you can comfort yourself that Brookefield is only a few miles away.'

Smith watched her walk off towards the garages. Miss Caro might seem to be quite the young lady now, but, since he had known her all her life, the chauffeur knew different. Very well, nowadays she was dressed in silk and tweed, but at heart she was still a tomboy, liking nothing better than to get into a scrape. And as for her driving – well, it chilled him to the marrow to think of what might happen if she met another car. Happily the distance between Chevrons and Brookefield House, as she had just stated, was only a matter of a few miles.

The distance between the two houses might be only a matter of a few miles, but if a measurement could also have been made of the distance between the lifestyles of the two houses, it might have stretched to a hundred, or even a thousand miles, such was the change in atmosphere once you entered Brookefield.

Robyn, tall, thin, and always accompanied by two small Cairn terriers, was already standing on the steps of the house, when Caro drove up with what she was now sure was practised élan, finally stopping at the bottom of the flight of steps that led to the front door.

'Well done, well driven! Gosh, she is a beauty, though, isn't she?'

Caro stepped out of the Fraser Nash. 'Hello, Robyn. Yes, she is. Just wish she was mine.'

The two girls kissed cheeks, and Robyn smiled appreciatively as Caro bent down to pat the terriers.

'Greetings Freddie, greetings Danny.'

Robyn found herself watching Caro with a detached eye, as if she was a camera photographing her friend. The world seemed yards warmer whenever Caro was about, probably because she was always so anxious for everyone else to enjoy themselves. Certainly it seemed to Robyn that Caro's underlying anxiety, her questing spirit, must actually fuel her enthusiasm for life.

'How's the Bentley?'

Robyn smiled. That was another thing about Caro, she always did ask all the right questions, and straight away.

'Very fast.'

They walked into the house.

'How's your father?'

'Quite the opposite.'

'How's your aunt?'

'Also quite the opposite.'

'Oh.'

'Yes, quite. "Oh" is about the only reply possible in the circumstances.'

They both laughed affectionately. Aunt Cicely had always been a law unto herself, and herself alone.

Caro followed Robyn across the freezing cold hall.

Although it was early summer outside, no matter what the weather it was always deep winter at Brookefield, due entirely to Mr Harding's refusal to entertain any form of heating other than the tiny and very desultory log fires that were permitted to be lit in the drawing room and his study, and then only really when it was snowing outside. Whatever the weather around the rest of the county Caro never expected life at Brookefield to be any different, which was why this morning she had taken care to wear a silk blouse and wool suit, and not a cotton frock.

'Come in, come in, no one's about.' Robyn beckoned to her to follow her into the drawing room. 'Father and Aunt Cicely are in London, and all the maids have taken French leave. You can't blame them, really. They only get a half-day a month off, courtesy of Father, so the moment his back is turned, *whoosh*, they're out of the door and running home as fast as Mrs Tiggy-Winkle up the hillside. Still, I've made us some sandwiches, but the only thing I could find to put in them though was, um, sardines.'

'They look, um, very welcoming. Well done.'

Caro stared in wonder at the pile of sandwiches being presented to her. To say they were elephantine was to say the least; and they were so charged with sardines that she realised that Robyn must have used around a dozen tins for the filling.

'I will make us both a gin and tonic. It's Aunt Cicely's gin. She keeps it in the boot cupboard. I took a bottle from the back so she won't notice for years and years and years, and by that time there'll be a war on, so it won't matter.'

'I love gin. Love the smell of juniper berries. I used to raid my mother's bedroom cupboard just to smell it.'

'I love gin anyway, never mind the smell of berries! Isn't this fun, though?'

They both watched with fascination as Robyn poured the gin into the glasses, followed by the tonic, until finally they raised their glasses.

'Here's to freedom,' Robyn said, after a satisfied sigh, having taken a good swig of her drink.

'Yes, here's to freedom, except there won't be much of it around to enjoy if Katherine has her wretched way, will there?'

Robyn knew all about Katherine and David, as did most of the county, but, unlike most of the county, Robyn was sympathetic to a degree.

'Anyone can have their minds twisted by the wrong person, you know, Caro, particularly if they are in love with them.'

Caro nodded. It was true, but as the gin started to do its work, she began to see life a little differently.

'Actually, if you really want to know, Robyn, if you really, really want to know, I could *actually* slap Katherine, and David, do you know that, Robyn?' she confided. 'The parents are feeling it so dreadfully about their intransigence. They don't say a thing, but it cuts into them so, so deep, I feel like giving Katherine and David the shake of their lives for going on these rallies with all those Blackshirts, and getting into the newspapers, albeit nothing that Papa reads, thank heavens, but even so, I could bang their silly heads together – really I could.'

'I don't blame you,' Robyn answered, but having

71

no sisters or brothers, only a father and an aged aunt, she found it difficult to put herself in Caro's shoes, so she changed the subject to something more general. 'Do you think there's going to be a war? Because I do, I'm certain of it now they've given Austria *and* Czechoslovakia to Herr Hitler. Well, there will be no stopping him, will there? I mean to say, talk about handing the horrid little man everything on a plate. I really don't see why these so-called great countries should eat up all the little ones. It's just not on. My father has been sure there will be a war for many years now. He says there will have to be conscription, even for girls, and if there is I am determined to join the FANYs—'

As Caro giggled at the name, Robyn went on to explain, 'No, listen silly, no stop. FANY stands for First Aid Nursing Yeomanry, and there's no hanky-panky, I promise you, about the Yeomanry. Aunt Cicely was one, and she says their uniform is just about the best, so that did it for me. Will you join them with me? Oh, do.'

'Of course,' Caro said quickly, without giving it much thought, and then after a few seconds, she frowned and asked, a little belatedly, 'What do they do, exactly?'

'I don't know in peacetime, but not just nursing, which was how they started, no, they do all sorts of things, I think. I know they don't just nurse, they drive officers about, and generally make themselves useful,' Robyn told her a little too airily, because the fact was that she herself was not too sure what being a member of the First Aid Nursing Yeomanry entailed, only that Aunt Cicely had told her a few days before that this was what her aunt was expecting Robyn to be, rather than a Wren or a Waac.

Of course it had more than surprised Robyn when Aunt Cicely had suddenly come up with this notion, it had actually astonished her; but as she got the picture that being in the Nursing Yeomanry was about a great deal more than just nursing, she became excited by the notion.

'You can drive well, Robyn, you have a good figure, you will look well in the FANYs. The uniform is most flattering. You will shine in it, believe me, especially if we make sure to have it tailored for you at your father's tailor, which frankly is *de rigueur* if you want to cut a dash.'

Robyn poured both Caro and herself another gin, before continuing, 'As a matter of fact my father's at his tailor this week, having what he keeps calling "The Last Suit" made, before the balloon goes up.' She paused, before continuing. 'Father has gone from being gloomy to being suicidal about Europe and its politicians. He thinks we should be making plans for a united government now, this minute, not hanging about waiting to see what the other side get up to.'

'That's just what my lot think we should do: form a united government *now*, and get on with it. But probably like your father they're *underneath* sad about Europe, but trying not to show it. I think that's why, when I suggested the mural, they thought it was a good idea. I think everyone has that feeling that everything is going to change, so we must get drawn how we were, while we're all still here, in case everything gets destroyed. Mind you, you have to feel sorry for poor Mr Painter, putting up with us lot. What a business for him. Gosh, this gin is good.'

73

Robyn nodded. 'How about a sandwich?'

They stared at the plates filled with the sardine sandwiches.

'Tell you what we might need, we might need a knife each so we can cut off the crusts, and then squish them,' Caro suggested.

'That is a good idea – I'll fetch some.'

Robyn was gone for such a long time that Caro, finally fed up with stroking Freddie and Danny, was just about to go and look for her, when she promptly reappeared.

'Sorry Caro, no maids to ask, didn't know where to find the knives. Kitchen knives all right?'

They both paused before starting to prepare to wield the kitchen knives, realising that, given that they had both had two socking great gins, it was as well to exercise caution when it came to cutting sandwiches.

Caro put a hand on Robyn's arm. 'No, no, Robyn, the first thing to do before you cut – I know this as a matter of fact because Cook taught me years ago – the first thing to always do with a sandwich is to *squish* it, and then cut.'

They nodded at each other, a little over-solemnly. Finally the squishing and the cutting ended with both of them chewing slowly through the now crustless sandwiches while the crusts they had cut off were thrown to the floor for the terriers to enjoy.

'What fun it all is,' Caro enthused. 'So much better than an ordinary lunch. I say, as soon as we've finished, let's take the dogs and go for a walk.'

'No, let's take the dogs and go for a spin in the Bentley.'

*   *   *

It was Aunt Cicely who had bought Robyn the Bentley.

It was not her father's habit to remember birthdays. She often thought he only really remembered Christmas because he had to go to church, but as always, Aunt Cicely was different.

Robyn's nineteenth birthday had fallen at the beginning of the year, and Aunt Cicely must have thought that a nineteenth birthday warranted some kind of rather special present.

She had entered the dining room where Robyn was having a lone breakfast, wondering sadly if her father had even remembered that she had a birthday.

'Happy birthday, dear.'

'Thank you, Aunt Cicely.'

'I will give you the card I made for you later, but just now it would be best if you go outside and look carefully, for there's a surprise for you that I think you will like,' she ended, patting her great bun of grey hair.

Robyn had indeed gone outside as directed, expecting to find at most some kind of outdoor present, perhaps a new tennis racquet, or a bag of golf clubs – a sport in which she was becoming increasingly interested – only to see a brand-new Bentley parked neatly at the bottom of the steps, the garage man, together with Mr Pilkington, chauffeur and handyman, standing beside it, smiling broadly.

As Aunt Cicely, who had followed her out on to the steps, looked from her niece to the Bentley and back again, she smiled, but seeing that Robyn was literally speechless, she finally giggled, a most unusual sound on the cold, quiet morning air.

'I've always wanted to have a Bentley motor car with a hood that went up and down. And one day I was passing that new show place in Speytesbury, and I saw it in the window. I'll never be able to learn to drive one at my age, I thought, but it's just the thing, I thought, for young Robyn.' She turned back. 'You see, Robyn dear, if only I'd had a motor car when I was young, it would have made such a difference. A motor car gives you freedom – for ever. I only ever had a bicycle, and that gets you a mere twenty miles or so, and then rather slowly. So get in, get in, and start her up, dear, oh, do! I can't wait to hear her throbbing sound once more. Pilkington here can teach you to ride it – I mean drive it, rather. He is a very good driver, as you know, tiptop at this driving lark.'

Happily, Pilkington was not just a *good* driver, he was superb, and as soon as she started taking the Bentley out with him, Robyn found herself impassioned by driving. From then on she and Pilkington talked cars, and nothing but cars. And what was more and what was better, Pilkington proved to be a splendid teacher. It didn't matter what the situation was in which they found themselves, Pilkington always remained as cool as the interior of Brookefield House.

Once when Robyn managed to get the gears stuck at the top of the highest hill in the county, and the car plunged giddily to the bottom of the hill, thankfully finishing up unharmed, Pilkington merely turned to Robyn and said, 'Quite right to just let her coast, Miss Robyn,' which was, to say the least, diplomatic.

'Are you ready then?'

Lunch over, and by now feeling perhaps a little too

carefree, thanks to the gins and tonics, Caro followed Robyn and the dogs into the Bentley.

'Will Freddie and Danny be all right in the back?'

Robyn laughed as she started up the engine. 'Be all right? They would balance on the bonnet if I wanted them to. The Cairns are just as addicted to motoring as I am. They would positively tear down the house if I didn't bring them with me. Now where shall we go?'

'How about up the hill to Speytesbury, and then on to the ridge, and round via Deacon and so home?'

They smiled at each other, neither noticing that the other's smile was just a little lopsided.

'Splendid.'

Robyn put the great car into gear, and eventually they turned out of the Hardings' drive into the main highway, along which a lone car was being driven at about twenty miles an hour.

'Poop, poop, cried Mr Toad,' Robyn shouted as she passed it. 'Out of my way! I am the captain of my soul, I am the commander of my boat.'

The fluttering sail-like sound of her silk scarf as it waved gaily in the breeze, the looks of doggy delight on the terriers' faces, their dark fur flattened by the wind, the empty road in front of them, it was all sheer bliss. And as always when motoring, Caro found that everything suddenly made much more sense. It was the feeling of freedom, the feeling that no one knew where you were, or perhaps cared. It was how life should always be, a heavenly drive on a perfect afternoon.

And then the feeling started that everything was going faster and faster, as Robyn failed to change gear properly, and a screeching seemed to be filling the air as the car hurtled down hill.

'Not again,' Robyn murmured.

'Bad luck . . .'

'More like bad driving.'

The car, now out of control, hurtled towards the hedge-rows to the side of the road and, perhaps because there was no Pilkington in the car, or perhaps because the road was smooth and dry, this time there was no stopping it at the bottom of the slope. It carried on as if it, like the girls, had been drinking too much gin at midday.

Robyn put out an arm to prevent Caro from being thrown through the windscreen, while Caro put out an arm to try to prevent the dogs hurtling into the front seats.

They both had just enough time to appreciate, rather too late, that something had gone more than a little wrong when the car headed through a gap in a fence at the side of the road and raged on over the pasture, behind a herd of fleeing sheep, only finally coming to a shuddering stop as it hit a log, at which point Caro opened her door and flung herself out rather than risk hurtling through the windscreen.

There was a short silence, which, given the circumstances, was only to be expected.

'Are you all right, Caro?' Robyn called.

'I'm fine.' Caro sat up. 'How are the dogs?'

'They're fine, they just shot under the seats.'

Robyn climbed out of the car, stood over Caro and offered her a hand.

'You can't have shut your door properly. Luckily,

no stinging nettles,' she added, looking round at the flattened grass.

Caro rubbed herself ruefully. 'It could have been worse. More important, how's the car?'

'Hardly a scratch. Amazing, she seemed to leap through that gap in the fence as if she was born to it. I'll have to enter her in the Grand National.'

Caro nodded, still rubbing herself.

'Hurt your backside?'

'No, not really, just bruised it a bit.' She looked up at Robyn. 'Come on, we're on Somerton land. If anyone sees us, we'll be for it. You know what they're like, they can traipse all over your acres, but drop a leaf in one of their fields and you'll hear about it for the next century.'

They started to climb back into the Bentley when Robyn stopped.

'No, look!' She stood up on the running board and pointed to a field beyond them. 'There's something going on over there.'

There did indeed seem to be something unusual taking place in the next field.

'It looks like an aeroplane has crashed, or landed, or something. We'd better go and see if we can help.'

The two girls made their way quickly across the first field, the dogs tearing ahead of them in happy confusion, Robyn calling out to them to 'leave' the sheep. When the girls reached the aeroplane, the two Cairns were running around it, barking.

Robyn, who loved aeroplanes almost as much as motor cars, at once recognised the aeroplane as being foreign. She turned to Caro.

'It's not an English aeroplane, so snips and snaps, as we used to say in the Girl Guides, and be on your mettle.'

The pilot was so far from being English as to be ludicrous in this rural setting, and although he was at pains to smile and shake their hands, while Caro tried out some of her nursery German on him, Robyn, under the pretence of trying to control the dogs, peered into his aeroplane. What she saw lying inside was unusual, to say the least. Nevertheless, she continued to scoop up the dogs, one under each arm and, having learned from Caro that the aeroplane was undamaged, and the pilot had merely lost his bearings rather than crashed his aircraft, she watched with cool eyes as the plane took off once more from the sheep-mown stretch of English turf.

'Well, well, well,' Robyn muttered, watching the aeroplane a little enviously. 'It seems the Huns are invading us already.'

'Oh, I don't think he's a Hun, Robyn,' Caro assured her. 'He spoke with a very cultured accent. In fact, he was really quite like my brothers' German tutor, who was a lovely chap.'

'Oh, I know, just acting under orders,' Robyn said sarcastically, striding ahead. 'If you find a German who has lost his bearings these days, believe me, his bearings were about nothing to do with doing England any good.'

'Oh I don't know . . .'

'Well, I do.'

'Anyway, thank God for a safe deliverance,' Caro said, assuming a pious expression as she climbed back into the Bentley. 'And,' she glanced backwards, 'just so long as the dogs are all right, that's all that matters.'

Robyn started to laugh helplessly.

'What's the matter?'

'You always say that,' Robyn replied, when she could speak. 'No matter what happens you always say, "Thank God the dogs are all right".'

On the way back to Brookefield both girls were silent, thinking over the events of the past hours.

Later, as they were saying goodbye to each other, Caro was the first to put their feelings into words.

'That was exciting, wasn't it, Robyn, the car and the German in the aeroplane? It really put us on our mettle, wouldn't you say?'

Robyn nodded and, bending forward, she pecked Caro on the cheek, still determined not to mention what she had seen in the aeroplane.

'I have a feeling we're both going to need rather a lot of that, of mettle, I mean, in the not-too-distant future.'

Caro turned away and went back to the *Blue Angel*, which although still as elegant as ever, seemed suddenly much smaller and more manageable, cosy even, after the Bentley.

She sang all the way home, parking the car carefully and neatly in one of the garages and then walked back into the pantry where Smith was waiting for her. She stared at him as he stared at her, looking her up and down in silence.

'I do declare, you're still where I left you, Smith.'

Smith continued to look her up and down, his face unmoving.

'Miss Robyn telephoned ahead of you.'

'Really?'

'Apparently you had an accident.'

'Not in *Blue Angel*, just in the Bentley. *Angel*'s fine.'

Smith nodded. 'You've got quite a bruise coming up on your face—'

'It's nothing, Smith, really.'

'Miss Robyn thought I ought to tell Mrs Grant to run you a nice hot bath with some Epsom salts, and after that she was to find you some ice on which to sit for a while, until things calm down a bit.'

'She's just fussing, Miss Robyn's fussing. She's got nothing better to do, all alone at Brookefield, just her and the dogs.'

'Be that as it may, she has made her suggestions, and I have told Mrs Grant what will be wanted, and no more to be said.'

'Oh, Smithy,' Caro groaned. 'Such a fuss.' Even so she followed him out of the pantry. 'You haven't heard,' she went on, enthusiastically. 'You haven't heard how fast we went.'

Smith stopped. 'I don't need to hear how fast you went, Miss Caro. I can *see* how fast you went.'

Caro shrugged her shoulders. She had to concede she was a bit battered and bruised, and covered in grass stains, and what not.

'Yes, but what a peach of a drive, Smith.' She smiled. 'And just wait until I tell you—'

Smith too was forced to smile. It was Miss Caro all over.

'Here's Mrs Grant, Miss Caro, I think you'd better follow her instructions, because there's no doubt about it, you're going to have quite a shiner by morning. A piece of steak under the eye, I would think might help, Mrs Grant,' he added, turning to the housekeeper.

Mrs Grant stared disapprovingly at Caro, who immediately smiled over-brightly at the housekeeper. Perhaps taking this to mean that she should get going Mrs Grant went quickly up the back stairs, and so on to the old-fashioned family bathroom where she ran Caro a bath and threw salts into it.

'That will help the bruises. Meanwhile I will ask Cook for some steak for your cheek, which we can only hope will be something she will spare for such a very worthy cause,' she added sarcastically, as she started to leave the room.

'Thank you, Mrs Grant. And don't worry about the steak, I can cover the bruise with some face powder.'

The housekeeper did not appear to have heard, because she merely closed the door behind her, which Caro promptly locked, before undressing, putting on a bath cap, and stepping into the welcoming warmth of the water. As she lay, allowing the water to soothe her bruises, she could not help feeling heroic. She had been through a much bigger adventure than she had ever had in the *Angel*, and she had come through it without feeling afraid. She sang a little as she soaped herself.

A moment later she stopped singing as she heard the sound of hurrying steps on the landing outside the bathroom, and then yet more hurrying steps above her on the third floor.

'Mrs Grant's parrot must have got out,' she murmured, staring up at the bathroom ceiling high above her.

Now there was the sound of doors being opened and shut, as if everyone was indeed searching for something or someone.

Caro sighed and, stepping out of the bath on to the thick Victorian mat, she removed her cap, and towelled herself down, gingerly admiring the deepening colours of her bruises, before sallying forth to her bedroom to dress.

It was then that she noticed that Katherine's bedroom door was open. She put her head around the door, and stared in.

'Katherine?' she called, feeling suddenly excited by the idea of telling her older sister about the adventure she had just enjoyed. She stopped. 'Katherine . . . ?'

Her feeling of excitement was quickly replaced by something quite different.

Why call Katherine when it was very evident that she was not in the room? Not only that, but why call Katherine when again, quite evidently, the room, normally a safe refuge for Katherine and her seemingly endless supply of clothes, was now empty of her elder sister, and she now saw all too distinctly, her clothes.

The doors of the old wardrobe were open, the rails occupied by dozens of empty cushioned hangers. A glance round the room showed Caro that the dressing-table drawers were open, and there were no silk stockings, no silk underwear, really nothing left of Katherine's belongings except her old worn felt riding hat, a yellow suit and a few other items – a brown evening dress with a sequinned jacket, and an old straw beach hat.

Caro quickly dressed in any old thing that she could

put her hand on, and ran down the main staircase to the hall where half the household seemed to have gathered.

'It's your sister,' her father said, as she stood looking at him. 'Your mother has just discovered a letter that she left for us this morning, it seems, after she had sat to the painter. She slipped out of the house – must have been by the side entrance – taking all her clothes and effects with her.'

Anthony was ashen, his lips trembling even as he spoke, but determined as always to hold on to his feelings.

'What can have possessed her?' Meriel wrung her hands, and she stared frantically at all the faces around her, as if she half expected Katherine to bob up behind one of the maids. 'It could all be just a wicked tease, couldn't it? I mean I dare say she will come popping back any minute now, don't you think?' she asked of no one in particular.

At this everyone looked embarrassed for her. It was common knowledge in the house that Miss Katherine had been nothing but trouble over the past two years, that her parents had begun to despair of her, that she had changed character beyond belief.

'I suppose there is hope, I mean that we can catch up with her, if she's not yet twenty-one, wouldn't you think?' Caro asked of no one, at the same time staring round her as if she expected suddenly to spot Katherine's beautiful face behind the people gathered in the old hall, perhaps with a finger to her lips indicating, as she used to say so often to Caro when she was young, 'This is our secret.'

But no one was standing at the back of the little anxious group, and no one was whispering, 'This is our secret.' Katherine was gone, and deep down in her deepest heart Caro somehow knew that she would never see her, or David, at Chevrons again.

Chapter Three

The moment that Katherine vanished from Chevrons the world became little more than a dust bowl of worry to Meriel. Katherine might have ceased to love her mother, but her mother had never stopped loving her, hoping, always hoping, that she would somehow, some time soon, change back to the glorious, fun-loving, beautiful girl that she had been before wretched David Astley came into her life.

And now, of course, the person that Meriel missed was that girl, that daughter, not the young woman she had turned into once she fell in love with the Astley boy. The very helplessness of it all made her long to go out and do something – search for Katherine, not just leave it to the police, or to friends in high places, all of whom had so generously pledged to help the Garlands in any way that they could.

Of course, the Astleys were blamed, albeit silently, by everyone at Chevrons, and indeed, no one from the Astley family had called at Chevrons. It was as if, in their shame at what David had done, they did not dare even to telephone the Garlands, guessing, as they surely must, that what the Garlands might be feeling was unimaginable.

'The Astleys have always been a strange lot, too idealistic, too *in* on themselves, too strait-laced, even too religious to be quite healthy. You have to allow children to *breathe*, not keep cramming their heads with ideas that they have no business thinking about until they're older. Personally the Ten Commandments do it for me; it's all there in the tablets. If all of us humans had stuck by the Ten Commandments we wouldn't be in such a mess now,' Anthony had been heard to mutter time and again over the passing years, and now it seemed he had been proved right, because, as in some much earlier age, a daughter of Chevrons had been carried off by one of the Astley sons, and that certainly was *not* in the Ten Commandments.

Ten Commandments or no Ten Commandments, Meriel, however, could not actually bring it on herself to hate poor David Astley. She could only feel sorry for him. He was young, he had come under the spell of extremists, and for what reason Meriel could only guess. Perhaps it had been foolish – it certainly seemed so now – but as parents, Meriel and Anthony had gone on and on hoping, with all their hearts and souls, that by tolerating David, by not banning him from seeing Katherine, the young man would come to realise that their way of life, their way of thinking, was the better way, that tolerance must rule if people were to go on from day to day in any kind of harmony.

To demonstrate their ideals not by words but by their way of life was something to which Meriel and Anthony

88

always aspired. When she looked at her sons, young Anthony, and his twin by five minutes, Francis, and of course Caro – and for some reason just the thought of Caro always made Meriel smile – and then at the people who came daily to the house to help them, Meriel tried to comfort herself that even if they could be said to have failed utterly with Katherine, they had not failed with everyone else.

Where Katherine and David had gone, no one knew; *why* they had gone was, if any of them dared to think about it, all too obvious.

'On that particular subject, my deah,' Caro stated to Walter a few weeks later, when there was still no news of the couple's whereabouts, 'no one, but no one, dares to utter the word beginning with G and ending with Y.'

'Quite understandable,' Walter called down to Caro from the top step of his ladder. 'But do *you* think they might have gone abroad to G ending with Y?'

Caro was sitting in what she now thought of as her 'morning' position, namely on the bottom rung of the set of steps at the top of which Walter was busy working. She knew he liked to have her nearby to chat to him, but also to keep quiet when necessary, and to keep herself ready to hand up what was needed, when it was needed.

The fact that Walter had fallen in love with Katherine the way (and really it was almost tedious) that every man who came within her orbit always seemed to had not worried Caro at first, but now Katherine had disappeared, she guessed that Mr Painter must be feeling Katherine's absence, feeling just a little more heartsore than he would have perhaps liked to admit, especially when he looked at how he had painted her, with the blue of the dress exactly reflected in the blue of her eyes, her beauty seeming to leap off the wall to the onlooker.

'My deah,' Caro said, once more deliberately using an over-bred County voice to make Walter laugh, 'my deah, *whooo* knows? They could be *any*where.'

Walter smiled at the tree he was busy outlining. Caro and he had now established a great many private jokes between them. The exaggerated way the 'County' spoke, not to mention their innate snobbishness, had become a source of much-needed fun, because unfortunately no one could be unaware of the change in atmosphere at Chevrons. Everyone was becoming tense and wary, as if the outer world, with all its particular horrors, could not now be kept at bay; as if they knew that with Katherine missing, believed lost to them, anything might now happen; as if they all sensed that everything was about to change for ever, and none of them would ever see her again.

It was for this reason that Walter had spent the last days encouraging Caro in her irreverence, allowing her to stay around the Long Room, even when he had what they both now referred to as one of his 'victims' sitting to him.

Caro somehow managed to make everyone laugh, even, of all people, Mrs Grant the housekeeper, and that was saying something. She also made Walter laugh, and that too went some way to help soothe his sense of failure over Katherine Garland.

'How can someone as beautiful as you hold such insane views?'

He had actually said that to her at the end of one morning's sitting, but she had merely looked away, shrugging her shoulders as if to say, 'Everyone says that.'

Once or twice, when she laughed, Walter had flattered himself into thinking that he was getting back the Katherine that she must have been before she became besotted with this godlike creature David Astley, but then the look in her eyes would change, and seconds later the hardened expression would return as if, like someone ill who can momentarily be distracted into thinking that they are well, Katherine had suddenly remembered the person she had once been, but then quickly reverted to the current reality.

All the time Walter had been painting Katherine, rather than anyone else, Caro had made sure to absent herself from the Long Room.

'If anyone can talk her out of her silly views, you can, you know, Walter,' Caro had confided, 'because I think, although you certainly wouldn't know it, she really quite likes you.'

'How do you know?' Walter had countered, turning away so that Caro could not see his face.

'Because I do. I am her sister.'

But evidently, and palpably, Walter had failed to talk her round. Now, looking back, he realised that his failure had probably been entirely due to the fact that he had fallen in love with her. Nowadays he found himself lying awake at night wondering, over and over again, why he, who loved and admired women to distraction, had not been able to charm her out of what had increasingly appealed to him as her trancelike state.

Over and over again, he had tried continually to make Katherine see that Hitler and the Nazis were nothing short of the devil incarnate. Yet, despite his increasing sense of failure, every day that Katherine Garland had sat to him he reapplied himself to the task of saving her, longing to pull her back from the brink of that horrendous darkness in which fascism revels and grows.

But he had failed, and now, most mornings, the Long Room was empty of everyone except himself and Caro. He was happy that it was so, because lately he had noticed that, alone but for young Caro in silent attendance, he could paint well and quickly.

'You know what you are, Caro Garland?' He looked down at the top of her head.

'No,' she said, sounding momentarily distracted, because one of the many Garland dogs had wandered into the room to find her.

'You are my lucky charm.'

There was a short silence during which Caro considered this statement, as she stroked the long-haired dog.

'When are you going to paint Dickie? He wants to be in the painting, don't you, Dickie?' she asked, as if Walter had not spoken, or as if she had no interest in being his lucky charm, or indeed anything else.

Walter looked down at the engaging black and white dog, with his tightly furled tail, and his habit of putting out his paw to be stroked, in which Caro was only too happy to oblige him.

'Tomorrow, perhaps. I might paint Dickie tomorrow. Why?'

'Oh, nothing. It's just that if you are going to start

painting Dickie pretty soon, I'll bath him tonight after the maids have finished.'

'Good idea.'

'You know old Miss Berenger's not come back, so she won't be able to be in your painting?'

'Miss Berenger?'

'She was the Belgian sort of maid person to my mother, but she was more than that really: she did all the sewing jobs, all the mending and making covers – oh, everything really to do with the needle. Made scarves for everyone every Christmas. But there you are, she's gone. We're all wondering if she's gone to help Katherine and David in whatever they're doing. Or just run back to Belgium before the war breaks out. The parents don't talk about it, but it's strange that she didn't even telephone or write. And when the parents reported her absence to the police no one seemed to care, Mrs Grant says. She also said she thought it was because Miss Berenger was foreign that the English police don't really care what's happened to her, which I suppose is understandable. Poor Miss Berenger, I keep thinking about her and wondering, but then I keep thinking about a whole lot of people and *worrying*, though really, there's no point. Worrying is quite, quite pointless. And if I take up worrying when there is a war, I will be no use to anyone. At any rate that is what I tell myself every night, before I fall asleep.'

Yet another short silence followed, during which Walter imagined that he could hear Caro thinking up her next question.

'What are you going to do when the wall is finished here, Mr Painter? Are you going to join the Guards or something, or the Artists' Rifles, or whatever they are called? Everyone round here is already making plans to take off for Salisbury Plain or Catterick, all stations east and west, even though nothing at all has really happened yet.'

'What am I going to do?' Walter paused. 'Well, I have a commission in Hertfordshire, from the Smythsons, as a matter of fact, to paint them in their drawing room – a large oil.'

'What about when the war comes, though, which everyone thinks it must – what will you do then?'

'Oh, I expect I will paint that too,' Walter replied, too readily and certainly too flippantly.

Caro was silent for a minute.

'No, but really. What *will* you do?'

Walter glanced down at her for a few seconds.

'I will do as my country requires, and since there is sure to be some sort of conscription, all will be made clear pretty soon, I should have thought.'

'Yes, Robyn Harding thinks they will bring in conscription for everyone, even for girls. She's joining up anyway. She can't wait.'

'She can't wait because she likes a fight?'

'No, no, she is actually really quite quiet by temperament, except when she's behind a wheel. No, it's because she feels a bit hemmed in at home, and because she doesn't want to be a débutante. If she joins the FANYs she will get out of all that. She will get out of everything, and just drive about in her Bentley, taking officers to lunch and dinner and mysterious meetings in the country.'

'Well I've heard of worse ways of defending your country.'

Caro stood up. 'I've changed my mind. I think I'm going to go and bath Dickie now. It's a good time because Mrs Grant will have gone home. 'Bye. See you tomorrow.'

Walter heard the door shut. Then he climbed down the ladder and, because the light was beginning to fade, switched on the lights of the Long Room.

He viewed the whole mural with critical eyes before going up close to look at the figure of Katherine Garland. Caro had said nothing about his painting of her sister when he had finished it, which had puzzled him, because in every other way his lucky charm had proved more than generous in her appreciation of what he was doing; but not, it seemed, when it came to her sister.

At first Walter had wondered if Caro was jealous of Katherine, which, given that Katherine was by far the more beautiful of the two, would have been only natural, but then, as the days fled by and he peopled the Long Room wall with family and servants, with sheep and deer and dogs, he had realised it was something else that was preventing Caro from commenting on his portrait of her sister; tantalisingly it had gradually become clear that it was something that she thought *she* could see in his portrait, which he could not. It irritated him when he saw her eyes travelling over the mural, but always stopping when they rested on Katherine.

Of course he wanted to ask for her opinion, but was far too proud. Besides, there was something about young Caro – an inner silence, if you like, a piece of her that she kept to herself – that he was finally forced to respect.

'You're a handful, Caro Garland,' he murmured as he finally packed up his paints for the night, preparing to retreat to the village pub, where there was mixed company of the kind that artists were traditionally meant to favour, and certainly, in that respect, Walter Beresford was no exception.

Aunt Cicely stared at Robyn.

'You must do as you wish,' she said. 'I quite understand, I truly do.'

'It's important to get going before the real need, don't you think, Aunt Cicely?'

The old lady nodded, her expression as inscrutable as ever. She had pale grey eyes, which, it had always seemed to her niece, looked out on the world with unblinkered objectivity. All during her childhood Robyn had found a sense of calm around not just Aunt Cicely, but many single or widowed women. There were so many of them living in the country: women made widows by the seemingly interminable tragedies of the Great War; women whose fiancés had been killed in the war to end all wars, and who had never thought to marry again, or who had never found anyone who sought to marry *them*.

Of course they were not all either passed up or lovelorn. Some, like Aunt Cicely, had been quite determined to stay single, having no desire to have children, and in consequence these women always seemed less confused and foolish than the rest of the world.

'I think you're right to go to London and get fitted for your uniform and so on, Robyn,' Aunt Cicely murmured eventually. 'There is definitely going to be another war, and it is just as well to get yourself lined up and ready in the right way.' She nodded. 'We have been sadly let down by the politicians – now and for ever, perhaps.' She sniffed. 'My father always used to say that professional politicians were always going to be a bad idea, because they were bound to be out only for self-advancement, as against men of standing who took decisions based on patriotism, thinking only of what is good for all, not what is going to enhance them.'

She picked up her glass and drained it.

'Do you want another sherry, Aunt Cicely?'

'I certainly do.'

Robyn could not believe her luck. Her father was still in London, sorting out goodness knew what. For once she had her beloved Aunt Cicely to herself. If all went well, Robyn could be packed up and gone before her father returned.

Robyn poured them each yet another glass of sherry, and sat down opposite her relative.

'You were in the Boer War, weren't you, Aunt Cicely?'

'I certainly was,' she agreed. 'I ran away from home to join the FANYs, as you know.' Aunt Cicely certainly did not mind being prompted into talking about her time with the First Aid Nursing Yeomanry. 'Couldn't wait to help, and we *did* help. For most of us it was completely against the wishes of our families, as was Florence Nightingale's work in the Crimea. The FANYs were different, of course, because we rode out, on our own horses, to fetch the wounded and dying. We brought them back to the field stations we had set up, thereby saving many lives.' She paused and her face became sad.

'Saw some terrible things, but we just had to do it. When the war was over, we came home believing we had done quite a good job, whereupon my family refused to have anything more to do with me.' She laughed. 'Everyone still thought nursing and being in the FANYs was tantamount to being a woman of loose morals, which of course it certainly was not. We were all respectable girls from good backgrounds, but we wanted to do *good*; we wanted to do something more than sit at home with our stitching, waiting for some young man to ask for our hand in marriage.'

'So what happened after, after your family turned their back on you?'

'I went to London and rented a flat just off Sloane Square. No money, of course, so I took in lodgers, just got on with it. You had to.'

'Well done, you,' Robyn murmured, and she looked at Aunt Cicely with renewed admiration.

'At first my lodgers were quite dubious people, raffish to a degree, I would say now, at any rate to start with; so much so I had to sleep with a revolver under my pillow. But after a while we managed to get a better class of person, and it all became quite jolly, until the Great War, and then off we went again, but to the Front this time.'

'Awful for you.'

'Yes, we saw terrible things, we didn't like it, but we knew that if we didn't stick it out, hundreds, no thousands, more would die, so we had to carry on. And by the time that was all over, your grandparents had been gathered to God, so your dear mamma and my young brother, your papa, asked me here. But then, of course, on your arrival into this world your mother too was gathered, poor darling, and so here we were left, just the three of us at Brookefield, my brother and I, and you, and here we have been ever since. But now,' she turned to look directly at Robyn, 'now everything is about to change once more, because here we go again – another war.'

It seemed to Robyn that the expression in her aunt's eyes had become clouded with the realities of war, with the horrors that she had seen, but sad though she was to see such a look on the older woman's face, Robyn imagined to herself that all these things grew worse when you aged, simply because you had more time to think about them.

It was not many seconds later when she became disabused of this notion.

'My dear, we must not romanticise the war that is undoubtedly ahead, not for a single second. War is terrible, terrible, terrible; and never more terrible than in retrospect. However much one tries to turn away from the memories of the things one saw when one was young, believe me, it is impossible. They are stained, and I mean *stained*, on your mind, never leaving you, returning to you again and again in your dreams, in waking moments, when one is half asleep, when one is waking. One smells and hears again and again the scents and sickening sounds of war, and the only thing that stops one from falling into an abyss of despair is the knowledge that one did *something* towards limiting the suffering, sending back the young men to their families – oh, and sending back the enemy to their families too, because when a young man lies dying in your arms, believe me, it doesn't matter where he comes from, he is just another young man dying for no good purpose. At least, to be honest, for no good purpose that I could ever make out, certainly not one that one could point to with any certainty, either then or now.'

Later that night, after dinner together, the younger woman and the older woman embraced each other and went off to their bedrooms in the great draughty house, knowing that they had reached a pretty perfect understanding. Robyn was being handed on the torch. She would take it up from where Aunt Cicely had left off.

Back in her room Robyn started to pack up her things preparatory to leaving before her father's return, which she knew – and Aunt Cicely obviously also knew, cunning old thing – might, to say the least, complicate matters.

Robyn could hardly wait to telephone Caro and invite her to join the FANYs with her. She knew she would be as keen as mustard about the whole idea, although she feared that, in the aftermath of Katherine's disappearance, the Garlands would be more than ever reluctant to let Caro off the leash.

'Don't worry about your father. I will explain everything to him when he returns,' Aunt Cicely murmured the next morning as she helped Robyn pack her suitcases, having sent for the Bentley to be brought round.

'Do you think Father will really mind?'

Aunt Cicely considered this for a good few seconds.

'Yes, but he won't show it. He will mind, of course he will, but knowing my brother he will also accept. He is very fond of you, you know but, being a Harding, he will never show it. It is not the Harding way. We do, I think, have the same feelings as everyone else, we just don't display them the way other people do.' She stopped in front of Robyn's bedroom window and stared out into the distant landscape. 'I don't know whether it is a good thing, or a bad thing. It is just how it is. If you are a Harding you don't complain, and you don't show your feelings, you just expect to get on with it, and for everyone else to do the same.'

Robyn, who was sitting on her suitcase, bent over to do up the buckles on the straps. She was terribly excited about going to London to get her uniform fitted, about leaving for her great adventure, but she was even more excited when she heard from Caro via the telephone half an hour later, to the astonishment of both of them, that her parents had agreed that she could come too.

'How absolutely too-too, my deah!' Robyn responded, because she, like Caro, loved to make fun of jumped-up county voices. 'What do you think made them agree?'

'I don't know. I just went in to them this morning, after your telephone call last night, and I said, "Robyn's going to London for her uniform, she's going to join the First Aid Nursing Yeomanry, and I would like to do the same," and so on. And guess what, Robyn? They said "yes" straight away. I mean the words had hardly left my mouth and they had agreed, which when you consider it, with Katherine gone, is pretty decent of them, don't you think?'

'Utterly decent,' Robyn agreed, her mind already straying on to whether or not she had topped up the

Bentley with its usual gallons and yet more gallons of petrol.

Meriel and Anthony had hardly given their consent to Caro going to London with Robyn, when Meriel rung for Mrs Grant to help Caro to start to get her things together for London – so much to do.

It was only when Caro had left them in hardly suppressed high spirits that on seeing Anthony's bewilderment, Meriel also saw the need to reassure him.

'It could not come at a better time, could it, Anthony? Robyn Harding going to London, Cicely Harding putting her Mayfair flat at the girls' disposal – it could not have come at a better time, really it couldn't. At least I don't think it could. Manna from heaven, if you think about it,' she murmured.

'If what you have said is true, it *could* not have come at a better time,' Anthony agreed. 'We can't have—' He stopped, before going on. 'We can't have any more troubles with our young, we really cannot. As it is,' he pointed to the newspaper lying on his desk, 'it seems that Katherine is busy ruining Caro's chances of finding a husband in the county. No decent young man will want to go near a Garland daughter *now*.'

'*She* hasn't seen that wretched piece, has she?'

Meriel went quickly to the desk, opened the drawer and pushed the newspaper into it.

'No, Caro hasn't seen it,' Anthony agreed. 'Nor must she. Happily she has very little interest in newspapers at this moment in time, if what you have told me is true – only in painters.'

'I must make it clear, Anthony, Caro's never said anything to me directly,' Meriel put in quickly. 'Never, ever said anything about Walter Beresford at all.'

'Then why are we, all of a sudden, in a hurry to send her to London?'

'No particular hurry, no, at least, certainly no flat panic. I just know that it would be as well if she leaves Chevrons sooner rather than later.'

'I dare say you're right, Meriel. My mamma always used to say that mothers always *know*.' Anthony sighed. 'He's a nice man, Walter Beresford, but hardly suitable for Caro, being a painter and rather older too, isn't he?'

Meriel laughed suddenly.

'What's so funny?'

Meriel touched his cheek lightly. '*You* were older than me, remember? As a matter of fact, you still are!'

Anthony frowned. 'That was different. Besides, we've made a success of it.'

Meriel turned away, still smiling. 'You're incorrigible, Anthony, do you know that?'

Anthony looked across at his wife. Meriel hadn't really smiled, not *really* smiled, since Katherine had run off. Maybe she was getting a little more used to the idea of Katherine's having left them. Maybe the coming war would give them reason to pretend that, like all the other young people around, Katherine had merely gone off to do her bit.

Whatever the truth behind the sudden encouraging warmth of his wife's smile, Anthony now knew that someone disappearing was in so many ways almost unendurable. Going to sleep with that dread of what might have happened, to wake every morning to what for a second you thought and hoped would be the dawn of a bright new day, only to be left wondering, always wondering, *how* she was, *where* she was, or even *if* she still was.

As it turned out Robyn had to leave for London immediately, as her father had telephoned to say he was returning home later that day.

Aunt Cicely, ever the diplomat, murmured, 'your father could complicate matters for you. I should leave as soon as you can, really I should. Much the best, in the circumstances.'

Robyn's precipitous departure within hours of Caro's telephone call meant that Caro was left feeling as if she had been let down, though of course she hadn't been, but somehow the idea of leaving by train a few days later seemed much less exciting than whizzing off to London in the Bentley with Robyn. Nevertheless she was far too aware of her parents' feelings to admit as much.

Perhaps her father realised this, or perhaps he had come to some new conclusion about his life, or her life, or all their lives, because the day after Robyn's departure for London, he came into the Long Room frowning and looking even more pensive than usual.

Walter, all too aware of the family situation, all but flung himself down his stepladders, and promptly repositioned them before flinging himself up them once more.

'Caro?'

Caro stood to attention, herself now also firmly in place

in front of the mural, while all the time edging slowly towards Walter so that they would make a solid front.

'Yes, Papa?'

Anthony stared from Walter to Caro, back to Walter, and then at Caro again, where his eyes remained fixed, frowning.

'I have been thinking.'

'Yes, Papa.'

'Yes, I have been thinking, Caro. As a matter of fact, I have been thinking quite hard, and I have come to a conclusion.'

'Yes, Papa?'

'And the conclusion that I have come to is this.' He paused, staring around him, and then at the mural, before his eyes dropped down to Caro's face once more. 'Yes, Caro. And what is more, as you might surmise, your darling mamma agrees with me too.' He nodded, obviously agreeing wholeheartedly with both himself and his wife. 'So that is settled then.'

Caro frowned.

'What is settled, Papa?'

'You'll have to come with me and check it through, of course.'

'What will I have to come and check through with you, Papa?'

'Why the *Blue Angel*, of course. Your mother and I have agreed that you should take the *Angel* to London next week. Most especially if you are to join the First Aid Nursing Yeomanry, Caro. You will have to have a motor car. Being in the FANYs without a motor car would be about as sensible as being a painter without a set of brushes. You can't drive an officer around town in a taxicab, can you?'

'But the *Angel* is—' Caro stopped, quickly rethinking what she was about to say. 'But the *Angel* is so special, won't you miss her?'

'No, no, not at all. Neither your mother nor I, nor your brothers use her, no, we don't use her at all, and Smith won't miss her. He is adapting a couple of vans to carry everything and anything for future needs, whatever they may be,' he added ominously. 'So if you would like to go to see Smith we can go through the various points again. I would like you to be able to tell everyone that you know how the combustion engine works, you see, Caro. I want you to be the first of your sex to know how a motor car really works.'

Caro thought of Robyn and her already very efficient approach to the Bentley and its needs, having been taught everything she knew by the brilliant Pilkington. Nevertheless, Pilkington or no Pilkington, she found herself wondering why it was that the opposite sex always thought girls were duffers when it came to engines.

'Can you spare Caro, Beresford?'

'Yes, of course, sir.'

The old man was to sit to Walter tomorrow. It was, Walter felt, going to be interesting, to say the least.

'Very well, cut along then, Caro. You mustn't keep Smith waiting.'

Caro hurried from the room. She knew how Smith dominated her father, how much in awe he was of him. They had grown up together, and Smith was not only a better driver than Anthony Garland, he was a better shot, and played cricket for the Chevrons village team like an angel in white flannels.

As Caro walked ahead of her father out of the room, Anthony paused and, turning back to Walter, said, 'Oh, and by the way, Beresford, very decent and sporting of you, and so on, but there is truly no need to cover up Katherine by standing in front of her every time I come into the room. Really, decent of you to try and hide her from me, but truly, there is no need.' He paused, nodding at the mural, which was now beginning to be closely peopled. 'I came in with her mother late last night, actually. We thought it very good of Katherine; strangely so, as a matter of fact.'

Anthony again paused, but Walter did not say anything, fearing to interrupt him.

'Fell in love with her, with Katherine, did you, Walter?' he asked with a sad smile, using the painter's Christian name for the first time, which had the effect of making Walter wish Garland hadn't, because he could hear from the older man's voice what an effort it was for him to speak about his beautiful daughter in such a purposefully casual manner, as if she meant nothing to him.

'Doesn't everyone, sir?'

'I am afraid you're right, Walter. I suppose I had hoped that you might make a difference, that you might get through to her in some way; help get rid of all her ridiculous ideas, if that makes sense? Women so often fall for painters. Such a pity she had to choose that so-and-so of a young man Astley, wasn't it? Just our luck, and hers, poor girl. But there you are, if a war breaks out, which we are told it will, sooner now than later, well, maybe that will change everything. Who knows?'

He went from the room, leaving Walter staring after him. After which he turned and looked up, frowning, at his painting of Katherine in her blue dress with the great silver wings.

Caro arrived on the dot of Smith's now famous 'naval time', that is, five minutes early, but Smith did not smile. Instead he stared at her as if he could not believe what was about to happen.

'Mr Garland has told me,' he stated finally in lugubrious tones, 'that he has it in mind to hand the *Blue Angel* over to you, Miss Caro.'

To her intense annoyance Caro found herself blushing, but she was helpless to prevent the wretched colour flooding her face. She was all too aware that she still had several traces of the accident in the Bentley on show, namely a bruised cheek, and that, privately of course, Smith probably believed that it was Caro who had been driving, because, grudgingly, and reluctantly, and only a few weeks before, Smith had been finally forced to admit that Miss Harding was a very good driver.

'Yes, yes, my father thinks I should take over the *Angel* because of my going to be in the FANYs, you see, Smith. I am going to London to join up, next week – Tuesday, probably,' she finished, trying to keep the excitement from her voice, because it was really rather not *on* to feel excited about the possibility of war. 'Will Trixie be going to London, do you think, Smith? Will she want to join up when the time comes?'

'I imagine that she will, Miss Caro, but for the moment she is studying hard, trying to improve herself. Apparently she had some idea of going on the boards – becoming an actress. Over my dead body, I have told her, so she has compromised and is going for lessons in elocution, to a Miss Reed in the village. Thinks the world of her, does Miss Reed, which surprised me, because frankly, Miss Caro, my Trixie has always been a handful, what with having no mother, and I know not what.'

Caro was just about to say, 'Her reading's whizzing along,' when she stopped, realising that it sounded all too patronising, and anyway she had no idea whether or not Trixie's reading lessons were something that her father knew about, so she kept her trap shut and contented herself with asking Smith to open up the bonnet of the Fraser Nash.

'Here is the motor, or *innards*, as you like to call them, Miss Caro. Here's where you put the water, unscrewing this cap here, and here's where the petrol comes into the engine, and that there is the fan, and fan belt. It's all very simple, as you will agree, until one of them gives out on you, and then, for some reason, everyone panics. Always carry a spare can of water, and of petrol, and above all a spare fan belt. The car can get overheated if you push her too hard, and she can get thirsty. Lack of water is a common problem with her.'

At the sound of approaching footsteps Smith looked round.

'Good morning, sir.'

'Good morning, Smith.'

'Just showing Miss Caro a few of the ropes, Mr Anthony.'

'Good, good, Smith, no one better, I am quite sure.'

Anthony stopped to admire the elegant motor car, which he loved for her elegant air and pretty lines. The *Blue Angel*, as she had quickly been christened by the family, had been his and Meriel's eighteenth birthday present to Katherine. He stroked the side of the car, finding it impossible to free himself of the memory of how Katherine's face had lit up when they had walked her round to the garages. He even knew that his face was softening as he remembered Katherine's first sight of the car standing in the garage in all its dark blue glory, and how, the night before, Smith and himself had polished her up, as excited as the rest of the family at the prospect of handing over such a beautiful motor car to Miss Katherine on her birthday morning.

'So, so – so.' Anthony cleared his throat a little over-loudly. 'Well, then – not much for me to do, I dare say, so I will . . . I will leave it all to *you*, Smith. Good hands, you're in good hands, Caro, as you know.'

Anthony backed out of the garage and sped off to the house, leaving his chauffeur and his daughter to stand for a minute gazing at the car, which was rather better than standing looking sadly after Anthony.

There was no need for either of them to say anything. After all, it was only too obvious that, in handing over Katherine's car to her younger sister to take to London, Anthony was finally giving in to the notion that Katherine would never be returning to Chevrons.

'Such a good idea to give the *Blue Angel* to Caro to

take to London,' Meriel murmured a little later when Anthony joined her for coffee. 'After all, with war coming there is no doubt that as a Fany she will be given special petrol allowances and so on.' Seeing Anthony sitting staring ahead of him rather than drinking his coffee, she continued smoothly, 'I can't remember what happened in the last war about transport. What *did* happen Anthony?'

Anthony looked at her distractedly, and then picked up his cup.

'What was that, dearest?'

'What happened in the last war, as far as transport was concerned?'

'Eight hundred thousand horses were killed, that was what happened to transport in the last war, Meriel.'

Meriel nodded. 'Yes, yes, of course, that's what happened . . .'

She looked away. At least with this war, whenever it came, at least this time no one would be coming for the horses. It would be all cars, except in the country when, in the event of petrol rationing, they would probably have to return to the horse.

In the garage Smith was lecturing Caro, something at which he was only too adept.

'You have to learn to look after your motor car yourself, the way you would look after Snowflake, Miss Caro.'

'You mean go over him with the body brush and the dandy brush, clean out his hooves and brush his mane and tail, always remembering to plait on hunting days?' Caro asked flippantly.

Smith nodded, giving a final polish to the already shining surface of the car's flanks.

'That is exactly what I mean, Miss Caro. A clean car is a car in which you take care to drive carefully. A dirty car will always be a victim of neglect.'

Smith nodded towards the two cars belonging to Jag and Francis, both of which, only that morning, he had spent some good time cleaning.

'Inside and outside, a car must be as shining an example of its kind as the day it left the factory. Just remember the *Blue Angel* was made in a factory where the workers took pride in what they did. They didn't turn out motor cars like this for people like you to drive them in dirt and filth. I hope I'm getting through to you now, Miss Caro?'

Caro nodded. It was a rare day when Smith didn't get through to her, but she couldn't help saying, 'Of course, the Fraser Nash engine was made in Ger—'

'Those brothers of yours,' Smith went on, ignoring her, 'I swear whether it's their ponies, or their motor cars – the truth is that those brothers of yours will be a hundred before they can be persuaded to wash a motor car, and that's a fact.'

'Oh, yes, but our mother says boys do come to those kind of things later. Alas, not everyone is like you, Smith, and what a much better place it would be if they were, is what she says.'

Smith coloured a little. 'Well, never mind that, I'm sure,' he murmured. 'Let's go through the engine parts again, shall we? The combustion engine, as you know, Miss Caro, was invented . . .'

Just for a minute or so Caro allowed her thoughts to wander from the business of the invention of the combustion engine, and to turn to Katherine's whereabouts. She imagined herself in London, perhaps parking the *Angel* in Piccadilly, or going down Bond Street with a smart officer as a passenger in the back, and perhaps suddenly hearing Katherine's voice.

Maybe Katherine would even bend down to look in the Fraser Nash's window and say, 'What are you doing in *my* car, Caro Garland?'

Caro was sure that if that happened she would forgive Katherine everything, and she would laugh and indicate that as soon as she could she would drive it round to wherever Katherine was, and they would be reunited.

Maybe they would even have a gin together, the way she and Robyn had enjoyed a gin together, followed by sardine sandwiches that were cut too thick, but which would squish beautifully. Yes, just maybe that would be what would happen when she was driving the *Angel* in London. It was certainly yet another reason to leave Chevrons, to motor towards that hope.

However, leaving home, at least in her mind, as Caro had been for the best part of a week now, was, imaginatively speaking, a somewhat casual affair compared to when her last few days at Chevrons started to begin their hurried march towards departure time.

Every moment seemed to be passing too quickly. People and events that she had taken for granted all her childhood, all her adolescence, seemed suddenly to have acquired a tender significance.

'I expect you're looking forward to going to London, Miss Caro,' Betty asked her for what possibly must be the twentieth time, as Caro carefully folded the clothes Betty

113

was handing her, everything having been in neat piles around her bedroom.

'Yes, yes, of course I am, Betty,' Caro agreed. 'I keep saying, why wouldn't I be looking forward to it?'

'Nothing, no, nothing, it's just that *I* keep thinking you've never really been abroad before, not really. Your whole life has been here at Chevrons, same as – same as mine has been, and now you're leaving it. It's a big step, Miss Caro, you must agree, a big step.'

Caro pushed yet another starched and folded blouse into the top of the suitcase, and then sat back on her heels.

'We keep going through this, Betty, time and time again, and what is the answer? There is none. I *have* to go to London. There is going to be a war, everyone says so. I have to go and start helping to win it, even before it begins, so perhaps we should drop the subject, don't you think?'

Betty's expression was mutinous. 'I can't drop the subject, Miss Caro, I just can't.'

'Why ever not, Betty?'

'Because it's on my mind all the time, because, well, if you really want to know, because I'm hoping to go to London too!' The words burst out of her before she looked across at Caro, guilt flooding her face as if she had broken a vow. 'I am,' she went on bravely. 'I am hoping to go to London to be a stenographer. I bought a book on Mr Pitman's Shorthand, in the church bazaar, seems like years and years ago now—'

'Pitman's shorthand? You mean like secretaries do?'

'That's right, but I practised and practised, and now I

114

can do it really fast. And the Vicar's wife, Mrs Armstrong, all this time she has let me use their typewriter to practise on when the Vicar was doing his churching of women, which Mrs Armstrong says, of late, he seems to do all the time. At any rate, she thinks I'm coming along really fast – at the typing I mean.' Betty leaned forward, her pretty face full of enthusiasm. 'You see I've been reading the newspapers these last two years – only after Mr Smith had finished with them, mind – but I saw what they were saying about war, so I thought if I could get to London to be a stenographer—'

'A secretary? But what about your painting? You draw so beautifully, I always thought one day you'd leave Chevrons to become an artist, like Mr Beresford downstairs. We used to talk about it, remember?'

'I thought about it, really I did, but I know I couldn't earn a crust with my art, Miss Caro, really I couldn't. But what I could do, I thought, and perhaps it's why I picked up the shorthand so quickly, is be a secretary to one of the high-ups; start making my way, as well as helping to win the war, that's what I thought I could do, and I could earn my corn at the same time.'

'Of course you could, Betty.' Caro folded yet another blouse and put it in her suitcase. 'Have you told my mother about this?'

Betty shook her head, silenced. Mrs Garland's kindness to the people who helped at the house was legendary, so naturally Betty dreaded telling her that she'd had it in her mind to leave Chevrons, not for weeks, but for months now.

'No, I haven't, Miss Caro. I haven't said anything yet.'

'Well, when I get to London, I will ask friends about what they can do for you, and then I will write and tell you, and after that you can tell my mother and, knowing Mamma, she will pull out all the stops to help you—'

At that moment there was a sound outside the open door. Both girls looked round.

'I am sorry, but I couldn't help overhearing what you were both saying.' Meriel stood in the doorway, smiling. 'It's all right, Betty, Mrs Armstrong has already told me about your typing, and I have to tell you that I guessed the rest when I saw you taking down my shopping list for the village a *good* few weeks ago. You wrote it down so fast I knew you must be mastering shorthand.'

She smiled across at Betty.

'As a matter of fact, I'll ask Mr Garland to put in a word for you with someone in government circles, get you into one of the Foreign or War Office places. In no time at all, who knows, I dare say you will be taking down shorthand from the dreaded Mr Chamberlain.'

She turned to Caro. 'I'll finish here for you, Caro, because you are wanted rather urgently in the Long Room. Walter has to put a few finishing touches to your hair, or some such.'

'Oh, I expect he's just fussing—'

'No, I think he really does need you for another hour or two, or so he said.'

'Painters! Anyone would think that the world revolved around them and their work, and no one had anything else to do.'

Caro left the room, sighing.

Meriel looked puzzled. It was certainly not like Caro

not to want to go to the Long Room. She kneeled down by her open suitcase. It was probably just nerves about leaving home for, of all Meriel's children, Caro had the sunniest of natures.

Downstairs, Caro pushed open the second of the doors that led into the Long Room, and then stood for a second or two looking up at Walter, who, as always, was perched at what seemed like the top of some tree, not just his borrowed ladder.

He did not turn but continued painting, calling down to her, 'Come in, come in, my lucky charm. I have missed you these last days. In fact I have had the decided feeling that you have been avoiding me. Could this be true?'

Caro stared up at the wall for a second, not wanting to answer him, not even liking him to use his joking reference to her as his lucky charm.

'You've been working very hard,' she said in a considered tone, eventually. 'And I see you've put Cook in, but not in the same way that Verrio put the cook at Burghley on *their* ceiling.'

Walter did not turn. 'Remind me . . .'

'With hardly more than a tea towel covering her.'

'Yes, yes, of course, Verrio detested the cook deeply, didn't he? Or he was in love with her, one of the two.'

'Poor Cook, imagine having to wield all those wooden spoons and pots and pans with a painter hanging around.' She laughed.

'What can I say except – *quite*?' Walter laughed, after which there was a long pause during which only the working of his brush on the wall could be heard.

117

'I'm going to London,' Caro stated.

'So I hear. I gather you're going to join the FANYs. Mrs Grant told me when she was sitting to me. In no time at all you will be driving some handsome young officer around town, and he will be falling madly in love with you. I predict it.'

Caro smiled. 'I hope so.'

Walter climbed down the ladder before turning and looking her up and down in silent surprise.

'You're looking very grown up today, Miss Garland,' he said, having taken in Caro's coat and skirt, her hair put up for almost the first time.

'I know,' Caro agreed. 'The skirt and coat are not new; they were, they were – Katherine's. I don't know why, but she left this and a few other things behind.'

'Perhaps she wanted you to have them, isn't that a possibility?'

Caro looked down at the coat and skirt, as if she too was surprised by them, before looking at Walter, and frowning. It had never occurred to her until that minute that Katherine might leave things behind for her. Why would she?

Then she remembered that she had actually admired the yellow ensemble, just as she had admired the brown evening dress with the sequinned jacket, and that too had been left hanging in the wardrobe.

'I expect you remember Katherine wearing these, don't you? I know I do,' she stated factually, willing herself to turn away from the idea that, even while planning her flight from home, even while perhaps hastily stuffing her clothes into her suitcases, and waiting for David to pick her up – heart beating in case someone caught them, or saw her suitcases – Katherine had nevertheless thought of Caro.

'Yes, of course I remember her in that. Anyone would.'

This time it was Walter who turned away. He remembered Katherine in everything that he had ever seen her in, but what he could not say was that he had dreamed of her in other things, clothes that he would put her in, clothes that she would wear for him, if she loved him.

'Yes, Katherine left a whole lot of things behind – ' Caro shrugged – 'so everyone decided that I should have them; that if she left them behind she probably didn't want them. But she is, was, is taller than me . . . than I . . . so Betty has had to alter the hems, which she's done jolly well, actually.'

Walter sighed inwardly. He had not expected to see young Caro in the yellow linen suit with the double collar, the top layer of yellow linen, the second of dark velvet. It was perhaps for this reason that he felt nothing but relief that she looked as different from her sister as it was possible to look. He really did not want Caro, his lucky charm, looking anything like beautiful, impossible, wrong-headed Katherine.

'The coat and skirt suit you wonderfully well,' he stated. 'Really, you look good enough to eat,' he finished, joking.

Caro gave him a sudden oddly grown-up look.

'I can't wear clothes as well as Katherine did, or does – I say, isn't it difficult to know how to refer to someone who has just vanished? – but there you are, everyone thinks the suit looks quite nice. But of course Katherine took the green silk paisley scarf that she used to wear with it, which is a bit of a pity, because that really finished it off.'

Once again Walter found that he was immensely relieved that Katherine had taken the green silk paisley scarf that had somehow seemed electrifying with the yellow linen.

'It suits you, anyway.'

Caro nodded. The whole subject of the suit was becoming just a little dull.

'I gather you want to repaint my hair?' she prompted Walter, indicating the mural.

'Yes, yes, I do. I've missed putting some of the lights in it. At the moment the colour looks too flat. There are quite a few reddish tinges.' He gestured to her chignon. 'You'll have to undo all that, I'm afraid.'

In silence, watched by Walter, Caro undid her long, shining brown hair, shaking it out and then combing it through with a small hair comb.

'I'll sit to you here, if you like?' She sat down.

Walter climbed up the stepladders, palette in one hand, brushes in another, and started to look from Caro's once more familiar brown hair to the wall and back again, and then again, and again, and again.

With the advent of his concentration, conversation ceased.

'My little helper is not in a very chatty mood now that London beckons.'

'No, no, I'm not,' Caro agreed.

'Quite an adventure.'

'So everyone keeps saying. I have been to London before. But only on a visit, not to live. I shall be with

120

Robyn Harding, probably at her aunt's flat in Mayfair, after which we won't know, until we have been kitted out with our uniforms and all that. Then we shall probably be sent all over the place.'

'It will be exciting.'

'I think it will.'

Walter narrowed his eyes, concentrating on the head of brown hair that he was painting, adding a few more of the lightly titian tones that gave some much-needed movement to it.

'You've grown up, haven't you, these last weeks?'

'Wouldn't you if – well, wouldn't you?'

'I dare say.'

Caro stared ahead of her, thinking of her father's carefully concealed distress when he handed the *Angel* over to her.

'Do you think that Katherine will ever come back to us, to Chevrons, Walter?'

'I hardly know.'

'You do, Walter, you do – I know you know.'

'She might.'

'But you doubt it?'

'Yes, you're right, I do rather doubt it.'

There was another long silence.

'I could honestly murder her, you know?' Caro finally confessed after a long, long pause. 'For what she and David have done to the parents, I could willingly murder her.'

'It's understandable.'

'At least the war coming will take their minds off her, off everything.'

'Yes, I imagine war does rather have that effect.'

'I wonder if David and she have married.'

'Probably, I would think.'

'She always told me she would never marry.'

'In that case, probably not.'

'They must have left the country or someone would surely have spotted them by now?'

'Yes, they probably have.'

'Actually, it's David Astley I could really murder, filling her mind with his twisted ideas.'

Walter smiled ruefully. 'You would be surprised at just how many people in this country share what you call Mr Astley's "twisted ideas", Caro. I certainly am.'

They chatted on in a desultory fashion until, all of a sudden, Caro stood up.

'I expect that's enough, isn't it?'

'Well, yes, as a matter of fact I expect it is,' Walter agreed, surprised. 'Yes, I think it is. Obviously for you it is quite enough. Were you bored, or just stiff, or both?'

Caro looked at her watch, and then quickly twisted her long hair back into a chignon at the nape of her neck, taking the pins out of her jacket as she did.

'Must go, meeting Robyn at the flat at six o'clock, and since I don't drive nearly as fast as she does, I have to give myself an extra hour or two!' She laughed suddenly. 'Pity the poor men who are going to be driven by me, Walter.' She leaned forward and kissed him quickly on the cheek. 'It's been such fun helping you.'

She turned away, but Walter caught at her hand.

'No, no, don't go—'

Caro looked down at his hand. He had long fingers with square-tipped nails.

'Take your hairy hand off mine, Mr Beresford,' she joked.

'No, no, no, I will not,' he insisted, pulling at her hand, while at the same time persistently drawing her back to the mural. 'You can't go until you have told me what you think, you haven't told me what you think.' He nodded up to the wall. 'After all, you've been here all along.' He put a hand on her shoulder, the way he had the first evening they had met, leaning on her in a brotherly fashion. 'You've been part of the mural all this time, what do you think?'

'It's good,' Caro stated, staring up at the painting. 'I think you've captured the parents really well, and the twins – they're really good too. I mean, Jag is so much a Garland, and Francis so much like our mother.'

She looked across at Walter, who was also standing staring at his work, half critical, and half admiring.

'The twins have gone to join Papa's regiment.'

'Yes, they said they were going. They couldn't wait, they told me, just couldn't wait.'

'Oh, that's Jag and Francis all over. They've been aching to climb into uniforms these last two years, but the parents – well, it's understandable – they kept hoping it wouldn't be necessary, that they would stay around the place, and take over eventually, you know how it is. Farming has been in the doldrums for so long now. Very little help around, because everyone has drifted to towns, for which they can't be blamed, of course. Still, everything will change now, Papa says. It will all turn about because of shipping being targeted, and so on; no food coming in. We will have to work even harder on places like this. No one knows what will happen to farming, except perhaps that people will suddenly realise that it is more important than they thought.'

Caro sighed suddenly, for even though she would be in London, far away from home, she knew she would miss the thought of her brothers not being around at Chevrons, driving their father mad, and always having to be chased up by Smith for not doing something or another, only to be forgiven instantly, because if the twins couldn't talk themselves out of everything and anything, no one could.

Still, no point in worrying about them. They would probably just carry on through the war the way they had carried on at Chevrons all the time they were growing up.

She moved closer to the mural, staring up at it appreciatively.

'You've got Betty and Trixie to perfection. Katherine too, she's brilliant. Except,' she leaned forward, frowning, 'except why is she balancing a ladybird on her finger?'

'I put that in because apparently that's what Astley calls her.'

'How do you know?'

'Because, Miss Caro Garland, Miss Katherine Garland *told* me. He calls her his ladybird.'

'So you painted it in, something that horrid Astley man called her, you painted it in?'

'Yes, but not for him, for *her*. She asked me to.'

'And did she like it?'

There was a small moment as Walter gazed up at

Katherine on the wall, Katherine in her beautiful blue dress, her lovely face looking oddly haunted, as if she knew that she was about to bring disgrace on herself and her lover.

'Yes, yes, as a matter of fact she did like it, she liked it quite a lot, but she wouldn't ask Astley in to see it, which was odd. I think she thought it might make him jealous if he saw that I knew about his nickname for her.'

'Yes, Astley would be jell-jell; that is Astley all over,' Caro agreed in a flat voice. 'I'm afraid we don't talk about him any more around here, he is so *persona* absolutely *non grata*. The parents think he's taken her abroad, he knows the Continent like the back of his hand, and of course he has so many contacts there now, seeing that he is such a Nazi.' She paused, then changed the subject.

'So, what have you done for me? Have you painted anything special in for me, after all the help I've been to you?' she demanded, mock crossly.

Walter put out his arms and shook her shoulders in brotherly affection.

'Ha! I thought you would never ask! Look, Caro, you haven't looked closely at yourself yet!'

Caro leaned forward frowning; she had been in such a confused state, what with all the packing, and Betty wanting to leave, as well as everything else, it was only now she noticed that Walter had newly painted in, around her neck, a gold chain with a lucky charm on it – some sort of animal. He took his hand off her shoulder and, turning to one of his many wooden painter's boxes, he took out a small leather box, and handed it to her.

'To remember me by.'

Caro opened the box and when she saw the gold animal she smiled and smiled.

'How did you know that was one of *my* nicknames? It's what the family always used to call me because of my thick fringe of hair, out of which they said I was always peering.'

It was Walter's turn to smile. 'I told you, I am a painter, I need to know everything,' he said, beginning to climb the ladders once more. 'It was some time before I could find a real-looking Mr Mole, complete with paintbrush for whitewash. Actually a friend made it for me.'

For a second Caro felt a rush of disappointment that he had not attempted to clasp it around her neck, but then she rallied and, taking the gold chain, she did up the clasp herself and then patted the small gold animal in the same affectionate way that she would pat Dickie. Then she left the room to go for a long walk around the lake, because, she said, she needed 'to think'.

When she returned Walter was packing up his paints, a mulish expression on his face.

'Is something the matter?' Caro asked in a vague voice, because she had just made a firm resolution not to think about *him* any more, except in a very casual 'oh, yes, I wonder how he is doing' kind of way.

'As a matter of fact, there is. Your father has just paid me a visit.' Walter breathed in. 'He has asked – no, demanded – on behalf of the family, that I paint your sister out of the mural.'

'Oh – no.'

'Yes, quite – oh no. That is just what I said.'

'And?'

'And I explained that if he wanted something painted out, he could do it himself, that she was as much part of my mural as everyone else. That if anyone else in the painting suddenly decided to murder someone, or die, would he ask me to paint them out too?'

'He *is* rather cross with Katherine, and I mean to say, you can't really blame him, can you?'

'Whatever his feelings, only a philistine would ask an artist to do such a thing.'

'Well, that is true. Quite apart from everything else, you are too close to your painting. It would be like kicking yourself in the ankle, or standing on your own foot.'

'Exactly so. Could you step aside now, and let me pack up my paints?'

Caro did not want Walter to leave. In fact every bit of her longed to say, 'Please don't go. Stay and finish the painting.'

'I will stop anyone defacing your work, Walter, I promise. I will ask Smith to speak to my father, and my mother too, before I leave for London. Smith and Mamma will step in for you.'

But Walter wasn't listening. He was too busy throwing brushes and paints into boxes, snapping the ladders shut, and generally indicating that a rapid exit was about to take place.

Caro left the room. She didn't want to see him drive off. Actually, since he had looked less than impressed by her volunteering to muster people to defend his work, she really felt she wasn't very interested in what happened to the mural.

Chapter Four

The hushed silence that had fallen over the assembled company was as if thick snow had fallen, so that even the sound of the heaviest of footsteps would be muffled, but since it was August the silence was due to something quite other.

Robyn stepped away from the dressing mirror as Mr Porter too stepped back, and they both turned to Caro, who shook her head.

'That is too horrible for words,' she said, determinedly tongue in cheek. 'Really Mr Porter, you could have done better than that, really you could.'

'You're next, Caro, so I should be very, very careful what you say in front of Mr Porter, lest he inadvertently pushes one of his pins into you rather than the suiting.'

'You look very much like your father in that uniform, Miss Harding, I am here to tell you, very much a Harding.'

'I'm not sure that this uniform would be *quite* what my father would order, Mr Porter.'

Robyn turned back to the mirror. She could not help admiring how she looked in the FANY uniform, which was very, very smart, enviably smart, but hardly surprising with so many special effects – blue and pink lanyards (FANY colours, as Mr Porter had explained) worn to the left, and the cap with its cocking-a-snook strap. Tall and slender as she was, with honey-coloured hair that she wore in a neat twist at the nape of her neck, Robyn knew she looked just as she should.

'Your turn,' she ordered Caro.

When Mr Porter drew back the curtain to reveal Caro, small, neat and brown-haired in her uniform, the tailor was fascinated to see that the whole effect of the uniform he had tailored for Miss Garland was altogether different from Miss Harding's. If Miss Harding was a commanding lady, needing only a Britannia-style hat and sword, Miss Garland was a slender impish Cleopatra, who might be expected to be brought in to tease some military Caesar into happy submission.

'We'll stay as we are, Mr Porter, if you don't mind, and pick up the next lot, say, in a fortnight's time?'

Mr Porter paused by his desk.

'Oh, I should pick them up before that, if I were you, Miss Harding,' he suggested in his detached, unemotional way. 'The war, you know. Any minute now, I hear, the war will be upon us. But then your lot, they've been training hard these many years, if the number of uniforms I have tailored for them is anything to go by, they've been busy keeping their hand in ever since – well, ever since the last war.'

The two girls walked proudly out of Mr Porter's Savile Row shop and strode down the street together, their civvy clothes in bags, together with their civvy shoes, and civvy attitudes too.

'God, if one more person tells me that the war is about to be declared "any minute now", I think I'll scream,' Caro grumbled.

'Let's go for tea, and see the effect our uniforms have on everyone. They'll probably refuse us, if people's attitudes to women in uniforms are anything to go by!' Robyn said gleefully. 'People still *loathe* to see a woman in a uniform, they really do. Aunt Cicely told me to be prepared to be jeered at, and have doors closed in our faces by servants and shopkeepers, and she knew not what. Such excitement, to be spurned by everyone, don't you think?'

Caro laughed and pulled down her cap, with its proud, distinctive strap across the front.

'Actually, now I'm kitted out, Robyn,' she confided, striding along beside her taller friend, 'I have to tell you I feel like arresting practically everyone I pass.'

'Enjoy the feeling as much as you can, Caro,' Robyn warned. 'This is probably going to be the best of the before-the-war moments, believe me.'

'You know something?'

Robyn rolled her eyes. 'I know too much.'

'Your friend Bob in the Foreign Office?'

'Of course.'

'And he says . . .'

'He says nothing – nothing at all – he wouldn't dare. No, it's the way he looks.'

'Which is?'

Robyn looked down at Caro for a second. 'Let's put it this way, no one in the know is very hopeful, and of course they all loathe poor old Chamberlain. They'd like to throw him over the white cliffs of Dover, Bob says, but

Bob also says that knowing men like that, he'd probably just float back to the shore because flotsam and jetsam always do.'

'Oh, well, no good news there, then. I say, let's dash in here for what might be our last chance to enjoy an ice-cream soda.'

The staff in the fashionable store must have heard the same gossip and rumours as Mr Porter the tailor, because hardly an eye was blinked at the entrance of the two uniformed young women, who sat down and demanded two ice-cream sodas.

'Delicious.'

After her first taste Caro stared dreamily past Robyn, and for a few minutes both were silent.

'We'll probably remember this over and over again, when all the world's on fire, won't we, Robyn?'

'What sort of people would we be, if we didn't? Now, come on, we've got interviews, fingers crossed we can swing it to be sent to the same place.'

Robyn stood up. Caro also stood up, and for a second or two she stared round the restaurant in an effort to remember every last detail of the morning. The ladies in their stylish hats; the men, some of them fresh from the City, in their morning coats of black, and black and grey striped trousers. Soon nothing would be the same, but nothing; just for that one minute though it was – and she loved it.

'Come on, time to report to headquarters.'

Caro hurried after Robyn, making sure to keep up with the tall slender figure, as she realised she had been doing so much of her young life.

'I don't know whether *you* know, but Aunt Cicely told me the other day that the rumour is that the new bugs, the ATS, are going to take us on, if not over, which is perfectly beastly, Aunt Cicely says,' Robyn confided as they walked along side by side when Caro caught up with her outside the shop. 'But she says because the Yeomanry *own* their own headquarters, fingers crossed that they won't be able to kick us around as much as they would like. Even so, if it happens – which she thinks it will – the ATS are sure to be looking out to take us down a peg.' She looked at Caro for a second, her nostrils flaring slightly, vaguely reminding her friend of a horse on a frosty morning. 'I forget how many military medals the First Aid Nursing Yeomanry have been awarded, but Aunt Cicely told me it was a great many.' She frowned and raised an eyebrow. 'At any rate rather more than the entirely new Auxiliary Territorial Service has yet achieved. Fanys are Fanys, and that is all there is to it. We are a *yeomanry*, the ATS is not: that's why we have lanyards, flashes on our shoulders, and straps on our caps, because we are a *yeomanry*.'

Caro had not really picked up on the significance of what Robyn was saying until she faced a committee full of officers an hour later.

'Drive, don't you?'

'Yes, ma'am.'

'Own your own car, do you?'

'Yes, ma'am, a Fraser Nash.'

The officer taking down the details looked up at that. 'Fraser Nash BMW?'

'Six cylinder.'

'How long have you been driving?'

'Do you want a fib or the truth?'

Caro glanced around at each member of the committee with a look of such solemn innocence that they all laughed.

'The truth will suit fine, I think, Miss Garland,' one of the lady officers finally volunteered, when the laughter had died away.

'I have driven since I was quite small, driven the fields around our house in the summer, when the ground is hard, but never on roads, until six months ago.'

'Chauffeur taught?'

Caro looked surprised. 'Well, yes—'

'Good, good. Well, you'll be off to Dorset tomorrow. Still have to pass a few tests, you know, before we can let you loose on unsuspecting personnel. So have a good evening, you and Miss Harding.' This was said with a wry look. 'Enjoy yourselves while you can.'

Caro left the room, only to meet up with Robyn outside.

'Bit of a narrow squeak that was,' Robyn confided, once they were clear of headquarters. 'But I managed to swing it for us to train together.'

'How did you do that?'

'Masses of charm needed, of course, especially since their senior officer is Aunt Cicely's best friend.'

They both laughed.

'Well, now, who are we meeting tonight?'

'Bill Forewood, and Eddie Napier. You'll like them.'

'How did you find them?'

'Easy as pie, my deah. Aunt Cicely donated me her little black book, which was so kind of her. The only trouble is that it dates from 1920 so everyone in it is well over fifty! These two, as it happens, are the *sons* of two of her old beaux. When I rang their mothers and fathers it turned out to be most fortuitous, because they've got what is known as twenty-four-hour "passionate" leave from the RAF. Goodness knows what they're really like, though.'

Caro shook her head admiringly. Between them, Aunt Cicely and Robyn seemed to know just about everyone or everything, whereas without Katherine and her brothers, with her parents always so preoccupied, Caro was feeling just a little helpless, as if she'd been thrown in the pool before she could swim, although she would never admit as much to Robyn.

They clattered up the steps to Aunt Cicely's flat, greeted the Cairn terriers, and at once started to prepare for the evening, running a bath, putting out fresh underwear, choosing dresses.

'Goodness, where did you get that?'

Robyn stared in admiration at the long brown evening dress, with its matching sequinned jacket, which Caro was now holding up against herself.

'It's Katherine's, actually. She left it behind.'

'Top marks to Katherine for good taste. I have put on so much weight from that ice-cream soda, I shall probably only be able to fit into one of Aunt Cicely's cast-offs,' Robyn joked. 'So let's hope and pray there'll be other people there wearing fancy dress.'

In the event Robyn reappeared looking breathtaking in a white piqué bolero dress with daisies embroidered liberally around the hem and bodice.

'One of Aunt Cicely's cast-offs, my foot,' Caro murmured,

and they both laughed before Robyn caught up her stole, and Caro followed her out of the door.

'Who are we meeting, did you say?'

'I told you earlier, the two chaps who were in Aunt Cicely's little black book.'

As Caro stopped and stared at her, Robyn started to laugh.

'But I thought—'

'I *told* you they are the *sons* of chaps who were in Aunt Cicely's little black book: Forewood and Napier were their fathers. Let's hope they're dishes, because Aunt Cicely, would you believe, has quite an eye – and not just for a motor car. I have told them to look out for a bright scarlet bag – and I don't mean me. I will stand waving it outside the Dorchester.' Robyn dangled a bag of immense bad taste, and laughed. 'They can't miss us with this!'

'What happens if we don't like them?'

'We kick them in the shins, and then come home. Stay,' Robyn commanded her Cairn terriers. 'And don't move until I get back, do you hear?' Both the dogs stared up at their mistress as if to say, '*Must* we?' as Robyn firmly closed the front door.

Outside the flats they climbed into a taxi and a few minutes later, out again, as the cab stopped outside the Dorchester.

'Ah, here they are!' a young man called from in front of the hotel. 'On time too, that is quite something.'

To confirm that it was indeed them, Robyn waved her flashy evening bag at the young man, who rushed forward, closely followed by a taller, more handsome companion.

'You are spiffing to come at such short notice. I'm Bill Forewood, and this is Edward Napier.'

Robyn turned to Caro and widened her eyes as if to say, 'How about *these* then?'

They all shook hands, and Caro could see that one look at them and the young men too thought they had fallen on their feet.

'We thought we could have a cocktail here, and then on to the Berkeley for dinner, after which perhaps the Grafton Galleries? What do you think?' Bill looked round at the other three.

'Splendid, we both love the Grafton Galleries.'

For a second Caro stared at Robyn. They had neither of them been to London before, let alone dancing at the famously chic nightclub, the Grafton Galleries.

'It's more fun than Ciro's, and the music's livelier.' This from the one called Edward Napier.

'Oh, ra*ther*,' Robyn gushed. 'Actually, we didn't want to say, but the Grafton Galleries, well, we agree, they are much more the thing, don't we, Caro?'

'So that's settled,' Edward said.

Caro turned to Robyn. 'I think we should disappear for a moment, don't you?'

In the elegant pink mirrored powder room, already filled with *soignée* ladies refreshing their red lips with even redder lipsticks, Caro murmured to Robyn, 'I've never been to a nightclub before, and nor have you, have you?'

Robyn rolled her eyes in the mirror.

'No, but we don't want *them* to know that, do we?'

'But, but – but what about – well, what about, what

136

happens if they follow us home and ask themselves in, and so on? What happens if they start to be frisky? With no chaperone?'

'Oh, don't worry. If they get above themselves we'll set the dogs on them, or do what Aunt Cicely always recommends.'

'Which is?'

'Ask them in for a cup of Ovaltine. Apparently it gives *quite* the wrong impression!'

Betty was feeling awful, and the fact that Mrs Garland was being so nice to her was not making her feel less so.

'Look, Betty, I know it's difficult for you to leave us, but it has to be faced that, from what I have heard on the grapevine, and on the wireless, you would be leaving us some time soon, anyway. We all know there is a war coming. Of course, as farmers we are probably going to be made a special case because the country is going to need what we grow, and we are going to need to grow twice as much. But you would not be right for farm work, Betty, any more than I would be.' Mrs Garland smiled. 'We are indoor workers, you and I, Betty, not outdoor workers, so take this opportunity you have been offered. Really, it would be best.'

Betty put out a hand to shake Mrs Garland's hand. Mrs Garland looked at it. It was a nice hand, well made, with a sensitive look to it, but she didn't take it.

'No need to shake hands, Betty. You're not leaving us today, are you? I'm just so sorry that Mr Garland hasn't been able to find you a position as a stenographer. As he told you, I think, there is such a crush for jobs in London now, among the young and single, of course, while all the mothers and children it seems are all coming down our way. Still, I dare say they'll be a lot of help with the harvest and so on.'

Betty returned her outstretched hand to the side of her apron in one oddly touching formal movement, where she finally clasped it with the other one.

'It is so kind of you not to mind us all leaving you in the lurch like this, Mrs Garland. I have had such a happy time of it at Chevrons, really I have.'

Betty turned to leave the room. The truth was that for weeks she had been excited about the prospect of London and a new life, and could think of nothing else, but now she had to face saying goodbye to everyone at Chevrons, she felt miserable.

'Very special place, this,' Mr Smith confided to her later when she was helping him clear out the boot cupboard under the kitchen stairs. 'Yes, Chevrons is very special,' he went on with some satisfaction. 'People often remark on its magical properties, as if all the people who have been here before us determined that they would leave behind them something that would keep it what we might like to call different.'

'And what you could call special, would you say?'

'You could call it that, Betty. My father and my grand-father, they all believed that it was something to do with its past, something of the happiness of the first Mr and Mrs Anthony Garland that has been left as a sort of, let's say, "buried treasure" hereabouts, and that is probably why none of us has ever left the place.' He held up what looked like a hastily rolled-up bundle. 'Now what do you think we might have here?'

'It looks like some sort of flag—'

Betty looked mortified as she recognised what the flag represented, and Mr Smith's face darkened.

'I wish you to know, Betty, that I personally will take great joy in putting – ' he breathed out audibly – 'in putting that *thing* on the bonfire this afternoon.'

Betty bundled the flag quickly into a piece of newspaper because, although they were alone, she felt mortified at the thought that someone else might see the wretched swastika.

'That Miss Katherine, she's been brought up here all her life, and this is the result?' Mr Smith nodded towards the newspaper bundle. 'It makes me feel sick to think of her supporting something evil like that. Beautiful child she was, beautiful young woman she grew into, and *now* look. We all had such hopes of her, and *now* look. Run off with that Astley man and broken her parents' hearts. I don't know – children.'

Betty looked at him, her head on one side. 'But you're proud of your Trixie, aren't you, Mr Smith?'

'I certainly am, Betty.'

'She's going to go far, isn't she, Mr Smith, your Trixie?'

Mr Smith smiled for the first time. 'Let's put it this way: if Trixie's got anything to do with it, she certainly is, Betty, she certainly is.'

At first Trixie had missed Caro's reading with her – or, more accurately, her elocution classes with her – as much as she missed gossiping with her, but just as her plans for leaving Chevrons started to become a reality, a letter arrived for Trixie from Caro.

Dear Trixie,

Well, here I am in London and having a wonderful time, as they say on all the best seaside resort posters, and thinking that you will love it here too. We went to a nightclub called the Grafton Galleries, and it was great fun to see all the fashionable ladies (some of them quite OLD!). I miss Chevrons and the dogs and everyone. But today we leave for training. I will write to you from there, snips and snaps, as we used to say when we were in the Speytesbury Girl Guides together (remember Miss Hodgson?!!?).

Take care of yourself.

Love from your old friend Caro

Trixie put the letter away in her apron pocket. She liked to think of Miss Caro in the Yeomanry. She was always such a below-stairs bolshie, was Miss Caro, but with her fighting for Britain there really wouldn't be too much to worry about. Miss Caro could take on Hitler and give him a bloody nose, *and* all the rest of them. What she couldn't do was to help her old companion in mischief Trixie Smith.

But first things first. She had to give in her notice to Mrs Garland, which her father had already warned would not be an easy matter.

Meriel rang the little bell on her desk.

'Yes, Trixie, do come in.'

Trixie had been brought up at Chevrons, it was her

home, and she thought of it as such quite as much as if she was one of the children of the house. So it was even more awkward for her to take her leave of Mrs Garland than it had been for Betty less than half an hour earlier.

'I am so sorry to bother you, Mrs Garland, but I have been offered a situation in London.'

Meriel stared at Trixie. What was there about this afternoon? It seemed suddenly that everyone had decided to leave Chevrons.

'Oh dear, Trixie, have you really to leave us? How sad.' Meriel could not keep the distress from her voice. First Betty leaving, and now Trixie.

'Yes, ma'am, I am hoping to join up, as a matter of fact. But don't tell Father, will you, Mrs Garland? What I have in mind is to join the ATS. I just felt that with everything the way it's going, and wanting to help keep our country the way it is now, I need to do what a boy would do, Father having had no boy, you see. I feel I could do my bit, as a boy would do his bit, as your boys are doing their bit, ma'am – and Miss Caro too.'

Meriel stared at Trixie. She knew her so well she sometimes felt when she was talking to her that she had been present at her birth, which, most happily she had not been, since Trixie's poor mother had died before the doctor could come from the village. All terribly distressing at the time, but everyone at Chevrons had done their best to ensure that Trixie had grown up surrounded by affection; and the truth was that she had enjoyed quite as good a time as any of their own children, running about their little estate, swimming in the river in the summer, fishing in the top pond, helping to feed the orphan lambs in the kitchens.

'Well, Trixie, if you have to leave us, and I perfectly understand that you do, there is no more to be said, of course. I also understand that you feel the need to join up – everyone is feeling the same at this time – and I only hope that the ATS can find some suitable work for you. I do know there is a great shortage of actual posts at the moment, due to so many people wanting to do something for their country, but if Mr Garland and I can influence anyone on your behalf, you must let us know.' She paused. 'I would very much like to think that you will always consider Chevrons your home as much as it is ours, and that whenever you are on leave you will not hesitate to come here; and wherever you are you will know that there will always be a place here for you.'

Trixie nodded. She knew that too much emotion at this moment would not be acceptable, so she put out her right hand and shook Mrs Garland's ringed one.

'You and Mr Garland –' She hesitated, and began again after clearing her throat. 'Mr Garland and yourself, Mrs Garland, have always been so kind to me. I am really most grateful to you, and I will always bear in mind –' she hesitated wondering whether 'that' or 'what' would be more correct – 'I will always bear in mind – what you have said to me this afternoon. Thank you very much, Mrs Garland.'

'I will tell Mrs Grant that you are to be let go whenever you wish, Trixie. That is the least I can do. After all, everyone is needed, and both my husband and Mr Smith are certain that the war will come sooner rather than later.'

Meriel watched Trixie slip out of the door. It was sad, but it was inevitable, the cygnet was determined to grow into a swan and, knowing Trixie as she did, Meriel was convinced that the young woman would make sure to grow into a really beautiful swan. She was a determined little thing and she had it in her to be whatever she wanted.

Meriel turned away from her desk and walked over to the French windows that looked out on to the view of first lawns, then meadows and then finally the river.

She knew from their old diaries that it had been a great day when the first Mr and Mrs Anthony Garland came to live in the house he had built for her, a day of much rejoicing. It was the house of their dreams, a family home where children could grow up in peace and harmony. Doubtless they would all have great days again, but for the moment everyone was leaving: Betty, Trixie, the twins and Caro; even Mrs Grant had already hinted at having her eye on a nursing job, something it now transpired she had always had a mind to do. Meriel smiled at the memory of how Anthony had taken that particular piece of news.

'Mrs Grant's becoming a nurse, you say? Good God, she'll kill more people than the enemy!'

As it happened, Anthony had heard on the grapevine that the government was already making preparations to evacuate the cities, and yet here they were again, against all advice, *still* hoping that they would somehow be able to make peace with Hitler. Meriel glanced at the date on the permanent calendar on her desk – nearly the end of August. In times gone by at this time of year, she would have been preparing for the boys' return to school, organising them to go to London for their uniforms. Now they were in uniform once again, but this time preparing to fight not in some rugby or cricket team, but in a regiment, for their country.

'Anthony?'

'Yes?'

These last weeks Anthony was nearly always to be found in his small library, reading one book or another, making notes for something or other. Meriel never quite knew what, and hadn't thought it her business to ask, whilst always hoping against hope that his reading matter would turn out to be something practical, something to do with the farm. She was not to be disappointed.

'There will be a petrol shortage. One doesn't have to be a prophet in the wilderness to predict *that*.' Anthony put down a large closely written tome and stood up as his wife advanced towards his reading table. 'And just as well we took so many to market in the spring and started to sow crops, Meriel, because I hear everything is to be given over to cereal and potatoes, even the London parks. It will not be long before we lose Smith, I am sure of it. He is quite determined to do his bit, and who can blame him?' He smiled, a rueful expression crossing his face. 'I dare say when winter comes I shall be glad that I learned to lamb all those years ago with old Wentworth, much as I grumbled about it to my poor father.' He shrugged his shoulders. 'Now what can I do for my beautiful wife?'

'I hate to disturb you, Anthony, but both Trixie and Betty have handed in their notice, one on top of each other, which is only rather to be expected, after all. But given that what you have just told me is true, I think I should start to prepare our cottages to take in evacuees from London.'

'Yes,' Anthony agreed. 'How many could we take, do you think?'

Meriel considered. 'I would think about ten, always provided they are not too big, of course!'

They both laughed even as they tried to avoid the thought that would keep coming into their minds, that would not be turned away – that they might be about to lose their whole world, and to a situation that should never have happened.

Anthony tapped a letter to the side of his book.

'Do you know old Tankerton told me the other day that Cynthia Asquith was warning everyone – her old friend Winston Churchill, the Liberals, the Conservatives, everyone – that Germany was rearming as far back as 1923, and what was the end result? No one took the slightest notice of her.'

Meriel touched her husband lightly and sympathetically on the arm.

'Well, why would they, Anthony dear? She is a woman.'

'They listened to Nancy Astor.'

'Because she is an American, and she frightened them. American women are very good like that,' Meriel stated. 'Besides, frightening women always go far. It is just a fact.'

She left Anthony then, because any further discussion on that particular subject was a backwards glance, and backward glances were always a melancholy, useless business.

Anthony returned to his books. Somehow, at this time of indecision, of no one quite knowing which way to turn and therefore unable to start making real plans, besides Meriel, and of course Smith, his books were his only source of comfort and escape. He just wished they could all get on with it. They had enough shelter, God knew. The cellars that ran under the house, as well as the vast old ice house, precluded the need for building anything new. Sometimes he woke in the night, after only a few hours, and found himself staring into the darkness, wondering, how soon, how soon?

The young officer had called out her name.

Robyn stepped forward, instantly, and understandably wondering what she had done wrong.

'Follow me, please.'

Robyn glanced back over her shoulder to Caro and pulled a little face. Their friendship had already ruffled feathers among the other girls training at the camp, despite the fact that they, in their turn, had already formed their own little cabals.

'Caught smoking in the la-la, was she?'

'She doesn't smoke.'

The tall, stunning redhead who had posed the question gave a short laugh. 'If she doesn't smoke now, she soon will.'

Caro turned. 'Why do you say that?'

'Because I've been here longer than you, Shorty, and because I know what is going to happen, that's why! I am not just omnipresent, I am omniscient.'

Caro held out her hand as the speaker – green eyes,

white, white skin, perfectly sculptured features – looked down at her.

'Caro Garland.'

The titian-haired beauty smiled. 'Pleased, I am sure. Edwina O'Brien, late of the Republic of Eire.' She shook Caro's hand. 'Shall we go for a cup o' tea?'

Caro fell in beside her new friend, feeling decidedly flattered that this stunner with the languid manner should have adopted her so readily. As they walked along to the canteen, Edwina glanced back at Robyn, who was being marched smartly off to one of the newly requisitioned buildings that housed the offices.

'My father's told me about the last war,' Edwina went on in the same languid voice, which held more than a hint of a lilt to it. 'You have to smoke to stop the old tummy rumbling, d'you see? I bet you half a crown,' she pretended to spit on her hand and extended it to the surprised Caro to shake, which she promptly did, 'that we'll all be smoking within the month. It's only normal, d'you see? Mind if I call you Shorty, Shorty?'

Caro shook her head then nodded distractedly as she looked back to see that Robyn had now disappeared. Caro followed Edwina into the canteen.

What had Robyn done? Or, to put it another way, what had Robyn done that Caro hadn't done? Nothing that she could think of at that moment. They had trained, they had changed wheels, they had driven, they had done everything that had been asked of them. Still, of one thing she could be sure, and that was that Robyn could take care of herself. There were few situations from which she could not extricate herself with a snap of her long, elegant fingers.

'What's worrying you so, Caro Garland?'

'I'm not worried exactly, I'm just curious as to why they should march my friend Robyn Harding off to head-quarters. Mind you, if anyone can take care of herself, she can.'

'And just as well, I would say.'

Edwina O'Brien rolled her eyes as they both joined the queue for tea and rock cakes. They sipped and nibbled in silence, each one wondering individually how anyone could make tea taste so disgusting, or bake cakes so hard.

'Take the varnish off your toenails, wouldn't it?' Edwina asked cheerfully, holding up her cup. 'Cheers! And as for the rock cakes, I think we should store them for ammunition. "Kill two Jerrys with one cake" – something the government could promote on the Underground.' She bounced hers on her plate and then rolled it up and down the table before continuing, 'Now your friend – Robyn, is it? – you say she can take care of herself? I hate to disabuse you of that notion, but when it comes to the Black Dame who is currently visiting us, not even Beelzebub would take her on, believe me. The Black Dame is one of the original forces behind women's recruitment. She has the reputation of gnawing her way through the opposition in a way that a deathwatch beetle would envy. And as for anyone taking *her* on – they are merely flies on the windscreen of her private plane, which, by the way, she still races at weekends, when she is not racing her motor car, that is. I can't remember which race she beat most of the men in, but beat them she did. Not taken well, as you can imagine.'

'Why is she called the Black Dame then, if she's so brilliant?'

'Because she always sports a black cane, has a bit of a limp, doncher know? Fell out of her plane at a thousand feet, and broke her fall by destroying a house, I dare say. But, at any rate, she is a dame. Happily for most of us we will never be given the privilege of more than a glimpse of her on parade, but it would seem that your friend Robyn is the exception, and the Dame is doubtless, even now, interrogating her.'

'Interrogating?'

'*Mais certainement, mademoiselle*. You don't think the Black Dame invites you into her office to ask for a tip for the Cheltenham Gold Cup, do you?'

Caro's eyes searched Edwina's face, longing to see something that would tell her that she was only teasing. She found no such look.

'I hope that you will remember my words of wisdom when I am proved triumphantly right.'

Edwina sighed with pleasurable anticipation as Caro finished her tea, and left her rock cake.

As they stood up Edwina glanced down at the cake. 'Put it in your pocket, Shorty. We may well, as I just indicated to you, find we need it for civil defence.'

Robyn saluted. She knew it was a good salute, she had practised it in the mirror for long enough.

'Miss Harding?'

'Ma'am?'

'Sit down, please.'

They were alone, her commanding officer, and Robyn, a mere pipsqueak recruit of a few weeks' training. Despite a calm exterior, Robyn's insides started to turn to ice, as they tended to do when there was, as Aunt Cicely would put it delicately, 'something afoot'.

She sat down on the chair in front of the desk, feet together. She didn't know why, but to cross your ankles was considered absolutely horrendous. She made a mental note to ask Aunt Cicely on her next leave.

'Miss Harding, before you joined the First Aid Nursing Yeomanry you had cause to report to someone at a Victoria office some kind of sighting, was this not so?'

'Yes, ma'am.'

'Why was that?'

'It was on the advice of my aunt, Cicely Harding—'

'Ah, yes, yes. I knew Cicely Harding very well in the old days.'

A brief affectionate smile crossed the face of the feared woman behind the desk. Encouraged by this, Robyn relaxed a little, although not as far as allowing herself to smile back.

'It was like this, ma'am. On hearing what I had noticed in the back of a civilian plane piloted by a German gentleman, my aunt gave me the address of a certain officer who runs a government department based in Victoria.'

'Precisely so, and it is for this reason that the officer in question has put forward your name to work undercover for us.'

Robyn stared at the Black Dame, and found herself immediately wishing that she had not taken Aunt Cicely's advice, and had not visited the officer in Victoria, and was not being asked anything other than to stay with Caro in Dorset, drilling and driving, and doing all the other tasks that she had fully expected to be doing, while all the time waiting to meet up with Eddie Napier and have a cracking evening out once again.

She could not bring herself to speak the words that she would have liked to have uttered, namely, 'Why me?' As it turned out she had no need.

'I expect you are wondering, why me?'

'I was rather.'

'Well, I will tell you. You have already shown initiative. Reporting the pilot's photographic equipment showed that you are alert to danger, but you are also discreet. For example, I notice that you did not disclose the name of the officer you went to meet in Victoria, even to me. After all, I might not be trustworthy. That is commendable. Then you have a good service background – aunt in the FANYs, papa in the cavalry – and are, I believe, a more than competent driver, not to mention already knowing your way around basic mechanics, such as changing wheels, when you arrived here. Not, I think, that you will be doing much changing wheels in the kind of work we have lined up for you.'

'I can't say that will cause me to lose much sleep.'

This time they both smiled.

'We shall not require you quite yet, but we shall require you to, let us say, behave in a way that is out of order, only in a minor way. Say, for instance, do you smoke?'

'No.'

'Do you go to nightclubs?'

'Not regularly, no, although I have been to the Grafton Galleries.'

'Are you easy, as the expression has it?'

Robyn cleared her throat. 'Good heavens, no!'

'No, of course not. Nevertheless I think we shall have to ask you to take up smoking, if you don't mind, and after that we will transfer you and the Bentley, back to London, where the fun will begin, if it can be termed as such.'

Robyn nodded. She didn't mind the idea of going back to London. It would make it easier to see Eddie and go to the Grafton Galleries, and even Ciro's and the Savoy, but the idea of taking up smoking was less appealing.

The Black Dame opened the drawer in her desk and took out a packet of cigarettes.

'Start in on these, after lights out, behind the sheds, and I'll make sure one of the officers catches you in a few days' time. You should have stopped feeling queasy by then.'

She stood up, extending her hand. 'We will be in close touch, but not through the usual channels. I don't need to say any more.'

Robyn went to leave, but the Black Dame stopped her. 'One more thing. If anyone asks you why you were interviewed, I was trying to recruit you for the nursing service, but you refused.'

Robyn nodded. 'I understand.'

But of course she didn't. She marched smartly across the green that divided the office from the sheds and the huts, all the time wondering what on earth she had let herself in for. She wished to God that she had not reported to that officer in Victoria on Aunt Cicely's advice. She wished she'd kept her mouth shut. She wished so many things, most of all that she did not have to take up smoking. Her father smoked, and she hated it. He had taken up smoking in the First World War to keep midges away, hunger at bay, and his spirits up. He had not stopped since, and of course she would never expect him to, but the idea that she would now have to take to nicotine was repellent.

A week later found Edwina O'Brien holding out her hand for the half a crown she now claimed Caro owed her.

'I told you it wouldn't be long,' she said to the astonished Caro. 'War and smoking go hand in hand, just as my old da told me.'

That was two days before the Sunday broadcast of September the third, when at long, long last, Great Britain 'got off her backside', as Edwina put it in her usual pithy way, and declared war on Germany, and just after Robyn had duly been caught smoking behind the sheds in the early hours of that fateful morning, and even as Meriel Garland led the small band of children who had been allocated to stay at Chevrons for the duration of the war towards their new homes, trying not to notice their bedraggled appearance, their tear-stained faces.

Chapter Five

It didn't matter that when the first siren blew it was afterwards found to be a mistake. It didn't matter that they had all started to say not '*if* the war begins', but '*when* the war begins', the sound of the air-raid siren wailing was enough to encourage everyone to run towards some place of refuge.

'I never thought I'd find myself *willingly* in a church on a Sunday,' Eddie whispered to Robyn, before he glanced down at his watch. 'I'll have to leave you here, I'm afraid. I must get back to camp.'

He leaned forward and kissed her briefly and lightly on the lips, which was really an outrageous thing to do in a small country church, and caused a stir among their fellow worshippers, but Robyn couldn't care less. She was definitely in love with Eddie Napier and, what was more, she didn't mind who knew it. They had not yet made love, but she knew she *would* make love with Eddie, before he climbed into his aeroplane, and flew off into the skies. She knew it with complete certainty. She also knew it would be quite the right thing. Not that she was easy, not that she had ever thought of love in that way before, only now it was war, everything was immediately quite different – most of all love.

Caro had returned to Dorset, after spending the weekend at Chevrons, to continue with her training. Upon hearing that they had at last declared war on Germany, Bill had immediately telephoned Caro and asked to marry her, 'before it is too late'. It seemed that suddenly everyone wanted to marry someone, and all for the right reasons. Several girls in their unit had already announced that they intended to get pregnant, no matter what, simply so that they could guarantee the next generation.

It was all too much for Caro, who, much as she liked Bill, did not want to marry him, or even make love to him. It was enough to have dinner and go dancing with him.

'You know you will have to one day,' Robyn announced to her some days later.

'Will have to what? Take up smoking?'

'No, you know what I mean. It.'

Caro turned away. She did not see why she should. Why should she do something just because they were at war?

'I'm taking a test today, can't think of anything else, big lorry type. I shall probably die if I crash it like I did that van,' Caro murmured, quickly changing the subject to avoid any more discussion of It.

'You'll pass with flying colours,' Robyn stated shortly, because she had just mentally made a note to tell their senior officer that a certain young lady in their ranks must be encouraged *not* to go home.

'Look, Caro. Sit down.'

Caro sat down on the edge of her bed.

'War is not just about bombs dropping and being invaded, it is also about being wet behind the ears, and you've had a pretty protected time of it, you know?'

'Well, so have you!'

Robyn shook her head. 'No pigeon pie, not like you. You were kept under wraps by everyone at Chevrons. Brothers, sister, mummy and daddy, even Smith and Mrs Grant. You were the baby of the family. I was an only child with a maiden aunt. I had to protect *her*, and look after Daddy, who as you know is quite incapable of remembering where he's left his spectacles, while Aunt Cicely suffered from what I can only describe as intermittent attacks of the Florence Nightingales.'

'How do you mean?'

'All that nursing in the Boer War and driving ambulances in the Great War had their effect, as they were bound to do. Gracious heavens, you can't go in for all that and not have some sort of after-effect. Aunt Cicely used to get prone for weeks on end, couldn't move. All those memories, you know, plus the fact that she never found love, as I think I have,' Robyn finished quickly.

'Eddie?'

'Yes.' Robyn was silent for a second. 'Remember Aunt Cicely's little black book? Well, Eddie's father, he was killed at the Somme. And now look.'

'I'm sorry, I don't understand?'

'Why should you?' Robyn looked down at her over-polished shoes. 'I think Eddie's father was the love of Aunt Cicely's life.'

156

Caro's heart sank as she realised that it was quite possible that Robyn was thinking herself into Aunt Cicely's shoes, first joining the Nursing Yeomanry, and now, obviously to bring everything neatly into a joined-up circle, falling for the son of her great love. She had heard this could happen to people, that they could become obsessed with the past.

'Don't you think maybe you're—'

'No, as a matter of fact, I don't.'

Robyn stood up abruptly and, going to her jacket, she plucked out a packet of cigarettes.

'I'm leaving for London later, once we've finished putting up the blackout in the offices, which is appallingly difficult because the windows are stone and nothing sticks – but let me know if you want to come.'

Caro, already unnerved by the prospect of her test, was now more unsettled. Everything was changing so fast, it made her feel odd, as if she had fallen down a hole and would soon bump into the Queen of Hearts. Indeed, she would not be at all surprised if a mouse didn't stick its head out of the canteen teapot and start to go on about *treacle*.

Later, after Caro and Edwina had not just taken their tests, but passed them with flying colours – Edwina managing to change the wheels on her vehicle in the fastest ever recorded time – she put her titian-coloured head round the common-room door and smiled sweetly at Caro.

'Come on, Shorty, we're wanted, sharpish. And from what I've heard I think we're going to be moving on, so better start learning some regimental songs.' She stopped.

'Do Fanys *have* any regimental songs? What they *do* have are pretty smart uniforms but, if the rumour is true, where you and I are going, dotey dear, we're not going to be allowed to display our pretty little pink lanyards no more; nor indeed the perky little straps on our caps, that make us so awfully distinctive. Ooh, no, our new guvs, the Auxiliary Territorial Service will be frowning on them. Rumour is we're going to be *absorbed* by them, doncher know?'

'What is happening? What have you actually heard?'

Edwina put her head on one side, her expression solemn.

'The new rumour is that we're being sent to the Outer Hebrides to ferry fishermen back and forth from their islands, so all these driving tests we've been so busy passing are going to be completely useless, and we won't even get to know all those lovely handsome officers about whom we have dreamed for aeons upon aeons, most especially those of us who hail from across the Irish Sea. So how are your rowing skills, Miss Garland?'

'Oh, I can row all right,' Caro reassured her. 'But I'm not quite sure *how* all right when it comes to the North Sea, and whatnot.'

Edwina laughed. 'You don't frighten easily, do you, Caro Garland? Sure, wasn't I teasing you in as cruel a way as I could think of? No, the rumour actually is that we are both being sent back to London, with our motor cars, to drive officers, just as our fond mammas had hoped, because that way we will meet young men from a beautiful background who will show us respect . . . I don't think! Now, what kind of sacrifice is that?'

Caro stared at her, hope dawning, because much as she was ready and willing to do whatever was necessary for her country, rowing around the Hebrides sounded a bit out of her league, not that she would have let on, least of all to Edwina.

'Is this true?'

'If this be not true then no woman ever bought a lipstick, nor put on silk stockings, nor dabbed French perfume behind her ears. Of *course* this is true. Have you ever known a rumour around this training camp not be true? Besides, I have a friend, or, since she drives such a hard bargain, some might call her a *fiend*, in the office, and in return for two packets of cigarettes, not to mention a pair of my best silk stockings, damn her, she let me know our orders-to-be, and London it is.'

'This is such good news. I'd much prefer to be in the thick of it.'

'Oh, I know, dotey,' Edwina drawled. 'And so much nearer for the nightclubs . . . not to mention the Dorchester and the Ritz, and you know, everything that is just so much more *us*. Now let us set fair to go like Dick the Whit with his cat to Londinium town, where your dearly beloved friend Robyn Harding is already about to hasten. And I do believe if we hurry she might just have finished her cigarette, and we can cadge a lift in the auld Bentley.'

At that Caro held back.

'No, I'll drive us in the Fraser Nash. Robyn won't want us trailing after her, not once we get to London.' As Edwina looked at her with sudden interest, Caro lowered her voice. 'Eddie Napier, you know, he has passionate leave. He might want to go for a drive with her, stay the night somewhere, and then we'd be without a lift. Besides, we don't want to go around trailing after her, feeling like lumps of unwanted cargo, do we?'

'No, of course not, being a gooseberry is only for fools!' They both laughed. 'But Eddie? Are you sure? Really? The Eddie you told me about? *Really?* So they really are going to make music, you think?'

Edwina entwined two elegant fingers, looking both amused and quizzical at the same time, which, because it was obviously going to be all too true, only succeeded in irritating Caro.

'None of our business—'

'Don't be such a hypocrite, Shorty. It's all of our business!'

'At any rate, it doesn't make any difference. The other reason to take our own motor is – is, well, for my money, Robyn drives too fast in the Bentley. So, all in all, I'd really rather drive myself in the Fraser Nash.'

'Very correct, Shorty,' Edwina said, but she still looked both quizzical and amused. 'I will therefore be most pleased to accompany you, because I myself have no Eddie at the moment and, what's more, none in mind. Besides, I drive dreadfully when I'm tight, and as I intend to be very-nicely-thank-you all weekend, I will willingly leave my dear motor behind and travel in yours.'

'I just can't wait to have some decent food.'

'We must try not to be late back on parade, as we were last weekend; most of all we must try not to fall in love with the chaps with whom we dine and dance. Mind you, no risk of that with the Algernon I was landed with last

Saturday night. However, now the dear old balloon has really gone up, love, as in falling in love, as in songs and such like, well, when you think about it, I think we should be well advised to avoid it. It is truly not practical.'

This was so much the opposite to what Robyn had said to her that Caro, who had been following Edwina at a fast trot down the corridor, instead overtook her, forcing her to come to a sudden halt.

'What do you mean by that?'

Edwina gave Caro a bored look.

'Well, now, Shorty, what do you think I mean by that, forsooth, if not fifth sooth? War, young men, love? Short-lived affairs are on the agenda from now on, but no time for Great Love. Dost thou twig now, or dost thou not twig? Pretty soon one will just be lucky to have a man, pretty well *any* man, to go out with, and that is the plain truth and nothing but the truth. In fact I am certain that in a very short time indeed, we will be grateful to go out with a fifty-year-old bus driver, let alone some poor Algernon de Montmorency, home on leave.'

'Mmm, perfectly understood,' Caro muttered, dropping her eyes.

'Never give all the heart, that is the message. If we allow ourselves to fall in love we will be sure to break our hearts, whereas if we just love, as in making love, it will be much easier.' Edwina shrugged. 'If we just love and send the men on their way, even if they don't return they will have something beautiful to remember, namely us, my dear. If we hang on to our hearts, we will not become useless to everyone and everything, for that is what happens when one loves and loses. One becomes useless, believe me, I know, because my mother told me, and she knew, if anyone did. Useless, hopeless and helpless, that is how one is left if one loves and is the one who is left.'

After which Edwina moved neatly past Caro, leaving her as always to follow, hurrying after her, for not only was Edwina a great deal taller than Caro, she was also more athletic. Edwina did not walk, she did not hurry, she did not stride, she loped. Tall, elegant and seemingly carefree, she loped ahead of her new shorter friend. Except from what she had just said, perhaps Edwina was not *quite* as carefree as she appeared to be.

Once they were in London, the three Fanys hurried round to Aunt Cicely's flat, so convenient for the London hotels, which, it had been announced, would soon be serving only five-shilling menus, as ordered by the law. The shops were already being prepared with tapes and blackouts, and they knew not what, for the exigencies to come. It momentarily lowered Caro's spirits to see all the preparations for war. Nevertheless, it was heaven to discard their uniforms and shimmy forth once more in civvies.

Caro stared at herself in the yellow suit, with the double collar of linen and black velvet in which she had originally travelled to London, and into which she had just changed. It was still stylish, and still very much Katherine. Well, why wouldn't it be?

She knocked on the bathroom door where she could hear Edwina splashing and singing 'The Mountains of Mourne at the top of a considerable, and happily tuneful, soprano voice.

'I'm just rushing off to the chemist's for some nail varnish remover. Anything I can bring you, Edwina?'

Edwina turned off the taps and stopped singing.

'Four thousand aspirins, please, for tomorrow morning.'

Next Caro went to Robyn's bedroom door.

'Need anything from the chemist?'

Robyn opened the door, and thrust a small white envelope at her.

'Would you mind . . . ? Only I won't have a chance to go myself later. Just hand it in to him, would you?' she said, and quickly closed the door again.

Caro drove round to the well-known chemist's shop Reading and Reading, a large establishment frequented by modish gentlemen and ladies, and according to Walter Beresford, supplier to the peerage of what had come to be known as 'Coronation bottles'. The Abbey's bathroom facilities being non-existent, the original and obviously obliging Mr Reading had had the foresight to invent a secret bottle, which, when positioned inside the lordly robes, helped relieve what might have been a quite insuperable problem for many a duke and belted earl.

Once inside the shop Caro made her own purchase, ordered Edwina's aspirins and paid for them, before thrusting Robyn's envelope at the grave-faced assistant, who, noting the poor young woman's heightened colour, disappeared with it, then reappeared and returned the envelope and the order, discreetly parcelled up in brown paper. After which Caro paid, and hurried thankfully from the premises.

Although it was now September she was still driving

the Fraser Nash with its dark blue roof folded down, still enjoying the fresh air, and the colours of late summer, while all the time feeling secretly guilty that she could enjoy anything at all, considering that the country was now at war.

She opened the boot, and put the parcel into it, and then walked round to the driver's door, which was when she saw it. There it was, curled up and over the steering wheel of the motor car, unmistakable in its bright colour, and its silk texture – the bright green paisley scarf that Katherine had always worn with the yellow suit that Caro was now wearing.

Caro untied the scarf and, without really thinking, she draped it around her shoulders while all the time looking around her for its true owner.

'Katherine? Katherine?' she found herself murmuring. 'Katherine, please come out from wherever you are.'

Katherine had always been good at playing sardines, hiding in places where no one would have ever dreamed of looking for her, nearly always having to reveal herself because the rest of them couldn't get on with their game if they never, ever found her.

Now it seemed nothing had changed, for even as she walked up and down that London street, Caro could have sworn that she could hear Katherine laughing, and she found herself hoping against hope that her beloved older sister would suddenly appear as if from nowhere, saying, 'Here I am, you silly thing!'

But walk up and down as often as she did, no elder sister appeared, so that finally Caro drove off back to the flat, leaving behind a note tucked into the envelope that

Robyn had given her, but which was now left sticking on the lamp post nearby.

'Katherine! My number is Mayfair 342. Please, please ring me. Caro.'

Robyn opened the door before Caro could even put her front door key in the lock.

'You've been gone long enough,' she snapped, immediately taking the brown-paper parcel from Caro.

'The aspirins are Edwina's, and the nail varnish remover mine,' Caro called after her.

She hurried off to her own bedroom, which, being double, she was now sharing with Edwina.

'Where did you get that scarf, dotey? Never seen that before. It is heaven on earth, and stars in the sky too.'

Edwina was standing looking not unlike a titian-haired Statue of Liberty, draped in a long, fluffy white bath towel, her red hair caught up in a silk bandana. She reached out a dry hand and stroked the paisley scarf.

'Perfect taste, well done,' she murmured.

Caro looked away. Who to tell? Must tell someone. Not to tell someone would be unbearable, and Robyn was understandably a bit nervy just now.

'Edwina?'

'Yes, dotey dear?'

'You see this scarf?'

'Yes, dotey dear. That is why I remarked upon it, because I saw it, noted it and admired it. Dot, dot, dot.'

'Well, that's just it, Edwina . . .' Caro sat down on her bed, staring first in front of her and then up at Edwina.

'What's "just it", Shorty?'

'This scarf was always worn by Katherine, with this

suit. And . . . and when she went, well, she left some of her clothes behind, including this suit, so everyone thought it perfectly all right to have it altered for me – the suit, I mean – because you know, she was, is, taller than me. So that's what we did, we had it altered.'

'So you did, dotey dear. *And* . . . ?' Edwina smiled in what she herself would describe as a 'kind-*ish*' sort of way, although her foot was beginning to tap. 'If you don't mind hurrying the narrative along *just* a little, I am about to drift into the bathroom and apply a mass of makeup to my beautiful visage.'

'But, you see, Katherine never left the scarf behind, this green paisley scarf which she always wore with this suit. She took it away with her, I know she did, but . . . well, I just found it wrapped around my steering wheel when I came out of Reading and Reading. So you see what this must mean?'

Edwina now sat down on the dressing-table stool, staring at Caro, all quips for once forgotten.

'I think I do see,' she agreed slowly. 'Your bad-girl elder sister, who disappeared with her very bad fascist beau, must be somewhere around in London, still being bad and a fascist, no doubt.'

'She must be! No one else could have seen me in this suit, this yellow suit, and left this green paisley scarf except Katherine. *It is just not possible.*'

'What will you do?'

'What can I do? What should I do?'

The expression on Edwina's face was unusually solemn. 'I would say you should report it to someone.

After all, she must be considered a danger to the state with her leanings, surely? They will have to be told.'

'But if they find her and David, maybe they'll think they are traitors and put them in prison.'

'So they will, dotey dear, and well deserved too, I'm sorry to tell you. They are both our common enemy now—'

'Katherine could never be common,' Caro put in quickly. 'She is too stylish, too beautiful.'

'No, but stylish or not, she is certainly our enemy,' Edwina continued in a crisp voice. 'And, sister or no sister, you will have to report that you know she is in London, as of now. I'm afraid it's your duty, or *mine*,' she ended firmly.

Caro stood up. 'You're right. I'll go and tell Robyn.'

'How will she help?'

'She knows where to go; she's been wherever it is already. Some friend or relative of her Aunt Cicely, an uncle or someone – he is the one everyone goes to, apparently.'

A few hours later Caro found herself, in full evening dress, calling round, but not at a Victoria address, for it appeared that 'Uncle Max' had moved on since Robyn's visit to him. This time he was to be found at a discreet address in Dolphin Square.

She rang the electric bell and the door was almost immediately opened by a sober-suited gentleman, who closed it behind her with a worried look, having first peered into the corridor outside the front door, perhaps to ascertain that no one had seen her.

'I quite understand that you were on your way out, but if anyone sees someone as glamorous as you visiting me, you might be followed. Do please sit down.'

The flat, far from being domestically furnished, was a series of rooms quite obviously functioning as offices. Certainly the room into which 'Uncle Max' led Caro was lined with official reference books and filing cabinets, leaving just enough room for a desk behind which he now sat himself, leaving Caro to sit opposite him.

'So, as I understand it,' he concluded after an exchange of dialogue that outlined the reasons for her visit and much else besides, 'you found this scarf, which you know to belong to your sister, Katherine Garland – ' he looked down at his notes – 'yes, Katherine, was Garland, possibly now Astley – a few hours ago, and it was, you say, draped around your steering wheel? And you now think that this proves that she and Astley, both known members of the British Union of Fascists and supporters of Hitler, are most likely still in London?'

'That's right, sir.'

'And this was outside that good old chemist's shop Reading and Reading at about four o'clock this afternoon?' He looked at his watch. 'They never do shut, do they?' he observed inconsequentially. 'I've been there for a hangover cure at four in the morning of a Sunday, you know, and one of them was still able to mix me his special cure with a smile and a joke. Marvellous fellows. They'll be needed more than ever now, of course. Quite a few headaches on the way, I'm afraid.'

He stood up. 'So there we are, you've done just the right thing, Miss Garland. I will make a note of what you have told me. Thank you for coming to see me. Not easy for you, given that it is your sister you are reporting. I hope you appreciate that I am most grateful to you?'

He shook Caro's gloved hand, and they walked together to the door, whereupon he excused himself and once more checked the corridor outside before letting her pass him, from where she hurried off to her car with a feeling that somehow she had betrayed her sister, who might be imprisoned, or worse, because of it. But since both Edwina and Robyn had said there was nothing else to be done, she felt that at least she had done her duty, if nothing else.

When she reached what seemed like the safety of the Ritz where they were all intent on dining early, because both Eddie and Bill were only on twelve-hour leave, Caro firmly put all feelings of guilt away from her. It was too late anyway to regret what she had done, too late to go back to 'Uncle Max', or whatever his real or unreal name was, too late to wonder what would happen to Katherine and David. Now she must enjoy herself, because at last they really were at war, and besides, there was always the sole bonne femme to be appreciated, albeit perhaps for the last time.

As Caro had predicted, Robyn and Eddie left the nightclub and drove off to somewhere or another, probably an old inn on the outskirts of London. Anyway, they certainly went somewhere other than back to the flat, leaving Bill and Caro, and Edwina and Tom – one of Edwina's seemingly endless supply of escorts – to go back and carry on in whatever way they wished.

With no streetlamps lighting their way, and no car lights allowed, actually getting back to the flat was an adventure in itself.

'I think the blackout's going to kill more people than the Germans will ever be able to!'

Tom, who had had the foresight to bring a small torch, was gaily if a little erratically leading the way in the dark, everyone following. Once in the flat, Edwina went into the sitting room and kicked the door shut behind them both, which left a more than startled Caro and Bill staring at the closed door, and with nowhere to go except the kitchen.

'Would you like a cup of Ovaltine?'

They both laughed.

'Would you be offended if I said a very firm "no" to that?'

'No, of course not, but tell you what – why don't we take a drink and go into my bedroom, but only, you know, just to drink and talk, if you know what I mean?'

Caro looked helplessly at Bill. He was not handsome in the way that Eddie was handsome, but he was good looking. Best of all he exuded good humour.

Despite being well dined, and certainly well wined, Bill gave Caro a brotherly look.

'I know *just* what you mean, Caro. Lead the way!'

Since there was no light coming from the kitchen, and no blackout material at the hall window, they were once more plunged into darkness, and obliged to feel their way towards the bedroom door, where Caro switched on a light, which she immediately draped with a scarf to dim its brightness.

'Phew. I suppose we'll get used to this.'

Feeling only too grateful that she had tidied their bedroom, Caro ducked back to the kitchen to fetch a bottle of whisky, two glasses, and also a jug of water for herself, on a tray.

When she returned, somewhat to her relief, Bill was not seated on either of the beds, but, having first removed the blackout, was standing at the window, staring out at the night sky.

'Hang on,' she protested, quickly switching off the light again.

'Look,' he said, 'a beautiful moon tonight, no planes, no Germans.' He turned back to Caro. 'Do you mind?'

By the light of the moon Caro placed the tray on a nearby table, and went to pour them both drinks, but Bill took the bottle of whisky from her.

'No, no, just water for me!'

'Come on! You can't expect me to drink alone!'

Bill splashed a little whisky into Caro's glass, and rather more into his own. 'Now let's enjoy the night sky while we can, with not a Hun in sight.'

Caro resolved not to drink, but stood firmly clutching her glass, because she really didn't want to be a party pooper, while obediently staring at the night sky. Soon, they both knew, perhaps any minute, it would be filled with the enemy, but, until then, they could talk.

'It's impossible,' Meriel sighed, indicating the blackout at the windows. 'We have tried everything, but with stone ledges and stone around the windows, the blackout is just refusing to stick.'

Anthony looked up briefly, and then went back to his accounts books. As far as he was concerned, blackout materials and the rest of it was women's business.

'I feel for you, I am sure, dearest, but at the moment I am trying to work out the accounts for last month, for what with getting the cottages ready for the evacuees, I have done nothing that I should have done for what seems now like weeks.'

Meriel nodded. It was at times like this that she missed both her daughters, and the maids. In fact, she missed her whole family. If Jag and Francis were here they would be climbing up Mrs Grant's ladders instead of her, and wielding tapes and scissors and ribbing everyone around, and it would all be such fun, the boys teasing her, and the girls protesting, and she knew not what. But with Mrs Grant and everyone gone to do much-needed factory work, and just Anthony and herself in this evening – Smith having today taken Trixie, and Betty too, up to London – there was no one with whom she could do such mundane tasks, no one with whom she could have a giggle.

She climbed up the ladders, as once again Anthony prepared to tot up yet more sums in the long columns of figures in front of him, eyes down, brow creased in frowning concentration.

He had just finished doing a complicated piece of multiplication of the kind that was fast becoming the dread of his life, when he heard a muted cracking sound, followed by a much louder one.

'Seventeen hundred and eighty—' He looked up reluctantly. 'Seventeen hundred and eighty-four—'

Meriel and the stepladders had parted company.

'Oh my Lord, Meriel, Meriel!' Seeing her crumpled body spread out on the dark old hard-wood floor, he ran from behind his desk, and without thinking, fatally, he kneeled, and taking her head and shoulders in his arms he managed to prop her. At once, and ominously, her head rolled sideways, and she made no sound.

He laid her back, calling her name over and over again, and then he rose to his feet and fled the room, calling for Smith. But Smith was out at the village pub, wetting his whistle, as he called it, after his long journey to London and back, and everywhere else in the house was only darkness.

Caro had never kissed anyone before and now that she was doing, she thought it was quite nice, but not as nice as she had always hoped that it might be.

'I think I'll stop now,' she said matter-of-factly to Bill, which made him laugh.

'I don't see why.'

'Well, I do,' Caro told him in a voice that, had Walter Beresford been listening in, he would have added in a warning tone, 'When you hear my lucky charm using that voice, take heed, young man.'

'How about if we lie down on the bed, and just hold each other, and go to sleep?'

Caro stared at Bill. 'No, I don't think so . . . not really.'

'You could lie on that bed then, and I could lie on this one, and we could talk.'

'What about?' Caro demanded cautiously.

'Shoes and ships and sealing wax, and whether pigs

173

have wings? Well, we know that they do, and they're called Hun-pigs and they most definitely have wings.'

'Go on then, you lie on that one, and I'll lie on this one, and we can talk.'

'We *could* push the beds together and hold hands?'

'We could. On the other hand, we could not.'

But they did, and they talked for some time, before finally falling asleep.

Bill must have been woken by the light coming in the unmasked window, the curtains left undrawn, for when Caro was woken by Edwina shaking her gently by the shoulder, there was no Bill, just Edwina staring down at her.

'Caro? It's your brother, on the telephone. Your brother Jag. He needs to speak to you urgently.' Edwina pushed a tangle of red hair from around her face. 'Hope it's not bad news, Shorty. But, well, I must warn you, he sounds just a tiny bit grim.'

Caro knew at once from Jag's tone, as people do, that it was not just going to be bad news, it was going to be very bad news. She tried to brace herself, and yet even as she listened intently to what he was saying, perhaps because his voice was so commandingly calm, she could not take in the reality. Anyway, why should she be able to? Their mother was both too young and too kind to die. Yet, it seemed, she had. How could she have? How *could* she?

Chapter Six

Even as Anthony's elegant gold pen moved across the name, even as the line went through the words 'Katherine Mary Elizabeth Sophia, 12 December 1918', none of them could quite believe what was happening. In some ways it seemed more unreal than their mother's death. Their mother had died in an accident; fate had decreed that their beautiful, kind, sensitive mother would be taken from them – 'suddenly as a result of an accident at home', as the obituary had read – whereas now that their father was taking his pen and crossing out Katherine's name from the Family Bible, it appeared to them all that in some strange way he was killing her by his own hand. Indeed, so final did that black ink look, so determinedly did the pen strike through her name, not once, but twice, that had she been laid out in front of the three of them, she could not have seemed more dead.

'Let her name never more be mentioned in this house,' Anthony said, and the words were so sonorous that they sounded to them all as if they were a quotation from that same Bible at which they were all staring, mesmerised. 'She is no longer my daughter, nor will she ever be again.'

He looked across at Caro. 'From now on I have only one daughter.' He glanced down at the Bible, as if he needed to remind himself who his one daughter might be. 'Caroline Elysia Constance, you are my daughter. I have two sons, and a daughter.' He stood up. 'Now I shall be grateful if you would all leave me alone.'

Jag turned at once, very much in a newly acquired military style, and headed the small sad group out of Anthony Garland's study, and Caro quietly closed the door behind them, after which Francis and Caro stared at Jag, much as they had as children when they were waiting for him to announce what game he had decided they were going to play on some rainy afternoon in the holidays.

'Come with me,' he said quietly. 'Let's go to the den.'

The den was a long room above the stables. They hadn't been there for years, and it was reached only by a long run of very old steps. The other two climbed up after Jag, hoping against hope that he would have some fresh words of comfort to offer them.

'I thought we'd better come up here because this is the only place where Smith has finished the blackout,' he explained, and then, from behind the hay stacks, he produced two bottles of wine. 'Pinched them from the old man's cellar,' he said, but he didn't smile. 'Thought we might need them after all. He's not very good at provisions, as you saw from the funeral tea.'

The funeral had been sad enough, but the catering had been even sadder, for with Meriel and all the female staff gone, and the estate workers and the village to be provided for, it was soon obvious that Smith and

Anthony had sadly underestimated how much tea and sandwiches and even cake was needed.

'Family Hold Back was very much the order of the day, wasn't it?' Jag muttered as he drew the cork from the first of the bottles. 'Caro,' he jerked his head backwards, 'you'll find some provender behind that sack of oats over there.'

Caro could not help feeling delighted when she saw what Jag had hidden: a whole seed cake, some cream crackers, half a pound of butter, some cheese, and even a couple of tins of corned beef, all of it tidily put together with picnic knives and plates, as well as teacups and saucers.

They were all silent as they ate their repast, and drank their wine from the teacups.

'Do you know, these last few days I have actually found myself happy that Mamma's gone, that she won't see what we're going to see, won't have to go through it all again? Not only that, I'm glad we're at war so I don't have to be here cooped up with Papa.' As his brother and sister stared at him, Jag went on, determined to be honest, 'No, it's true. With Katherine gone, with you both gone, with everyone going – Miss Berenger, Trixie, Betty – I know it's shocking, but lately I've been really glad that I have a reason to leave too. If there wasn't a war, I wouldn't have. I'd have had to stay and farm, and you, Caro, well, you'd probably be just cooped up here too, an old maid with only the dogs and Smith for company.'

'I know what you mean, but I don't think you should be glad for war, Jag, really I don't. It's as if the war is getting us out of having to be normal, and as if normal is somehow more difficult than war, which of course it isn't, but that's how it seems.'

Caro stared ahead of her, silent, still disbelieving of everything that was happening. She had always been so close to her mother, and had never really considered leaving Chevrons, at least not for long, but now that Jag had said he was glad to be leaving, perhaps it was true of all of them. Perhaps if everything had stayed the same, she would, as Jag had just said, have become an old maid, stuck at home with Smith and the dogs.

Now she remembered how reasonable her mother had been when she'd overheard Trixie talking about leaving Chevrons, and how bravely she had borne her suffering when Katherine had disappeared, seemingly into thin air. Their mother had always been at such pains not to let her feelings show; so Jag was right in a way: perhaps it was just as well that Meriel had gone, because now she wouldn't have to worry. There would be nothing more to be brave about, nothing more to pretend about.

'I don't think Father would ever have crossed Katherine's name from the Family Bible if . . . if Mamma was alive,' Caro stated suddenly, out of nowhere.

Jag gave his sister a vaguely patronising look. 'Yes, Caro, we know that, for the very good reason that if Mamma was still alive Katherine wouldn't have missed turning up for her funeral.' He drained his cup of wine, and then promptly refilled it. 'That was the last straw really. You can't blame the old man. I mean she must *know*; someone must have told her. She must have been *told*.'

Caro too held out her teacup for more wine. Jag was right: Katherine must know. She must still be around

London somewhere, because of the scarf left tied around the *Blue Angel*'s steering wheel. But although he hadn't said as much, she guessed that 'Uncle Max' would not want her telling even Jag and Francis about the scarf. So she sat on, listening to her brothers talking, holding her cup, and wondering what their father might think if he heard them. He would not think much of them, of that she was quite sure.

'I quite understand,' her father told Caro, while his eyes were saying 'Not you too?' 'You must go where you feel your duty will take you; must go where you hope to be of most help. Smith and I can manage. Mrs Warburton will still be coming from the village to clean, and she thinks her daughter might help out with the evacuees because two of the mothers have already gone back to London.' He gave a flicker of a smile. 'Apparently, like Beatrix Potter's Johnny Town-mouse, they have already found Chevrons too quiet.'

Caro had decided to don her uniform for what she realised might turn out to be the most awkward interview of her life, in the hope that if she appeared in the library in full fig, her father would guess at once where her determination might lie.

'I quite understand really, I do.'

As always Anthony found it easier to look down at his eternal accounts books.

'The thing is, Papa, I know with Mamma gone I should perhaps stay behind with you here, that I should stay behind, and help with everything, but I feel I will be of better use in London.'

179

'Of course you do, Caro. It's only natural that you should want to be with young people, at this time. Young men visiting London will be wanting to take you out, and you will be driving young officers who will naturally also want to take you out, and so on. You want to be where the gaiety is. It is quite understandable.'

Anthony looked up at Caro, who was standing almost to attention in front of his desk. It seemed to her that her father had quite deliberately not asked her to sit down. It also seemed to her that he was not just hinting but suggesting that he had expected her not only to be selfish, but *fast*.

'No, it is quite understandable, quite understandable,' he repeated, his eyes once more returning to his columns of figures.

Caro decided to ignore what might be his insinuations, and begin her defence afresh.

Her father was admirable in many ways, a good father, but he had it in him to be subtly unkind, which meant that unless you took care you could become indignant, and that was no good.

Once you became indignant, as she had been moved to be once or twice when she was growing up, then on realising this he would immediately move in for the kill.

'I asked Smith about the household arrangements, and he says that he knows that you can both manage. He says that you will probably be moving into the wing, so there will be less on his shoulders. And he says that being a widower he has begun to get used to foraging for himself, and that, after all, all the trade vans still visit;

they can bring him whatever he wants,' Caro stated in as calm a voice as she could muster.

Her father dropped his finger at the bottom of one of the columns of figures, which he had obviously been mentally adding up, and looked up at her with an irritated expression on his face.

'Look, do as you wish, Caro, really do as you wish, because you are obviously going to anyway. In the end, in this life, we all have to get on with it. Believe me, I *perfectly* understand that you do not want to stay cooped up at Chevrons while you can be in London having a good time, and behaving just as you wish. With the war on there'll be no chaperones, and it'll be *laissez-faire* everywhere. With Jag and Francis at Catterick Camp, and you and I, and of course Smith, here alone in this house, alone without your mother, what possible use could you be to me anyhow?' He stopped, his eyes going back to his columns of figures. 'You never were particularly domesticated. Your mother used to despair of your cooking and sewing, your dress sense, everything about you, now I come to think of it.' He sighed sadly. 'As I remember it she always used to say, "Caro's such a tomboy, she should have been a boy, really she should."'

At that Caro dropped her eyes to the all-too-familiar Persian rug on which she was standing. It was a stab to the heart to hear her father talking about her in that, albeit lightly, despising way. More than that, she couldn't believe that her mother, of all people, would have talked about her to her father in quite the way he had just described. In her mind she tried desperately to conjure up her mother's voice, tried to remember how low-toned and gentle it had always seemed. She knew that Meriel couldn't have used that tone of voice about her. Her mother had always been so kind, so gentle, never demanding, always at pains to set a good example, making you *want* to be like her.

Caro waited a few seconds before saying, in a valiant tone, 'Mamma used to say my sewing was *quite* good. I know I don't sew as well as she did, but then who does . . . who did? And I never had a chance to cook, living here at Chevrons – why would I? No one else cooked, not me, not Ka— not Trixie, not even Mamma.'

'You were always hopeless domestically,' her father carried on as if Caro had not spoken, and as if he were speaking to a forty-year-old spinster on whom he had quite given up. '*Hopeless.*'

'In that case, Papa, perhaps it is just as well that I will be driving through the war, and not cooking.'

Her father looked at his watch. 'What time do you intend leaving?' he asked, his manner becoming even more formal, as if Caro was his house guest, not his only remaining daughter.

'I, er . . . I, er, I don't know,' she stammered. 'I could leave whenever you wish. As a matter of fact I was actually going to make you a steak and kidney pie before I left, something like that.'

'Oh, very well, but let me know when you are leaving, and I'll come and say goodbye.'

Anthony reached forward and picked up yet another of his large leather-covered accounts books, which Caro knew of old was his way of dismissing her.

She walked smartly from the room, and was about to

close the door when he called her back. Caro turned and as she did she could not suppress the hope in her heart that now he was about to be less censorious towards her, that he would have some words of comfort, or even tenderness.

'By the way, I have paid the tailor's bill for that uniform of yours. I hope there are not too many more like that coming my way?'

'No, no, of course not, no. And I will pay you back, out of my wages, really I will.'

'Hmm.'

She slipped back out of the room and, having closed the door, she leaned against it, her eyes half closed. In some ways it had been a much worse interview than even she could have imagined; in other ways it had been better than she could have hoped. She did not now have to stay behind at Chevrons as the main prop to her father's grief, to help him through his lonely days. She could go and join her generation, go and be one of the young, not a stay-at-home spinster daughter waiting around for her father to ring a bell for his evening drink, or facing some mound of ironing before wiping the noses of the evacuees. She could go back to London and her driving. That was really a great escape, if ever there was one.

'Miss Caro?' Smith beckoned from a doorway. 'Can I have a word?'

'Yes, of course, Smith.' She followed him downstairs to the kitchen.

'I'm sorry to tell you, Miss Caro, but I overheard Mr Anthony talking to you.' As Caro looked vaguely shocked, Smith went on hurriedly, 'As a matter of fact

I made it my business to overhear him today, for the best reasons, I hope you will agree when I explain. You see, I've known Mr Anthony all my life – well, most of it, at any rate – and the truth of it is he is so unlike his normal self at the moment, and knowing that this was so, I was really anxious for you. He doesn't mean anything that he's saying or doing at the moment.' He stopped, sighing. 'It's difficult to explain, Miss Caro, but I've seen it all before. Grief, well, it often takes men like that, more than women. I know because I was like that when I lost my Polly, so early on too, only a year into our marriage. I loved her so much, I never did get over it, never have. But to begin with, that was how it took me, Miss Caro: it made me angry. And that's how it takes so many of us men, God help us, when we lose our loved ones. And, of course, Miss Katherine having been taken the way she was, lured away by that David Astley and his views, Mr Anthony has turned in on himself and out on everyone else. In time he will change back, but it will take time, Miss Caro. Can't expect it not to.'

Caro nodded. She actually felt so done over by her father, she could have swigged everything in his cellar, but now that Smith had explained it the way he had, it was different.

'Thank you so much for telling me that, Smith.'

Caro shook Smith's hand, and then on impulse she leaned forward and kissed him quickly on the cheek. Smith coloured slightly.

'I don't think you should stay here at Chevrons now, Miss Caro, if you don't mind me saying? And if it is any comfort to you, I think you are quite right to want to go back to London. Staying here is the last thing that you should do. You have your life to lead, same as my Trixie has her life to lead, same as Betty, same as all of you. You're young, you have a war to fight, and you must go and fight it the best you may, as you will, I know. And God bless you!' He cleared his throat. 'Now off you go.'

'No, no, I can't go yet, Smith. I promised I'd make my father a steak and kidney pie.'

Smith sighed again, shook his head wearily, and then he started to laugh.

'God bless you, Miss Caro, but I'd rather eat my own shoes than serve up something you've cooked. I can make steak and kidney pie until the cows come home for milking, and back again into the pastures too. How do you think an old widower like me has managed all these years? Steak and kidney pie, my foot! By the time you've finished making it anyway, we'd all be dead of hunger, and the kitchen would look like a bomb had dropped on it. Steak and kidney pie! What an idea. Now, off you go.'

'I must say goodbye to my father.'

Smith put out a fatherly hand and pressed Caro's arm. 'No, no, you go, Miss Caro. No more words, really. I've filled the Fraser Nash with petrol, so off you go and good luck to you. I will cope with your father. You just leave him to me.' He glanced up at the old wooden clock. 'Believe me, he'll have fallen asleep by now. That's how grief takes you. You fall asleep at the oddest times, and then when it comes to going to sleep at night, you can't. Normally, at this time, Mr Anthony would have been out and about the place, but that's all changed. Now he'll sleep until I take him in his cocktail at six, and by that time he won't have remembered what you said, or what he said, or who made the blessed steak and kidney pie, or anything else. He'll listen to Alvar Liddell, or Bruce Belfridge – he likes him – on the news, then I'll take him round for his night-time tour of the cottages where he'll talk to the evacuees, see what's needed and that, and by the time we get back, it'll be the news again, and so to bed, where he'll keep his light on until dawn. So, no, don't you worry about a thing, not any more. Smith's here, Smith's in charge. You do the same as the others – they've all gone, so now it's your turn to go.'

Caro stepped away from him, and saluted.

'Thank you, Smith,' she said. 'You're one of the best.'

Smith nodded approvingly at Caro's salute, which she was holding for him.

'Well done, Miss Caro, you're officer material alright!'

Betty looked up at the man behind the desk.

'You don't want me?'

'It's not that we don't want you, Miss Thomas, it's just that at the moment we have no room for you. Your speeds are excellent, in fact you are everything that we should want, but it is very difficult at the moment. Everyone is pressing us for this kind of work, and there are just not enough jobs to go round.'

The man, sober-suited, kind of eye, was to Betty almost frighteningly pale of face, bloodless, pallid, most especially when compared to the men at Chevrons, with their bronzed summer faces ending in white necks where their shirts began.

'Now where personnel is badly needed, where we

need to concentrate our efforts most especially, Miss Thomas, is in the factories. There, if I may suggest it, you will find a welcome on the mat indeed.'

'Yes, I have heard that. My friend and I keep being told that.'

'Well then, why not go too, and see if you like it?'

Betty stared at the gentleman. He had quite obviously not spent the last year practising and practising his shorthand, pounding on the old Vicarage typewriter, sending off postal tests. If he had, he would not be dismissing her so easily.

'I think what you really mean is that I'm not quite the type you're looking for, sir.' Betty picked up her handbag. 'I haven't been to a secretarial college, and you fear I might not get on with the rest in the typing pool, who probably have.'

'No, no, not at all. It is just that there are no vacancies, nothing more than that.'

Betty nodded, while at the same time drawing a small amount of satisfaction at seeing that she had actually embarrassed him with what must, after all, be rather too near the truth.

'Well, thank you for seeing me, sir. I think I will probably end up, as you have just suggested, in a factory.'

Betty walked out into the London sunshine. She and Trixie had been in London, staying in a bed and breakfast near Paddington Station, for what seemed for ever, but was in reality rather less than a fortnight, and neither of them could get the kind of job that they wanted.

Loath to spend any more money than was necessary, she ignored the buses and walked back to her lodgings, to be greeted by an equally morose Trixie. Trixie had been very cast down by the death of Mrs Garland.

They sat on their thinly blanketed beds and regarded each other.

'I think it'll have to be factory work, Trixie. I don't think we have a chance at anything else. You see, all the top-notchers, they've all descended on London too, and they want all the driving and secretarial jobs. It stands to reason. And a lot of women have been taking courses this last year with just that in mind; I know, I read about it in the newspaper a few days ago.' Betty pulled a face. 'But they do want women in the factories, all right. The factories are out of town, most of them, so I guess we'll have to follow our noses and get work out of town, which is probably going to be safer anyway, from what everyone is saying.'

Trixie thought of all her efforts to change and become someone who *wouldn't* be doing factory work, and she really felt quite like swearing long and hard, if only she had the words.

'I could say a bad word or two, you know that, Betty?'

'Well, go ahead then.'

Trixie looked mutinous. 'Bloody bluebottle!'

Betty was impressed. 'Expect you feel better now.'

'As a matter of fact, I do.' Trixie exhaled a little too noisily even for her taste. 'If we don't get something in the way of work soon we'll be walking back home, you know that?'

They had both been back to Chevrons for Mrs Garland's funeral, and that had taken a large bite out of their purses. Betty had quite expected to want to stay behind in the quiet of the English countryside, but the truth was that Chevrons had already changed so much it was hardly bearable, and it was certainly not somewhere where either of them wanted to be any more – not with everyone so sad, and Mr Smith, Trixie's father, preoccupied with all the arrangements for the evacuees from London, and so on.

The truth was, work or no work, they had both been very glad to get back on the train and return to the Smoke; but now, it seemed, the Smoke didn't want them.

'Apparently, even the likes of Miss Caro and her friends are finding it difficult to get the positions they want, Miss Caro told me, you know – after the funeral, at the tea. It seems everyone wants to be in the thick of it in wartime, all heading for London and the top jobs. Miss Caro said she was lucky to get a job at all, but since she's got a motor car, she did. Starts next week, driving officers about, or at least that is what she is hoping.'

Trixie picked up the evening paper, and pointed to an advertisement.

'There's this place advertising for workers in a factory in Sussex. I think we'd best telephone this number and find out whether there are any places left before we have to turn tail and head back for home, don't you?'

Betty watched Trixie putting on her coat, preparatory to going to the corner to use the public telephone.

'Come on, cheer up, we'll be together, won't we? That's not so bad, is it? You can't blame people wanting to hold on to their jobs, war or no war, really you can't, in the same way you can't blame all those evacuee people coming back from the country. I mean, one minute there they are minding their own business, and the next they're dumped in the middle of nowhere with only a cow for company. The country's frightening to town people. I know because we had a cousin to stay once, and she lasted only a day. Heard a cow moo, and that was enough. She and her little boy jumped straight back on the train!'

Betty gave a wan smile, but her face remained a picture of misery, so Trixie hurried off.

She knew just how Betty felt. She too hated the idea that they would have to leave London. Even with the blackout and all the rest, London was still an exciting place to be.

Betty was still sitting looking down in the dumps when Trixie returned from her telephoning mission.

'Well, that's something, at any rate. This Mrs Ludgrove wants to see us tomorrow. So we'll cross our fingers, shall we, Betty? Cross our fingers and hope that if we buy ourselves one-way tickets, that's all we'll need, eh?'

Trixie took off her hat, and started to brush her dark curls. It came to her that if she did get to work in the munitions factory she would have to tie her hair up in a scarf, that she would need ear plugs to drown out the noise of the machinery, that pretty soon her feet would ache more than they had ever ached before, even when Mrs Grant put her to do the dusting of the Long Room pictures, not to mention the music room and the dining room. The last thing her father had wanted was for her to take factory work. They had both hoped for something better, but it seemed it was not to be.

'Come on, Betty Boo Hoo!' Trixie gave Betty's arm a

playful shake. 'Let's take a walk before it gets too dark. We might even see the King and Queen going by in their gold carriage; or the princesses at the window of their house. But if this is our last day in London, let's see a few sights. We might even get a couple of admirers to buy us a drink.'

But Betty refused to respond to this enticing notion. Instead, she put her head in her hands. She'd worked so hard with one end in sight: to get a position as a stenographer, and now it seemed all she was going to be doing was standing in a line making ammunitions, or whatever they were going to be asked to do.

Trixie kneeled down and put her arms around her.

'Look, dear, I know it's hard for you. Frankly it's not a bowl of cherries for me either. Neither of us wanted this, but we can't find anything better, and that's just a fact. It's war, and we've got to go where we're needed, so that's what we'll do. But once we're in this factory, who knows that we won't find it leads somewhere else? One door opens, and another closes is the best motto at this moment. So, pull yourself together, eh?'

Betty nodded, wiping the tears from her eyes, and standing up.

'Sorry, Trixie. I'm not as strong as you, bit of a wet blanket.'

'No, not a wet blanket. You're just a bit of an ar*tiste*, same as that man that was painting us all. You see under and over things, and round the sides, all at the same time. Now, come on. This may well be our last night in London, and we're best to be trying to enjoy it, no matter what.'

*　　*　　*

191

Caro too was having problems getting the kind of work she wanted. Instead of being ordered to start driving some dashing young officer around town, soon after she reported back to headquarters after her mother's funeral, she was ordered to start work out of town, at a secret address, which was just what she did *not* want.

'But I don't . . . I don't really think I will be suited to undercover work, really I don't,' she'd protested to the panel of lady officers.

'You're just the type,' came the brisk reply. 'We don't want conceited misses with ideas above their station.'

'I find it very hard to remember secrets, and so I really wouldn't trust me not to give them away, by mistake.'

The smile on the officer's face was peculiarly understanding.

'You are perfect.'

Caro saluted, and left the room in a cloud of desperation. Just as she had settled down, off again. It seemed so unfair. She had the car, she had won her freedom, and yet not the work. The only sop to her unhappiness was that Robyn had also been posted to this secret address.

'Not that there is much chance of keeping a place like this *secret*,' Robyn said when she showed Caro round their new quarters. 'It is without doubt one of the most staggering houses we're ever likely to stay in, isn't it?'

Caro gazed around her. Robyn was not exaggerating. The house, it seemed, was the product of one man's dream to build an everlasting monument to his own taste.

'No stone that could have been turned into something new and strange has been left untouched by human

192

hand,' Robyn stated, rolling her eyes in a droll way before indicating the heavy marble columns underneath which they were standing, then waving a hand towards heavy marble fireplaces, to marble floors and marble statues. 'I hope the noble lord who built this had shares in marble, because if he didn't then he must have gone through an awful lot of his pocket money.'

Later when they repaired to their attic rooms on the fourth floor of the house, rooms that gave them a sweeping view over beautiful parkland towards the sea, Robyn helped Caro to unpack.

'Please, please, *please* tell me you've brought some female furniture with you, because I only went and forgot it,' Robyn murmured. 'And apparently we're about twenty miles from the nearest chemist, which in the event of the little visitor, is *not* going to be funny.'

Caro coloured, but nodded towards a small suitcase, which she had not yet unpacked.

'Before I left London, Mr Reading wrapped up enough for the whole army.'

'Just as well, since you and I and half a dozen others, and most of them are in the kitchens, are the only females in the whole building.'

'Gracious.'

Robyn shook her head. 'No, ducks, there's going to be nothing gracious about our situation, I'm sorry to tell you. It is just us and about forty men, none of whom speaks English, and all of whom, I'm equally sorry to tell you, are suspects of His Majesty's Government. While they are questioned, interrogated, and generally kept an eye on, on account of being very, very foreign indeed, it will be up to us to make sure they have clean hankies, stay in the grounds and, in the event of an invasion, apparently it will even be up to us to shoot them – if they're naughty. This is undercover work of a really rather tame kind, unless we have to shoot them, of course, in which case it should cheer up matters no end.'

Caro sat down on her bed.

'I don't really want to shoot anyone, at least not yet,' she murmured. 'Perhaps in a little while, when they're crawling up the sides of the buildings with rape and pillage in mind, but not yet.'

'Best if we change into civvies for after-supper activities. There's a concert tonight, as it seems there has been most nights.' Robyn rolled her eyes. 'Just don't try dancing to it; it's not that kind of music. Go down like a cup of cold sick at the Grafton Galleries, believe me.'

As Caro looked at her questioningly, Robyn shrugged and pulled a little face.

'It seems at least a dozen of our suspects – I mean inmates – are professional violinists, and at least another dozen are cellists, and most of those are Austrian, bless them. Not fair really to coop them up here, but there, I expect they'll be let out soon, at least as soon as the authorities find out they haven't been parachuted into the grounds dressed as nuns. God, how I miss the dogs!'

Caro looked sympathetic. The Cairns had been sent back down to Aunt Cicely for the duration, while the Garland dogs had retired with Smith to his cottage because Anthony had never taken quite the same interest in them as Meriel.

A string quartet played for them after supper in the

smallest of the large reception rooms. From the moment they began, Caro listened intently. Meriel had played the piano to a high standard, practising most mornings after breakfast, and while Caro was no musician, from the time she was small she had loved to be asked to sit in and listen. Her mother had often remarked that, of all her children, Caro was the one who fidgeted least, sitting happily still, watching and listening.

Tonight, too, she sat still, watching and listening, the pieces familiar to her. Robyn, on the other hand, had twisted her legs together, and never stopped snapping the top of her handbag – click, click, click – until Caro put a restraining hand on the top of the small decorative evening bag, and gave her a 'stopping this would be a good idea' look, which made Robyn tighten her entwined legs ever more frantically.

'What a martyrdom,' she murmured to Caro as they all applauded. 'Please don't tell me we're going to have this every evening. I never thought to say it, but how I long for my *wireless*. Aunt Cicely will have to have Carter Patterson or Trollopes send it to me *toute suite*, because this chamber music, or whatever it is, will drive me completely dotty, truly it will.'

But Caro wasn't listening to Robyn's paean of protests, she was already making her way across to the group who were still bowing, or half-bowing to the warm applause. Caro waited until it ceased, and then stepped forward.

'That was so good, thank you so much.'

'Sank *you*,' they all chorused and, bows still in hand, they bowed and smiled. 'We luff to play for your audience. The English always so warm and appreciative.'

'Yes, quite,' Caro agreed, trying not to think of Robyn and her crossed legs. 'I am Caro Garland,' she went on. 'How do you do?'

One by one they introduced themselves, and shook hands with her, the last one holding her hand a little longer than was absolutely necessary.

'Until we were put here we never knew each other, Miss Garland, but now that we enjoy so much fun together, we have teamed up. We are thinking of calling ourselves the Wiener Schnitzels. What are your thoughts, maybe, about this, Miss Garland?'

As Robyn joined her, wearing a commendably appreciative expression, Caro considered the question.

'The Wiener Schnitzels? Rather good,' she replied, keeping a straight face. 'Speaking for myself I would always book straight away to go to a concert featuring a quartet with that name. Not *quite* sure that the BBC would be so enthusiastic at this particular moment,' she added.

'Oh, surely, Miss Garland, you and your friend, both of you being so pretty, they could be persuaded, no?'

They all laughed, and Carl, the youngest and tallest, put his violin under his chin and started to play once more, this time gypsy music. Faster and faster the music sang out, until finally he finished and they all laughed once more, knowing that his encore was a celebration of the moment.

'You want to watch that Gypsy Ned and his wayward fiddle,' Robyn teased her as they climbed the many stairs to bed. 'He likes you. He lit up the moment you spoke.'

'I hardly think so.'

Quite suddenly Caro lay down on her bed, still clothed. She didn't know why but all the time she had been listening to the music playing she had imagined she could smell her mother's perfume and hear her laughter, most of all that, because Meriel had loved to laugh.

When Katherine had disappeared she seemed to have taken all their mother's loving laughter with her. It was that, more than anything, that Caro had so resented. If Katherine hadn't taken up with fascism, if she hadn't run off with David Astley, everything would be so different. Meriel might even be alive. Everything bad seemed to have started with Katherine's disappearance. Tears poured down Caro's face.

Robyn sat down on her bed, and took her hand.

'I wondered when this was going to happen,' she murmured.

The factory to which Betty and Trixie now directed themselves was a long, low, single-storey building. It was not inviting in appearance, and even less so when entered. The noise was appalling, not just from the machines, but also the girls, in their headscarves and factory wear, who were all singing along to a radio blaring out some morning tune. Despite the autumn rain, or perhaps because of it, the heat inside the building was intense.

Betty and Trixie exchanged looks. After Chevrons, where the sound of the ducks on the river, or Cook singing in the kitchen, or the distant whirring of the Hoover was about all that could have been heard of a morning, this noise was terrifying, literally sick-making, so that the girls instinctively moved nearer to each other. It was as if they were two wild birds who had been thrown into a cage filled with creatures of a very different kind.

'I don't think we can stay, really I don't, Trixie,' Betty murmured.

'And I don't think we have any choice, not for the moment, anyway,' Trixie replied crisply. 'The rumour is that there's going to be conscription of one kind or another, and for everyone except nursing mothers, and you're not one of those, are you?'

'I don't know what I am,' Betty murmured, 'but I'm not one of these kind of girls, that I do know, Trixie.'

She looked down the room. She knew these kind of girls: hard as the materials they were so busy assembling. She had been at the orphanage with a whole heap of them. They were harder and faster than anything you'd ever come across anywhere, except down at China Docks, perhaps.

Betty nudged Trixie's arm. 'I'm leaving, Trixie, and if you've got any sense, you will too.'

Before Trixie could come up with one of her spirited ripostes, a middle-aged woman, a great deal larger in width and height than either of them, came towards them with purposeful tread.

'Follow me!'

The noise inside the office where Mrs Ludgrove interviewed them was almost as deafening as that on the factory floor. Nevertheless she managed to take down the girls' details before nodding towards a changing room some way down the main room.

'You'll have no difficulty with the work. I'll put a

foreman on to you and you'll pick it up in no time. Meanwhile, you'll find everything you need in there,' she said with some satisfaction. 'Scarves, boiler suits, and flat shoes – scarves for safety, boiler suits to save your clothes, and flat shoes, because without them your feet will kill you. Well, they will anyway, but never mind that.'

Betty followed Trixie down past the rows and rows and rows of women, and so into the room that the manageress – if that was what you called her – had indicated.

'We can't stay here, Trixie, truly we can't.'

'We stay here until we find something better, Betty Boo Hoo.'

Betty knew what Trixie meant. They were down to their last few shillings, they had left Chevrons on a wave of patriotism; there really was no going back. Besides, there were only the men and the London evacuees in the cottages now, apart from Mr Smith. Mr Garland was moving into new quarters in the wing, and the main house was being prepared to take in badly wounded officers and the like. The girls would not be wanted back at the old place now. Quite apart from anything else, there would be no room for them.

Betty started to put up her hair in the scarf provided, and turning to a large pile of boiler suits she took the top one off.

'Quite glam, dear, don't you think?' Trixie sashayed up and down the floor. Betty smiled, and then they both looked across at the shoe basket.

'Oh God.' Trixie's face fell. 'They've all been worn before.'

'Put your best foot forward.'

Trixie shook her head. 'Not in those shoes I'm not. We'll catch verrucas. I believe in being like the Garland sheep and looking after my feet. No, definitely not going to be seen in those, dear. In those it will be worst foot forward and no mistake; we could catch anything.'

She sat down on the side of the bench and, taking one of her own shoes, started to knock it against the side.

'What are you doing now, Trixie?'

'Taking the heels off my shoes, and if you've any sense you'll do the same.'

Betty sat down beside her. The din was terrible, and the ventilation so bad that the damp in the air was palpable. She felt faint, but she found herself following Trixie, and they began the first of what would seem like endless days and nights learning to put pieces of aircraft together.

Dear Father,

Betty and I have landed ourselves on our feet all right – all day, and all night too, sometimes. Anyway it seems like that! We're doing something we can't tell anyone else about, same as everyone in this war, if you ask me. But we have nice digs with a lady who usually takes in theatricals, but they've all gone to be soldiers, and such like, so she has to take in the dregs, and make do with us instead! It is hard work, Father, but we know that we must do it for our country, and please God, there will be an end to it all soon.

Please send all our best to Mr Garland, and to Mavis, if she's still there, and the fox hasn't got her. I hope she behaves herself and doesn't go broody on you. Betty sends her best too. She has done some drawings of us in the factory which she is putting in the envelope along with this. I hope you keep well, Father, really I do. Well, must stop now, my eyes are shutting. Lots of love and kisses to you, and Mavis too, Father. XXXXXXXXX

Trixie

Trixie put down her pen, and stared out at the night sky. It seemed that the war had begun in earnest, but if so, where was it? It was nowhere near them, it was nowhere near Father and Chevrons, it was nowhere near London. The lads that they'd met at the pub that last night in town had said they thought it might never begin, and there would be no war, ever, and they were off to Catterick or somewhere to have themselves a bit of fun with guns and such like. The *Phoney* War, they were calling it all over London, and the South-East, the lads had said.

And yet there was so much going *on*. Why else would they be working so hard to make all this weaponry except to wage war against Hitler?

She pulled the rough bed sheet and blankets up to her face, and slid one sly finger out to pull back a tiny bit of the blackout at the window below which she lay.

Betty was still at the factory trying to beat her record of five consecutive hours. Trixie had just completed six. They had a bet on, a pair of nylons to the winner who did the most hours, but judging from the expressions of the other women, no good would come of their enthusiasm. All the others seemed to care about was staying within their union rules. Working to time, they called it – or something like that – but it was more as if they didn't want to cooperate, as if they thought the government was taking advantage of them, not trying to build up arms so they wouldn't all end up being shot, or put in prison camps.

Through her tiny gap in the blackout Trixie watched wisps of what looked like smoke drifting across the moon, and for a few minutes it seemed to her that she was back at Chevrons in their cottage, and Father was out at the pub playing cribbage, and she could hear a fox crying somewhere, and an owl hooting.

In what she now thought of as the old days, she had, of a summer evening, been able to sit at her open bedroom window and listen to the sound of the grass swaying and rustling, as real a sound as any human step; as real as the moon above the factory was now real, but just now, also as far away from her present reality as that same moon.

Although she was left alone in Robyn's Aunt Cicely's flat, and she missed them, Edwina did not envy Robyn and Caro being seconded to a secret address more than an hour from London. She too had her own car, and although not as swanky as Robyn's Bentley, and not as elegant as Caro's Fraser Nash, nevertheless she loved her Morris, almost as much as she thought she might love her new job, driving the tall, handsome Colonel Atkins wherever he wanted.

Colonel Atkins was, at any rate to Edwina's mind, an unlikely man for the military, not least because from the moment he stepped into the car, he applied himself to his embroidery, at which he was most surprisingly talented, stitching swiftly and without pause even as he chatted to her; and that was all before she dropped him off at his flat for his after-lunch snooze, for which he informed her, without the slightest embarrassment, it was his habit to take off all his clothes to allow his body to breathe.

'Doesn't sewing in the car make you feel a little unwell, sir?' Edwina finally asked him one afternoon as they sped out of London towards the same 'secret address', that they had been to half a dozen times in the past fortnight, the secret address belonging to someone whom the colonel had no hesitation in referring to as 'the next PM'.

'No, never felt sick when stitching, probably because I learned to sew on the journey back from India to go to boarding school. Rough passage took my mind off it, that was why Nanny set us all to do it, I should have thought. Had to stop when we got to prep school, though, as you may imagine. Not the kind of thing headmasters and matrons understand. Start getting put down as a pillow chewer if you sew.'

Edwina, who never had much idea what the good colonel was talking about on their drives, certainly had no idea of what he might mean by 'pillow chewer'.

They arrived at the secret address, where she planned to stay by the car, avoiding all eye contact, looking as anonymous as possible.

'Still driving the good Colonel Atkins, are you, Miss Carrots?'

Edwina straightened up and saluted the next PM, smartly, crisply, thank *God*, but she did not move from the side of the car.

'Yes, sir.'

'If there are any more developments, Miss Carrots, I think I'll put in for you to drive this old body, I do, really. Just remember that, *mademoiselle*.'

Edwina did not know whether to nod or smile, so she merely stared ahead. The next PM's French accent was comfortingly atrocious.

'I will, of course, sir. Thank you, sir.'

He turned back and smiled. 'Ah, just a touch of the Irish in the voice, I hear. Mmm. Interesting. I have Red Indian blood, you know, as well as Jewish, my mother being of that noble race. It's good to be a mongrel, gives you a sound mix of ancestral memories.'

He was gone, leaving behind him a strong smell of the best kind of cigar on the English air.

Not very much later Colonel Atkins climbed back into the rear seat. They had hardly rejoined the main road when he started to pluck once more at his tapestry.

'So, I saw you caught the old man's eye.'

Edwina said nothing, avoiding looking at her passenger in her mirror.

'No good will come of that, be warned. I'll lose you as my driver, sure as eggs are eggs.'

Edwina reduced her speed as rain started to fling itself against the windscreen. She had the habit of rain, having been brought up in Ireland, but nevertheless she always dreaded having to brake hard, in case Colonel Atkins's needle caused him some kind of damage. As she chugged demurely back into the capital she considered Colonel Atkins's words. Why would he think that Winston Churchill MP might cause him to lose her as a driver? After all, Mr Churchill, although by no means popular in Ireland, was known for his marital fidelity, for which he was admired, it being so very rare among those in power, so that could not be the reason for Colonel Atkins's remark. Would she be wanted to drive him? He'd surely rather be driven by a man, especially if he became Prime Minister. Why therefore had the colonel noted the old man singling her out?

She put the matter quite out of her mind, which was understandable, since the next officer she drove was Captain Robert Plume.

'Terrific day for a spin,' was his opening remark as Edwina held the rear door open for him.

The day before, if asked, Edwina would have thought that it would take a great deal for dear Ben, the latest of her adoring tribe of beaux, to be driven from her mind, but the moment that she caught Robert's sparkling eyes underneath his naval cap, it seemed to her that she could hardly remember much about Ben, except that he was very eager, and in the RAF.

For the rest of the drive to Portsmouth, she tried silently repeating to herself, 'Never give all the heart for love,' but found to her confusion that somehow the words were not making the same good old sense any more, and that the seemingly sound advice she had dished out to Caro about keeping emotion at bay, about loving, but not falling in love, about how to behave in war, simply did not pertain to herself.

A few days later, having driven down to Portsmouth yet again, only this time not on official business, Robert and Edwina had dinner, and unsurprisingly to her, made love in a hotel suite, which he had booked.

'The funny thing is,' Edwina told him, just a little crossly a few hours later, when she lay in his arms staring up at the old beamed ceiling, 'I am not usually like this. I don't usually sleep with people on a first date.'

'It's war.' Robert kissed the top of her titian head and sighed with contentment. 'We can only blame the war for our behaviour—'

'Because we certainly don't want to blame ourselves. I should have kept myself for – after the war, don't you think, dotey?'

'Too late for that!'

They laughed, and Edwina propped herself up on her elbows, and stared down at Robert's head lying on the pillow beside her.

'And to think I was determined on taking Mr William Butler Yeats's advice.'

'Which was?'

Edwina hesitated, frowning. 'Never you mind. As my wise old Irish nanny used to say, "There's a time and a place, Miss Edwina," and this is not it, Master Robert,' she told him, before once more sinking back into the delights of lovemaking.

After all, if the words had been ignored, and she had indeed given her heart for love, what was the point of dwelling on it? And, as she had advised Caro Garland, this was war, no time to think too hard about the heart, only to love when you could. Yet if Robert had not been in the navy, but a gentleman farmer, living in his native Norfolk, and she a carefree young girl, living perhaps in a flat in Mayfair, staying with a friend for a few days, would they not have said they loved each other? So what was the difference? Everything was the difference, and nothing was the difference.

When she lay back against the pillows again, but this time out of reach of Robert's arms, and he brought a rose from the hotel vase and placed it carefully on the pillow beside her, Edwina found she had changed her mind. After all, life was too short not to be honest.

'I love you, Robert,' she stated, looking from him to the rose and back again.

He kissed her hand, his eyes sad.

'I would love to marry you, if there wasn't a war.'

Edwina smiled ruefully. 'Of course. And I would love to marry you, if there wasn't a war.'

She stared ahead of her, wondering how many times she was going to hear that said.

PART TWO

'So this *is war!'*

Chapter Seven

'. . . I don't have the right qualities to deal with homesick Frenchmen, and cooped-up Polish gents,' Robyn finished in briskly unrepentant tones.

'A pity, but understandable.' Aunt Cicely's great friend and Robyn's commanding officer replied, looking unsurprised, just as a junior officer put something on her desk marked 'Urgent'.

'I've stuck with it for months, but the cool hand that calms the fevered brow is not my forte, I'm afraid,' Robyn added, and her eyes too strayed to the piece of paper. 'To be honest, I found it a bit much when the Free French kept complaining that since they'd arrived they hadn't *once* been taken to the cinema. I felt like boxing their ears, not lending them a hanky to wipe their tears.'

'Horses for courses,' came the vague reply as Captain Agnes Hastings's focus was still on the piece of paper in front of her. 'Your family have a beach house in Sussex, I seem to remember, so you're familiar with the route. In view of this news,' she tapped the piece of paper and looked up at Robyn, 'it is just as well you're here. You can take your car, and drive like the clappers to the coast.

All hands are needed. It seems our army's stranded at Dunkirk, sitting ducks on the beaches, being strafed by the enemy at every turn.'

Aunt Cicely had always emphasised that Fanys were independent, proud, daring, and now, as one of them, thank God, Robyn realised, *active*!

'I've gone,' Robyn told Captain Hastings, her eyes alight. She saluted and was out of the door before either of them had time to say any more.

Caro had also been only too relieved to return to London. Not that she did not care for looking after the refugees, but once the Poles and the Czechs had all been cleared for active service with the RAF – their experience in aerial fighting now being second to none – the Fanys had been left with a nucleus of Austrian suspects and grumbling French, which was an unhappy mix, to say the least.

'You're better off sticking to what you love, motor cars and driving,' Robyn had told her affectionately. 'The art of winning a war is to follow the WVS rule: use every person for what they're *best* at, and then, little by little, you will find, against all the odds, you will win. You have to. It makes sense.'

Now they practically collided as they raced for their car keys, and then for their cars, both shouting out 'Goodbye' as they shot off to pick up their very different transport.

As Robyn started up the Bentley, thanking the gods that by dint of her special pass from MI5 she had managed to fill the car up with petrol, she set about calculating how long it would take her to get to the coast to pick up the men detailed in her orders. She had to hurry, to do her bit in her country's hour of need. Apart from anything else, she knew that this was what *Eddie* would expect. Should she fail, she could never look him in the eyes again. Even as she backed the car out, she knew he would be taking off in his Spitfire.

'Come on, come on,' she urged the Bentley, and the magnificent car seemed to understand and respond, as if she too wanted to do her bit. 'We've got to give Hitler a bloody nose. We've got to get our army back,' Robyn shouted over the sound of the rushing wind.

As Caro too drove towards the coast, probably faster than she had ever driven, she was not thinking of giving Hitler, or anybody else, a bloody nose; she was thinking of the mass evacuation of the troops, and she could not suppress the idea that among them might be her brothers, or someone they knew, sitting on those beaches, waiting and waiting, while the Germans picked them off at their leisure. Even as she tried to think in a more positive fashion, another thought would keep coming back to her, and would not be blanked out.

It was because of Katherine and David, and people like them, that they were all in this spot. How she hated them. She hated them in the same measure as they loved Hitler. Damn them, damn them both for ever and a day. She hoped she would never set eyes on either of them ever again.

The town in which Katherine had found herself after her long journey was beautiful. Black and white buildings, a great river running past, an old château with fortifications

213

on the hill above – everything about it exuded prosperity and tradition. A glance down its main streets suggested worthy city burghers and their wives strolling on a Sunday, nurses pushing prams with exuberant offspring lying back contentedly against lace cushions. It was a town that spelled ease, good food, wine harvested and bottled – not war. For these reasons, just before the outbreak of hostilities, David and Katherine had thought it ideal for their purposes, and rented a house in one of its calm backstreets.

David soon left her to go on Nazi business, so that Katherine, for the first time in her life, was left to cope on her own. They had both agreed on their plan, and it was up to her to implement it, get to know who the neighbours were, observe the townspeople, to understand the life that was about to be invaded. Indeed, they had hardly put their key in the door before it seemed that the fall of France had begun, her army dropping back from the advancing Nazis.

The house they had chosen to live in belonged to a Swiss businessman into whose numbered account the monthly rental was paid. The building was tall and thin, and the front door opened out on to the street. It was normally a quiet street, lit by faded eighteenth-century lamps, which at night gave a faint glamour to the figures that walked with feigned ease up to the house next door before knocking on the door – two raps only. With her first-floor sitting-room window open on summer evenings, Katherine was interested to note those two sharp knocks, and then to hear the old, narrow, eighteenth-century door opening and shutting with almost equal rapidity.

With David away it was up to her to watch, make notes, but, above all, to keep herself to herself.

For this reason she made sure never to leave the house for the marketplace except at dawn, nor to make friends with any of the local concierges, nor employ a daily *bonne* for the cleaning, or the shopping. Concierges could never be trusted not to talk, and everyone in France knew that the daily *bonne* was a source of information second to none.

Not a day went by when Katherine didn't find herself feeling thankful that, on being sent to learn a second language, and quite against her parents' wishes, she had insisted on living in France with French people, rather than settling for some smart Parisian finishing school. There she had not just learned French, she had learned the French way of life. If the devil was in the detail then from that time onwards she would cross her sevens, dip her bread in her early morning chocolate, and use her hands to gesture, as naturally as any *citoyenne* of the French Republic.

Not that the people who had placed her where she was imagined for one moment that she was French. She was there to work for them, and the last thing they wanted was for her to be exposed as a Nazi before the war began. They had made sure that she understood this, just as she, and David of course, had made sure to leave England before they aroused suspicion, and well before the first siren had sounded the previous September now what only seemed like a matter of a few months later, her dreams of living with David in an old house under an English heaven were as absurd as those people who had spent so many years refusing to take Hitler seriously.

All through the previous scorching French summer, Katherine had tried not to think of English rain washing warmly through the streams of home, of English meadows swaying in an English breeze, most of all of a distant figure, walking his dogs between tall grass, making his happy way down to a meandering river where he would watch the fish rise, and listen to the larks overhead singing of the gentle delights of the season.

An unusually loud sound on her neighbour's narrow door drew her cautiously to the window. The street-lamps had been lit, and the sky had darkened, but still distinguishable was the large, open-topped Mercedes motor car outside, a military figure holding the passenger's door open for a tall officer, who stepped out of the car and walked straight up to the door, which was already opening in response to his driver's sharp knock. An exchange of greetings in German and French followed.

Katherine's curtains having fluttered momentarily in the warm breeze, she withdrew quickly, but not before the driver had looked up to the house.

She hurried upstairs to take a bath, and go to bed. Being on her own, she was always waiting – for messages, for someone whom she had never seen before to arrive with a parcel that had to be taken on to some new address. In between her sending messages on her radio and her other duties, her bed had become both a refuge and an escape, a place where she read uneasily.

Tonight she had hardly fallen asleep before she was awoken by a knock on the downstairs door that seemed to echo through the tall house, with its bare wooden stairs and its empty rooms. She pulled on a wrap and some slippers, and ran down to answer it, hoping as always that it was David.

To see him again would be bliss. On the other hand, given next door's evening visitor, given the Mercedes, and the black-gloved driver, a much larger part of her hoped to God it wasn't him.

It should have been a relief to open the door and find the German officer whose cap she had seen disappearing into the house next door, but somehow it wasn't, because she was not so indoctrinated that she found the sight of a German uniform reassuring. He removed his cap to reveal that he was not just blond, but, it had to be admitted, handsome to a fault, something that Katherine was able to appreciate to the full as he smiled slowly, showing a set of perfect white teeth.

'Mademoiselle de Messadiere?'

He bowed slightly, and as he did so Katherine curtsied, because she had quickly sensed that he was *that* kind of Nazi, the old guard who liked old-fashioned customs, liked his women to be clinging vines, dependent on him for everything, eyeing him always with adoring eyes. Besides, he had a very educated accent.

Katherine smiled. 'How can I help you, General?'

He smiled at her upgrading his rank, realising from her droll look that they both knew that in reality he was several notches down from a general.

'Might I come in?'

Katherine hesitated. To say 'no' would be a mistake, to say 'yes' might be taken as the wrong kind of invitation. However, remembering that he had already been next door, she opened the door wider to let him in.

'Please come up, yes.' She paused on the stairs, smiling down at him. 'I will change, if you will give me a moment or two, after which we can perhaps enjoy *une petite coupe*, no?'

He followed her up to the first-floor drawing room and she left him, returning within a few minutes wearing a stunning red dress, her hair up, scent behind her ears, a pair of high-heeled shoes showing off her slender, shapely legs.

'How can I help you?'

He turned, smiling.

'You can allow me to sit down and appreciate your beauty,' he said calmly.

'Yes, please do.'

They sat looking at each other, and as they did so it occurred to Katherine that the two of them would make a good painting. The young woman in the scarlet frock with the black stockings, and the red and black shoes, and the German officer with his tall boots and magnificently cut uniform.

She wondered fleetingly what a painter might call it, and could not help smiling inwardly and thinking that if Walter Beresford chose them for a subject he would probably call it *The Ladybird*, because Katherine was wearing red and black. It was just one of many nicknames that David had given her; now it was just one of many code names that she used – some for the British, some for the Nazis.

'So – so you are "Elvira"?' the officer said a little later as they sat sipping some superb cognac, with which David had stocked their little wine cellar. 'You are just how I imagined you, Fräulein, just; and how often can one say that of someone?'

'This is our fourth lift!' the naval officer announced proudly to Robyn as she beckoned him and his companions to the Bentley. 'And seeing that it's a Bentley motor car, I think, with your permission we will make it our last, eh, boys?'

She laughed. 'Where to?'

'Pompey for us all, please, miss.'

'Portsmouth it is then. Hold on to your stripes, gentlemen, we are on our way.'

The car shot forward, but not before Robyn had time to take in the sparkling eyes of the uniformed young man seated beside her.

'Robyn Harding.'

'Robert Plume.'

He closed his eyes for a second as they appeared to be going round a hairpin bend on fewer wheels than was perhaps normal.

'And the two in the back are Tony Marston, and Julian Love.'

'Good morning, gentlemen. Now I suggest before we reach our destination—'

'You mean Dunkirk?'

'If you like, yes, although I'm not sure how useful this car is on water. But, as I was saying, before we get to Pompey I really think we should stop off to wet our whistles, because I don't know about you three, but, personally, I am parched.'

Robert smiled, and turned to the other two in the back.

'I agree with the officer here. After all, this might be the last time we can take a pull before we reach France.'

Tony Marston started to whistle something to which he had been dancing the night before. It didn't seem quite right to him, stopping at a pub when the others were God knew where, or God knew how. But he was outvoted.

When he eventually boarded a powerful motor boat, and steered it across the Channel, the day being sunny and clear, he reached France in a much shorter time than expected. And as the boat started to grind across the shallower waters, and a Stuka seemed to be making it its business to dive towards him and his boarding party, Tony found he was really rather glad that he had stopped at the Spread Eagle, and that was all before, the orderly line of soldiers having crowded in, the boat was found to be too heavy to move.

On hearing the news that the British Army were marooned on the beaches at Dunkirk and being picked off by the Germans from the air, and on the pretence that he had been robbed of his radio equipment, David made his way to Belgium now happily dressed as a french farm worker. Here he immediately changed disguises and assumed the uniform of a now, alas, dead staff officer of the Royal Fusiliers. Unfortunately he was just in time to witness the German bombing of the refugee camps, a sight far worse than any battle.

'Shoot me here, sir, please, shoot me before the Germans find me, please, sir.'

David could hardly bear the pleading look in the eyes

of the young girl who had just confronted him. He tried to move away from her but she followed him.

'There are rules that govern us,' he told her gently. 'The rules of war, the rules of the International Red Cross.'

She looked at him, despair now replacing pleading.

'It is such a little thing to ask of you, sir,' she told him. 'Such a little thing to ask you to do, to save me from a far worse death, an agonising death.'

David looked around – dozens of despairing faces surrounded them.

She reached forward suddenly, trying to grab his gun and turn it on herself. David wrenched the gun back.

'Mademoiselle, believe me, if I could do so I would certainly do as you wish, but if I shoot you, I in my turn will be shot! Take courage.'

The young girl turned away. It was impossible. She would have to kill herself some other way – a knife perhaps, or some sort of poison. Or the river beyond the camp, under cover of darkness. That would be the solution: to lie face down in the river, and stop breathing, before the Germans, now bombing them from the air, arrived in person.

Approached by a senior officer, looking as if he had just witnessed the massacring of his whole family, David took his gabbled orders with a sense of despairing relief. He was to take a petrol convoy to Dunkirk. The journey suddenly seemed very long, yet the task very small compared to trying to cope with the massacre, the despair, the horror, of these refugee camps.

*   *   *

Katherine looked with even greater appreciation at the German officer as he took his leave of her. He seemed taller and more handsome than ever, but then that was not very surprising, since both he and she had consumed several very smooth and very delicious cognacs from the very old bottle that she had brought up from the cellar.

'May I visit you again, Mademoiselle?'

'Elvira, General.'

'Ah yes, Elvira, an enchanting Mozart heroine, but quite naughty.' He glanced momentarily down at Katherine's red and black dress, stockings, shoes. 'You look so beautiful in red,' he murmured.

'Shocking colour for a respectable young woman, but I do look good in red, my mother always said as much,' Katherine replied, but as soon as she mentioned her mother the word 'home' came to her mind. She had not thought of home for so long – home, with its fires and its paintings, its lawns and its river, home as in faces lit by candlelight, and dogs barking delightedly, and the mix and cross of voices floating up as you came downstairs. Home, as in her mother looking beautifully composed, playing the piano, laughing with her brothers. Home, and all that went with it, was what she was fighting for. All this went through her mind, not as a sequence of thoughts but as a kaleidoscope of colours, a beautiful pattern held up to the window, the better to match it with that one precious word.

'You, I think, Mademoiselle, would look good in every colour of the rainbow.'

'Yes, but not all at once, perhaps.'

'All at once,' he retorted, straight-faced. 'And in a

rainbow sequence. Now what information shall I take back to my superiors?'

'What would you like to take back? Life here is very quiet, as you may imagine, at the moment, General.'

'That will not be acceptable.' He shook his head. 'No, I will have to report some suspicious goings-on in the countryside, but you know how it is in France: so many woods and valleys, so easy to lose people, most unfortunate the suspects got away.'

'Very good.'

'And so,' he paused, 'I will have to return.'

Katherine smiled. She couldn't believe she was smiling, but she *was*. She shook his hand before she shut the door, and in the seconds that followed, during which she heard his car being driven off, it seemed to her in her loneliness that she was already missing his courteous company. It was the cognac, surely? It could not be anything else. She missed company, any company, because she was missing David. Away for so long, it was only natural, but perhaps like so much that was only natural, she knew that she must not dwell on such an emotion. After all, between so many people, all the lines that David had been setting up through France and Belgium, she of the many names – the Ladybird, Elvira, Black Beauty, Diamond Lil – she was their link.

It had been David's idea to rent the house next door to the town brothel, and like so many of David's ideas, it was brilliant. Their people, his people, could come and go without either the men, or indeed the girls, arousing any suspicion. No one questioned the right of Madame Prosciutto, as she called herself – because, as she once told David, she was thin and salty – to entertain the gentlemen of the town, and lately the officers of the invading German Army, or anyone else for that matter. Of course, if the war was won by the Allies, the fate of Madame in such a quiet and respectable town would be perilous, yet Katherine was sure that Madame would simply disappear before anyone could punish her, only to reappear in another disguise somewhere quite the same, to begin all over again. It was no one else's business.

She walked slowly up to her bedroom. Soon it would be time to send a message. Sometimes it seemed to her that she was quite alone, because invariably she had so little to report, and yet now she might have a German officer in the palm of her elegant hand. Maybe she would at last receive a reply from the nameless people who worked at the other end in wherever it was. She took her shoes off, lay down on the bed and gazed up at the ceiling. It was not long before the brandy took effect, and she fell asleep in her clothes – only to be awoken a few hours later by yet another pounding on the front door.

'You silly bloody idiot!' the officer roared at David, who, still dressed as a staff officer, had helped him to push a heavy and powerful motor boat off the beach and into the sea. The driver, only too glad to be afloat at last, his boat now filled to overflowing with men, immediately sped away, leaving the officer stranded on the beach.

'Don't worry, sir, there'll be another one along in a minute.'

Not surprisingly, the officer, as he flung himself beside David, both of them being narrowly missed by bombs from a Stuka, did not find David's light-hearted remark amusing. Despite his face being now decorated by sand, despite the noise – and, boy, was it noisy – the officer continued to rage.

'Oh, do shut up, old boy,' David finally heard himself saying. 'You're truly not the only pebble on this beach, and you're not a very important one either!'

'I will have you shot for insubordination,' the officer screamed.

'Oh, I don't think you will,' David told him, turning his back on him. 'I am not one of your officers, sir. I take orders only from a code name, so stand in line and wait for the next bus to come along like a good chap.'

There must have been something in his tone, because the officer fell silent, eventually falling into the seemingly endless line awaiting rescue by any number of assorted craft – everything from paddle steamers to small sailing boats. For a second David reflected wryly that he would not have been very surprised to see a rowing boat from the Serpentine fetching up on La Panne beach that day.

'Take a trip round the bay?'

David turned and found himself facing someone who obviously knew him, but whom he did not recognise. Incredibly, the man, wearing a French beret and workman's overalls, was busily sketching the scenes on the beach as he too waited to find a place in one of the bravely approaching craft.

'Shall *I* shoot you, if he doesn't want to?' the man asked, still sketching briskly. 'Or are you waiting to shoot one of *us*, Mr David Astley?'

'And you are?'

'Walter Beresford, sometime mural painter at Chevrons, from where, I seem to remember, you absconded with the elder daughter.'

Walter felt a sudden punch between his shoulder blades, as David pushed him to the ground, throwing himself across the painter as he did so.

The explosion was very near to them. It ended in the screams and groans of its victims. For a few seconds, stunned as he was, Walter was convinced that he must be one of them, before David pulled him by the shoulder and helped him to his feet.

'Sorry about the drawing, old chap.' He leaned forward to speak into Walter's ear, covering his mouth as he did so. 'Whatever you may think or have heard, we are on the same side. My code name is Stendhal. When you get back to Blighty go to Dolphin Square and ask for Colonel Max. He'll cut you in – probably recruit you too, knowing Max.'

A moment later he was gone, weaving his way through the bloodied chaos of conflict, or in this case, as a fleeing body dropped in front of him, the massacre of conflict.

'Makes you sorry for ducks,' Walter heard someone remark as yet another line of men were dive-bombed by a Stuka.

Walter shoved his regrettably sketchy drawings back into his rucksack and joined the end of a long line waiting for a boat. It seemed hardly days since he had been quietly painting the portrait of an eminent French lawyer in the Midi when the Germans broke through the French defences. In common with just about everyone, he had foolishly imagined that he had time on his side, not appreciating that the Germans would march through France virtually unopposed, the result being that he had reached Dunkirk and the coast at precisely the same time as the German Army. Now, despite the bombardment, or perhaps because of it, he was glad to find himself still alive, but doubtful that he could count on any more luck. He tried to concentrate on the detail of what was around him: boats coming in, others being pushed out, the overhead warfare, the blood red of the blue sea, the incongruous brightness of the sunshine determinedly floodlighting and highlighting the horror around him.

Someone ahead of him muttered, 'Where's the RAF? Why is no one defending us?'

'They can't send in the RAF because, in the event that we are invaded, we would have no air power left to defend ourselves. It is just too much of a risk.'

'Balderdash,' the man seated opposite Robyn stated calmly. 'Utter balderdash. Our army should be defended now, not allowed to become target practice while most of the RAF sit on their backsides and do nothing to defend them.'

'The whole idea was ridiculous, sending a British Expeditionary Force over to France to say boo to Hitler. What did they imagine was going to be the outcome? Germany, frightened to death, throws in the towel and surrenders to an underequipped British force? If you ask me, there is no such thing as British understatement, only underequipment.'

Robyn leaned forward, putting her finger to Eddie's lips.

'No, not another word of this seditious talk. If anyone hears us we will be thrown in jug, and left to moulder there for the rest of the war, and that is the truth.'

Robyn could see that the word 'seditious' meant almost nothing to Eddie. He was still determined to fulminate.

'I can hardly go anywhere in RAF uniform without someone muttering, "And where were *you* when you were needed at Dunkirk, old boy?" It's a crying disgrace. We could have taken them on and put them to flight.'

Robyn still said nothing, but sipped at her drink instead. She knew that the whole idea of not sending in the RAF was anathema to young pilots like Eddie, who were fed up with not being allowed to get at the enemy, and the sooner the better, but she also knew that when Eddie said he could hardly go anywhere without being asked where the RAF was when needed at Dunkirk, he actually meant that he was feeling too embarrassed to go to the pub, and that was making him uncharacteristically irritable.

All the talk everywhere they went was the same. The humiliation of Dunkirk was a hair shirt to the nation as a whole, and a particular horror to those, like the Nursing Yeomanry, who had been drafted in to help with the horrifying injuries, particularly oil burns.

'Come on, ducks . . .'

'Not a good word to use at this time, Robyn. Those poor so-and-sos at Dunkirk, that's all they were: sitting ducks for the Stukas to enjoy their fairground fun – blam, blam, blam.'

'Come on anyway, Eddie. We're meant to be going out for a dance, not staying in for a grumble.'

Eddie looked at her. Robyn was the epitome of every girl with whom he had ever thought he might fall in love. Tall with a proud head carriage, slim figure, and fabulous legs.

'How about staying *in* and not grumbling?'

'Sorry, Eddie old thing, just not possible at this moment.'

'Why?'

Robyn gave him her sweetest smile. 'I am starving with hunger, and dinner at the Berkeley is heaven on wheels.'

'*Allez, allez* then, *cherie*, and the first one to touch the table has to pay!'

Naturally Robyn was the first to reach their table, but she could not have cared less; she would have paid for dinner for eight if need be, so much did she feel herself to be in love with Eddie.

Edwina was dining at the next table. She waved at Robyn, and blew Eddie a kiss from her long, elegant fingers.

'Obviously someone you know?' Colonel Atkins stated drily, feeling an unexpected dart of jealousy as the young man blew a kiss back to her. 'Known each other long?'

'No, not really. He is going to become engaged to one of my friends, that's all.'

Colonel Atkins did not smile. Everyone was getting engaged, marrying, starting wild affairs with unsuitable people – that was the effect war had. The behaviour of the normally quite respectable had become quite extra-ordinary.

'I take it, as of this minute, you are not becoming engaged to anyone in particular, Miss O'Brien?'

Edwina gave him a smile that would have launched the Queen Mary. 'No, not anyone in particular, just everyone in general, Colonel Atkins.'

The smile was so compelling, the small teeth so white, the green eyes so fascinating, that for a moment Colonel Atkins forgot that he was meant to be having dinner to recruit a new agent.

'Well, well, well, that is entirely to be wished for, as it happens. That suits our purpose most admirably.'

Edwina's heart sank. She knew that in some way she was being singled out, and she had the feeling that she knew who in particular had chosen her, and he was a stocky, cigar-smoking politician, who was now leading the country in place of Neville Chamberlain.

'I have to confess I am actually in love with one man, though, Colonel Atkins,' Edwina said, a little too hastily. 'Nothing to do with the war particularly, everything to do with *coup de foudre*.'

'Ah, the old lightning bolt. Well, no one can argue with the force of that, I am sure. Struck by lightning, struck by love – no difference, I understand.'

'No, perhaps not,' Edwina agreed, remembering Robert's expression.

'He has actually just returned from Dunkirk, and pretty miffed he is too at all the incompetence: no air cover, French troops pushing our lot aside, our lot rescuing their lot before our lot, and heaven only knows what else has gone on, or not gone on.'

'It isn't good – hasn't been good – but we can't give them the air cover we would like, for obvious reasons.' Colonel Atkins gave Edwina a significant look.

'No,' Edwina agreed, realising that the look must mean 'no aeroplanes to spare for that particular enterprise'. 'Perhaps not. However, the fact that most of the Expeditionary Force have returned is surely a miracle.'

'And they are still returning, my dear. Even as we speak our people are still returning in their hundreds, and on board every kind of craft.'

'I wish I'd been allowed to get over there instead of being ordered back to London. I mean, what does it look like if one is in uniform but not taking part in any of the main events?'

'You will not be in uniform for long, my dear, believe me. If what I think is going to happen to you does indeed happen, you will be very far from being uniform-clad. Not that you don't look handsome in your uniform,' he added quickly, seeing the look in the green eyes.

'Flattery will get you everywhere, Colonel, dotey,' Edwina murmured, at the same time only too happy to see the potted shrimps arriving, albeit that they were being presented in such a very round shape they could only be tinned. '*Ah, les crevettes sont arrivées.* How delightful.'

'Yes, the shrimps are indeed arrived at last.' Colonel Atkins put his napkin across his knees. 'Delicious. I used to love to go shrimping. Did you shrimp in Ireland?'

'Naturally, Colonel Atkins, in fact I shrimped so long that I once got caught by the tide, and was forced to spend the night on the rocks, before being rescued by the local fishing fleet.'

'Is that so?' The colonel looked momentarily impressed.

'No, of course not. But I did always hope that would happen. I loved adventure, but was never let off the lunge rope for long enough to enjoy any for very long.'

'So that was the reason you came to England from Ireland?'

'Naturally, as so many of us have, leaving behind a sighing, regretful—'

'But neutral nation.'

'Whatever gave you that idea, Colonel Atkins?' Edwina dabbed her lips with her napkin. 'No Irish man or woman is ever neutral, gracious no. They are fiercely partisan, never *neutral*! So it is now that those that can't swim across the Irish Sea to help in the war are staying at home and sending parcels of food to everyone and anyone, most particularly their thousand upon thousand of kissing cousins in Liverpool and Manchester.'

All this chatter, all this talk, why would the English never get to the point? Edwina wondered.

If you dined or lunched with an Irishman he would settle down to the point straight away, after which everyone could enjoy the rest of the meal. Not so the English – with them it was always silence, and then the weather, more silence, and then more weather, yet more silence, and yet more weather.

'How's your tapestry coming along, Colonel Atkins?'

The colonel's expression was solemn. 'It is finished, and ready to be mounted.'

'Well, that is good,' Edwina replied over-brightly. 'And what is going to happen to it now, I wonder?'

'I have an idea it will be made into a cover for a foot-stool, that sort of thing.'

232

Colonel Atkins looked momentarily regretful. Edwina could see that he could not quite come to terms with his beautiful stitching spending the rest of its days under the weight of someone or other's feet, but much as she was sure that his tapestry deserved a better fate, she could bear his procrastination no longer. She determined to come to the point before the fillets of sole were placed in front of them.

'Colonel Atkins, I wonder if it would help us both if I reminded you that I had hardly walked in the door, hardly parked my car outside the flat, all freshly returned from my seventh trip to the coast, bringing back and taking, bringing back and taking, when you telephoned through to say that you wished to see me on *urgent* business.'

'I did, didn't I?' Colonel Atkins feigned surprise.

'Yes, you did, and I hurried round to meet you here, after the quickest change since Gertrude Lawrence in *London Calling*—'

'Ah, now that was quite a show, delightful. He's been in America, you know, Noel Coward, on government business, and now questions are being asked in Parliament, and I know not what. Press can't mind their own business, Beaverbrook gunning for him and all that. All disgraceful, and unnecessary. Anyone would think we should have better things to do than go for our own people, but there you are, that's newspaper barons for you.'

'Colonel Atkins, what is it that you want from me? Please put me out of my state of animated curiosity.'

Colonel Atkins looked embarrassed. 'Are you sure you want to talk about it before we have pudding?'

Edwina's eyes flashed. 'I certainly do,' she assured

him. 'Because once I hear what you have to say, perhaps I will not feel like eating pudding, Colonel, dotey!'

As the sweat ran off Betty's forehead, and she quickly wiped it away with the sleeve of her boiler suit, lest it drop on one of the items she was making, she was sure she could hear the jeering voice of the principal of the orphanage. *'You'll never make anything of yourself, Betty Thomas, never! You'll always be an also-ran, sitting at the bottom of the pile, Miss Going Nowhere.'*

She had made it to seven hours at a sitting, or rather a standing, because they had to stand to assemble everything. Foolishly she had been quite determined to notch up that seven hours, and of course she had paid for it, as you surely always did with factory work, even in wartime. She had paid for it with aching limbs and cracking headaches; she had paid for it with Trixie's teasing her, endlessly, but not it seemed without reason. Worst of all she had paid for it by being marked out as a goody-goody by the rest of the factory women.

She glanced up at the clock. Five hours would have to do today, five hours and five minutes. She stepped away from the line, her place soon taken by a newcomer, and peeled off to the changing room, if that was what you could call it, before staggering back to their digs.

'I tried to warn you,' Trixie told her, almost smugly. 'You might take half a crown off of me—'

'Off me, not off of me, Trix—'

'*Off* me. Anyway – *that*!' Trixie laughed. 'My grammar is going backwards from being in the factory. At any rate, you might take half a crown off me – and my fault for betting you, I grant you – but even so, seven hours! Mind you, I did try to warn you that by notching up the best time ever and being singled out by the supervisor, you would make enemies of just about everyone except the supervisor.'

'Mrs Ludgrove did say she was pleased, that no one else had ever notched up seven hours at a go.'

'Of course she's pleased, now she's got your hours to beat the rest of them over the head with so she's pleased all right. And, as I said, you have made three hundred enemies at one go. And that too is something to be proud of, all right.' Trixie looked resigned. 'Still, seeing that they work in shifts, you won't be seeing all of them at once. So you might get let off lightly – only get your shoe laces tied together and your handbag rifled, and castor oil put in your tea.' Trixie gave a short sarcastic laugh. 'I, on the other hand, have made more friends than you've made explosives, my deah. Full of popularity, I am, because me and the work is chalk and cheese, and that's for certain.'

'Well, you were right,' Betty stated, lying back down on her narrow bed, while deciding not to correct Trixie's grammar yet again, 'and I was wrong, and nothing to be done about it now.'

'No, nothing,' Trixie agreed. 'Except to say I'm a bit worried about you, because what with one thing and another, it could really turn in there for you, you know? I mean, it could get dangerous, with all of them being the kind they are.'

She sat down on her own bed opposite Trixie.

'I don't think you should stay, Betty, really I don't. I

235

mean, the work's dangerous enough without all those cats waiting to scratch your eyes out.'

'I'll be all right. Spiders in my tea, cutting off the bottom of my boiler suit, whatever else they do, I'll be all right. You forget I was brought up in an orphanage.'

Betty glanced at Trixie and then stared up at the ceiling. Actually, if she was to be honest with herself, she knew Trixie was right to be worried. Since the infamous moment when she had clocked up seven hours, there had been an unpleasant incident every day, sometimes more than one. Only this evening a gang of women had stopped by her station and jeered at her. They had only fled when Mrs Ludgrove fetched up unexpectedly.

After a long pause, during which she set herself to think about the situation a little more seriously than usual, Trixie spoke.

'The trouble is, Betty, we have to face it, there's no one else like us in the factory. I mean, we stick out like sore thumbs, and sore thumbs is what we got and all, for all the trouble we've been put to, and that's a fact. It's funny really, here were we – me the chauffeur's daughter, and you Little Orphan Annie, well, Betty, from the institution down the way – and yet we're not like the rest of them, and you know why? Because of being at Chevrons. Because I was born there and you were adopted there, we wanted to better ourselves, and now that we *have* bettered ourselves, like I said, we stick out like sore thumbs, and go in fear of getting ourselves taken out. I mean, let's face it, it's dangerous enough work all right, but if I'm going to have danger I'd rather it came from the enemy than from some long-faced girl on the assembly line who's just got in the straw for the third time.'

Betty sat up. 'Language, please, Trixie!'

Trixie shrugged. 'Once upon a time, what seems like fifty years ago, I was learning to speak like a lady to fit in at Chevrons, so now I'm learning to speak like that lot, because I'm in a factory making things to blow up little children just because they happen to be German.'

'They started it.'

'I know, I know, but even so, it's not nice, is it? I can't help thinking of the innocent people we're going to kill with those things.'

'War's not nice.'

'No, is that the truth?'

Trixie now lay down on her bed and stared up at the ceiling in similar fashion to Betty, hands behind the head, expression glum.

'It all seems like another world, doesn't it? Us being at Chevrons, and Mrs Garland taking you out of the orphanage, because she was one – an orphan, I mean – and she took such an interest in the place. I often think back on Dad taking us on trips in his car on Sunday afternoons, and picnicking with him on the hill above the town, and going looking for things he'd hidden on a treasure hunt, and all that. Seems like another world.'

'It *was* another world, and it's not going to come back, and we know it.'

Trixie glanced sideways at Betty. 'Well, what are we fighting the war for, then?'

'To try and hold on to it, bits of it, not all of it but bits of it, so we can try to bring it back . . . bring back bits of the old life, if we win.'

'We've got to win, Betty. I mean to say, what else is there to do except win? We'll be in a prison camp for the rest of our lives, or on a chain gang, if we don't win.'

'Much good we'd be breaking up rocks!'

'Knowing you, Betty, you'd break up so many you'd spoil it all for everyone else.'

Betty started to laugh. 'Maybe you're right, Trixie. Maybe I'm nothing but trouble, just as they used to say at the orphanage.'

'You're not trouble, Betty, you're a saint. I know, because Mrs Garland used to say, "The trouble with Betty is, she's a saint. She can't help it, it's how she is, and I fear her bleeding heart will get her into trouble."'

'Did she really say that?'

'Yes, she did.'

Trixie was silent then, because she felt she'd gone too far. She remembered now that Mrs Garland also used to say that she knew what it felt like to be rescued, and that like all rescued creatures Betty would always feel grateful for the rest of her life.

'First thing we've got to do is to get out of this factory,' she continued eventually. 'Especially you,' she added, half accusingly. 'We have to think who could help us. There must be someone.'

'No one can help us, Trix. We've got to help ourselves. I wasn't going to tell you in case nothing came of it, but a letter arrived for me this morning when you were out, and I'm going up to London again tomorrow.' Betty sat up, and after a minute of searching she produced a piece of paper from her handbag. 'I've been asked back to see that gentleman in the War Office again.'

Trixie stared at the letter. 'How did he know you were here?'

'I don't know, but he did, so I'm going back to see him, and maybe this time I will get a job as a secretary.' She pulled some of her books down from the meagre shelf beside the bed. 'So, if you will, just start dictating to me, Trix, because I'm afraid I've got stale, and I don't want that. You see, this could be an opportunity for me to prove what I can do.'

Betty picked up her pencil. Her hands still hurt from the assembly line, her back hurt, her head hurt, but once the phrases started to come back to her the old feeling of contentment stole over and finally through her, that feeling of being at peace with herself. After all, this was something she could do. A hundred and fifty words a minute, that's what she had been doing before the war, and that was like doing seven hours on the factory floor; that was a bull's-eye of a speed.

Trixie read at a good speed, which she could now, and as she did so she remembered Caro Garland and the sessions they had enjoyed together: Miss Caro correcting her pronunciation, Trixie revelling in the attention, both of them taking secret enjoyment in the idea that Trixie was determined not to stay a maid. Trixie was going to become a lady, and drive a car like her father, and wear nice clothes like Miss Caro.

'Getting on is what it's all about,' Caro had agreed. 'We all have to. I have to because I'm not a beauty. Oh, yes, I have to get on too, you know, Trixie. I will never be sought after the way Miss Katherine is sought after, but that doesn't matter. I am determined to really live my life, not just sit about waiting for something to happen, which it never does unless you give life a good shake and kick it in the shins. Otherwise it will settle round you like a fog, and you'll never find your way round it, not ever. I know this the same as I know my own name.'

Now Trixie read on, taking a pride in her voice, refining it as she imagined herself back at Chevrons, and as she did so she could not help filling up with pride. Betty must have been written to by the man at the War Office because of Trixie's scheming.

Trixie had been so worried about the enemies Betty had made at the factory that she had written to Miss Caro, begging her to find Betty a position as a typist, or just as something, *anything*, in an office, before she came to harm in the factory. Miss Caro, bless her cotton socks – or rather, her shiny French nylons – must have come up trumps or Betty surely would not have received that letter.

Trixie gave an inward sigh of relief. She could manage all right at the factory. She had a way of getting round the cats that worked alongside her, having learned to become a chameleon, pleasing everyone all the time. At Chevrons she had learned to duck under the invisible barriers and make good friends of everyone. It was an art that poor old saintly Betty had not yet acquired, and perhaps never would.

The man who had taken the decision not to send the whole of the RAF to take on the Germans at Dunkirk was being proved right. As the London Blitz began, the plucky little aeroplanes manned by young men barely out of their teens took on the invasion from the air. Whatever the outcome – and please God, against all the odds, they would win – the man who had stood firm against everyone knew he would never be forgiven, most particularly since he was being proved right.

As he watched the young Waafs moving the pieces, representing his precious Spitfires and Hurricanes and all the rest, across the boards, while others chalked up losses and victories on the wall blackboards, he was aware that he had long ago resigned himself to his fate. No one would thank him for keeping back so many of his planes from Dunkirk, but what would that matter if they could win this battle of the skies? The important thing now was to give Hitler a thrashing, put off the invasion, and begin to turn the odds against him.

As the news vendors broadcast the scores of enemy planes shot down, and played down the home team's losses, as people grew so used to seeing aerial battles overhead they sometimes did not even look up, as telegrams arrived at households that had never known loss, but now would know too much, the man responsible for saving England from invasion went outside and lit a much-needed cigarette.

It was not being proved right that was gnawing at him. No, what was eating him up was the idea that had he not held out for what he believed, he just might have given in to the pressure to throw everything that he had at Dunkirk – and in so doing would have lost England.

Chapter Eight

Edwina glanced down at her watch. It was well after half past seven. Robert was meant to have picked her up at six thirty, and they were to have gone dancing at the Savoy. Well, drinks first, and then dancing, and dinner. She snapped open her evening bag, and taking out a new small gold cigarette case – a divine present from Ben, bless him – she lit a cigarette, not caring that she was wearing evening gloves, not caring very much about anything at all except that Robert was late, not there, had not arrived.

Over their dinner together Colonel Atkins had hinted that he knew Edwina to be a bit of a goer. How had he known? Edwina knew she should have felt angry at his impertinence, but somehow war put paid to all that too.

'I'm not a goer, Colonel Atkins,' she had finally said, 'but I do believe in being just a little, what you might call *loving* to those who know they are about to die. There is nothing wrong with their last memory being of the smell of French scent, the sight of pretty legs in silk stockings, and a pretty girl's kisses – nothing more. In fact, it should be obligatory for the services to supply them! That is all I have offered our gallant young men. I have beaux, Colonel Atkins, admirers, worshippers, not boyfriends. I am after all an Irish girl. We are not the same as those from here.'

Edwina knew, from the look that Colonel Atkins had given her, that if he could have blushed at her dignified reply, he would have done, but he really was not the blushing type. Instead he allowed his blue eyes to rest on her face as he looked at her over the top of his wine glass. He was more than able to appreciate that Edwina O'Brien was a beautiful woman, and now he could also appreciate that she was an intelligent one. All this was to his advantage.

Of course, the files back at the office had already told him that Edwina O'Brien had never been a goer, but now she had confirmed this he felt both encouraged and disappointed: encouraged because, like so many attractive men of his generation, he enjoyed the thought that not all beautiful women were easy; and disappointed because he was sure, from the look that she had given him, that she was about to spin his idea.

However it was, and whatever she thought of him, he was proved right, for the dinner had finally ended with Edwina turning down his proposed offer.

Colonel Atkins had taken it very well, stating calmly that he had thought she might react as she had, and that being so, he would never mention the matter again. He would wait for her to come back to him if she changed her mind. After which he had called for another bottle of wine, and they had fallen to talking about the good old days in Ireland, when it seemed he had known Edwina's esteemed grandmother, and had stayed at Clonakilty Castle – not, he was forced to confess, that he could remember a great deal of it.

'Hunting all day and drinking all night rather puts paid to the memory, you know.'

Edwina had laughed at that, and been surprised too, because she somehow could not imagine Colonel Atkins having been young and drunk, but she did not say as much.

Oh, but *where* was Robert?

An American officer stopped momentarily and stared at her admiringly. Edwina stared right back. Look your fill, her glance said, but I have what I believe you would call 'a date'.

She moved off into the thick of the people milling about the foyer. It was a miracle that during the recent air raids the Savoy had not yet been hit. The Dorchester was actually proving to be the most popular of the London hotels, because it was rumoured, rightly or wrongly, that it had concrete foundations, or some such idiocy. As if that would make any difference if it took a direct hit! But nevertheless all the old dowagers, and God knows who else, now crowded its basement every night, carrying Dorothy bags filled with their precious jewels. As if jewellery would make any difference when you were dead.

The truth was Edwina had never before been in love, until now. So, much as she did not regret being the comfort of first Tom and then Ben, her heart had been captured by neither of them. No, her wild Irish heart had, for some reason best known to the gods, been stolen by beloved Robert.

'Edwina O'Brien? Edwina O'Brien?'

The page was calling her name. But why? Why should he be calling her name? Who would know that she was here except Robert? But why would he be sending a telegram to her? Why would he not want to meet her? After all, he had been to Dunkirk and back, and back and back and back and back.

'I'm Miss O'Brien.'

'Miss Edwina O'Brien?'

'The very same.' She stared into the fresh face of the page boy. 'I'm surprised you're still here,' she joked as she took the telegram. 'Shouldn't you be in the army?'

The page boy grinned. 'I'm only fourteen, ma'am. Give me time.' He nodded at the telegram, and then his grin grew wider as Edwina took a shilling from her evening bag and placed it in his palm.

'Take my advice and stay fourteen, gossoon, you hear me?'

He saluted her. 'Yes, ma'am. Whatever you say, ma'am. For a shilling I'd stay anything!'

'I bet you would, you rascal!'

Edwina opened the telegram. 'Have been posted. Nothing to be done. Think of me. Love you always my Ginger Nut – ROBERT.'

Edwina stared at the telegram, and then folded it very carefully and put it into her evening bag.

'Talk about all dressed up and nowhere to go,' she remarked as the American officer passed by her once again.

'Not bad news, I hope?' he asked with genuine concern.

'Not bad news, no, just not good news. My date's been posted.'

He stared at her, allowing unadulterated admiration to flood his face as he took in her tall, slender figure, her vibrant hair, her pale skin, her green eyes with their vaguely promising look.

'In that case, ma'am, may I have the privilege?'

'I don't see why not.'

Edwina flicked her cigarette into a nearby ashcan.

'This is my lucky night, ma'am.'

'And you are . . . ?'

'Gene Hawtrey.'

'I see. Well, I am Edwina O'Brien, and I am very hungry, so I hope you are too.'

He held out his arm. 'Booked?'

'Booked.' Edwina slid her hand through his arm. 'Since you are my date for tonight, I hope you can dance?'

'All Americans can dance. You can't become an officer unless you can dance.'

'How very civilised.'

Edwina sashayed ahead of Gene down the Savoy steps, and as she did so, she put out of her head any more thought of Robert. It was the only thing to do. So he had meant a lot to her, so what would 'a lot' finally mean? He would probably be gone as soon as all the others. They all would be – she glanced back towards Gene Hawtrey – perhaps even him.

Only later did she take the telegram and lay it carefully under her pillow with her holy pictures, praying, 'Are you there, God? Take care of him, bring him back to me. I'll be so good if you will just do this one thing for me. Bring Robert back.'

Caro looked at herself very seriously in the mirror, leaning forward and staring into her eyes as if she was someone else, which just for a moment she imagined she might be.

Outside she could see the fires burning, the great searchlights sweeping the sky. At the beginning of the week an incendiary bomb had taken out two houses in the next street. Yesterday night had found her driving much-needed supplies to the East End, together with a few VIPs who had wanted to see for themselves the growing legend of what was now being called 'the plucky spirit of the East End'.

What they had seen had indeed surprised and impressed them; the singing, the huddling together for cheer and warmth, the utter resignation of those who had lost everything that they had ever possessed.

'These are ordinary folk, not trained for battle, as we have been. Nothing could have prepared them for what they are going through, and yet see how they are?'

The journey there and back had been tortuous, as night-time London journeys now were, passing screaming fire engines, ambulances tearing through the narrow streets, stooped figures sorting through the rubble of their homes, their bent outlines lit by the vast fires of the burning buildings around.

The blanket bombing of London had begun at last. Yet, everyone seemed to agree, it was almost a relief. Nothing but nothing could have been worse than actually waiting

247

for war to begin. Everything that you had ever dreaded in your imagination turned out to be less in reality. The duration of the 'Phoney War' – when all the children had been evacuated, the people trained by the Red Cross been put on alert, everyone waiting, waiting to start their new duties, from fire fighting to driving canteens, but then nothing, just more ominous waiting, everyone trying not to think too much – had been intolerable.

'You're not going back tonight. You've done six nights driving the canteen. I'll go in your place,' her senior officer had told Caro, giving her an old-fashioned look as if to say she had her number all right. 'Besides, doubtless it's your night for fire watching, isn't it?'

As a matter of fact it had been, which was why Caro now found herself staring at her red-lined eyes and grey expression in Aunt Cicely's bathroom mirror. There was the sound of sirens, followed all too soon by the inevitable hum of approaching enemy bombers. She wanted to go down to the basement with whoever was also in the building, but she found she couldn't. For some reason she seemed to be rooted to where she was standing, clinging to the basin, watching herself losing what remained of colour from her face, with vague fascination, as if she was someone else.

If only she weren't alone. If Robyn was with her they would both have dived under the kitchen table with a bottle of gin, but Robyn was out driving some officer or another on a date. (Robyn kept complaining that she was fed up with driving officers back from nightclubs and trying not to watch them necking in the back of the Bentley.) Probably because she didn't have to pretend to be calm in front of someone else, Caro now realised she was actually scared stiff. The apartment block was shaking so badly that she would not have been surprised to find herself, together with all the furniture, flying out of the side, as it crumbled. She shut her eyes. Please, please God, she would stop trembling soon.

It was the noise mostly, she kept telling herself, the incessant noise that seemed to get you down the most. That was why it was so much better to be *doing* something. No one would or could believe the noise that a bombing raid threw at you. And it did seem to have been actually thrown *at* you. While she was driving her car, or the canteen, she was fine. It was now, when she was just being ordinary, that the air raid became a nightmare and she felt herself longing with sudden passion for someone to grumble and be afraid with. She picked up her torch, her tin hat, and a blanket, and the notebook telling her where to clock in for fire watching on the roof, and made her way out into the now darkened city.

Sandbags sheltered the doorway of the flats, and rubble filled the pavement when she turned the corner, lighting her way gingerly past the silent, darkened houses. As usual the docks and the East End were taking the brunt of the bombardment, but there were always a few surprises in store. The night before last, making her way from the Underground where she had been taking much-needed succour of tea and blankets, she had stepped on a dead body. It was no good pretending that she had not been horrified, because she had, but happily, or unhappily, the sound of destruction all around her had drowned out her scream.

She was in dread of the same thing happening tonight, and it seemed that she would never find her way to the right door, but at last she found the stairway that led to the rooftop where she was to take up her duties. She climbed the hollow-sounding stairs, frightened now of meeting up with someone that she wouldn't like. Stories of girls who had been raped in the blackout, or in some godforsaken bomb shelter, were now going the rounds, and the sight of figures stealing out with torches to search ruins for money and jewellery was now a commonplace. Rats would also creep in and out of abandoned buildings, stealing what remained from the human occupation left behind, as eager as so many humans to take advantage of the Nazi destruction.

Caro stopped.

There was someone else on the roof, torch in hand, a tall figure in a strangely old-fashioned hat. On hearing the door to the roof opening, which, in the weird lull of the aftermath of the raid, for some reason sounded fire-cracker loud, he turned at once and shone his torch in Caro's face, just as she shone hers right back.

'Good God!'

Betty too found herself staring in the mirror. She had taken a long time to choose her clothes, and the result was a navy-blue suit with pleated skirt, navy-blue shoes and matching handbag, gloves, of course, and a white blouse with a slight sailor-boy look to the cut.

'You look as if you want to join the navy.'

'Or I already have,' Betty agreed, turning from the rust-marked mirror to Trixie. 'The thing is, Trix, I have to look respectable, or they will not believe I can do the work, and I have to look as if I have class, the kind of class that a secretary should have, discreet, and trustworthy.

'Oh, you look discreet all right,' Trixie told her, packing up her own things before leaving for the blasted factory. 'You look so discreet, Betty, that, quite honestly, if it were up to me I'd employ you in the Prime Minister's office, really I would, or, seeing that you look so good in navy, put you to work in the Admiralty!'

'Wish me luck, Trixie, please. I am awfully nervous.'

Trixie gave her an old-fashioned look. 'Gumption, Betty Thomas, not nerves, that's what's needed. Never let them see you're nervous or they think you've got something to be nervous *about* that you're hiding from them, which wouldn't be good, would it? Unless, of course, you have?'

Betty reddened. 'I have nothing to hide, Trixie, you know that.'

'Oh, I don't know . . .' Trixie gave her a sly look. 'What about seven hours at the factory bench? Now that is something to hide all right, seeing that it's brought you into disrepute, Miss Thomas.'

Betty pulled a face. Trixie was not taking her interview seriously.

'No, really, wish me luck, won't you?'

'Nope! No, I will do no such thing.'

'Why?'

'Because I know you'll get the job, that's for why.'

Of course, what Betty did not know was that the old grapevine that ran from Chevrons to London had, it now seemed, done its really rather efficient magic.

Trixie had already written to Caro that Betty was about to be lynched. Caro, as she was meant to, had casually mentioned this to Edwina, who, while at dinner with Colonel Atkins, had mentioned the name of Betty Thomas not so casually to him, recommending her as trustworthy and with a known provenance at Chevrons.

Colonel Atkins, recognising a good, sound recommendation when he heard one, contacted his old colleague Max, now at Baker Street, who told his old colleague at the Park, as it was now known. The colleague requested Colonel Atkins to conduct an interview on his behalf, under the guise of being a colleague of the man at the War Office who had, albeit with some regret, turned down Betty Thomas in the first place.

'It's quite simple work, really. By that I mean a bright girl like you will cotton on straight away, but it is also very, very high on the security list.' Colonel Atkins looked pensive. 'In fact, it is top, top security, but you have come recommended, despite the fact that you are not, as it were, in uniform.'

Miss Thomas certainly looked as though she was in uniform.

'If you are offered the post it will mean signing the Act, and living out of town. Not much nightlife at the Park, you know. In fact there is no nightlife at the Park. You might be better joining the WAAC, wouldn't you say?'

'No, sir.'

'So you wouldn't mind no nightlife?'

'No, sir. I have never been fond of nightlife.'

Betty hoped what she was feeling, which was not just nervous, but actually hopeless, was not showing itself.

Certainly she was speaking nothing but the truth when she said she had no fondness for nightlife, since she had never actually experienced it.

'These Fanys, you know, they drive all day and dance all night. Nothing stops them.' Colonel Atkins shook his head and the look in his eyes was so admiring that Betty found herself wishing that she did have a penchant for nightlife after all, if only to be able to see that same appreciative light in the colonel's blue eyes, for he was a handsome man, almost absurdly so, with thick wavy blond hair, and perfect features.

'I think what we will have to do first is to get you to sign the Official Secrets Act, not that it amounts to much; except now, of course, it amounts to a little more, because if you disobeyed anything in it, you would, of course, receive the death penalty.'

For a second, Betty wondered if she had heard right, because the colonel made everything sound so casual, as if signing the Official Secrets Act was no different from passing a driving test – and that too, it seemed, was on the curriculum.

'You should learn to drive while at the Park, in case of invasion, you know. Very useful in that kind of circumstance, if you're fleeing the enemy, having first burned everything interesting, of course. That is always the first duty in times of invasion, to set fire to everything. So now, first things first, you must sign the old Act, and then I'll pass you on to a Wren, who will kit you out in WAAC or, more probably, WRNS uniform. In case of invasion, a service uniform is obligatory, or the Nazis will treat you as a spy. They will not believe you have an official role if you are in mufti, and will just go ahead and shoot you. So here we are, sign along the line, and then on we go.'

It was not until Betty had uncapped her fountain pen and was signing the Official Secrets Act that it came to her that if she was signing this piece of paper, and if Colonel Atkins was talking about passing her on to a Wren to kit her out in some kind of uniform, she surely must have the job. But she didn't dare ask. Instead she meekly signed the Act, and replaced the cap on her fountain pen.

'What about my things?' she finally did ask as he ushered her towards the door.

'Your things?' The colonel looked confused. It was as if he thought there was no more to Betty than Betty herself, her handbag, her navy-blue skirt and jacket, and her shining navy-blue shoes.

'Yes, my things, Colonel Atkins. Back at my place I share with Trixie Smith, where we are working, at the factory, and so on. I have left all my things there.'

'Oh, I see, your *things*. Oh, don't worry about your *things*, Miss Thomas. They're all taken care of. They'll be at the Park already.'

Betty felt suddenly both shocked and indignant. Of all the cheek! Supposing she had said no to the job?

'You're wondering how I knew you would be suitable, Miss Thomas?' The colonel did not smile, but indicated for her to go through the door. 'You came strongly recommended, by trustworthy sources. How else do you think we get the right people? Certainly not by advertising for them.' He gave a short humourless laugh, and Betty walked quickly ahead of him. 'Life in wartime moves very fast, Miss Thomas,' he murmured, as they went back down what seemed to be endlessly grey corridors, passing a sea of navy and army personnel, all hurrying purposefully. 'It has to move fast, or else we will never win the accursed thing.'

Caro thought she was going to faint when she saw the torch suddenly lighting the familiar features of Walter Beresford under his tin hat.

'I thought you were – ' she paused, frowning, looking up from under hers – 'I had thought you were, well, somewhere or another. I think it was France, yes, I think my father said you were in France. You and he quarrelled, didn't you? That's why you left suddenly, wasn't it? Wasn't there some sort of dispute over the mural?'

Walter kissed her briefly on the cheek. It was a brotherly kiss, the kiss of someone who was preoccupied with matters about which he wouldn't care to speak, the kiss of someone who might have been physically present, but was certainly not spiritually present.

'I do have an idea that I was in France,' he agreed. 'But a little thing called the German Army, and then Dunkirk, stopped short my enjoyment of life over there.'

'I wondered what had happened to you,' Caro lied, probably because she hadn't at all, although she had gone on wearing her lucky golden mole, which she now pulled out by its gold chain and showed Walter. 'Still wearing my lucky charm. See?'

The truth was that despite his present to her that day at Chevrons, so much had happened in the months between her leaving home and their present meeting, she had most determinedly not given him a thought.

'How have you been?' Walter's tone was one of a man who, after their last meeting, had also not given his companion another thought.

'Dunkirk was pretty beastly, wasn't it?' she asked as they both fell to the ground, bombs dropping on buildings all around them.

'Yes, yes, it was. But guess who I met up with there?' Walter raised his voice above the shattering sounds of a building being hit.

'Shan't, can't, won't. Quite apart from anything else I'm rotten at pretending to guess at things about which I haven't a clue,' Caro answered, also raising her voice.

'I'll give you a hint. Someone you used to know.'

Caro frowned. 'Someone nice?'

'No, I'm afraid not. Someone not at all nice – David Astley.'

'Good gracious.'

'Funny thing was, he was dressed as a staff officer and helping our lot, which led me to wonder if he has seen sense after all. Or do you think he was just busying himself, preparatory to making beckoning signs to his friends the Nazis, who were bombing us defenceless creatures?'

The mention of David was a blow to Caro's normally buoyant self-confidence. The disappearance of David and Katherine was for her somehow inextricably linked with her mother's sudden death.

'I don't know anything about David, or Katherine, for that matter.'

Caro's voice must have reflected her perturbed state more than she would have wanted. It had been bad enough having to find her way to that chap Max's place in Dolphin Square to do her patriotic bit and report finding Katherine's scarf in her car, God knows. As she had left him, she had felt like some sort of traitor, not at all patriotic, just shabby, telling on her sister to someone who might throw her in prison, but now the thought of David at Dunkirk was more disturbing.

'What did you say to him? I mean, did you say anything to him? You never met him, though, did you, so how would you know it was him?'

'I never met him, no, but I saw him that time, with you, remember, that first evening I was at Chevrons? I knew his face straight away. He does look just a little like a Greek god, damn him, and of course being an artist I rarely forget a face like that.'

'Not a very nice person behind the face, though. David is so "inside beastly", it would make you prefer him to be ugly, wouldn't it? Did you report that you had seen him when you got back?'

'Of course. But no one was interested. You know the War Office: people pushing files of closely written papers around during peacetime, then war breaks out and they employ even more people to push files of papers around, only just a little faster. Oh, no, I told them all right, and they pretended to be interested.' He put on an interested officer's voice. '"Thank you very much, old boy. Done the right thing, absolutely. Dressed as a staff officer, you say? Well, well, cheeky chap. Of course we will pass it on to relevant quarters, et cetera, et cetera. So if there's nothing more to tell us, why don't you go and jump in the Serpentine, what?"'

Caro laughed. She hadn't realised how much she had missed Walter's mocking nature, his lightness of touch.

'I wish I could feel sorry for Katherine and David, but I can't,' she said after a few seconds' silence. 'In fact, I feel quite the opposite. I feel nothing but contempt for them, and their stupid ideas. Look what it has brought us!' She nodded to the chaos around them, the sound of dull crunches, the groans of buildings, or were they people? The sky lit not just by the moon but by the flames of the burning buildings. 'Just look what a plain little house painter who parts his hair on the wrong side can do, thanks to the stupid people who believed him and his rotten ideas?'

Walter nodded. 'Yes, I must admit, if I'd had a gun, I might even have been tempted to shoot Astley in the back, but I only had my sketchbook. Besides, if you broke the line at Dunkirk, you never got back into it again, so I'm afraid I put myself before the security of my country, which is not very admirable.'

'I would have shot him in the back, no matter what,' Caro asserted. 'No hesitation, I'm afraid.'

David had been issued with the cyanide pill. It wasn't difficult to reach the damn thing, and reach for it, he now realised, he would have to. As a matter of fact the only thing he felt at that moment was grateful for it, and to the Miss Abel who had doled it out to him on one of his flying visits to see Max. She kept it in the bottom drawer at SOE in Baker Street.

'You're only allowed one,' he remembered her telling him. 'Not that anyone ever needs two,' she had added suddenly, and finally they had both smiled, because, after all, it was quite funny.

She had been a very pretty woman: dark hair and dark eyes, cracking legs. He remembered those with sudden clarity as he flung the pill into his mouth.

'Fifteen seconds, not more,' she had told him. 'Very efficient, but I hope you don't have to – well, I always say this to our people, I hope you don't have to discover its efficacy.'

Her voice had been as pretty as her face, nicely modulated, gentle. He remembered it now quite clearly. And she was right. It was taking only a few – only a few. Quick. Shan't get me. He smiled as he fell.

Sorry, Katherine, so, so sorry, so sorry. How much I love you, darling. Let you know that. I love you, love you, love you. Always. David.

'Do you want to cuddle up to me?' Walter asked Caro matter-of-factly, shortly after they had finished fantasising as to what she was prepared to do to David. 'It's cold enough tonight, God knows.'

Caro shook her head.

'No, I'm fine, really. I don't like cuddling up to people.'

'Why not?'

'It's against my religion,' she replied, very much tongue in cheek. Edwina had told her that was a phrase that Irish girls used, with apparently great effect, whenever young men went too far.

'I didn't know you were religious,' Walter said, sounding vaguely appalled.

'It's not something you should talk about, religion.

259

It's something that is in your heart, in your mind, but not something you should talk about, ever. Not to my mind, anyhow. I'm sorry, but I think it's wrong. You should keep your opinions of every kind to yourself, and so say all of us, especially now. Signed Miss Perfect.'

'You're quite right. No one should talk about their religious beliefs, especially not now. In fact if you can point out to me, please, which religion has taken a stand against the Nazis, I will join it immediately.'

'Well, that's not something you should talk about either, so you've broken the rules already,' Caro remarked, and then she sighed. 'As a matter of fact no one talks about anything much nowadays, if you ask me, except which nightclub they're going to, which bomb missed them, and where to get something which tastes like food!'

'I have some chewing gum. Like to try a piece?'

'I don't think I will, as a matter of fact.'

While a vague smell of peppermint filled the air Caro felt her spirits plummeting. Somehow Walter was turning out a disappointment, not at all how she might have imagined him, had she given him any thought over the last months, which of course she had made quite sure not to do.

'Are you going to climb into uniform and join the Blues and Royals, or something?' she asked, pointedly staring at his long civilian coat and old-fashioned hat.

'Now you mention the Guards, I heard a funny story about them,' Walter said suddenly, still chewing on his gum. Perhaps in reverence to the story he suddenly took the gum out of his mouth, and stuck it behind a chimneypot. 'A friend of mine was taking the parade at Knightsbridge Barracks with their colonel. All the troops were brand-new recruits, and all that, so naturally the colonel expected the usual chaos, but no. "Good God, Captain," he murmured to my friend. "Never in my life have I seen such brilliant marching from recruits." My friend replied, straight-faced, "Well, you wouldn't have, sir, because what you are watching are the first two rows of the chorus from Ivor Novello's *The Dancing Years*!"'

They both laughed, after which Walter put out a hand and leaned on Caro's shoulder as, it suddenly seemed to her, he had been doing since she first met him.

'To continue, since you asked, no, I am *not* climbing into uniform, as you put it. Neither the army nor the navy want anything to do with me on account of my weak chest, so it seems I am destined to join the Artists' Rifles. Tomorrow night I shall be going down to the bowels of the earth to paint the people in the Underground.'

'I don't know why they all want to go down there.'

'Quite simple. The above-ground shelters are, to put it plainly, above-ground coffins. They are built not of concrete, but of sand and lime, which means they have the nasty habit of collapsing on anyone who takes shelter in them. That is why the people use the Underground stations.'

'The smell is already terrible. One of our officers told me she nearly passed out on her first-time duty down there. I'm on tea duty again next week, lucky me.'

Walter didn't look in the least bit interested by this, but went on after a few seconds, still leaning on Caro's shoulder, 'The trouble with all-out war is it means there's

261

actually too much to paint, but, as they say, someone has to do it, and when it comes down to it, I am not cut out for soldiering. What artist is? So I shall be down the East End or down the Underground, or wherever I am needed, to record this terrible struggle which our nation is undergoing.' He paused. 'The trouble with the British in peacetime is that we will insist on enduring in silence when we shouldn't, but when it comes to a war, precisely *because* we have the habit of endurance, we are masterly.'

A part of Caro thought that it was cowardly not to join up, and yet another part of her realised that Walter had been chosen to paint the people, to paint the war, and since he would be in London he would be putting himself in the line of fire, and since he was brilliant he would be using his talents to their best ability. So, all in all, it really made sense not to send him where he would be less than useful. She stopped feeling let down and started to look at him in a different light – literally too – because the lights of the city fires seemed to be filling the sky. For a short time they were silent, watching, watching, always watching. It seemed to Caro that the whole of London was on fire, and only they were not.

Once the sound of the fire engines, the ambulances, and the people had eventually died down, Walter turned to Caro as if he had suddenly remembered something he had long wanted to ask her.

'I wonder where Katherine is now. I meant to ask Astley when I saw him at Dunkirk, but – you know how it is – so busy regretting that I was unarmed, I forgot.'

Caro saw at once from the expression on his face that

he still minded about Katherine: that it still mattered that she hadn't noticed him, that she taken nothing from his arguments against the Nazis, that he had had to resign himself to the fact that Katherine's mind had been turned by her obsessive love for David.

Caro knew she shouldn't tell him about Katherine's scarf, and yet she couldn't help herself.

Of course Walter remembered the scarf, as he remembered every detail of that unimaginably beautiful young woman. He could even recall her voice, still the light voice of a girl, and yet at times suddenly becoming oddly deep as if she smoked too much in secret, or went to bed too late, or stayed up too much, or was prone to nervous attacks.

'Could the scarf have been put there by someone else, do you think? I mean, is that a possibility? Perhaps she could have given it to a friend, who, seeing your car open, passed it on for some sort of joke?'

Caro shook her head.

'I hadn't been long in London. No one else would have known my car, or rather Katherine's car. No, somehow Katherine must have seen me in her old coat and skirt, the one she had left behind for me at Chevrons, or the one she failed to pack because she perhaps didn't like it. Whatever the truth, the sight of me in her suit must have reminded her of the fact that she still had the scarf that she wore with it, and knowing her as she *used* to be, before David did something to her mind, she would have taken it off and tied it to the steering wheel, and then watched me, from somewhere secret, go back to the car and find it. She would have loved that. That would have been the old Katherine. And of course when I did find it, she would have found the whole thing killingly funny. She laughed a lot in the old days, and that was really why she was more beautiful then than later, when *you* knew her, because she loved to laugh or, as they say now, shriek. "My deah, we *shrieked*."' Caro paused, but neither of them laughed at her customary mimicry. 'She so loved life in those days, when we were growing up. Life was her – well – her beach ball, really. She always seemed to be running about with it, throwing it above her head. She seemed to have all the promise of a golden summer day, but now who, please tell me *who*, finds anyone beautiful who has no laughter in them?'

Walter gave her an odd look. 'I'd forgotten your queer old-fashioned way of expressing yourself,' he murmured, and the hand on Caro's shoulder grew a little heavier as he sighed as if her chatter had brought back memories of happier days or, perhaps more realistically, as if it had brought back the particular happy days when Katherine was sitting to him, and Caro would be at the bottom of the ladder talking to him while he was working.

'But as you say,' Walter continued, 'where would Katherine be now? If she had been in London before war broke out, she would certainly not be here now. She might be in Germany, she might be anywhere.'

Caro stared ahead of her. Katherine in Germany? With the enemy? It was a terrible thought. Her beloved sister might even now be standing beside Hitler, or Goering. She might be wearing a swastika on her arm.

Caro put out her arm to steady herself.

Walter bent down, staring at her anxiously.

'Are you all right?'

'Of course. I just haven't eaten since God was a boy; felt a bit faint suddenly.'

Walter pointed at the now lightening sky.

'We've done our bit for the moment. Come to my flat. I'll make you a dried egg omelette and a very large gin.'

'What an irresistible offer,' Caro said, laughing a little shakily.

'You'd be surprised how tasty I can make a dried egg omelette.'

She followed him down the stairs from the roof. It was nice to be with Walter. It was like being at Chevrons, only not, and it really did not matter that he still held a torch for Katherine, not a bit, because wherever Katherine was, she certainly wouldn't be feeling the same about him.

As it happened Katherine was somewhere in France, lying in bed unmoving, woken by the sound of David's voice calling to her urgently in the darkness.

Growing up in an unspoiled part of the English countryside, Katherine had always accepted as natural that spirits and ghosts existed, that there were two worlds, the practical and the spiritual. She and everyone else at Chevrons frequently saw the spectre of an old gardener in eighteenth-century-style clothes walk past the kitchen window, and watched the ghost of a cat walk through a bedroom wall, or heard sounds of a choir singing where once there had been a family chapel.

This particular night she had woken up as if she had heard a shot, or as if she had fallen from a height of some kind, and as she did so she had quite definitely heard David calling to her. It was not surprising, because he had always been able to do that. He could call to her in his thoughts, and she would know the time and the place exactly. It was something they had taken pride in being able to do ever since they were children growing up on neighbouring estates, recording the time and the thoughts exactly, and when they were older, and fell in love, it was only natural that they should continue.

'Heart on heart, the two beating as one,' David would murmur to her, after they had made love the first time. 'No one will ever understand our relationship – no one, not even us. It's just a fact when two people have always been as close as we are, twin souls, a matching half making one whole, we will always and ever know what is happening to the other. There will be no need for spoken words.'

So it seemed that David had called to her. She was sure of it. He had called to her that he loved her, that he had been caught, but that he would always wait for her. Her heart seemed to grow leaden with the weight of the knowledge that she would never see him again in this world, and yet when would she be told?

She stared into the darkness, calling back to him in her thoughts, willing him to answer her, but knowing that where there had once been a voice there was now only silence, and the sound of the wind rattling the windows, and a world so empty that she might have been the only person left in it.

*   *   *

Later, when the doorbell downstairs had rung out, and Katherine, now dressed in black, went down to answer it, she hoped for one long despairing minute that she might be wrong, that it might after all be David, and briefly her step grew faster and lighter, and she ran to answer the heavy old oak door. After all, if David was dead, someone would have let her know, and since she had as yet received no message, perhaps, oh please, please, perhaps she had been wrong. She flung the chain aside and pulled forcibly on the old door, peering out into the night, hoping to see David's handsome face, the blue eyes sparkling with his particular brand of daredevil mischief, hear his infectious laugh.

But it was not David. It was 'the General', as she had nicknamed him.

Katherine opened the door wider.

The General smiled and walked in, removing his cap.

Katherine stared after him as she shut the door, and because she had momentarily, and unforgivably, forgotten that she was meant to be a Nazi, for a few moments it did not occur to her that he, of all people, would have news of David.

'Elvira.'

His boots were making that oddly military sound that tall boots on male feet always did, bringing back memories of other floors, other riding boots on other feet.

'You are early tonight, General,' she smiled, calm-eyed, beautiful, but at the same time glad that the high neck of her dress would be covering the pulse in her neck, hoping that he would not notice if she had lost colour.

'Yes, yes, I am early, Elvira.' He looked troubled. 'It has

not been a good day. I fear that two or three of our people might have been uncovered by the Maquis.'

'Really? Oh, but that is terrible.'

'Yes, it is terrible. They were brave young Nazis, like yourself, posing as members of the Resistance.' The General sighed, his patrician features momentarily filled with compassion. 'Well, perhaps we should thank God that they are dead. No one would want to fall into the hands of the Maquis, Elvira, not if they think you are a traitor.'

'No, indeed not.'

Katherine turned away to hide her fear. David had been posing as a communist, a member of the Maquis. He had been working for two sides. To the Nazis he was pretending to be a member of the Resistance, and to the Resistance he was a British spy working for them. Only London knew his double identity, and that he was, in fact, working for them. What had gone wrong? Katherine closed her eyes momentarily. Had she heard him calling to her? Maybe spending so much time alone meant that she had gone mad; maybe it was not he who had been caught or uncovered, maybe it was someone else.

'I have put out our favourite cognac,' she called back to the General, who was following her up the stairs to the first-floor drawing room. 'I had a strange feeling that you might be early tonight.'

'I was quite certainly in no mood to visit Madame's establishment next door.'

As Katherine started to pour the precious liquid into what now seemed to her to be increasingly familiar glasses, the General continued, 'It seems that the

Resistance became suspicious of two or three of our people, and they came after them just as one of them was contacting Nazi headquarters in Nice by radio.' He sighed, taking his glass from Katherine. 'There will be reprisals, of course, but they will be a waste of time. Nothing will stop the Resistance, or the communists, and reprisals will only fuel their determination.'

Katherine sat down opposite the General, trying frantically to assemble her thoughts. As she sipped her cognac the General talked on, the look in his eyes still understandably sombre, his conversation revolving again and again around the problem of an occupying army dealing with civilian resistance.

'If the invading force takes too harsh a line, it inevitably leads to panic,' he murmured disconsolately. 'Rein in too tightly and your horse will start to fight you. People are the same.'

Katherine stared at him, suddenly suspicious of his all too reasonable attitudes. Determined to keep up some pretence at polite conversation, she questioned him further about his ideas, but even as he began to talk, Katherine's inner attention left him, as she suddenly remembered that day in London, just before the war really took off, when David and she had been flown in for one of those mad twelve-hour visits that Max sometimes insisted on, and how, out of the blue, she had seen Caro, wearing her suit, parking what had formerly been her car, and how David had mischievously untied Katherine's scarf from her neck, and tied it around the steering wheel, and how they had watched Caro's expression from afar, and then heartbreakingly, much later, found her message on the lamp post, her Mayfair number, then, 'Please, please ring me.'

It had been so like Caro to imagine that Katherine was around and to hope that she would telephone her. And also not to mind whether or not Katherine and David were marching behind Hitler or working for the Gestapo – to hope only that they could talk – probably, knowing Caro, in the hope that she could talk them out of whatever it was they were actually doing. Caro had always been behind Katherine, somewhere, all her childhood; walking behind, talking the hind leg off anyone and everyone, always cheerful, always happy, 'a tomboy in petticoats', their father called her, except in Caro's case, her petticoats usually ended up bandaging some poor lame duck or other.

The General finally left Katherine to attend a meeting, but he was back all too soon, knocking sharply on the front door, which Katherine once more opened to him.

'You have to get out. You must come with me, leave the house within the hour. No, now, you must leave at once, take no risks,' he told her urgently, and as he spoke he quickly turned the hall lights off. Then, making his way up the house, he switched off every light that was burning, before returning to her, so that finally the two of them were in the dark, talking in low voices. 'The reprisals I predicted have begun. They have captured and interrogated some communists. One of them weakened when they went to work on him. They know who you are, or at least they hope they do. They are already celebrating with a large dinner, so confident are they.'

'Who are "they"?'

'The Gestapo.'

Katherine's heart missed two dozen beats.

'So – who *am* I, General?'

She knew he was looking down at her, and the hold on her arm tightened slightly, which frightened her, yet his voice became even lower, and his tone was suddenly gentle. 'You are Elvira, but perhaps you are not just Elvira. Perhaps you are also – ' he started to push her ahead of him out of the room – 'you are also, perhaps, someone else. Frankly, Elvira, I do not mind *who* you are. All I mind is that I do not let you fall into the hands of the Gestapo, even if it means the end for me too.'

Katherine wrenched herself free.

'How am I to believe you?'

'You have no means of knowing how to believe me, but you must. And you know you can,' he breathed, 'because I am in love with you. You are the most beautiful creature. Indeed, you are the loveliest young woman that I have ever met, and I will love you all my life, and you must know it. I have thought of what to do as I came here. Leaving my car and my driver at the restaurant, I slipped out the back way, and I think I have found the perfect hiding place for you. We have time. The Gestapo are presently eating bouillabaisse. With large bibs around their necks to save their uniforms, they have the air of hideous babies. However, with bouillabaisse and many courses to come, they will be several hours before they reach the cheese and fruit.'

'I can't leave—'

'You can, and you must.' The General pulled Katherine after him. 'Whatever you have here, believe me, will

271

be useless to you now, and nothing is to be done about it.'

Katherine thought quickly of her wireless, of her codes, and her gun, and then realising there was nothing she could do *except* hope for the best, she followed him into the street.

He pushed the front door to behind her.

'Don't worry. I will take care of everything for you. I will bring you all your things.'

For a second Katherine felt reassured. Then the thought came to her. She was standing out on the pavement, in France, at ten o'clock at night, trusting a German officer not to deliver her into the hands of the Gestapo. Where were her brains?

Chapter Nine

Edwina was smoking. Caro stared at her, frowning.

'You're smoking too much.'

'Of course,' Edwina told her, her voice flat. 'And to think I once hated smoking worse than sin, but now I find it stops me feeling hungry, and so on and so forth, dotey dear. And anyway, what is the point of giving up, tell me do?'

Caro looked away. She knew what Edwina meant. Every day something awful happened, and because there were so many reasons to despair, it seemed to her that they had to find an equal number not to do so, although she had to admit it was tiring.

Robert had been posted. Everyone knew that Edwina of the carefree heart had flirted with Tom and Ben, but had fallen for dashing Robert, waited for him to return from Dunkirk, made love with him, waited for him to take her on a date to the Savoy, been stood up, and had then gone off and made love with someone else – Gene someone or another – and was now, it seemed, rather regretting it.

'How can smoking stop you feeling hungry when you haven't eaten for days?'

'That's why I haven't eaten for days, dotey dear, because I am smoking. I want to keep my figure.'

'Let me make you a dried egg omelette. I have a secret recipe. It is truly brilliant.' As Edwina turned to look at her, Caro went on, 'Walter gave me the recipe.'

'Ah, Walter, the painter who believes he loves the elder sister, who in her turn has eyes only for the Nazi?'

'The very same one. But never mind all that, the recipe is better than you could hope, truly it is.'

Edwina's eyes slid sideways to watch Caro's retreating back. Shorty was being very maternal towards her. It was almost alarming.

'I'm not sure I can eat an omelette at four in the afternoon, Shorty, really I'm not.'

'And I'm not sure you can go on living on air. Your skin is suffering.'

Edwina quickly stubbed out her cigarette.

'How so, dotey?'

She went to the mirror and stared at herself. It was true, her skin *was* suffering. She looked like something the cat would leave on the doorstep.

'You're right. I have gone a kind of greyish fawn, haven't I?'

'Yes,' Caro called cheerfully from the kitchen. 'And what is more, having nothing to eat for so long will do little for your figure either. You will only look gaunt, and gaunt is so unattractive to men, my deah.'

Edwina sat back down again.

'Oh, blow men,' she told the cushions on the sofa. 'And blow everything else too.'

She sat back listening to the sounds from the small

kitchen. Caro was turning into a proper little mother to everyone. Only yesterday Edwina had found her cooking some recipe of Marguerite Patten's, which she had taken down from the wireless. Nowadays it was nothing to hear her muttering about how to make scones without butter, or rice pudding without rice, or something equally disturbingly unusual.

Caro put down a tray in front of her. Edwina looked from the tray with the dried egg omelette, to her friend, and back to the tray again.

'It looks like an omelette, Shorty. I have to at least congratulate you on that. But will it taste like an omelette, I am asking the gods above us?'

'No, but it will taste of something perfectly all right. It's got a secret ingredient, you see, as well as those mushroom stalks that Trixie brought us up from her factory.'

'Is Trixie making mushroom stalks in her factory? I thought it was aeroplane parts,' Edwina asked without curiosity, as she began to tackle the omelette with all the enthusiasm of a young woman who is convinced she is about to die from food poisoning.

'Yes, she is making aero parts, but now that Betty's gone, Trixie's been able to make friends with someone who is growing mushrooms in her free time. The factory is so near to the countryside, they get more of a go at food stuffs than we do here. Trixie wrote me that she gets real eggs, and tomatoes, and bacon too, and no hanky-panky needed. They just leave it at the back door of her digs, and she shares it with the other lodgers. So I told her to bring us up anything she can spare, and she did – so here we have, mushroom stalks.'

Edwina looked up. 'This has got a funny taste, Shorty.'

'That's the secret ingredient – toadstool. Very fortifying in a war.'

'Ah, yes, we have that in Ireland. My mother's cook did it – it was called bye-bye potato pie.' Edwina polished off the omelette as quickly as anything, and then she sat back.

'Now I think I'll have a gin.'

'Why ever not?' Caro agreed, her spirits lifting as she saw some colour coming into Edwina's cheeks. 'A gin it shall be.'

She hurried over to the drinks table, poured each of them a large gin, to which she added some tonic, then hurried back to Edwina.

'You must be feeling better if you want a gin.'

Edwina nodded. She was feeling much better.

'I've been a damn fool, Shorty, dotey, do you know that?'

Caro knew that this was true, so of course she said 'no', but she said it too quickly for comfort – at any rate, for Edwina's comfort – which meant that Edwina nodded, staring ahead of her, not at Caro.

'I knew you would agree with me,' she went on, slowly sipping her gin. 'First of all I tell you we mustn't get our hearts involved, and then, not two seconds later, I ignore my own advice. What a fool I've been, what a silly, silly fool.'

'Oh, but we all have, some time or another,' Caro told her with a little too much enthusiasm. 'Even Robyn. I only just stopped her falling for an absolute shocker, after Eddie was shot down, and she imagined that . . . well, she thought that . . . well, you know how it is. It sometimes

276

seems better to think that someone isn't coming back, rather than cling on to a tatty bit of hope.'

There was a small silence as they both remembered the news coming through, and then how they had all made up their minds to think of Eddie as dead, until they had a postcard from him from a prisoner of war camp.

'Of course, now he's been taken prisoner, it's not so bad. And Bill's taking her out whenever he can.'

Caro fell silent, remembering when she and Robyn had been newly arrived in London and had met Eddie for the first time, and how they had pretended that they had been to the Grafton Galleries before, when in reality they had never set eyes on the place.

'Bill's all right. Did I tell you? Bill's fine. He's notched up, I think he said it was ten and a *half* kills, because he agreed to share one kill with someone else.' She sat back, sipping her own gin and tonic. It was still only tea-time, but who cared, really? 'I hope Bill keeps on going the way he has been. He says if you don't think you'll be killed, you won't be. It's the chaps who think their number's up who cop it, apparently.'

Edwina nodded in a desultory way, still staring ahead of her rather than at Caro. Her father had said the same thing about the Great War.

'I've had an offer, a bit ago,' she suddenly announced, a little too loudly considering that Caro was sitting close by her. 'Yes, I've had an offer from Colonel Atkins.' She turned to Caro. 'What do you think?'

'Not a legal one, since he's married, isn't he?' Caro joked.

'Well, actually, since you mention it, he is a widower,

277

I think. No, apparently, he and others are of the opinion that I am some kind of a loose type.'

'You should have kicked him in the shins for even thinking such a thing.'

'No, no, he means as in loose *cannon*. Anyway, it seems he would like to set me up in sumptuous style in a large apartment, in competition with that well-known lady our Prime Minister's dear daughter-in-law.'

'Oh, her.'

'Yes, her. I would have a maid, a chauffeur, plenty of food and drink, a large wardrobe of clothes, everything, except I must not get personally involved with anyone that comes to the flat whom I have to entertain. That, apparently, is just not on.'

'I should take up the offer at once, Edwina. If you don't, I will!' Caro drained her gin. 'Gracious heavens, if I'd had an offer like that from Colonel Atkins you would *not* see my heels for dust.'

'Do you really think – but I mean, what about personal feelings? Supposing I have some, dotey? Supposing I fall for a Free Frenchman?'

Caro pulled Edwina to her feet. 'Edwina, all Frenchmen are free – you know that!'

'No, but seriously, dotey, supposing I fall for one of the people I'm meant to be spying on, or entertaining, or whatever it is I'm meant to be doing?'

'Just don't tell Colonel Atkins. But just now, *do* go and tell Colonel Atkins that you have changed your mind and you will accept his offer to set you up in a sumptuous apartment. Except, just a minute, what do you actually have to do?'

'Oh, I don't know, nothing too much, You know, be nice to the right people, have what they used to call a "salon" where every kind of person can come, where there is always some kind of party going on, and people of all types drop in, and then you know . . .' she shrugged. 'Then I have to tell him about them. What they like to drink, how they dress, what their preferred type of lover is – all that. Simple really, and no strings attached, which is good, I suppose.'

'That's not a job, that's a sinecure. Run to the telephone and say "yes" before he changes his mind.'

'No, no, he said to tell him when I'd made up my mind.'

'No, no, yes, yes, ring him now.' Caro smiled, and reached for the telephone. 'Is it to be me, or you?'

Edwina stood up, walked across and snatched the telephone receiver from her.

'Buzz off, dotey, this is woman's business. You don't qualify; you are still not yet a woman.'

Caro turned away. Everyone was always teasing her about that, about It, but there it was: if you don't want to do something, you shouldn't do it, or at least that is what her mother had always said – or was it Trixie? Someone at any rate, someone from the old days at Chevrons, when such subjects did not really come up, thank goodness. Conversations in the days when she was growing up revolved around whether or not to go fishing, or have your hair cut, all really beautifully important, and in the scheme of things, delightfully unimportant.

'Not everyone *wants* to be a woman, at least not until they're ready, you know, Edwina,' Caro murmured, but because Edwina was now on the telephone busily rotting up 'Colonel Dotey', as she called Colonel Atkins, she did not hear her. Anyway there was another distraction just at that moment when Robyn emerged, dressed and ready to go out, from the bathroom where she had been soaking in a statutory six inches of tepid bath water.

'Oh, for the days when the water was allowed to cover your body, and not just your little toe,' she said to Caro in a distant voice, while inspecting her makeup in the hall mirror.

'Oh, for the days when sleep was something one thought necessary,' Caro responded. She paused before going on. 'Did I tell you, last night I met Walter Beresford, fire watching?'

Robyn turned to Caro. She knew they both had black lines under their eyes that were not makeup. She also knew that they were both busily burning the candle at both ends, and in the middle too, but what else was there to do?

When not driving, they were fire watching, when not fire watching they were driving, and when not doing either of those things it was straight to a nightclub, or somewhere like the Savoy for dinner and dancing, all the while knowing that the young man you were dancing with, or you, or both of you, or all of you, might not be there tomorrow. So no wonder no one thought about tomorrow, only of today. Indeed, the statutory toast at the flat had become 'Here's to now, and let the next minute take care of itself.'

'No, you didn't tell me you saw Walter Beresford again. Was he still interesting?'

'Yes.' Caro frowned, turning over the question in her mind, concentrating on it. 'Yes, yes, he was,' she said, sounding vaguely surprised. 'He's going to paint the war, you know.'

'Makes a change from painting your father's wall, I suppose.'

Caro was silent for a minute. She knew that Robyn didn't really mean to sound disparaging about Walter painting rather than joining the Blues and Royals, or even the Pioneer Corps, but it certainly sounded slightly sarcastic.

'He never finished the wall, you know?' she said, after a short pause. 'As a matter of fact, he fell out with my father before he could finish it, but that's another matter. Apparently he's going down the Underground tonight, to paint the crowds sheltering from the bombs.'

But Robyn wasn't listening. She hardly knew Walter, and anyway, she was looking disapproving.

'My dear, did you hear about Bill's narrow escape?'

'No, tell me. He's always having them,' Caro replied, and this time it was she who turned away.

She had quite put Bill out of her mind, as she put aside the thought of every young man once he wasn't actually in the room. It was the only way. Nowadays everyone had one phrase and one phrase alone engraved on their hearts and that was 'you assume the best until you hear different'.

'Yes, he was shot down, Bill was shot down,' Robyn continued. 'But being Bill, and a lucky devil, he opened his parachute over Dorking. What a bit of luck!' Robyn laughed. 'Typical Bill, because, as he said, it meant that it was only a short walk to his local to enjoy a pint . . . which, unsurprisingly, he downed in one. Apparently his landlord's face was something to behold.'

This time they both laughed although it wasn't particularly funny. Everyone laughed in war whenever it was even remotely possible, perhaps because quite simply there was so little to laugh *about*.

'He's off again today, is Bill.'

There was a second of silence, barely that, and then they both started to talk volubly.

'I'm driving that naval bod and one of his dates to-night.'

'Not the one that's always trying to go the whole way before he even gets to dinner?'

Now they were both pushing out of the front door together, car keys already dangling from their fingers.

'The very same. I don't know what life must be like at Admiralty House, but it certainly must be lively if *he* ever gets near the secretaries, poor souls. The sound of slapping in the back of the Bentley is enough to put you off going to sea for the rest of your life, truly it is.' Robyn shook her head and sighed. 'Still, here goes. *Bonsoir*, dear girl, and see you much later, I hope, *chez* Ciro, perhaps.'

Edwina had watched the other two leave the flat, laughing and talking, with envy in her heart. A part of her longed to be driving canteens, fire watching, and taking tea to people, running them to hospital, a bit of this and that. Why did she have the bad luck to catch the Great Man's eye, and why, oh why, did he remember her? Most likely quite simply because she had red hair. Was it always the colour of one's hair that meant you were singled out? Italians literally worshipped red hair. She knew that for certain because her mother had been a tiny bit Italian; although if she was in a temper, it seemed to be a great deal more than a tiny bit.

A little later Colonel Atkins rang the doorbell. He had hoped that Miss Carrots, as he secretly called Edwina O'Brien, would come round to his point of view, and now that she quite obviously had, he felt quite excited. It would be a challenge to see whether he could set up a beautiful young woman as a pot of beckoning honey and then watch to see which bees came buzzing round.

'It was the fact that you inferred that I was "loose" that put me off; I think that's what you said, at some point,' Edwina stated, very much tongue in cheek, as she handed the colonel a zonking great gin.

'What I actually said was that you would have to *pose* as some sort of a political loose cannon, someone who gave allegiance to no one, but hospitality to everyone. If successful you will find every kind of nationality feels at home at your table, in your apartment, but not necessarily anywhere else. A loose cannon is someone who raises a lone standard, walks a lone path, very useful in peace, even more so in war.'

Edwina lit a cigarette and nodded, before raising her glass.

'Here's to my firing power, Colonel, dotey.' She paused. 'As a matter of fact that is not a bad cover name, is it? Now I come to think about it. What do you think, Colonel? "Operation Loose Cannon"?'

The colonel smiled, the blue in his eyes seeming to

become more pronounced. This was very good. Miss Carrots was beginning to think like a professional.

'So be it,' he murmured, and he removed a superb thin gold cigarette case from his inner pocket, extracted a slender Turkish cigarette, and lit it with a slim gold lighter, before exhaling slowly and appreciatively. 'So be it, Operation Loose Cannon. I can see it on the top of a file already.' He made a gesture as if underlining it. 'Yes, very good. Now.' He looked at Aunt Cicely's small gold clock on the shelf behind Edwina. 'I think we had better get our skates on. Word has it there is going to be a bit of a battering tonight, throwing everything at us, so we'd better hurry on before it starts getting interesting.'

They both quickly drained their glasses, and made for the front door, Edwina snatching at a light summer coat of silk muslin and lace, the colonel snatching up his hat and stick. As he did so the walking stick started to come apart.

'Gracious, Colonel, dotey, how very Scarlet Pimpernel,' Edwina commented as she saw that the walking stick actually clothed a sword.

'Wilkinson sword stick, quite excellent. Should have put it back more securely.' He smiled briefly, and secured the stick. 'Had to use it in a bit of a hurry a few hours ago.'

Edwina turned away. The colonel's world was becoming a trifle real for her tastes, and now she had signed herself up to it. Would she have to carry such a weapon too? All of a sudden driving randy young officers around London seemed infinitely preferable.

*   *   *

284

The Gestapo had searched everywhere and found nothing. Madame could see that it was making them irritable, and so she made soothing noises, and brought them a tray of drinks. Soon they would be fixed up with local girls, and then they would be gone, and that would be that. She hoped.

'The Gestapo are usually more refined,' she murmured much later to one of the girls as they too murmured, and grumbled, then grumbled and pocketed their earnings, leaving before any more unsavoury customers from that particular branch of the invading army arrived.

Finally, after the last girl had gone, leaving no one but Madame herself and the new arrival, she switched off the lights, and climbed the stairs to the top room. She knocked softly on the door, and when it was opened to her she found herself momentarily pausing to stare at what she saw.

'*Mon Dieu*,' she said softly. 'Mademoiselle, the changes you have made, they make you unrecognisable.'

Katherine nodded. It was true. Following her sudden exit from Chevrons, Katherine had been sent to The Beeches, an old house that the newly reorganised pre-war MI5 had turned into a school for potential saboteurs and agents. Here, in addition to many other arts, martial and otherwise, she had been trained in disguise by a distinguished veteran actor from the Old Vic Theatre.

'The trouble with most people, when they change their appearance, is that they change too much,' the darling old actor had told the fledgeling agents. 'And that makes them look startling. Better by far to do something small that will change your whole look, but still not make you stand out. So *no* to blond wigs that get knocked sideways, and moustaches that drop in the soup, and *yes* to changing your parting from one side to the other, shaving *off* a moustache or beard, or leaving *off* makeup where you once wore it, or putting it on thickly where you once did not wear it. Change the way you walk, the way you speak. Don't put on a stammer, rather adopt a slight hesitation, or lower your voice, or heighten it. It is by these subtleties that you will find yourself changed from within, and that is the most important part of changing yourself. It is what a good actor must do, and frankly that is what will save your life if you find yourself up a gumtree – which you well might.'

Katherine was up a gumtree at that moment, albeit a heavily ornate one. Her General had hurried her from the house next door and up to a room where he had shut them both in.

'The Gestapo are on to you, Elvira. Your only hope is to be kept here by me, and for me.'

As Katherine's expression changed to one of potential fury, he put out a comforting hand.

'No, no, my dear, I will look after you. Don't worry. Madame is a friend of long standing, long before the war, from student days, when we all ran about France learning a great deal more than French, you may be sure.'

His face had softened as he remembered the carefree feeling of being a student, to be replaced by an almost fatherly concern.

'It is here that you must stay. The worst that can happen to you will be that you will become bored, but Madame will give you food, and whatever else you may need, and soon we will find you a safe house. The Gestapo, you see, are convinced that you are a double agent, planted by the British since before the war. The person that gave you away under torture – I don't know who it was.'

Katherine could not hide the fear in her eyes, but it was not for her, it was for David.

'Surely they are all dead?'

'Oh yes, they all died – eventually.'

The General shook his head. He was an officer in the German Army, and a gentleman. The men that made up the Gestapo were recruited from a very particular kind of scum.

'War is terrible, but the human muck it throws up is more terrible than we can perhaps imagine.' He sighed briefly, then left her, and she locked the door after him.

The sound of his retreating steps, the sounds from the arrival of the official cars, the Gestapo and much else, happily came together, drowning the sound of Katherine's sobs as she pushed a pillow against her face and gave way to grief and fear.

She fell asleep hoping against hope that – of all things – David was indeed dead. Please, please God, he remembered his cyanide pill. Please, oh merciful God, tell me he reached for it before they reached him. Please, please God it was indeed he whom she had heard calling to her.

When she was at last asleep she dreamed of many things. Images came and went: faces – many faces, so many of them from the past – so that when she woke up she was not surprised to find that her own face was still wet from fresh tears.

Once she had pulled herself together, she realised

she had to assess her situation. She was a prisoner of a German officer, living in a French brothel. She didn't know why but, as she sat on the end of the ornate carved French boudoir bed, and perhaps because of her dreams, Caro's face came to her. She could see her walking along beside her, in some woodland somewhere near Chevrons, and she imagined what her younger sister would say to her.

'You're a prisoner in a French brothel? Gracious heavens, Katherine, that's slightly original, isn't it?' Then as Katherine paused to let her catch up – Caro had always been a few paces behind her – she would say, 'Could be worse, though, couldn't it, Sis? I mean, you could be a prisoner in an English brothel, and it wouldn't be nearly such good food. Still, probably a good idea to plan your escape, otherwise things might get a bit hot, wouldn't you say?'

And Caro would be right. Katherine stood up, self-pity falling away to be replaced by practicality. She had to escape, but it would not be possible without the help of the General. Certainly Madame would be on her side only as long as the General paid her for Katherine's services. She closed her eyes. Was it possible that she was here? Was it possible that her wretched patriotism, her idealism, could bring her to such a pass? She would have to go as soon as possible. She could not become the *chère amie* of a German. Quite apart from anything else, there was nothing in her training at The Beeches that had taught her how to be a lady of easy virtue.

For a minute she imagined the old actor attempting to teach her.

'Now, dear, sit on the edge of the bed, and start rolling down your stockings, and while you're doing it tell yourself, "This is for England, for freedom, for this sceptred isle, this precious stone set in a silver sea . . ."'

'Oh, do shut up,' Katherine murmured to herself. 'Fantasies do not an escape make.'

And then she remembered that same old actor demonstrating turning himself from a railway official, all whistle and cap, into an old woman. It had taken so little, a few blackened teeth, a headscarf, wrinkled stockings. She stared at her hair in the mirror. What would it take to make it yet more different? Perhaps a pair of scissors, a few curling papers, and maybe even she would not know herself? She stared at her reflection yet closer in the mirror. Then, taking a mascara brush from her bag, she carefully blackened one of her front teeth, before standing back and smiling at herself.

Hours later her disguise was complete. A stained blouse, a skirt with the hem hanging down, wrinkled stockings (not difficult with suspenders) and flat shoes, one of whose heels she had knocked, so that it was askew. Her hair stood out in a satisfactory matted bob, and with her shoulders pulled down and hunched, clutching some now disreputable-looking bags with what remained of her essentials in them, she set out from the room. The General had taken what he could find of her belongings from the next-door house, and Madame and she had burned much of what little she had left.

It was early afternoon, a time when both the girls and Madame were resting. Katherine moved quietly past their doors, hearing with satisfaction the sounds of wine-induced snoring. The next moment she was in the street outside, and passing two Gestapo officers. Happily her stance was such that, despite her height, she could not catch their eyes. Happily also their own eyes were quite obviously being directed towards the door of the brothel, for they passed her on the trot as she turned into the main thoroughfare, and gave her not a second glance.

Katherine hurried on. After some time she turned into the station yard, shuffling along slowly, and made her way to the ticket office where she bought a ticket to Paris, stopping off all the way up France. Once in Paris, she could lose herself. But first she would take the usual precautions, and change trains many times. It was a tip she had learned at The Beeches, and a wise precaution, which Katherine would never ignore. If you were on a train for any length of time, people stared at you, often out of boredom or curiosity, or, in her present disguise, probably out of disgust. Hop on and off whatever method of transport you had chosen, and no one would be able to put their hand on their heart and say they had seen you.

'You! Old woman!'

She turned.

'You've dropped something!'

Katherine put out a dirty mittened claw, only to receive something quite revolting in return.

The boy ran off laughing. Katherine put the filthy piece of rubbish in the nearby litter bin, and climbed on the train, at the same time allowing a glow of satisfaction to wash over her.

Her disguise had worked.

                              *   *   *

Edwina was impressed. Colonel Atkins was purring. He
had secured for her the best kind of apartment, situated
as it was, fashionably, in The Place. It had a large first-
floor drawing room with a double door leading to a large
dining room filled with period pieces, all of which, in
the event of the hostess wanting to give a large party,
could be folded up or put against the wall. The whole
suite of rooms was done up in the best kind of country
house taste, with grand curtains decorated with rosettes
(at least the colonel thought they were called rosettes)
and heavy brass handles that pulled them backwards
and forwards with sumptuous ease. There were Knole
sofas upholstered in velvet, and flowered sofas covered
in patterns of roses. There was a plethora of china
ornaments and carved Nubian slaves with turbans and
gold waistbands supporting both candles and flowers.
The whole look was rich, sensual and, when you glanced
at some of the paintings, tastefully naughty.

   'Why, Colonel, dotey, did you do this all yourself?'
Edwina turned to the colonel, widening her large green
eyes, her head on one side.

   'I did have a little help,' Colonel Atkins lied finally, because if Miss Carrots from Ireland knew the truth, it was
that he had personally chosen everything that had gone
into the apartment. This was not because he considered
that he had faultless taste (the late beloved Mrs Atkins
would have split her sides at the very notion), no, it was
because he did not trust anyone else to know what was
wanted.

   If the colonel's association with Miss Carrots was to be

productive, everything had to be right, and the immense cost of what he had done would be entirely justified. But his plan could not work, would not work, if there was one detail that was out of place.

'Careless talk costs lives' was on posters all over the London Underground, all over the stations, anywhere the authorities considered that it would be effective, and Colonel Atkins had no doubt whatsoever that it *would* be effective. Put simply he did not think that anyone standing on a dirty station, or in a comfortless railway carriage, or outside a hospital, would be particularly tempted to give away information that might be considered useful to the enemy; but give those same people nice wine, nice food, and a beautiful woman paying them particularly sympathetic attention, and they would probably betray their nearest and dearest without even realising it.

The colonel's vision for the apartment was to present to the casual visitor a picture of the utmost taste, interlaced with a hint of something else. With this in mind he had chosen classically painted nudes, some male, some female, but in particularly tasteful settings. There was nothing on the walls of the flat to which the modern person, under the age of forty, could take exception, and nothing by which anyone over that age would not be mildly stimulated. All in all the apartment stank of taste and, with it all, was just a little sensual and roguish.

'Oh, Colonel, look! Your tapestry!'

Edwina held up an elegant stool, which was acting as a partner to a very pretty inlaid desk.

'Yes, well, since the colours suited, I thought we might

as well make use of it here. I dare say you may well have an objection to it, in which case we can always bring round some sort of substitute. Some people take exception to tapestry; makes them feel woolly, I believe.'

Edwina walked up to the colonel and kissed him lightly on the cheek.

'Well, your tapestry doesn't make *me* feel woolly. It's very, very pretty, an absolute treasure, and it certainly fits in beautifully, of that there is no doubt. Did you do it with this place in mind, do you think, Colonel?'

The colonel looked momentarily taken back. He had not thought of that. He looked round the flat, and his colour deepened. Was Miss Carrots suggesting that this place in which they found themselves standing might be his ideal apartment? He was used to examining his conscience. Every man must do so if he was to be just or honourable.

'Yes, I have a feeling that I must.'

'How lovely.'

Edwina sashayed down the drawing room, her silk petticoat making a delightful rustling sound. She sighed happily before she looked down the room, imagining herself receiving guests, manipulating them into having conversations, into sighing for the old days, or longing for new ones, into admitting their taste in love, or denying it – either could be most revealing, she was sure. She had a task ahead, but what a pleasurable one.

'Now I have hired you a cook, Mrs Cherry, and a retired manservant, Mr Fleming – they are both our people – but you will need a personal maid. Would you have anyone you could suggest? Someone who was reliable, someone you might have known in the old days, from the old life?'

'Not a person, Colonel, dotey. But I have a friend who could help.'

'In that case pursue the matter, if you would. Now what about social contacts? The Office will expect you to entertain a great many of what are usually known as British sympathisers and, let us face it, there are plenty – British-born Italians, Czechs, Free French, Americans, naturally. Will you be able to build up your list on your own? Or shall you need my help?'

Edwina looked down the drawing room at the beautiful furniture, the paintings, the rugs and the statuary, and sighed with regret.

'I am afraid you will be about to give me my coat now, Colonel. I know no British-born Italians, no Free French, and only one American.'

'No matter, I know plenty. Ask your American round as soon as maybe.' He smiled. 'After all, you have to start somewhere, and it's always best to start with someone you know. Builds up the confidence; gives you a bit of a boost.'

Edwina looked down the drawing room and smiled. She had passed the test, she had told the truth, and she was still hired.

'I will leave you now, and let you settle in, but when I return I expect to find you using the place as if it were your own. No need to have your clothes sent round. We have filled the wardrobes, or as your American friend would call them, the closets. I think you will find we have your measurements and, more importantly, that you will like the clothes. I think you will be happy with the overall taste.'

He left Edwina, walking off into the lift, carrying his stick and replacing his hat on his head at a really rather dashing angle.

'Goodbye, my dear, goodbye. I shall, like the bad penny, turn up sooner than you think, I'm afraid.'

'Goodbye, Colonel, dotey, and just make sure you are back soon. I shall miss you.'

The colonel passed the ancient hall porter. He knew he had heard what he had just said, and that was satisfying. The colonel wanted him to think that he was one of Miss Carrots' older beaux, that this was the reason he visited her often. So he made sure to wink at the old man as he passed him, and then to put his stick in rifle style over his shoulder, before walking off, whistling a saucy tune.

Inside the flat, Edwina found it hard not to bolt to the wardrobes in her grand new bedroom. She flung open the mirrored doors and, having looked inside, pulled out one dress after another, each of them the prettiest she thought she'd ever seen. She finally plumped for a beautiful cocktail dress and flung it on the bed, where it lay like a person, its silk skirts flung wide.

'What a beautiful creature you are, to be sure,' she told the dress, and then she picked up the elegant telephone beside the bed, and lay back against the silk-covered button-back chair.

It wasn't difficult to imagine being a great grand lady in this bedroom, nor to imagine being a beautiful spy. And to think that she tried to turn the role down – for it was a role. She was being asked to act out being someone quite different, while all the time staying herself. It was a delicious thought, but she must not let herself become conceited or over-confident. The role could be dangerous too. If she let the colonel down, she could put others in danger. If she became over-confident, she would put herself in danger. She must not be naïve.

'Gene? How marvellous that you are in. Do come round and see me, won't you?'

She stared at the ceiling. He was sounding hurt, just because she hadn't been in touch. Really, men were so difficult.

'No, I understand, Gene, really I do. But you must remember there is a war on. I was called away. I can't say more, you understand? But what I can do is give you my new address, and tell you that if you should come round, say at about half past seven, we could dine *à deux*, Hitler permitting, and then go dancing. I believe my new cook is too-too, with reserves of food that we must never ask about, but del-icious.'

Of course he was coming round like a shot. It always worked with men. Not the promise of dancing, or being alone, but a good dinner.

She replaced the telephone, and then shot off out of the bedroom to go to meet her cook and butler. As she pushed her way into the kitchen the smells were already so delicious she would have fainted with desire if she did not have fitting into her new clothes at the forefront of her mind.

'Mrs Cherry? How do you do? I am Edwina O'Brien— Dear heavens, I know you!'

Mrs Cherry put her finger to her lips.

'The colonel thought it a good thing if we had known each other in the past, if you know what he means? In case we have to work together in an unexpected manner,' she said, speaking in a lowered tone.

'Of course I know what he means, but golly! I haven't seen you since you were in the sixth form at that horribly misnamed school – Angel's Court.'

Mrs Cherry continued as if she had not heard Edwina speak. 'We are not to tell Mr Fleming, the colonel said. Mr Fleming imagines that I am a professional cook, albeit he knows that we are both hired by the colonel. At the moment he is out at a secret rendezvous.'

'How impressive. The colonel or Mr Fleming?'

'Mr Fleming. If he can bring it off we'll all be very pleased.'

'Is it something I shouldn't know about?'

'It is something you will soon know about, Miss O'Brien.'

Mrs Cherry's eyes flickered momentarily, and she made a small movement with her head towards the back door, from which Edwina knew that she was to gather that she had heard the butler arriving back from his mission.

Mr Fleming was of medium height with thinning hair. As Edwina was soon to discover, his habitual expression, no matter what happened, was of implacable melancholy. He was therefore entirely suited to the role of solitary butler-cum-general factotum.

'There we are.' He placed a small parcel on the kitchen table, but on seeing Edwina, he gave a small bow. 'Pleased to meet you, Miss O'Brien. Mr Fleming, at your service at all times.'

Edwina shook his hand.

'I gather you have been entrusted with a mission about which I shall soon know, Mr Fleming?' Edwina stated, while at the same time she had the uneasy feeling that since moving into Wilbraham Place, she was beginning not just to feel grand, but to sound it too.

'I have to tell you, indeed I am pleased to tell you, Miss O'Brien, that the mission has been successful. A pound of the best beluga caviar, expressly brought to you by unknown forces working for the government, and also some pure Russian vodka.'

Edwina smiled slowly as she took in both items.

'Well done, Mr Fleming, well done! If we can keep this up The Place is going to be the talk of London in a very short time.'

Mr Fleming nodded at Mrs Cherry. 'She will make magic with it, Miss O'Brien, believe me. No one prepares food better than Mrs Cherry.'

Edwina drifted out through the green baize door. She knew that somehow, somewhere, there must be other people, other young women, who would give anything to be in her position, and she knew that she should feel sorry for them, but the truth was she didn't. The Prime Minister himself had taken account of her that afternoon when she had been waiting for Colonel Atkins. The colonel had said as much. When it came to this particular assignment, they had both remembered her most particularly, and it was certainly not because she was a mousy brunette.

Chapter Ten

Trixie did not know whether she was pleased or not to be pulled out of the production line. It had taken her some time to get over the unpopularity that had come about from being friends with Betty, but now that Betty was long gone, she found that she was gradually being taken up by her fellow workers and was friends with most of them too.

'What's up?' she asked, trying not to look anxious as she hurried after the young woman sent to fetch her.

'I dunno, do I?' she answered, shouting over the noise. 'All I know is that the boss wants to see you.'

'I hope I haven't done anything wrong,' Trixie yelled back.

'I told you, I *dunno*! I dunno *why* she wants to see you. I'm going for my dinner break, good luck to you,' she added, as she nodded towards the supervisor's door.

Trixie straightened herself, though she didn't take off her headscarf, tied modishly into a bow at the top of her head, but merely wiped her hands down her boiler suit. She thought quickly. They wouldn't send a telegram here if it was anything about Father, would they?

'Ah, there you are, Smith.'

The new supervisor was a great deal nicer than the old one, who had departed in a great hurry, due, it was rumoured, to having got banged up in an air raid.

Trixie gave the supervisor's desk a quick look. It was a mere flick of her head, but Mrs Teal noted it at once.

'It's all right, no telegram, Smith. Not bad news. No, nothing like that, dear. You're wanted in London. They're waiting for you.'

Trixie stared at her. 'Who wants me in London?'

Mrs Teal leaned forward. 'I don't know, dear.' She looked suddenly both impressed and frightened at the same time. 'A car came for you; it's waiting out there.' She nodded to outside the factory. 'Tell them to take you home to change. You don't want to go to London in your factory things, do you?'

'But it could be anyone.' Trixie looked stubborn. She had been brought up never to get into a stranger's car, not ever. 'Anyone at all.'

'No, dear.' Mrs Teal pushed a card towards her. It bore a name with letters after it, and when Trixie turned it over, it said, 'I have recommended you to Colonel Atkins', and it was signed 'Caro Garland'.

'You know her, I think?'

'Oh yes, I know Miss Caro, all right,' Trixie agreed. 'But I wonder what she's doing recommending me to this Colonel Atkins. I haven't any military experience.'

'Whatever it is I should hurry along, dear. Can't keep the military waiting.'

Trixie did hurry along, and by the time she was stepping out of the discreetly official car to dash into her lodgings to change, she had relaxed enough to realise she was enjoying herself. A chauffeur's daughter being driven, coo, coo, look at her! She even heard someone saying, 'Cor, look at her,' as she stepped out of the back of the motor.

And whatever Miss Caro was up to, knowing Miss Caro and her mischievous ways, it was sure to be something Trixie would enjoy. Perhaps she might not even have to go back to the factory. Perhaps she was on her way at last.

'Betty Thomas!'

The caller waved to her, and despite feeling more tired than she thought she had ever felt in her life, Betty waved back. It was her new friend at the Park, Mary Mullins.

'I hoped with all my heart that I'd catch sight of you, seeing that it's four o'clock, and the end of your watch.'

Mary slipped her arm into Betty's and they started to walk down the wide paths towards the lake where various military figures were busy fishing, taking advantage of the evening rise.

'Phew, what a business this decrypting and filing is. It has my poor head in a spin, it really does,' she said, looking round her with the air of someone who had just been born. 'I don't know about you, but I have half a mind on my work, and half a mind on what's happening over there, which means I am less than useful at it,' she confided, lowering her voice. 'There was a terrible hurry on last night, telegrams and messages flying in all directions. Night watch is meant to be four until midnight, but

I didn't hit my bed until the birds were waking up and yawning.'

Betty was silent as they walked along enjoying the sunny, cold air, the sun beginning to sink down into its early spring bed with a sweet pink glow that was reminiscent of the inside of shells.

'I keep thinking, if I make a mistake, what will happen? It will cost someone, or many people, their lives,' Mary went on, leaning down on Betty's arm, hurrying her along as they breathed in the fresh air – air not filled with the dust of filing cards and that rang with the song of birds before they retired, and not with the shrill sound of telephones.

Betty remained silent. She knew exactly what Mary meant about worrying. She too could not help worrying about their work, so much so that she went to bed at night turning over and over in her mind what she had done, just in case she had done it wrong. To make a mistake would not just be disastrous, it would be calamitous.

'You stare at what you do, you do it, but then you keep on worrying and worrying and thinking and thinking. Where was the agent who went under the code name of Grey Fox? Why have his radio messages suddenly stopped? And then the dread of seeing "*Goodnight Sweetheart*". And you go to bed knowing some brave creature has been blown, and praying and praying that they are dead, and not captured.'

Mary was not exaggerating. Even as you did your work, the facts behind what you were doing – well, they bit into your imagination – why was there nothing more from the one that calls herself Jezebel, or the Ladybird, or the Old

Crow, or whoever? The shifts were long – seven hours without a break was normal.

'I could never do what they're doing over there,' Betty confessed at last. 'Sometimes I just want to bring them all home, and give them a slap-up lunch – you know, roast beef, Yorkshire puddings, roast potatoes, and all that, tell them they've done enough, but that's not what we're here for, is it? And they wouldn't come. They believe in what they are doing – that even if they have to sacrifice their lives, they will have been saving the world from a new darkness, and we have to believe that too, even though we're only here to do the decryptions, file the cards in and out, not think too much, because it slows us down.' She paused, the look in her eyes changing from pensive to dreamy. 'As a matter of fact I wish I hadn't said that.'

'What?'

'Roast beef. I can hardly remember what it tasted like.'

'Oh, I know what you mean. Dear Mother of all that's holy, if we have any more baked trout, fried trout, potted trout, or any other kind of trout from that lake over there, I think I will find I'm growing fins and a tail.' Mary's eyes too turned dreamy. 'Come to think of it, now you mention food, I'd give an awful lot more than I would like to admit for just a taste of my ma's boiled bacon with some of her special parsley mashed potatoes and golden roast turnips. Oh, and to see a great slab of golden Irish butter on the table in front of you – wouldn't you give your eyeteeth for that?'

Betty looked at her. 'I know it's none of my business, but if you don't mind my asking, why didn't you go home to Ireland when you could? After all, it is your home country.'

Mary smiled, and shook back her long blonde curly hair.

'For the same reason that those boys and girls are battling their way through France over there, putting their lives on the line every hour of every day, for the very same reason as them, bless their hearts and souls. I hate bullies worse than sin. A dark age indeed it would be if we let the fascists in. A fine thing that would be if we all fell into that kind of slavery.'

They walked on in silence for a few minutes.

'Sometimes before the war seems like one long beautiful dream, doesn't it?' Betty said at last.

She thought back to those gentle days. Even the boredom now seemed entrancing; when afternoons seemed to be somehow just a little too long, and going to sleep at ten just a little too early, and waking up to the song of birds that had already been busy from first light vaguely irritating.

'Certainly the pre-war days seem like a dream, but perhaps when peace comes again we'll look back on these days now as being brighter and better, because we were all needed, so? Because we were all pulling together, being one people rather than many?'

'It doesn't seem possible, but maybe you're right.' They turned back, their short attempt at exercise now finished as they headed towards their billets.

'I do hope it's not going to be trout again at dinner,' Mary moaned.

*   *   *

Trixie's eyes had once more grown immensely round, and the look in them had become immensely serious, which was understandable since the sight confronting her was shocking.

She turned to her companion. 'I do believe that nothing I have yet seen in the war, *nothing* is so dreadful as this, Miss O'Brien.'

Edwina had the good sense to look embarrassed. Of course this Trixie person, Caro's childhood friend, was right. It was a very, very shocking sight, and she was not proud of it, but there, what could they do? When all was said and done, they were at war, and you had to do some pretty funny things in war.

'I know, I know, Miss Smith, and I share your opinion, of course I do, but it was Colonel Atkins's orders. He is the boss and this is how he said it should be. He chose everything himself, and with great care, d'you see? He chose it all.'

'Then he should be shot!'

It was Edwina's turn to look shocked.

'Do you really think so?'

'I certainly do. Why, there are children out there who are hard put to find a crust off a loaf, and look what we have laid out here.' Trixie pointed an indignant finger at the buffet table. 'Whole salmons! Chickens! Vol-au-vents with real pastry! Iced cakes with twirly bits! This is a feast fit for King Solomon, Miss O'Brien, and even he would never have touched it at a time like this, when all of us could end up dead or in a chain gang.'

Trixie was so cross, Edwina could see it was time to guide her out of the dining room, and into the drawing room.

'And that's only luncheon, Miss Smith, you know?' she said, solemn-faced. 'You should see what Mrs Cherry has laid on for the dinner party tonight. It would shock the ribbons off your camiknickers.'

Trixie followed her into the drawing room, and because she was half impressed that Miss O'Brien had taken it for granted that Trixie Smith wore camiknickers – which frankly she could never have afforded – her indignation did start to subside.

And yet, as she was guided through the double doors into a very large drawing room, she found she was not impressed by the décor. After all, she had been brought up at Chevrons which was full of fine things; beautiful objects were familiar to her.

Nevertheless, as she looked around, it dawned on her that the décor at The Place was of a very different nature from that of Chevrons. There were no family portraits, and no heavy velvet curtains that had been hung perhaps even a hundred years before. Neither were there old vases holding spills for the fire, nor worn Persian rugs. Here was much gold, and paintings that were roguish in content, and fabrics that were new and bright, more like something in a magazine, although not like that either.

'You were brought up at Chevrons, weren't you? With Miss Caro?'

Edwina and Trixie were now seated opposite each other.

'My father was chauffeur to Mr and Mrs Garland, and now helps out on the estate. My grandfather was coach-man to Mr Garland that was. And I have been a maid there, personal maid, finally, to Mrs Garland, and only left to help with the war effort, doing factory work because I could get nothing else.'

Edwina nodded. She had been both amused and impressed by Trixie's display of indignation when she saw the sumptuous buffet laid out in the dining room.

'If you want to come here you will be working for Colonel Atkins, but you will still be working for me here, even though you're really working for Colonel Atkins, if you understand me?'

Edwina put her head on one side, satisfied that she had explained herself very succinctly.

There was a slight pause, and then Trixie, having recovered from her burst of indignation, finally gave Edwina a calm look.

'You're really very Irish, aren't you?'

'So why wouldn't I be? I was born in Ireland. Naturally I'm Irish. Now we must get down to business. You will pose as my maid, but you will also *be* my maid. You will have to double as *parlour* maid too, with Mr Fleming as butler.'

Edwina had agreed with Colonel Atkins that no good could possibly come from Trixie knowing that Mrs Cherry and Mr Fleming also worked for Colonel Atkins. The rule at Baker Street and Dolphin Square was that the less people knew about each other, the better.

'I used to look after Mrs Garland, in the old days, before the war, when Miss Berenger, her Belgian maid, had her weekend off, and such like.' A nostalgic look came into Trixie's large eyes. 'It was wonderful looking after Mrs Garland. Her clothes were quite beautiful – clothes like you never see now.' She sighed deeply. 'But then women could be women before the war, couldn't they, Miss O'Brien? Not like now; now we're all in boiler suits, or slacks, or uniforms.'

Edwina sensed the rivalry in these casual observations, and her natural competitiveness rose to the bait.

'Yes, yes, of course, looking after Mrs Garland must have been a joy. Let me take you through to see my wardrobe, provided for me, by the colonel, bless his sacred socks.'

Of course there was mischief behind what Edwina was saying, and a part of her could not help hoping that Trixie would again be indignant at the sight of her sumptuous clothes.

When the colonel had shown her what she was being asked to wear, Edwina had not asked the source of such beautiful clothing. She realised that it was, as it were, camouflage, as much as anything that a soldier would wear. It was also intended to be used as propaganda. If the Queen of England's couture outfits were a source of inspiration and delight to the bombed-out poor of the East End, if her Majesty's beauty and charm were considered a brilliant propaganda tool against the enemy, then Edwina knew that Colonel Atkins was thinking along the very same lines.

If Edwina was to set up a salon that would attract the right kind of sympathisers from other countries, who, looking round London's bombed-out buildings, its nightly battering by Hitler's Luftwaffe, must be convinced that England was finished, it was vital that the beautiful Edwina O'Brien should look groomed within an inch of her life, and as beautifully dressed as it was possible to be. By being so she would be telling both England's enemies and her friends, 'Don't you believe what you see around you. Don't believe old England is done. How can she be when I'm looking like something dropped from heaven?'

Edwina now found herself staring at the contents of her new wardrobes, because although she had been through them many times, the truth was she still couldn't believe what they contained.

'The colonel acquired all these dresses and coats and skirts for me. Chosen for me by himself, I believe,' Edwina added swiftly, before Trixie could jump to any unlikely conclusions.

'The colonel must certainly know his stuff if he bought all this for you,' Trixie remarked, and her large brown eyes once more widened as she tried to take in row upon row of beautiful dresses and coats, and the contents of the multitude of mahogany drawers that Edwina was opening and shutting to demonstrate where the more personal garments were stored.

'Oh, the colonel has taste up to his elbows, believe me. Why else would he be choosing thee and me to work for him, do you think, Miss Smith?'

They both laughed.

'Please call me Trixie, Miss O'Brien. Everyone else does.'

Edwina shook her head. 'No, Trixie, I will not call you any such thing. I will call you "Smith", and that is, I am afraid, an unbreakable rule. A lady's maid in a London household is always called by her surname. Of course, when we are alone, if there is definitely no one else around, I expect I will call you "Smith, dotey" or "TS" or anything else that comes into my head, but when we are, if you will excuse the expression, professionally occupied, we will call each other Miss O'Brien and Smith, and we mustn't forget that.'

Trixie nodded in agreement. She didn't really care what Miss O'Brien called her, she just wanted her to get on with showing her everything that was so beautifully hanging on cushioned hangers and polished dark wooden hangers, inside those hand-carved mahogany wardrobes.

But for some reason Miss O'Brien seemed disinclined to do this yet. Instead she walked around the room pointing out where she kept her shoes and handbags, her gloves, and her lace-edged handkerchiefs, and all the other items that were so indispensable to a lady. Her makeup was in a leather case, stored neatly, and her silver hairbrushes and combs were on the dressing table, together with the largest scent bottles that Trixie had ever seen.

'So that is that,' Edwina finished. 'There are the clothes, and there are the things that go with the clothes.'

'From my experience with Mrs Garland,' Trixie announced, 'it is always necessary to show the personal maid the dress that will be worn that evening. And all the underpinnings, as well as the other – ' Trixie paused – 'as well as the jewellery, and such like,' she finished, looking around pointedly for a jewellery box.

Edwina was silent. She knew that this Trixie person was someone that Caro Garland had recommended, someone whom Caro had known all her life, but in war nothing was certain, and she had no idea whether or not she should show Trixie Smith where the jewellery was kept. Perhaps if it had been her own jewellery, it might be different, but it belonged, as it were, to the colonel, and he had only muttered in his gentlemanly way, 'Might be a better thing to wait to show the maid where the beads are kept, but I'll let you make up your own mind about that.'

'Let me show you some of my dresses that the colonel has picked out for me from some private pre-war collections – nothing that would contravene the expected ration regulations, all second-hand, some unworn, some worn once.'

She reached up into the wardrobe and took down a dress.

'I was thinking of wearing this tonight, for my dinner party for sixteen. Look at the embroidery on it, duvetyn stitching, and all this travertine lace – I think that is travertine – on the edging, quite a good thing in the V of a dress, I suppose.'

Edwina smiled slyly. She could see that Trixie was enthralled, that by showing her this wardrobe full of carefully selected dresses and coats and skirts, of short furs, and long rabbit-lined coats, of every kind of sophisticated wear, she had awakened the dormant personal maid in Smith, formerly known as Trixie.

The simmering indignation displayed in the dining room had completely disappeared, to be replaced by reverence, and she was already, with a look of great piety, laying out a dress that she had obviously singled out for Edwina to wear that evening. It was black and full-skirted, its many petticoats shot through with a cerise

311

silk, the silk echoed in the bodice, and the sleeves. It was very beautiful.

'I would suggest this one for tonight, Miss O'Brien.'

Trixie looked up expectantly at Edwina. It was a challenging moment, and they both knew it.

'Just what I would have chosen for myself, Smith,' Edwina said in a smooth voice. 'Exactly right for the kind of gathering we can expect.'

Happily it really was what Edwina herself would have chosen, because if it hadn't been there might well have been what Edwina had heard Caro nowadays sometimes call 'a teeny momento'.

'Mrs Garland always said that red hair and red or pink were a beautiful combination. She had it from Mr de Laszlo, *the* Mr de Laszlo. Mr Philip de Laszlo. He designed the dress for Mrs Garland to wear in her portrait. It was, is, a most beautiful dress, and the portrait, is, was, a great success in every way. It was the last thing I dressed her in before the annual ball given by the Lord Lieutenant, which she always attended. This particular year she had sacrificed her dress allowance to Miss Katherine's needs, so that she could have a fashionable wardrobe, but then that was Mrs Garland all over. She would rather have starved than not share what she had with someone who might be in need. Not that Miss Katherine was in need, but she *was* due to come out the following spring, and she had to get used to wearing beautiful things, and – as Mrs Garland always said – no good throwing Miss Katherine into the arena like some unschooled horse. She must not just learn elegance, she must experience it.'

Edwina smiled, despite actually wanting to scream.

Obviously the sainted Mrs Garland, mother of Caro, was someone with whom she would have to get used to living.

'Mrs Garland was obviously a lovely lady . . .' Her voice tailed off, ending on a deliberately vague and bored note.

'She was a beautiful lady,' Trixie affirmed. 'She will always be missed. If we all live to be a hundred, we will always miss her, everyone that knew her.'

Edwina sighed inwardly. Just her luck to inherit a personal maid who was used to working for a saint.

'I am awfully afraid that I shall prove to be a trying sort of disappointment to you, Smith, after Mrs Garland,' she said, adopting a sad tone. 'I am more sinner than saint, but I do love to laugh, as you doubtless will notice. Laughter is the safety valve of a nation, and we need all of that at this time, I think you will agree.'

But Trixie was not listening. She was busy searching for suitable shoes and stockings to go with the cerise and black dress. Whatever her feelings about Miss O'Brien, after the din and the gloom of the factory, the contents of the wardrobes, the scent and feel of all that sophistication were intoxicating.

That night the London bombing raids were so ferocious that Trixie was not even able to return home to collect her things. Miss O'Brien forbade it, saying, 'Now you're here we must try to keep you whole. I will lend you whatever you need.'

However, the planned party went ahead. No matter that the noise outside was horrendous, what with the sirens and then the bombs, it seemed that everyone had become used to it. Either that or their hunger was stronger than their fear.

It was not just Trixie's first evening as a personal maid, it was also her first evening helping in the dining room. She dressed in her new black dress – perfect fit, how did they know? – and then placed the starched cap on her head and looked at herself in the mirror.

'You were meant to be getting on with your life, Beatrice Smith,' she told her image, 'not going back into service.' But then she smiled at herself, because she couldn't help realising that she looked really rather perky.

Mind you, she'd have to watch her rear end with the gentlemen, but that was only to be expected when you were dressed as a maid. Why there were any frustrated spinsters left in the world had always been a source of amazement to Trixie. After all, when all was said and done they would only have to put on a maid's uniform, and there'd be a queue of men waiting for them halfway down the road.

The sirens started up as Trixie entered the kitchen. It was a sound she had heard many times, but in London, because the buildings were so close together, it seemed to be a great deal more sinister.

Mr Fleming turned to her. 'Don't show fear in front of the guests, will you?'

'No, Mr Fleming, of course not.'

'If the building shakes it is permissible to retreat under the dining table, or if the building might seem to be about to be hit, to a cupboard under the stairs in the downstairs hall. Otherwise we just carry on.'

'Yes, Mr Fleming.'

Trixie picked up her tray of hors d'oeuvres. How would they know if the building was 'about to be hit'?

Still, life back at the factory was hardly less noisy, and at least here at The Place, the work was more varied. She straightened her black dress and parlour maid's cap, and proceeded out of the green baize door. She would do as the others did. She would carry on as if nothing was happening, no matter that her insides had turned to water, no matter that she had a job keeping the tray in her hands steady. There were a great many foreigners present, all talking at once, but if they were prepared to carry on, so was she.

Days later, having been given a room in the basement of the building, which was to serve her as a bedroom for the rest of the war, Trixie began to realise that, since the Blitz, and the devastation of the unprecedented bombing that had been unleashed on London, the number-one rule of life in the capital was to enjoy yourself whenever you could. Hours spent driving ambulances, or taking food and drink to firemen, whose endurance was such that sometimes their hands froze to their hoses, were swiftly compensated by as many hours spent dining and dancing. The pace of life was ferocious. Yet while she learned to admire it, Trixie had no intention of following suit. She would rather be down in the basement with her books and her knitting, or under the kitchen table with Mrs Cherry, than out dancing with someone new.

'I couldn't go dancing knowing that young men were dying,' she murmured piously.

Despite the fact that they were spending their

umpteenth night under the basement stairs, Mrs Cherry managed to give her an old-fashioned look.

'That's exactly why they do go dancing, Smith, to amuse the young men, take their minds off what's going to happen tomorrow. That is the whole point, don't you see?'

Trixie did see, but dancing was still not for her. Besides, she had to look after Miss O'Brien, whose social life was becoming something to behold. She only hoped that good would come of it, or else it would be a proper waste of everyone's efforts, not to mention a crying scandal when you saw all the people who came to the apartment disporting themselves, eating and drinking in such a fashion you would have thought it was their last meal.

Walter was up and about early. He had spent the night fire watching yet again, standing in for his neighbour, and then snatched a couple of hours' sleep, shaved and dressed, and was now making his way along the endlessly empty roads that would take him to the place where his next subject would already be at work.

The previous evening he had been down the Underground, sketching the crowds, the turmoil, the people, the bunks, the sleeping bags, but avoiding some of the less savoury sights. He saw it as his duty to ignore the squalor, to concentrate instead on the relentless courage of the people, singing and picnicking, reading to their children, joking and laughing, playing cards, pretending, as they all must, that tomorrow was going to be just another day – if only they could hang on, stick it out, make sure that there *was* another day to which to look forward.

An hour or so after leaving London, showing his identity card for what seemed like the hundredth time, he was at last coming to grips with the subject of his painting, the gun turret.

As he saw the magnitude of the task ahead – the crew's not his – he became fearful, and at the same time excited.

The crew were in rehearsal, but the way they were setting about their business with the gun turret, which weighed near enough a ton, they would seem to be doing the exercise for real.

Of course, since they were only practising, the men were not wearing 'flash' gear but wearing training uniform. Sooner than Walter expected the breech was shut, and almost immediately the machinery appeared to him to be a monstrous creature weaving around the crew. The atmosphere, claustrophobic, increasingly fetid, became heavy with sweat and human effort, shiny with dripping moisture, but Walter sketched on, his own sweat starting to impede his efforts, his life seeming to become one with that of the perspiring crew. He knew, as they knew, that they were learning a grim ballet that had to be foot- and arm-perfect. They would never know until the moment arrived whether they would be a success because that demon of the unknown was waiting for them, thousands of miles of its great dark body, the unknown devil that could be charmer or slayer – the sea.

'I will be back tomorrow,' Walter murmured finally to the gunnery officer, who regarded him with passive disinterest.

The fact that Walter was from some Artists' Rifles

brigade, or whatnot, that he had arrived not in uniform but in a painter's smock and white shirt, in drill trousers and light shoes, and was now leaving, wrung out with sweat, wearing precisely the same clothes, did not mean that the officer was going to let him off producing his identity card.

'I'll be back tomorrow at the same time,' Walter murmured, and he could almost hear the officer in question sighing, doubtlessly thinking: infernal painters, what use were they when the battle was on, endlessly daubing and doubtless getting in everyone's way too.

Walter felt the same himself. The truth was that in war an artist, a painter, was just what no one needed, hanging around the people that really mattered, getting in the way. Every day, and every night when he finally went to bed, the urge to put in for something else overwhelmed him. He had to find another role, before he lost all self-respect.

Katherine straightened up and paused by the dark alley, head bent, looking up and down the narrow street of small shops that ran from her cavern-like hiding place under the bridge.

No one was about, not that it would have mattered if they had been, because there was so much poverty on the Left Bank, one more tramp, one more drunken woman would arouse about as much curiosity as an empty bottle lying in the gutter.

Happily she knew Paris like the back of her hand, and she also knew the concierge of this particular block of flats, had known her long before the war, which was why she would not trust her as far as she could throw her. She knew her habits, her failings, her greed. For if madame the concierge was not greedy, if she did not worship a fresh baguette, and croissants, and filet mignon done to perfection, then Paris was not beautiful.

Katherine had planned to wait until the old woman left her little set of narrow rooms by the entrance to the courtyard, and went down the street to pick up her early morning bread, and then Katherine would cross from her dirty, smelly hiding place and make her way to the block of flats.

She had spent the night under the arches at the top of the street, where tramps and drunks were famous for sitting and drinking, sleeping and waking, only to fall asleep scratching and groaning. Her night had not been the best she had ever spent, but it had been more than useful for making her look as authentic as the rest of the company. She looked and smelled dreadful.

As soon as she saw the concierge leave, hardly after dawn, for there was currently a flour shortage in Paris, Katherine moved from the shadows of her filthy hiding place, and through the door cut into the large shuttered barrier that guarded the courtyard, then made her way up to the flat.

Marie-Christine opened her front door with the chain still on, and stared at Katherine, but such was the efficiency of the underground movement in France, she had long been expecting the Ladybird. Quickly she closed the door and reopened it to her.

'*Mon Dieu, vous sentez mal!*' She stepped backwards, putting one long-fingered elegant hand over her nose, and then forwards again to reattach the door chain behind Katherine. '*Ma pauvre*. You will excuse me if I do not kiss you, eh? The things you do for England I am surely not prepared to do for France.'

They both laughed, but Marie-Christine immediately stopped and stared in horror at Katherine's teeth.

'*Mais – quelle horreur!*'

'*C'est nécessaire,*' Katherine informed her in a low voice, before following her old friend down the narrow dark corridor to the sloping-floored kitchen, with its one tap and its food cages, and its window overlooking the Seine – and many other things too.

Once in the kitchen Marie-Christine raised her finger to her lips, and opened the door that should have led to a larder. Katherine stared in. Inside were no winter stores, precious pots of jam or bags of flour, but what seemed like half a dozen pairs of dark eyes staring back at her. She kneeled down in the doorway.

'How long have they been here?' she asked in French.

'Many days, madame,' one of the children said finally, after looking towards Marie-Christine to make sure that it was all right to answer.

'They have to stay here. It would be impossible to move them now,' Marie-Christine told Katherine in English. 'Paris is so crowded, you understand, not just the Boche, but the Gestapo too. They make lightning visits everywhere. Last night it was Montmartre, today it is St-Germain-en-Laye. It is tedious not knowing, but then war is tedious.' She shrugged her shoulders, and nodded towards the window. 'We have a lookout on the Pont des Arts during the day. You see, there? That small boy standing by the bridge? He is very quick. As soon as they approach we will know. He is a cousin of mine. He knows nothing, only to watch for the Boche, or the Gestapo. Not even the concierge knows of the little ones' presence here. We trust no one. We can't.' She put a cafetière on the stove and lit the gas under it. 'Soon the war will be over, I know it, and soon we will see the back of these filthy Boche, but until then we make certain no one knows our secret, eh? This coffee is not the best, but it is all we have. Food is getting harder and harder to find here. I am hoping all the time to find a way to get these little ones to the countryside where it will be easier to hide them.' She stopped, her eye caught by something beyond the window. Her face lost colour. *'Mon Dieu*, the little *gosse* is waving his handkerchief, and running off. *Mon Dieu*, the Gestapo.' She turned to Katherine. 'Where shall we hide them?'

'Where are you? Where are you?' the voice called.

For a second Caro felt disinclined to reply.

'I'm up here!' she called down to Walter. 'On the roof,' she said in a fed-up voice.

Walter appeared. He looked worried.

'I have been waiting downstairs for you for nearly an hour. Didn't you get my message?'

'No,' Caro lied, because she didn't want him to know that she had scrambled out of the ATS uniform, which was now obligatory, into her better cut, and altogether more flattering FANY uniform. She didn't want Walter to know in case he teased her. And also, he might get a big head, feel flattered that she had rushed back to change in order to look nice for him.

Walter looked momentarily put out. 'I gave the message to Robyn to pass on to you.'

'Robyn has been driving non-stop this week, and dancing until dawn. She wouldn't remember anything you told her.'

Walter looked at his watch.

'Look, it's Saturday, in case you hadn't noticed, and it's Bob's watch tonight. Come to the Berkeley for dinner, and then on to the 400, if you like. Time we had ourselves some fun before the Yanks get here, and snatch all the girls from under our noses.'

'Well, if they're in it now with us, at least we have a better chance, don't we?' Caro stated.

'Of course. It's what the old man has wanted all along, we all know that. But you know how it is, once the Americans occupy a place, well, we Englishmen don't get a look in. Their uniforms are so much better cut, and they're not made of scratchy material.'

'You're not in uniform.'

'I will be next week.' Walter looked proud. 'I'm off to do something that not even you can know about.'

He made a pretend moustache-twirling gesture. He had finally finished his painting, finally come to the end of the sweltering days spent in the gun turret, and was ready for action of a quite different kind.

Caro looked at him. She could never tell Walter how anxious his news made her feel.

'Come on, my lucky charm. Let's go to where the wine will flow, and then on to where the band will be playing tunes of today for the folk of tomorrow.'

'You sound like Vera Lynn.'

No one in the services now changed to go to dinner. It was the rule. They kept their uniforms on at all times.

'You've got great legs you know, Lucky,' Walter announced to Caro and the rest of the street as he followed her into the taxi, even as the sirens started. 'Great pins. As soon as this war is over I will paint you again. You will fill the canvas with your charm, Lucky, and I with my genius.'

Caro gave him an old-fashioned look and sat back in the taxi, holding on to the strap at the side, sighing.

'Shorty? Lucky? I don't know what it is about me, I seem to attract nicknames,' she complained.

'Who calls you Shorty? That is absolutely not on, Lucky. You are not short – your legs are too long to be short – but you are let us say, petite, and that is something different. You are Shaw's Cleopatra, that's what you are,' he finished meditatively, still staring at her as if she was on her way to sit to him instead of, Caro devoutly hoped and prayed, on her way to dinner. 'Perhaps that is how I will paint you, as a petite Cleopatra. Will you sit to me as Cleopatra, Queen of the Nile, Lucky?'

'I will sit *on* you if you go on talking such drivel,' Caro told him, but before she could say any more she found herself sheltering in his arms, with her head against his chest, clinging to him for dear life.

A bomb had just dropped in front of the taxi.

'Get out of my way, old woman!' the Gestapo officer looked contemptuously at Katherine, who was seated at the bottom of the stairs. She did not move. He attempted to spit at her, but missed, and she merely smiled and waved the bottle of wine she was holding in her filthy fingers.

He stepped back, and his companion nodded towards the ironwork grille in front of them.

'Come on, let's take the lift. My God, that old woman smells.'

They pressed the button for the old-fashioned cage-like lift. It creaked and groaned its way to the ground floor, while Katherine drank on from the bottle of wine, grinning wildly at the officers between gulps.

'Let's start at the top and make our way down.'

'The top flats are empty; have been for years. No, we'll go to the first floor, that's our tip-off.'

The lift stopped at the first floor, creaking and swaying as if just reaching that far up was asking too much of it.

Katherine prayed. In a way her prayers were answered almost immediately, for any extra sounds that might have been noticed, any scratchings or whisperings, were immediately covered by the Gestapo kicking and knocking at Marie-Christine's door.

Katherine's thoughts darted in every direction, as random and confused as the pigeons in the courtyard had been as the Gestapo passed them. She heard the door above her opening, the chains having first been removed. Who had betrayed them?

'Gentlemen?' Katherine could hear Marie-Christine's cool, educated voice.

'We have the authority to search these flats.'

'Of course you have, and by all means, please go ahead, gentlemen. But first, would you like a cup of coffee, or *une petite coupe*, perhaps an eau-de-vie to warm the heart and soul?'

Katherine remained seated on her steps, her heart racing. God alone knew how long the wretched Gestapo would be, but worst of all, God alone knew, if they took their time, what would happen to the children.

'You all right?' The taxi driver turned round. His tin-hatted head appeared at the now open door of the cab, his eyes the only part of his face that was not covered in dust.

'Yes, of course, quite all right, thank you. Carry on to the Berkeley, shall we?' Walter asked coolly.

The driver nodded.

'Right you are, governor, so long as you're all right, then course I'll take you on.'

He restarted his engine as Caro sat up, straightening her uniform jacket as she did so.

'Sorry about that, Walter. I don't usually fling myself on men.'

'Don't be sorry.' Walter put his arm back around her shoulders, but not in his usual brotherly fashion.

'It's the bombing,' Caro explained, staring ahead and then clearing her throat. 'I dare say it's succeeded in making us all look fast.'

'No, Lucky, not fast, just human.'

Caro moved away from him so that she could open her gas mask case, out of which she then removed not the usual dreaded black mask, but a powder compact and lipstick.

Walter started to laugh as she repaired her lipstick and tidied herself.

'You know what I love about girls?'

'No?'

'Everything, that's all. Just everything.'

Caro smiled, and having put her compact and lipstick back in the case, she surprised herself by settling back into the comfort of Walter's arm. After all, it was wartime, anything could happen. Seconds later there was another explosion, but this time they both flung themselves to the floor of the cab as part of a building collapsed ahead of them.

'Will we never get to dinner?' Caro moaned. 'I'm so hungry I could eat my tie.'

'We'll get there in the end, Lucky,' said Walter, 'if it's the last thing we do, which, judging from the aim of the Luftwaffe tonight, it might well turn out to be. But of course we will get there, because you are my lucky charm, and we will have ourselves a great time, you'll see.'

The bar was packed with uniforms, both male and female. Walter bought the drinks, and Caro was ashamed to see that despite her best efforts, when she was at last able to find her lighter and light a much-needed cigarette, her hand was shaking.

Walter put his hand out to steady her.

'Blast and damn – so embarrassing when that happens.'

'It's all right, Lucky,' he told her. 'My hand's not too good either.'

He held it out to show her that it too was shaking. Caro looked rueful for a second or two, but nevertheless managed to blow a perfect smoke ring. It floated across the group of people behind her, still perfectly round.

'I should be better at all this by now. God knows I've been in London long enough.'

'What, smoking? You're great at smoking. Look at that ring, kid, expert stuff!'

'Actually I can do better than that,' she nodded at the disappearing ring, 'but what with one thing and another my puff's not so good after that taxi ride.'

Walter leaned forward and kissed her lightly on the lips, the merest brush.

'We'll bolt our dinner and then go dancing. Come to think of it, I have a half-finished bottle of something delicious I left at the 400 a week or so ago. Maybe there then?'

Caro gave him a brilliant smile. 'You bet.'

Then she frowned. Hang on, what had just happened? Oh, yes. Walter had just kissed her.

'Table's ready.'

He took her by the hand, and she quickly followed him. Whatever happened tonight there was a war on, and when there was a war on anything could happen; and then whatever did happen could always be blamed on the war, couldn't it?

Marie-Christine had succeeded in giving the Gestapo everything that they wanted – drinks, coffee and even a little something to take back to their headquarters. Now Katherine was determined to delay them on the stairs.

'Out of my way, old woman!'

They lunged at her and snatched her bottle of wine away. She moaned in a drunken manner, which was not difficult since by now, given the hour, she was actually feeling more than a little tipsy.

'Get her out of here.'

'*You* get her out of here – phew!'

They walked off laughing, slamming the doors to the courtyard after them. Katherine sprang up, went to the half-glassed porch doors and watched them crossing the paved area, the pigeons once more flying up and circling about them. Finally they stopped by the concierge's door and called to her. Judging from their shoulder shrugging and gestures they were telling her that they had found nothing, that her so-called tip-off had been a mistake. Katherine did not hear her reply. She did not need to. So *that* was who had betrayed them.

'You'll regret that, Madame Defarge,' she muttered before turning away and haring up the stairs to the first floor to help Marie-Christine unload the children.

'Wait, wait! We must wait at least twenty minutes. They could be back. Sometimes they do that, you know? They comb a place through minutely, and then they come back almost immediately, counting on the fact that you will think the coast is clear. It happened down the way at the old bookshop near the church. They were hiding an old gentleman in the cellar. They thought the coast was clear, but then twenty minutes later . . .' For a second Marie-Christine's eyes were heavy with regret, and then Katherine could see she turned away from the memory, whatever it was, because pursuing it was a waste of time. 'It is very cruel, but it is very effective.'

In the end they let several hours go by, all the time calling softly to the children to be brave, to keep still, and then, at long last, they lifted them from the top of the lift to which they had been clinging, and hurried them back to their hiding place off the kitchen.

They made coffee, twice used, three times used – it didn't matter, it calmed the nerves.

'We'll have to get them out of here, but how?'

'It was the concierge who betrayed us, and she will do so again. Probably she is doing it in return for some relative being allowed to escape, or for money or rations, or for all three. Whatever happens, the children must be moved on.'

The two young women stared at each other. Of course the children must be moved on, but how?

'There is no time when that woman is not in her *cabinet*.'

Katherine shook her head, and lit half a cigarette, passing the other half she had cut to Marie-Christine.

'Yes, there is, when she goes for black market bread. Not long, but enough time for us to smuggle the children out – about ten minutes, at dawn, when it is still dark. She likes to gossip with the baker, pass on details that she knows or has seen, and in return the baker smuggles her a baguette or two.'

'Very well, we could move them on in the dark of dawn, but after that, what do we do? You can't hide six children in the suburbs of Paris, can you? That is where my mother lives, but they would be noticed. They look too foreign, they would be too obvious in the suburbs.'

'If we use the river and one of the older barges, the ones they are all so afraid of now in case they sink, we could move them on without anyone noticing.'

'One of them sank only last week, and with God knows who or what on board.'

'Yes, but the authorities care less at the moment. Most of the pleasure boats have been abandoned down the waterways, and they are so rat-ridden no one minds if they sink. I will go and buy one, or steal one. Whichever, we will find a way to escape by river. It is truly our only chance.'

Katherine had reverted to a guttural Parisian accent. Marie-Christine smiled.

'You are very good at accents, *chérie*, but how good are you at being a bargee?'

Katherine smiled. 'I grew up beside a river. Talking of which, I must wash just a little of my stink away before we both pass out.'

'Yes, yes, I will boil some water, and then you must wash, and then we will talk again, but only after you have rested. Sleeping under the archway with the *clochards* is not a restful thing, I would say.'

Katherine washed, no, she scrubbed, knowing she could stay clean for only a while. Soon she would have to become decrepit again.

As she towelled herself dry, and felt fatigue dropping off her, as if her body was a candle and she was melting, she remembered what the old actor on their survival course used to say to them.

'You need only do a little to suggest that you are an undesirable. A little earth under your nails, sleep in your eyes, hair unwashed, that will be quite enough. You must look pitiable rather than objectionable, as if you would like to wash, but just haven't the facilities. That way people will hurry away from you, rather than take a closer look. Nothing truly ugly really scares people, you will find, but nothing is more frightening to them than the idea that you might be *asking* for their sympathy.'

Soon Katherine was fast asleep. Perhaps because of their talk about finding a barge to hide the children and spirit them away down the river, she dreamed of Chevrons, and of David. He was coming towards her, always coming towards her, but she was always backing away from him. However hard she tried to reach out to him it was as if her arms were weighted, and although she put all her strength into willing them towards him, they would not reach him, and all the longing in her heart would not make them. This was terrible because there was David, as real as anything, and he was just as beautiful as ever, but most of all his blue eyes were filled with such a humorous look. As he had always said to her, life was really just a game, and they all knew it was not the winning that mattered, but the taking part. Which of course he did not believe at all, but it made them both laugh, that hearty 'play the game' kind of thinking, the pipe-smoking Scoutmaster attitude that they had never believed in.

'We're far too beautiful for tweed-suited heroics,' he would tease Katherine. 'We are Greeks, not Romans.'

In her dream she couldn't hear him, but she was laughing, and he was laughing with her. But when she woke up there were tears on her face, tears that marked her freshly scrubbed cheeks, and she left them there, along with the sleep in her eyes, because it was time to become someone else again. Time to find out about the boats that lay about the Seine, some still with the remains of ruined cargo, some empty, their hulls rotting, their paint peeling.

'You will be taking a boat with us,' she told the children, a few days later. 'It will be a great adventure, but you will have to be very quiet, as you have been here. You have to be hidden again, and perhaps there will be rats, and bad smells, but you will try to sleep, and when you wake up you will find that you are far away in the countryside, safe, and with plenty to eat. Until then, you must pretend you are deaf and dumb, you must not move, or make a sound. You must be like little ghosts, not there, but there all the same. Now follow me when I call for you, and not a word or a sound from you. It is tiptoe and silence, tiptoe and silence, all the way.'

Across the courtyard, and into the empty street – they had just those few minutes before the wretched concierge returned. Under the arches where the tramps and the drunks groaned and slept, and then on to the river, and within a minute or two, the river being so close to the old block of flats, there was the barge that Katherine had managed to buy from a vendor along the banks, lying waiting for her. Whether the vessel truly was his or not, the sight of her cash had quickly bought his silence, along with the boat.

Nothing seemed so silent as the Seine that particular dark morning. There was no one about, not a soldier, not a gendarme, not a prostitute, not a bus, no one. It was as if the enemy was sleeping in that morning, as if, despite America having come into the war, despite Hitler's troubles in Russia, they knew themselves to be safe, safe in the one place that not even Hitler would dare to bomb – Paris.

Soon the city familiar to the two young women was far behind, and the Seine was bearing them along in almost silent conspiracy, only the grumbling of the motor leaking out across the water, only the sight of other vessels making their way back to the capital, to distract their early morning ears and eyes.

The children were asleep in the hold. If they could get them into the countryside, to the remote farmhouse owned by Marie-Christine in the Loire, they would be safe.

'There are cows and sheep, and chickens too. An old man lives above the stables and he looks after everything for me, but I have not been there for more than three years, not since the war came, but it is so remote, I doubt that any but he has been there either. When we find it, we will be able to eat again, until then we must make what little we have last.' Marie-Christine looked philosophical, and shrugged her elegant shoulders, pointing down to where the children lay hidden. 'At least there are no rats down there; they are too intelligent to go where there is so little for them.'

They both knew the truth of this. The barge chugged on. They must make good time before the light became too bright, when they would have to hide in a backwater, and once again wait until the comfort of darkness before continuing their long journey. All too soon they would have to abandon the barge and make their way across the countryside to another river, to a tributary where

333

once again they would have to beg, borrow or steal a vessel. So their journey would continue, not just along the waterways but across short stretches of land, but always in the dark, and away from the towns and the cities where the enemy was concentrated. Thank God that France was so big.

As they travelled the two young women kept conversation to practicalities, because anything else was a waste of energy. They had carefully dressed the children in poor, nondescript clothes, and hats and scarves, so that they looked for all the world as if the little party appeared to be merely two women travelling alone with their brood of children across Occupied – or in their case, largely unoccupied – France.

At last they came to the farmhouse in the clearing. It was near enough midnight, so it was not surprising that there was no one about, or that no light burned in the flat above the stables, or that there was no other sign of human life.

Marie-Christine pushed open the unlocked door of the old farmhouse. A hen ran out from under the table, leaving not one egg, but what looked like a dozen or more.

'Never surely have we seen such a splendid sight!' Marie-Christine whispered.

The children crept in past her. She shut the door and lit an oil lamp on the side. The farmhouse was dusty, it was dirty, but there were eggs, and soon there would be a pan, and she would find something – oil, something – in which to cook the eggs. In the morning she would find a cow, and all the usual comforts would start to appear, but before she could do any of these things, she felt a pair of arms around her neck, and Katherine was giving her a fierce hug.

'We did it! We did it! Don't you realise, we're here!'

They all joined hands and started to dance around the old stone-flagged kitchen, with its low ceiling and its cobwebs, with its ancient range, and its strange old-fashioned oil lamps of every shape.

After that there was much to do to make everything more comfortable. Hands helped to pile up logs in the fireplace, feet ran to search for matches and oil, for everything and anything that would make their refuge cosier. It was the gayest of sights to see the children's faces become roseate, lit by the gentle spill from the lamps, and that was all before they smelled the eggs cooking. Katherine found some old potatoes, which she made into tiny chips, and they all wolfed what was put before them, thinking, as they did, one communal thought – nothing would ever taste as good again, surely?

It was not long after cooking the eggs for the children that Marie-Christine found a bottle of wine and, having tucked up the children in the upstairs rooms, knowing that they would fall asleep almost immediately, the two women crept back down and broached this hidden treasure – a rare and beautiful bottle of wine, happily one of many.

Again, never had anything tasted so good, or felt so warming. So much so that after turning the lamp off to save oil, they sat drinking by the light of the moon well into the small hours before they too fell asleep, Katherine insisting on placing her mattress across the door, because, as she said, old habits die hard and, anyway, she wanted Marie-Christine to sleep until she woke.

What Katherine didn't say to her was that she would not be staying with her and the children. She would be leaving within a day or two.

She lay staring up at the moon – not a French moon, not an English moon, certainly not a Nazi moon, but everyone's moon – which was at least a constant in an inconstant world. She closed her eyes and for the next minutes it seemed to her that she was back at Chevrons, and a child again, and then she and David were running through the bluebells that grew under the ancient beech trees on his father's estate, and he was looking back at her and saying, 'When I grow up, Katie, I am going to be a hero,' and seeing the look in his eyes, that glowing blue-eyed look that all heroes must have, she knew she had to be the same. She remembered saying, 'And so am I, David. I'm going to be a hero like you' and he was laughing and telling her that girls couldn't be heroes, they had to be heroines, and then she recalled her challenging reply: 'That's what I shall be then – a heroine.'

PART THREE

'Who says we can take it?'

Chapter Eleven

If Katherine could only dream of Chevrons, to Betty and Trixie the old house was at last becoming a reality.

Their train journey was taking so long, standing all the way, stopping, and changing what seemed like every hour. And being pinched and kicked by more uniformed personnel than Montgomery could command was gruelling, to say the least. As Trixie opined later, it had been a worse experience than any bombing raid.

Trixie looked across at Betty. She was a horrible colour, pale green or, at the very best, a tasteful eau-de-Nil would be a fair description. Of course, after the awful journey, it was hardly surprising if she looked done in.

But that was not all. Betty was pale green for another reason too, which was more worrying to Trixie.

'I can't ask anyone to give up their seat for you, because you don't look pregnant,' she murmured. 'Anyway, there are so many foreign soldiers on the train I wouldn't know how to ask them, *truly* I wouldn't.'

'I'm all right, Trix, really I am.'

'Of course you are, you've never been better. You wouldn't swap places with anyone else in the whole world, would you?' She sighed. 'Would you ever believe that a journey could take so long? I keep thinking when the train finally reaches its destination we'll find we're in Hong Kong, and there'll be a rickshaw ready and waiting to take us up to the old place.'

Betty nodded. Trixie was a real friend, and the truth was that without her she wouldn't have known which way to turn.

In recent weeks Betty's life had become a nightmare. Of course, there was no point in moaning, 'If only I hadn't gone to London with Mary Mullins, if only I hadn't sheltered next to a Frenchman in that nightclub she took me to, if only I hadn't been so frightened . . .'

Of course, there were so many 'if onlys' surrounding her condition at the moment it was a wonder she could go on from one minute to another without collapsing from the weight of her guilt, from the burden of her despair, from the horror of what had happened to her – and the fact that it had happened to so many others was no comfort at all. Very well, this was what did happen in war: people became frightened, people acted out of character, people were not themselves when they were terrified, but her excuses fell on her own deaf ears, and lying awake at night, tussling with such feelings helped nothing, least of all herself.

If there was one thing she would have said would never, ever happen to her, it was that she would get pregnant; and worse, that she would get pregnant, as the old-fashioned saying went, out of wedlock. But she had been so frightened, and, as she thought, so alone, with only the darkness and the rubble, rats running squealing, and the sounds of people somewhere else moaning and screaming. Mary had disappeared into the crowd, leaving Betty and someone else, someone she had never met or seen, or ever would again, the other side of all that rubble.

They had gone up to London for the evening. It was not like Mary and Betty to take an evening off, in fact they hadn't even been to London together before. At the Park, Mary and Betty had been known to be the goody-goodies, always volunteering for extra work, never wanting to sleep when they could be awake and helping, but the ever-increasing workforce at the Park meant that there was less need for even the most enthusiastic to work for more than the statutory seven hours by day, or even by night. So they had gone up to London to have dinner and to dance, to enjoy themselves, but they had only been there a few hours, coming out of the restaurant into the blackout, waving their torches at the pavement, and giggling a little because it was all such an adventure, with the crowds, the singing they could hear coming from somewhere or other – down the Underground, was it? They had been heading for a nightclub when the siren had gone off, and so, together with just about everyone else, they had headed for the Underground, which was conveniently near. But it seemed the Luftwaffe was quicker than they could be, and the crowd panicked. In the mêlée Betty was borne one way and Mary the other, and then the world seemed to explode around her as she and others dashed down some steps into some kind of basement, where they were sheltering when another bomb dropped.

They had clung together, perhaps the only ones alive, who knew? Certainly she had clung to him as she had never clung to anyone in her life before, experiencing the inner ice of terror for the first time. Betty wouldn't have cared who he was, she had clung to him as if he was her saviour, which he wasn't. He had been as frightened as she, sweating with fear, scrabbling at the rubble until his hands bled, calling and calling until he had collapsed with exhaustion, crying and clinging to her the way she had started out by clinging to him.

She couldn't now remember a great deal of what had happened, at least not in sequence, but she did remember that after some hours she had attempted to comfort him, stroking his hair, holding him in her arms as if he was her child.

That they had eventually emerged had been a miracle; that they had made love before that, in some ways was another miracle, because finally she could not deny that she had wanted him, as much as he perhaps had wanted her at that moment, not for anything more than comfort, but to find temporary peace, to expiate the terror, the claustrophobia, to take his mind off everything that he was feeling, the shame of it to be replaced, eventually, by another emotion, a sort of strange peace.

Then, when daylight came and, eventually with it, rescue, it was almost a disappointment for Betty – the sudden shock of other faces, of the brightness of the sun behind them, of their voices, which now seemed too loud – and then to turn and shake hands with someone to whom she had just given herself. It was both a nightmare and dream at one and the same time, the two set neatly side by side. And then for days and weeks to pass before she was forced to face the undeniable fact that she was having a baby, a baby that was the result not of love, but of terror.

There was no question but that she had to tell her superior, no question that she had to make arrangements, and no question that there was only one person to whom she could turn, and that was the now London-based Trixie.

Except it seemed that Trixie was no longer Trixie, that she had grown as grand as her surroundings. *Beatrice Smith* was what she now was, and yet Betty had to admit that it suited her, except on a long journey such as they were undertaking now, when she somehow became very much her dear old Trixie again.

'You'll have to get fixed up.'

Those had been Trixie's first words to Betty when she had confessed to her situation.

Betty had looked at her calmly and with compassion. 'Do you know me so little that you would expect me to do something about my condition?' the look said. 'No question of that now, Trix – I mean Beatrice. Besides, it is not the sort of thing that a girl like me would do, is it?'

Trixie had the grace to blush. She leaned forward, dropping her voice because there were other people in the tea shop, which was continuing to trade despite its blown-in glass door, and its rubble-filled windows, and its notice that said 'OPEN FOR WHAT YOU CAN GET'.

'No, no, not like that, I don't mean that kind of fixed up. No, I mean you'll have to get fixed up with somewhere to live, somewhere you can be peaceful and all that.' She

343

thought for a minute. 'I'll get Miss Caro to root out something for you. You can't stay in London, not now, with the bombs, and needing somewhere to live and whatnot. The air raids will be enough to frighten the poor thing into arriving too early, they will. And you'll have to be married. We'll have to get you a ring and make up a story about your husband being taken prisoner in Singapore or North Africa or somewhere, that's what we'll have to do. Everyone does, you know. Nothing to be ashamed of, truly it's not. There are more so-called married women going around with missing husbands at the moment than there are grains of sand on Bognor beach, and that's the truth.'

Betty sipped at what was little more than a cup of hot water. 'You don't have to do all this for me, Trix, really you don't.'

Trixie put a hot little hand over Betty's larger cool one. 'I know I don't, Betty, but I will and I shall, because you're the best friend anyone can have, and that's the truth.' As Betty looked anywhere except at her, Trixie continued as if the subject was now closed. 'Do you know, if I wasn't having the time of my life with Miss O'Brien, the truth is I would leave London myself now, and go bomb dodging with the rest of the population, truly I would. Miss O'Brien tells me the same, but what can she do? As she says, she can't leave London; she's got a job to do, same as we all have.' She sighed, and looked rueful. 'Just when I have my chance to be a lady, make my way up the ladder, on comes the war, and out comes this job, and I'm back being a ruddy maid again. It's enough to make you weep. Still, it could be worse.'

'Yes, it could be worse. You could be me,' Betty told her sadly.

Trixie put her hand over her friend's hand again, and this time she squeezed it.

'You know what I mean. I had ambitions before the war, and so did you. We wanted to get on, and now look at us! Still, that's war, and no amount of grumbling's going to help. That's one good thing about the sort of people we know from the old days at Chevrons: they can pull strings for us. Not like some, who get abandoned by their folks, or worse. Miss O'Brien'll understand your situation. She'll help us, or I'll want to know the reason why.'

It was a very quick route from Edwina – who brimmed with sympathy for Betty's situation – to Caro, who while being sympathetic to a degree was more practical, and quickly had Betty invited back to Chevrons where, following a telephone call, Trixie's dad had promised she would be loaned a cottage.

'All the evacuees have gone back, said they can't stand the quiet and they're missing their friends,' he told Trixie. 'Betty can have one of their cottages.'

'But what if they come back, Father?'

'I tell you, sure as eggs is eggs those evacuees will not be back. They'd rather be down the Underground playing cards than in the good clean air here. Just can't stand the quiet.'

Trixie didn't say what was up with Betty, only that she was just 'a little unwell'. She was too discreet to explain. Besides, she thought the truth would upset her father, a very conservative gentleman. To say exactly what *was* wrong with Betty might put him off having her at Chevrons, where it had to be faced, he now ruled the roost. When, a little later, he did ask her to elaborate, Trixie hinted that Betty was having a nervous breakdown because of the war generally, and her husband of only a few months had gone missing in the Far East.

'Nervous breakdown my foot,' Smith had said, putting down the telephone and turning round to address the dogs, who were sitting by a meagre fire in the hall. 'Nervous breakdown nothing doing; much more to do with like daughter, like mother – or like mother, like daughter, whichever way round you'd have it. Young Betty's in the straw, mark my words. That's what her coming back to Chevrons is all about. But that is what happens in war. It's not just the dead, it's the living that gets in a muddle during a war, and if that isn't true, then my name's not Raymond Smith.'

But Smith hadn't voiced his suspicions to Mr Garland, for the same reasons that Trixie had not said anything to him. Mr Garland was a gentleman, and Smith did not want to shock him. He merely informed him that Betty Thomas 'needed a rest' and would be coming back to Chevrons to stay in one of the cottages for a while.

'Nice to see Betty again,' Anthony had said absently, and then he returned to his books, which nowadays he never seemed to leave, not even at mealtimes.

It broke Smith's heart to see Mr Garland, of all people, sitting alone with a book propped up against the water decanter, reading, reading, reading as if his life depended on it. In the old days, when Mrs Garland had been alive, the dining room had always been a place of great gaiety, with the two of them laughing and talking the hind legs off several donkeys, but now, the little dining room in the wing was as quiet as the village library, with only the occasional sound of a page being turned, or a book being shut, preparatory to Mr Garland leaving the room.

Now the girls had finally arrived, Smith hoped Chevrons would become a little livelier.

'Ahem,' Smith, alternating between the roles of chauffeur, butler, and even boot boy, had become quite practised at coughing to get attention.

Mr Garland turned slowly, as if he had a permanently stiff neck, which doubtless he did as a result of sitting still and reading for such long hours. Seeing Smith, he picked up one of the small terriers he had adopted and put him on his knee. It had become a habit, as if he wished to guard himself from everyone and everything that was not in a book.

'My Beatrice – ' Smith had been strictly instructed by Trixie to revert to her baptismal name – 'my Beatrice wishes to know what you would like for supper, since she's intent on taking over in the kitchen this evening.'

Anthony gave a wan, sad smile.

'How kind, how very kind,' he said. 'Well, what is there in the kitchen, do you think, Smith?'

His old friend and servant frowned. What there was in the kitchen was chicken, and some lamb shanks, not much more. Gone were the days when the game larder was so stuffed with contents that they had to give away pheasants to the parson, or whoever would take them. Gone were the days when Cook would put a vast leg of lamb on the old spit and he and the others who used to help him could smell it cooking from across the stable yard.

'The daughter was thinking of making an old-fashioned chicken pie, in the old manner. She has found the receipt and is intent on making it.'

'Let her be intent on making it, by all means . . .'

Anthony replaced the terrier on the floor and returned to his book.

But it seemed that Smith was not done with him yet.

'Beatrice, the daughter that is – well, not just her, all of us – we were all wondering if you would like to join us in the kitchen? They had it as a thought that it might be nice for you to come below stairs, just for a change, huggermugger; but they will quite understand if you don't wish to do anything of the sort, and I said as much . . . that I thought you would not want to do anything of the sort, that it might indeed be seen as the thin end of the wedge, and that, Mr Garland.'

Anthony frowned. He was too intelligent not to be aware that he was lonely; too sensitive not to realise that Smith was coping with two young women who were brimming with suggestions with which he probably did not agree. And yet? And yet.

Supper in the kitchen, with the old fire crackling, and the old ranges beaming brightly with the brisk rubbing they received from the maids in the morning. Supper in the kitchen, with eggs from under the hen being washed, and pastry being rolled, and the endless murmuring conversations of the servants as they moved around him, and he a small boy, not bothering to listen, but leaning forward, head cupped in his hands, watching everything, enjoying the privilege of that most splendid of treats – supper in the kitchen.

'I think that would be a perfectly splendid idea. Supper in the kitchen, all huggermugger and cosily warm. Can I bring the dogs?' he finished, the look in his eyes as anxious as when he was a small boy, and Smith and he used to come in from fishing and he would ask the same question of Cook.

'Oh yes, Mr Anthony, bring the dogs. We will be serving at seven thirty.'

'In that case I will bring my whisky and soda down at seven. Haven't been asked to the kitchen for I don't know how long,' he went on nostalgically, and he stood up and left the little dining room, closely followed by the terriers.

Smith stared after him, and then back to the table, because Mr Anthony had left his book at his place.

He went across and shut the book, placing it carefully on the occasional table. If Mr Anthony had forgotten to take his book with him, things were indeed beginning to look up.

In the kitchen Betty sat watching Trixie roll out a very special pastry.

'Butter pastry. There are some things which you forget that you have missed,' Betty sighed. 'I don't know when I last even thought about butter pastry.'

'Can't get margarine on a farm!'

'The new cows in the barn, sheep and the chickens, not to mention the game, are still providing a modest standard of living for everyone at Chevrons, it seems, which is comforting to know,' Betty added drily.

From the moment they had returned to the old house, even with convalescing soldiers in the main rooms, it had seemed to both girls that they were back in the midst of life, not as in London, forever in the midst of death.

'Supper is going to taste like heaven,' Trixie said happily.

Robyn regarded herself in the mirror. For the first time for days she was going out, and not driving someone *else* who was going out. She knew she would enjoy it more than she could say.

She looked at her watch. Bill was late. She lit a cigarette. The list of friends whom they had lost was growing. Perhaps for this reason just waiting for someone was now a sort of martyrdom, because your imagination started to play havoc. Hurry up, Bill. Don't be too long. Make sure you do arrive. Don't you be posted missing too . . .

God knows, and only He did, she had waited long enough for Eddie. Made supper for them both, in the flat, and then she had waited and waited, and waited some more. Drunk some gin, drunk some more gin, before subsiding into the sofa and falling sound asleep, only to be woken by the siren, blast it!

She mustn't do that now. She must not drink too much gin, she must not get tight and fall asleep, just mustn't. She hadn't forgiven herself for falling asleep waiting for Eddie, not that he would have known, but it had created a fierce kind of guilt that lasted for days and days. Eddie not arriving, she asleep, it shouldn't be something that

350

would make you feel guilty, but the truth was that it had, particularly because he hadn't come back, because he had been shot down and taken prisoner, because they had thought they were in love, because . . . well, because if he had come back she might have married him.

She looked at the clock. Still no Bill. Her eyes strayed to the gin bottle. Must keep away from that. She started to walk up and down, once again trying not to think about how many friends they had lost. Only last week three of the bomb disposal boys who occupied the basement flat had been blown up trying to dismantle a bomb in the East End. They were easily recognised, were the bomb disposal boys, Edwina always said. They had a bright-eyed look to them, strangely bright, as if they were anticipating their end long before it came.

'How do they do it? Or rather, why do they do it?' Robyn had asked Caro once or twice, but Caro had had no answer.

Every now and then they had news from Chevrons that Jag and Francis were still alive, although quite how, none of them liked to think, for Italy was not exactly the home of good news for the British Army.

Still when, and if, Bill turned up, he would undoubtedly argue how lucky *he* was, particularly since he had been grounded, shoe-horned into a desk job, which was driving him crackers.

'Losing an eye is no reason not to go on flying a plane, Group Captain Bader was flying one with no legs, for God's sake!'

That he was in love with Robyn was now quite clear to both of them, and since poor Eddie had been shot down over France, and been taken prisoner, Bill, with the youthful ruthlessness that war seemed to bring about, immediately saw that his chances with the tall, long-legged Miss Harding had been greatly increased.

All alone in the London flat, as she so often was, Robyn was finding her thoughts turning to Bill, who was there, rather than poor Eddie, who was not there. Eddie seemed to be more and more unreal, a prisoner of war, a recipient of letters and food parcels, not real the way that Bill was real. However often Robyn could read and reread Eddie's letters, nevertheless he was not a shoulder upon which she could lean, or a chest against which she could place her head. Never mind that Bill was not as handsome as Eddie, at least she could drink with him, joke with him, dance with him.

'Oh, there you are. For God's sake, I thought you would never arrive!'

As soon as she saw Bill standing outside the front door, Robyn threw her cigarettes and lighter into her gas mask case, and ran down the flat stairs to go to dinner, and then to dance, dance, dance the night away, because that's what they all did nowadays. They danced not as if their lives depended on it, but as if their world would end any minute.

'Let's go to the Savoy. Let's dine and dance in the same place, and that'll save a bit of bomb dodging, won't it?'

Robyn nodded. The Savoy had a non-stop cabaret. Nothing seemed able to come between that music, those songs, the dancers, the band.

Cocktails and laughter, and what came after really were all that seemed to matter once they were inside those safe confines, once they were lighting their cigarettes and looking round at the other couples, waving to some, admiring others, quite able to forget everything except the moment, because outside was reality, and who needed that?

They had just been served their first course when there was the most terrific blast from a bomb dropping on the Embankment opposite the hotel, blowing in all the doors and windows.

'Oh, for God's sake, and just when I started my soup,' Robyn protested as she threw herself to the floor.

Bill, who had followed her to the floor, put his arm round her, and there was the usual strange silence that always seemed to follow an explosion, a kind of amazed quiet, followed by noisy relief as they all realised the good old Savoy, famed for its iron girders, was still standing, as everyone believed that it always would be. Eventually, picking themselves up from the floor, to everyone's astonishment, they prepared to resume dining and dancing, quite as if nothing had happened.

It was, after all, just one night, like many that would follow or that had already been, when you might be killed, or the girl or the boy beside you, or the people eating opposite you, and that was why you had to keep on dancing and drinking and laughing, because to stop would be to give in to the enemy, to give in to the idea that you might not win this wretched war.

'The Windmill's not the only place to be able to boast that they never close!' someone nearby shouted out, as the band scrambled back into their places, and everyone laughed.

Back to their table for a much-needed drink, Robyn murmured, 'Light me a cigarette, Bill? Because frankly, I don't know about you, but I could smoke one of my fingers!'

Bill lit one for each of them, after which they looked round at everyone else, and started to laugh weakly, because they were all doing the same thing, and the whole place had become a blasted fog of cigarette smoke.

A young chanteuse grabbed the microphone and started to sing 'A Nightingale Sang in Berkeley Square'.

For some reason for the first time in her life Robyn started really to listen to the words of the song, and as she did – as the song sang out of young love and a certain night when love and kissing was all that was on anyone's mind – for the first time since she had climbed into uniform she had the feeling that she was going to give way.

Perhaps it was because it had been, might still be, one of Eddie's favourite songs. He had played it over and over again, whenever possible. That was one of Eddie's most endearing characteristics – when he loved, he loved to shreds. A song, a poem, didn't matter how often he heard it or quoted it, if he loved something or someone, it could never be enough for him.

Bill looked across the table at Robyn. He must have sensed what she was feeling because he put a hand over hers.

'Come on kid, back on the floor. This is one of my favourites.'

Robyn followed him and as they danced she forgot that there was anyone in the room except herself and Bill. She could see other couples dancing, other couples clinging to each other, singing and dancing, clinging and smiling, laughing, kissing, one or two, quickly, between everything else that was happening, and yet she was certain there was only herself and Bill, not just on the floor, but in the world. She frowned. Where were all the other people? She could see them, and yet they weren't there.

'Bill—'

He held her away from him. He was dark haired and even featured, his eye patch actually succeeding in making him appear even more masculine.

Robyn leaned forward and murmured, 'Let's go back to the flat and make love?'

For once in his life Bill found he could think of nothing to say and, seeing this, Robyn at once burst out laughing.

'What is so funny, Miss Harding?' Bill asked eventually, knowing exactly.

When Robyn was able to speak she said, 'It's just your face. I don't think I've ever seen you silenced before!'

Bill caught her hand, and pulled her after him.

'Come on, before some blasted bomb puts an end to us and the evening.'

Caro turned away from Walter.

Walter put a hand to her head, stroking her long hair down over her shoulders, making his fingers into a comb as he did so, and then again, and again.

'I will fetch you a cup of tea,' he whispered, and he slipped from the bed.

Caro turned, but only momentarily.

'Coffee, anything but tea, not tea.'

Walter made two cups of chicory-smelling coffee. It was all he could find. No more pure coffee left. He felt exhilarated, but knew that Lucky felt less than the same.

He took the cups back carefully on a tray, and he placed the tray on the bedside table. Caro sat up eventually and, pulling the curtain beside the bed a little open, she saw that dawn was breaking.

'I wonder why people say dawn is "breaking",' she murmured, sitting back against a tier of pillows that he had just arranged for her, and holding the sheet up against her body in a gesture of belated modesty.

'Because the advent of dawn breaks up the dark sky of night,' her painter lover told her, as he slipped in beside her.

The bed was too narrow, but that was not why Caro moved away from him.

'You're not happy,' he said, stating the obvious.

She looked at him, silent, her eyes large with veiled accusation, before she picked up the cup of coffee he was offering her and sipped at the hot sweet mixture he had made of condensed milk and strangely diluted coffee.

'Why aren't you happy, Lucky?'

'Because,' she stated in a dull voice, 'I do not believe that you love me. I suppose that is why I am not happy.'

Walter stepped out of his side of the bed, pulling a counterpane around his nakedness, throwing the spare bit over his shoulder, as if it were a toga.

'Why do you think I don't love you when we have just made love, Lucky? Do you think we could make love like that if I didn't love you?'

Caro turned once more away from him on her pillow.

'Oh, you know – it's war. Everyone seems to be making love *because* there's a war on. Love is being made quite as often as war, and for all the wrong reasons.'

'War is wrong, love isn't.'

Caro sighed. She would never say what was foremost in her mind, would never say to Walter, 'You made love to me as second-best; it's Katherine you really want. You want my Hitler-worshipping sister – that is who or what you want, Mr Walter Beresford.'

Walter put a hand once more to her head, but he didn't stroke or comb her hair.

'Love is very difficult, *particularly* in war,' he told her in a tender voice. 'But believe me—'

'Why should I?' came the interruption.

'Believe me,' he insisted. 'I am in love with you. I couldn't make love to you, we couldn't make love the way we just have if I wasn't in love with you, and if you weren't in love with me. We fused, didn't we?'

'I don't know. I've never made love before. You tell me. No, don't tell me.'

Caro sprang out of bed, and catching up a dressing gown she started to leave the room.

'Where are you going?'

'I'm going to have a wash, because you certainly couldn't call it a bath . . .'

Walter put his hands behind his head and stared ahead of him, coughing slightly as he did so. Too many blasted cigarettes had given him some kind of infection. He sighed. He would be gone soon to the North Sea, paints and pencils with him, to join the convoys making their way across icy seas, running much-needed supplies back and forth between the mines, and the submarines, gone to record the courage and the bravery of the men who went unremarked, and perhaps, even like himself at that moment, unloved?

Caro bumped into Robyn outside her bedroom door. It seemed that Robyn was also heading for the bathroom.

'Sorry, sail before steam, Caro.'

Caro looked at Robyn, her head on one side, determined to remain unflustered, unembarrassed, and nearly succeeding.

'And by that you mean . . . ?'

'I am a beautiful sailing ship, that's what I mean!'

Robyn laughed. Unlike Caro, she looked exhilarated, as if she had just made a discovery.

'And I am a . . . I am a . . . ?'

'That I will not answer. I treasure my life too much!'

Caro could see the outline of Bill's body in Robyn's bed through the open door. So that was what was happening, and perhaps that was why Robyn was looking energetic, beautiful, and bubbling with life.

She took Robyn by her naked arm and drew her into the kitchen.

'What are we doing?' she asked her in a low voice. 'I mean, what have we come to? Let us ask ourselves. We're meant to be nice girls, and look at us!'

'How do you mean?' Robyn looked genuinely puzzled.

'What would . . .' Caro searched for a suitable name, avoided her own mother, and then plumped for someone close to Robyn. 'What would *Aunt Cicely* say if she suddenly came into the flat now, Robyn?'

The very idea momentarily startled her companion. She put out a kindly hand and laid it on Caro's bare shoulder.

'"Caro, calm down. This is war." That is what she would say.'

Caro looked up at Robyn, who suddenly seemed taller than ever.

'What? I mean, do you really think so?' she asked, frowning, but only after a long, long pause, during which Robyn made sure to keep the expression in her eyes both calming and understanding.

'Of course. Aunt Cicely's been through two wars already. What do you think she was during two wars, a vestal virgin? Of course not. She must have fallen in love, and certainly I know men fell in love with her. The past is not what we think it is, not ever.' Robyn leaned forward and touched Caro lightly on the shoulder. 'The past is full of secrets, and that is how it should stay, but people are not saints – why should they be? Why should the older generation be any different from us? Do you honestly think they were?'

'Well, no, I don't know, truly I don't. I always thought the older generation, well . . .' Caro nodded her head one way, then the other, the movement taking in both the bedrooms and, by implication, both the males in the bed-rooms, in their beds. 'I always thought they all waited, people like Aunt Cicely, until they were married.'

'Aunt Cicely never married!'

Caro smiled suddenly. She felt comforted and at the same time a little disillusioned, as if she had in some way been deceived, or had been deceiving herself.

'Oh, I see what you mean. At least I think I do. You mean things happened then too, but no one talked about it?'

'Of course, ducks. Human beings are human beings. Now I must go. I am going to be hours late even if I hurry.' Robyn leaned forward and chucked Caro under the chin as if she were a child who needed cheering up. 'Don't think too much,' she advised. 'Not too good at a time like this. Keep all thoughts for later, when we've won the war, and all that. Now I'm having first splash, so get out of my way.'

Caro turned back to her room. Walter was still lying across the pillows, both sets, as if in her absence he had taken possession of her half of the bed and claimed it.

Caro climbed back into bed again, and they started to make love once more.

Anthony looked at Smith and smiled, and then he smiled round at the two girls. He didn't realise it but it was the first time he had really smiled since Meriel had been killed.

'Thank you so much. Truly, thank you. That was a really happy evening,' he said, and he shook the girls' hands as if he was a head teacher, and they were pupils at a prize giving, before leaving the kitchen, closely followed by his terriers.

'He enjoyed himself for once,' Smith told Trixie. 'I haven't seen him enjoy anything since Mrs Garland was taken from us so suddenly. The shock, you know, that as much as anything was enough to make him fold his tent and put away his character. But tonight, well, tonight he almost seemed himself again.'

'I can see what you mean,' Trixie said with some satis-faction.

'To give you an example, that's the first time I've seen him eat anything without a book propped up against the water carafe.' Smith started to clear away the plates one by one, in the accepted manner. 'And he ate everything, which is another miracle. Developed the appetite of a bird, he has, since Mrs Garland went. Like doves, they were. So close that they could have been a pair of doves. And you know what?' He paused to add water from the kettle to the tepid water at the old kitchen sink, filling up the washing-up basin. 'When doves mate, they mate for ever. And when one of them goes, the other shortly follows, and that is the truth.' He swirled the water in the basin with one of his large red hands. 'I too would have liked to have gone when Beatrice's mother was taken from me, but I couldn't, could I, not with the little one relying on me? But if it hadn't been for the baby, I would have liked to have gone.'

He started to put the plates, one by one, carefully in the soapy water. He washed each with all the care that he must have taken over his baby girl, and then he let the water out and rinsed each plate in the fresh water he had drawn.

Trixie watched him. He had always done ordinary tasks meticulously and with concentration, because he believed in doing everything the right way, and that there was only one way to do it: by the book.

She picked up an immaculately laundered tea towel, and started to dry the rinsed plate being held out to her, and as she did so she felt as if she was four, or would it be five, standing on a small wooden stool, helping her father, and he was saying, 'There's only one way to wash a plate. First you rinse it, and then you soap it, and then you rinse it again, and then you wipe it with a clean cloth.'

Although there were three of them to do it, the washing-up took more than an hour, what with the soaping and the rinsing and the drying, and the boiling of kettles to make hot water. Betty made conversation with Trixie's father while Trixie ploughed on with her thoughts that life at The Place was really one long party compared to Chevrons in wartime.

Of course Mr Garland had been right, it had been a very happy evening, but even so, glad though Trixie was that Betty would be looked after, glad that they had all thought up a good story about her missing husband, and even bought her an engagement and a wedding ring, Trixie was even gladder that she would be leaving Chevrons the following morning.

It was disappointing, but though she loved the old place, and although it was as much her childhood home as it was that of the Garland boys and girls, she was only too aware that being home, being with her father again, was making her feel shut in. At Chevrons she was still the chauffeur's daughter; up there at The Place, although still a maid, she was also someone else.

She was 'Beatrice' the personal maid, but she was also the ears and eyes of the place. She was Miss O'Brien's shadow, the person upon whom she relied, her best friend. They laid plans and made schemes together, they laughed and cried together – cried when the bad news came, laughed when Miss O'Brien brought off one of what she called her 'trickeries', which meant that the colonel was left purring with delight and not a little quiet pride. The colonel liked success, Trixie could see that.

Of course, given Miss O'Brien's stunning looks, the success of her schemes always and inevitably involved men. That was the point of her having a salon. Miss O'Brien was there to do, as she called it, her 'Mata O'Hari'. A little too much to drink, a little too much to eat, a little something in their whiskies, and when the men woke up in the morning, they could only remember pleasure, not sedition.

'The silly eejits think they've been in the arms of an Irish witch all night, which of course they haven't, but don't they always leave kissing the tips of their fingers to me, and with a look to their eyes like they've just lain with Helen of Troy herself. If only they all knew that I am really and truly a nun at heart!'

However, unless and until Edwina joined a convent, it seemed that they were all succeeding admirably in the task that they had been set by the colonel, which was, principally, the dissemination of wrong information, an essential part of defence work, and a very subtle one.

It was not just that Miss O'Brien was now a well-known beauty maintaining a much-graced salon, but to the apartment at The Place also came many others who were not guests, and here the kitchen played a vital role. Mrs Cherry cheerfully gave away 'secrets' to drivers and chauffeurs, all of whom reported back to their bosses such tasty items as that Mr Churchill had lost his mind and Mr Attlee had to stand in for him most of the time; that the British had run out of bombs; that there were no more Hurricanes or Spitfires to fly; that they were going to stop night bombing; that the King was dying and the Queen having an affair with Anthony Eden.

'All jolly good stuff,' the colonel said to Edwina one day. 'But the most important rumour is to come, and when it does come, no one will be privy to this particular piece of misinformation except you and me, and two others. That is all.'

Edwina had felt both flattered and horrified, but had the good sense not to question the colonel any further. Besides, she had other things on her mind at that moment. Robert was missing.

Following their reunion dinner at Chevrons, and, as Trixie joked with Betty, worn out from all that unaccustomed washing-up, both girls slept in the following morning.

'Good God, is that really the time? I shall miss whatever train is not going to arrive!'

Trixie hurled on her clothes, then snatched at her overnight bag. Her father would be champing at the bit, waiting to take her to the station in the old Austin 7.

'I won't bother with breakfast,' she told Betty, not because she didn't want any but because she knew that the smell of cooking and coffee and all that in the morning made Betty feel ill.

She stopped by the front door of the cottage. Betty was seated at a small table looking so forlorn that, despite the hurry she was in, Trixie was forced to hesitate before lifting the latch.

'Been sick again, have you?' she asked kindly.

'Yes,' Betty admitted. 'I have been sick, quite a lot really.'

'It will go. It will pass soon.'

Trixie knew that this was far from being the case, but what was the point of saying as much to Betty?

She pulled on her coat. 'Look, Betty, I know it's not much, being here, the cottage and that, but it's all we could think of, isn't it? I mean, it's the best we could do, and maybe we will come up with something better, but you've had to leave your job, and there's no point staying in London with the air raids and whatnot. Well, it wouldn't be good for either of you, would it?'

Betty shook her head in agreement, and then, to Trixie's horror, she leaned forward and, putting her head on the table in front of her, started to cry.

'I don't want you to go. I don't want you to leave me, Trix. I feel so lonely already.'

They both knew that she was feeling as she had at the orphanage: alone, no one to help her cope, friendless, without family.

'I told you, Father will look in on you from time to time, and you can go up to the house and eat in the kitchen with him.' Trixie looked helplessly at the dark head, the hands covering the face. 'I wish I didn't have to go,' she said, lying. 'Truly, I do. But Miss O'Brien needs me for everything. She can't do her work without me, and some of it is quite vital, although you wouldn't think so to look at the way we go on.'

Betty straightened up. 'Of course you must go,' she agreed. 'I'll be all right. You've been so good to me. But . . . but I – I feel so afraid, somehow.'

'Don't be. Everything will be all right, you'll see. And I'll come and visit as often as I can.'

Betty wiped her eyes on a tea cloth, and followed Trixie to the door.

'Yes, I know you will,' she agreed, also lying. 'But, but one thing, Trix?'

Trixie turned at the door.

'Yes?'

'How are we going to cope with my husband? I mean, when shall I get the bad news that he's been killed? I don't know what to do about that.'

'I'll let you know. Don't you worry, Miss O'Brien will think of something. She's a wizard at that kind of thing, or I should say Irish witch, really.'

They bumped cheeks.

'Try to keep zipped, as Mr Fleming would say.'

Betty nodded. 'Of course. Sorry, I was just being silly.'

'No, you weren't. Understandable, really. After all, you've never had a baby before, but I believe when it gets nearer the time you will feel much better, and then Father will fetch the doctor and all that. You know, he has promised.'

Betty tried to smile. 'Off you go,' she told Trixie. 'He'll be waiting to take you to the train.'

She waited until she could no longer hear Trixie's high-heeled shoes crunching across the gravel, and then clattering on to the path that led back to the main house. Then she went back to the kitchen table and, putting her head in her hands, she started to cry once more. She sobbed until she could cry no more, and then she lay down on the bed and fell fast asleep, only waking when daylight was fading.

Edwina looked at Trixie, and said nothing for a minute or two.

'I don't know who can help you with that kind of thing,' she admitted, before turning back to the bed where Trixie had laid out an exquisite evening two-piece consisting of black trousers and a white embroidered jacket sparkling with tiny false diamonds and jet beads. 'The colonel would be the only person who might be able to help you,' she went on in a much lower voice. 'He does false passports and suchlike things. But I can't ask him. You'll have to ask him. He'll start thinking wrong things if I ask him, start thinking I'm asking for one for myself. You know the way people do: "My *friend* would like a false driving licence."'

Trixie held up the evening jacket, searching it for the slightest imperfection, and finding none she waited until Miss O'Brien had stepped into the evening trousers.

'To think that no one would speak to you if you wore slacks before the war,' Edwina murmured. 'And now look at us. No one will speak to us if we don't.'

'It's not quite come to that yet.' Then returning to her original subject, Trixie said, 'We won't need the telegram for quite a few months.'

'Best to wait until there's a dust-up somewhere, and then kill him off,' Edwina said absently. 'Although why Betty can't just say she's lost him and that's that, I don't know.'

'It's a small village where Betty is. No one would help

her if they knew . . . you know. And it's not what you could call salubrious, is it, Miss O'Brien, having a little baby with someone you'll never see again?'

Edwina looked quizzical. 'Absolutely not, no, I don't suppose it is; but then war's not exactly salubrious either, is it?'

'No war is a dirty business, I agree, Miss O'Brien. Now sit down at your dressing table while I arrange your necklace for you.'

Trixie placed the brilliant piece around Edwina's neck, and as she did so she thought of Miss Katherine and her long, swanlike neck, and she thought of how much they all hated her now, and how she had betrayed her country. She hoped that what they were doing was right, bombing and bombing and more bombing, laying waste everything that lay between them and victory, and she couldn't help hoping that one of the bombs had hit Katherine Garland.

Marie-Christine stared at Katherine. She understood exactly what she was saying, she appreciated exactly why she was saying it, but she wished to heavens she did not have to hear it.

'Of course this one will be different,' she agreed, shrugging her shoulders. 'But of course. And I understand for you there is only one way, and that is forward, and more, and more forward. You have been so much on these short missions, but now you must take on something much bigger, of *course*.'

'And you – you will be all right?'

'Why not?' The words came out too forcefully and yet

368

why wouldn't they? 'This is a place I love.' This was a place they both loved, a place where they had spent long summers before the war. Marie-Christine went to speak again, but Katherine put a hand on her arm.

'The Boche—'

'The Boche will not come here. Besides, I will take care that the children stay in during the day, while I go to market. They can play games in the evenings in the old barn.' She shrugged her shoulders a little helplessly. 'Not even the postman comes here, not any more.'

'It is good you know nothing.'

'Of course. I know nothing.'

'And whatever happens, I want you to know I'll be all right. Really.'

Katherine turned on her heel, and at once became someone else, adopting a different walk, a frowning worried demeanour, her back a little stooped, her prop an ancient bicycle. Marie-Christine had worked hard to make Katherine look as close as possible to a photograph, which, together with new papers, Marie-Christine had found for her. Dark hair pulled back, a pair of tin spectacles, a woollen floral scarf tied in the French manner, a wide skirt – fashionable circa 1924 – and a pair of heavy walking shoes completed the spinster look. The new papers were of course forged, but then that had been Marie-Christine's speciality. 'And to think I used to want to be a great painter like Berthe Morisot!' she had joked as she had completed the papers with her usual care.

Now she did not joke but watched her companion in arms, her friend of many years, walk off down the narrow grass path that led to the forest, pushing the old bike in front of her, head bent.

Mademoiselle Chantelle Thubron was on her way.

God go with her, and if not God, then at least her patron saint, Marie-Christine prayed.

She turned back to the house. It was time to start digging vegetables. Thanks to old Jacques they had enough growing around the place to make soup of every kind for many weeks. She should not think of what might happen, perhaps inevitably would happen, to Katherine. She must think only of the children in her charge. It was up to her to see that they remained safe at the farm, and that was going to be hard enough. Katherine she could only pray for.

Chapter Twelve

The elegantly dressed Italian gentleman was besotted with Miss O'Brien, but although he was anti Mussolini, and had a reputation for being more than trustworthy, he was fast becoming what Mr Fleming called 'a social nuisance' to his mistress, and neither Mr Fleming, nor Trixie, appreciated that.

The worry was that Miss Edwina, as they all now called her, had fallen into the habit of allowing him to stay too late. It was up to Trixie to make sure that he did finally leave, employing whatever ruse came to mind.

Trixie already knew that even if this Roberto creature had not, as yet, proved useful to their cause, the same could not be said of his chauffeur. Mr Fleming with his usual ruthlessness had already used the chauffeur to disseminate some really rather ripe little mistruths about the war situation – a rumour about cessation of night bombing over Germany, and many more similar lies – so for that reason alone it had been well worth entertaining the driver's employer. What was not all right was that it was quite evident that Miss Edwina was now drinking too much, and staying up far too late – and far too often in the company of the said Italian gentleman.

Tonight when Trixie went to help her undress Edwina was once more half seas over, and Signor Roberto had only just been persuaded to leave the flat, by dint of his chauffeur's joining forces with the staff to ship him off – not an easy task since he too was what Mr Fleming discreetly called 'far from better'.

To Trixie's irritation, she found Edwina, still fully dressed, lying on her vast bed, her copper-coloured hair spread about the stack of linen pillows, looking up at the ceiling, an expression of vague despair on her face.

'Will the war never end? I'm getting tired, so tired.'

Trixie stared down at her. She would have liked to have thrown a glass of water at her, because that would sober her up all right. The only reason Trixie didn't actually do that was because she didn't want to stain the Chinese wallpaper behind the bed. She finally settled for pulling off Edwina's evening shoes a little too roughly to be polite, but even that had no effect.

'It's the noise, and the news, and more noise, and more news.'

Trixie propped Edwina up in a sitting position and started to undo the buttons on her dress.

'You're not the only one in the war, you know, in case you hadn't noticed, Miss Edwina? And war or no war, what you're doing to yourself isn't helping you – or, for that matter, the war either.'

'What about you, dotey? Aren't you feeling a mite banjaxed by the war, Trixie, dotey?'

'I might be. On the other hand, I might not be,'

Trixie stated tersely. 'If you ask me,' she went on, at last whisking Edwina's evening dress away, 'most people have given up thinking about it at all. Most of us have taken to the idea that either our name is on a bomb or it's not on it, and that's all there is to it. Mr Fleming says that hardly anyone even bothers with their Anderson shelter any more, and the numbers down the Underground are halved. So, if that's what you mean by being tired of the war, it's true. People *have* got tired. They've got tired of feeling afraid. They know that it's all about luck, and nothing else, just luck.'

She handed Edwina her wrap, while actually wanting to throw it at her. There was something so *irritating* about people when they were one over the eight, like her father at Christmas after he'd finished serving their lunch, or Cook at Chevrons on any Saturday evening after a hard week catering for everyone.

Edwina pulled on her wrap slowly, oh so slowly. Whether or not Trixie was right, and the people had stopped being afraid and become resigned, everyone she knew was moving about London, either from St James's to Chelsea, or from Chelsea to Belgravia, in a kind of mad dance to get away from the gaping windows, the shrapnel marks on the buildings, the sight of twisted car wrecks in the middle of streets.

Horror stories abounded, of course. She tried not to listen, but somehow, between the sirens, and the fires, and the crump, crump, crump of the guns, they got through to her. People who you'd been having a jolly with the night before, blown to extinction, nothing left of them except an earring or a cap. The hall porter

373

downstairs – gone to visit his mother, her house blown out and nothing left of anything.

'Let's get our makeup off now, shall we, Miss Edwina?'

Edwina nodded. Standing up, she went obediently to her dressing table and sat down in front of the mirror.

'I look terrible,' she complained.

'You'll look better for a good night's sleep,' Trixie told her, without changing the brisk tone she had chosen to adopt.

'Yes, you're right, Smith, dotey.'

Shortly afterwards Edwina climbed into bed, and Trixie tucked her up tightly as if she were a child and she wanted to make sure she felt secure.

'Goodnight,' she called from the door, switching off the light.

'Goodnight,' came a small voice from the bed.

Trixie closed the door, and then waited, as she had recently become accustomed to doing. A few seconds later came the sound of sobbing. Trixie shook her head and sighed. It had been the same every night for the past weeks, ever since Captain Robert had been posted missing.

The following night, Roberto-the-all-too-eager, as he was known in the kitchen, stayed so late, and there was such a long silence in the drawing room, that Trixie went through to Mr Fleming.

'What shall I do?' Trixie whispered, taking him aside.

'Cause an upset,' Mr Fleming told her, in a low voice.

'Telephone call?'

'Anything.'

He crossed his eyes at Trixie behind the chauffeur's back.

Trixie managed to keep a straight face, and went out of the room to the hall where there was a cupboard fitted with a number of different telephones, official and unofficial, while Mr Fleming turned back to the chauffeur.

'I say, old boy, I've suddenly remembered that tomorrow is your birthday, isn't it? I'm sure you want to get back to your wife, don't you?'

The chauffeur put out his cigarette and nodded, surprised.

'Signor Fleming! 'Ow did you know it was my birthday?'

Mr Fleming managed to look both patronising and benevolent at the same time. It was a ridiculous question. Of course he knew it was the chauffeur's birthday. He didn't just look up someone's personal file, he memorised it too. He made it his business to know everything about everyone who came to the flat, even the delivery men – most especially the delivery men, most especially if they were new delivery men, however old, and however tired from the bombing and the lack of sleep.

'Scribble your master something to the effect that you have just heard that there is someone coming round to see him at midnight – on urgent business,' Mr Fleming, at his most dangerously benevolent, instructed the chauffeur.

'And when there is no one there, when the boss discovers I am making a false excuse, I am a dead man, no?'

Mr Fleming smiled. 'There will be someone there,' he stated.

Trixie, who had returned to witness the last part of the conversation never really liked it when Mr Fleming smiled. Mr Fleming was not a man to cross, Mrs Cherry always said, but then Mrs Cherry was not a woman to cross either. Miss Edwina had once confided to Trixie that Mrs Cherry had told her that she knew more about poisons than Trixie knew about herself. Trixie remembered this, especially when the cook was in a bad mood and making some of her foreign-sounding sauces.

'It was a pity Roberto had to go so early,' Edwina moaned later, if anything, even more drunkenly than the night before, as Trixie once more set about helping her undress.

Trixie raised her eyes to heaven. Women, and men, her father had told her many times, so often fell for the same *name*. You would think it would occur to them at some point that someone of the same name was not the same person – but no, apparently not. So Captain *Robert* Plume had been substituted in Edwina's affections by a *Roberto* – although the two men must have been as unalike as it was possible to imagine.

'You're getting like the gamekeeper at Chevrons,' Trixie told Edwina, as she hung up her dress for her.

'And what was wrong with him? Did he also drink too much?'

Before she climbed into bed Edwina drained the glass of water by the side. Trixie replenished the glass from the water carafe, before going back to the dressing table, and taking all the necessaries to remove Edwina's makeup.

Then she sat on the side of the bed and tried to apply cream to Edwina's face, which was not easy, since she kept sliding down the pillows.

'Sit up.'

'No . . .'

'Sit up.'

'No, why?'

'I don't want you getting lipstick on that pillowcase, Miss Edwina. It'll never come out.'

Edwina finally lay back against the pillows, cleansed but not sober, and Trixie sighed inwardly. Miss Edwina was getting like this far too often. She needed to brace up, and shut up. Or, if that were not possible, she needed to have a change. Something must be done.

Edwina opened her eyes and stared blearily at Trixie.

'What was it that you were saying that I was like, did you say, Smith?'

'I said you've got . . . you have become like the game-keeper at Chevrons,' Trixie told her, her voice raised, as if she was talking to a child. 'He had seven different dogs, but they were all called Mike.'

Edwina frowned.

'I don't have any dogs, and I don't know any Mikes, not any more, anyway. Except I did know Mike Darlington, but he was killed in North Africa; and I knew Mike Partridge, but he was shot down over France, right at the beginning of the war. So I can't be like whoever it is that you think I'm like, this person who likes Mikes, because all mine are dead.'

Trixie wanted to say, 'Oh, do shut up and go to sleep' but instead she merely put out the pink-shaded lights on the dressing table, and carried on lecturing Edwina as if she hadn't spoken, because that was the effect drunkards had on you: you kept on talking *at* them, and in a raised voice, as if they were deaf.

'No, what I am saying, Miss Edwina, is that you've got yourself in a confusion over this missing Captain Robert, and now you're convincing yourself that you should fall for this Signor Roberto, but only because he has the same name – except it's in Italian, of course. What you need to do is to realise that a name is only a name, the way the gamekeeper at Chevrons never did, if you know what I mean? You need to understand that Captain Robert and this Signor Roberto are nothing like each other, any more than the gamekeeper's dogs were alike. Anyway, who's to say that Captain Robert *isn't* going to come back to you? He's only been reported *missing*, not dead, Miss Edwina.'

Trixie sighed and started neatly to replace the precious makeup removal items in their small basket. So many of the items were impossible to get now, unless you were lucky enough to know a smuggler, or a black marketeer.

She looked down at Edwina, and a very beautiful sight she was, even when she was tight. Judging from the amount she had drunk, she would soon be asleep, and would not wake until morning, thank the Lord, and pass the butter – if you could find any.

Trixie tottered off to her own room, a pristine little place, set quite apart from the rest of the flat, hidden behind the kitchens. She shut the door, leaned against it and sighed with gratitude. She was always glad to enter her little kingdom, for with its flowered wallpaper and old oak furniture, it had a strangely countrified air. It reminded her of her room at her father's cottage, what with its framed picture of *The Light of the World*, and its patchwork quilt of many colours. She undressed, brushed out her thick curly hair, and climbed thankfully into the narrow bed.

Trixie was wrong about Edwina. Drunk or not, this particular night she did not fall asleep straight after Trixie had turned out the lights. She lay staring into the darkness. Trixie's words had been said without either rancour or sentiment. They had been plain words, crisp words, words that had not pierced her heart, but given her hope. It was true. Robert *had* only been posted missing. He *might* not be dead.

What was it they all said nowadays when they parted? 'Expect you when I see you.' That's what she had to say to herself. She must expect *to* see Robert, not expect *not* to see him.

She turned over on her pillow and, after giving a large and heartfelt sigh, she, like Trixie, was soon fast asleep.

Colonel Atkins looked across the table at Edwina.

'You've done well, O'Brien,' he said kindly, 'so well, that the powers that be,' by which of course he meant himself and Max, 'think it would do you good to have a change for a few weeks.'

Edwina frowned. She liked her apartment, and she liked all the people she had met, most particularly Roberto, though for some reason he had not telephoned her the morning after he had left her, and not the morning after that. Not that she had found that she was missing him in the least, for with the thought that Robert might still be in the world came the thought that Roberto was not what she wanted. A person could have enough of flattery.

'Where were you thinking of sending me, you and the powers that be, Colonel, dotey?'

'We were thinking somewhere quite different, a complete change of scene.'

'So you just said, but may I know my fate?' Edwina leaned forward and whispered dramatically, 'Could you not write it on the napkin and I will swallow the information with my rissole?'

'We were thinking a few weeks in the country first of all, but then we thought by the sea would make a nice change. Somewhere you can rest up a little, put the war behind you. It's been non-stop for you, after all, a bit of a jazz-age rhythm to your life, which might need to be set aside for a couple of weeks.'

He put down his glass and stared at Edwina with interest. Trixie had told him what a handful she had been over the past weeks, but what she had not said, indeed was too kind to state, was that Miss Carrots had rather lost her beautiful looks. Too much good living was bad for a girl's complexion. If he and Max's plans were to succeed, and they both knew they had to, then he needed Edwina on tiptop form, not pallid as a peeled potato, lines under her eyes, a weary tone to her voice. He needed her as glossy and gorgeous as a favourite for the Derby.

'I know. You must feel sorry for me! Everyone must

drip tears at my predicament.' Edwina's laugh was just a little shrill. 'Non-stop food and drink, non-stop entertaining, non-stop cocktails and laughter. Dear, oh dear, and to think I could be out there having fun, and more fun on the convoys! Or in Italy. *Saach* fun, the hills beyond Rome, doncher know?'

Colonel Atkins smiled. 'My dear, you can mock my concern for you, but one of the most important moments in the war is about to occur, not just the turning point, but the actual point, and you will have your part to play in the drama. For this I want you fit and well, not tired. You have to be fit, fit, fit for battle, for upon you and a few others will rest the outcome of something so big that if we last for a thousand years, the world will say not that this was our finest hour, but our most dangerous. If this fails, fighting this war will have been for nothing.'

Edwina stared at him.

'Am I to be dropped into France?' she asked, a little flippantly but also a little fearfully. 'Because if I am, I think you should know, Colonel, dotey, that parachuting is not quite my *métier*.'

'No, no, nothing like that. Of course not. No, what we are going to do is to give out to all your contacts – everyone who has ever been entertained at the flat – that you are going to the country for a few weeks of fresh air. You have a nasty cough, which needs ozone, sea air, that sort of thing. When you come back the party will resume, of course, and by that time you will be as fresh as the proverbial daisy.' He smiled. 'As a matter of fact I envy you, going where you're going.'

'I shan't guess, but I think I will probably be able

381

to. No second language needed, I take it? No need for Baedeker's guide to the ancient cities of Europe.'

'I haven't said a word . . .'

'And I haven't said yes yet, Colonel, dotey.'

'Oh, but you will,' the colonel told her in a firm voice. 'I know you will. You're too sensible not to.'

He was quite right, of course. Edwina *was* too sensible to say no to such a proposition. Besides, she had felt that she had grown so stale of late, all the time feeling as if she was some kind of smart shopping bag with the shop's name emblazoned in gold on the side, and nothing inside. She needed to be somewhere else, somewhere quite different. She needed to *feel* different.

'I wish you could come with me,' she said to Trixie the following morning, as they packed a suitcase for her.

'Oh no, you don't,' Trixie told her, smiling. 'Besides, you need a clean break. You need new people around you, people who aren't making the same old sound in the same old way. A good belt of sea air will do you the world of good.'

'I will miss your snooty English ways, Beatrice Smith,' Edwina said, for once quite serious, and she seized Trixie's hands and shook them up and down as a child might before starting a game.

'Get on with you.'

'Get on with you too,' Edwina rejoined, and she hugged Trixie because it was Trixie's words that had brought Edwina back to life as it should be lived, in hope.

'It's very kind of you to think of me, but I don't want to go anywhere at the moment. I want to stay here with Mr Fleming and Mrs Cherry. I want to be right here in London when we hear the news that Hitler's been hanged, drawn and quartered, except that would be too good for him, wouldn't it?'

'Well, you're probably right, but sitting by the sea with no one to boss me I shall feel like Sally No Friends, and that's the truth.'

Edwina turned away, as Trixie picked up her suitcase, and then went to answer the door to the colonel, who had arrived to drive Edwina to Sussex.

'Ah, good morning, Miss Smith.' The colonel looked appreciatively at Trixie. 'Do you know, every time I say that I feel as if I am using a pseudonym for you?' he confessed.

'Well, you would,' Trixie agreed, smiling.

As he kicked his heels in the drawing room, waiting for Edwina to appear, the colonel found himself staring at Trixie, who was checking the flowers, the glasses and drinks on the side table, in fact just about everything in the room, to make sure it was as perfect as possible, something of which – since he had been the *force motif* behind the furnishing of it – the colonel could only approve.

He watched the young woman in a charmed kind of way as she moved about. Dark-haired and slim, in her own way Trixie Smith, although she did not possess the beauty of Edwina O'Brien, was a very pretty girl. Mentally he removed her maid's uniform – in the nicest possible way, of course – and dressed her instead in the kind of wardrobe that he had provided for Edwina.

'Miss Smith?'

Trixie turned as she went back to Edwina's bedroom, where she knew she would be still dawdling in front of the mirror – keeping 'Irish time' as Trixie now called it, because Mr Fleming had told her that the Irish had a different sense of time from everyone else, based on thousands of years of playing music, listening to stories, and making sense of the world with a pint of Guinness and a pipe.

'Yes, Colonel Atkins?'

'I wonder if you would care to come and see me tomorrow?'

'Certainly, Colonel, if that is what you want.'

He produced a card from his wallet.

'Make it early, and then we can really get down to business.'

Trixie looked from the card to him, and back again. She had noted some time ago that the colonel was a very handsome man.

'Will there be other people there?' she asked, just a little sharply.

'Of course. My colleagues will want to be there for your briefing,' he said in a reassuring tone.

'Really?' Trixie managed to look innocent. 'That's a pity, then.' She turned away.

'We could have lunch afterwards, of course.'

She turned back. 'That sounds more like it.'

Trixie left the room smiling. Really, men like Colonel Atkins were so easy to see through.

Inside the drawing room, the colonel too turned away and in doing so caught sight of himself in the mirror. He too was smiling.

*　　*　　*

It seemed that the colonel had found Edwina a cottage by the sea, on an old Edwardian estate, once frequented by crowned heads. It was small and cosy, and furnished with dark oak and bright fittings that owed everything to someone of taste.

'How delightful, Colonel, dotey,' Edwina said. 'And how beautifully furnished, how tasteful, how perfect in every degree.'

'Yes, it is pretty,' he agreed. 'Now you'll be all right, because there's a maid that comes every day, and she will bring you whatever you want. But meanwhile, there is a pie in the Frigidaire and gin on the drinks table, and so on. Everything you need for the first twenty-four to forty-eight hours, at any rate.'

Edwina leaned forward and kissed him on the cheek.

'I never realised how tired I had become,' she told him, suddenly serious. 'But now I'm here, I do. I am so tired, I think I shall spend the whole of the next week sleeping.'

The colonel smiled. 'You can drop me back at the station, and then take the car on from there. You have a special petrol allowance, which I don't expect you to need. There are shops within walking distance, and what with the sea and the sun, you should be back to rights in no time.'

When Edwina returned from dropping the colonel at the station, in the old rented Morris, the cottage, with its holiday air, was such that, from the moment she entered it, she could have burst into tears from relief. Instead she lay back on the chintz sofa and stared out at the sea. It seemed never ending.

Edwina's green eyes grew dreamy as she realised that

somewhere Robert might be alive, and perhaps even well, maybe not even missing, and certainly not dead. She rearranged a cushion, and as she did so she saw it looked familiar. It was exactly the same tapestry pattern as the footstool cover the colonel had been stitching when she first drove him, and which was now in the apartment.

She frowned at it, and then shook her head disbelievingly. The cottage must belong to the colonel. Typical of Colonel Dotey to lend her what must be his own cottage by the sea, and not say as much. She started to inspect the rest of the oak-beamed rooms. Everything was just as it should be in such a place, but there were no photographs anywhere. Not that there needed to be, for Mr Fleming had told her that since the colonel became a widower, he lived only for his work, adding, 'as the ancient saying goes'.

Edwina never knew whether Mr Fleming had quoted such phrases because he was posing as a butler, or whether they were his natural way of speaking.

She lay back against the cushions on the chintz sofa once more, half closing her eyes, not wanting to shut out the distant blue of the sea and the bright sunshine outside. She realised that by cutting herself off from nature, being in a city full of streets, buildings, people, more streets, more buildings, more people, bombs and bodies, suffering, she had been on the verge of a breakdown. Now, staring out at the beach, the water, the horizon, that poor bombed place that London had become seemed to have no reality at all, to be just a nightmare.

Edwina sighed a long shuddering sigh, as if she had just dropped something very heavy and was only now beginning to appreciate just what a burden it had been. For the next two or three weeks, at any rate, for as long as the colonel saw fit to leave her by the sea, she would try to reassure herself that only the beauty of the scene in front of her was real. Obviously the colonel had brought her to this place because he knew she had forgotten that there was a world outside of the war. Never mind the defences on the seashore, never mind the curls of barbed wire, the sea was still coming in and not even Hitler had been able to stop that. The sky was still blue, and he hadn't been able to do anything about that either. And what was more . . . she couldn't actually think of what was more and, quite suddenly, it didn't seem to matter.

Even as Edwina rested and then slept, her head on the colonel's hand-stitched cushion, Betty was woken by the first of many pains, intermittent, some strong, and some less so.

'Oh gracious, oh dear, oh dear!'

She staggered to the door of her cottage. She had to fetch Mr Smith to take her to the hospital, but when she eventually managed to push open first the door of his cottage, and then the door of his snug in the house, where he liked to repair after lunch, there was no Mr Smith, and what was worse, although she called and called, she soon realised that there was no one in the house, not even the dogs, everyone had gone for walks or drives, and she was miles from the doctor's surgery, and still more miles from the cottage hospital.

'Oh, why did I come back here, when it's so far from everywhere?' she asked the swaying trees and garden plants, the clouds overhead, the sheep beyond the river. 'Please, please, God, let someone come back to find me, before it's too late.'

Caro and Robyn had thirty-six-hour passes, courtesy, they both suspected, of Aunt Cicely pulling strings for them.

'Unheard of, quite unheard of. When they called me in to tell me – well, you can imagine,' Robyn said as she made her way towards the garage where she kept the Bentley. 'And to give us enough petrol to get us home and back! I nearly passed out.'

Caro could imagine.

'Did they say why we've been given all this?'

'No, but you know that friend of Aunt Cicely? Well, she just said that she knew that it was necessary. That was all. Talk about strings being pulled. Ours not to reason why, old thing. Ours just to jump into the great beast, and thank God for Aunt Cicely and her friends, for a sunny day, and for a great clear road where no one but us will be motoring – well, next to no one but us.'

In fact there were a great many vehicles on the road back to Brookefield and Chevrons that day, and since they were all military, and the dear old Bentley was far from being so, each time they sped past them, Robyn and Caro kissed their fingers to them and waved.

The men in the crowded vehicles, seeing a couple of uniformed beauties, waved and cheered in return. Caro, because she wasn't driving, constantly found herself looking back at the smiling faces, and each time, for a few seconds it seemed to her that she saw Jag and Francis or

Tom and Eddie, or others she knew, so that she seemed to be passing all of her friends, all waving to her and cheering.

She finally stopped looking back, determinedly shaking off the idea that she was somehow passing the missing, the untraced, those that she had not yet heard from, might never hear from again.

It started to rain as they were nearing home, and the woods and fields were taking on a familiar look, so that Caro felt her spirits lifting at the old sights and sounds, even the uneven roads taking on a soothing familiarity as Robyn steered the heavy car between the potholes, at the same time trying to avoid the banks of mud and the fallen branches at the side of the roads.

'Oh my God! Look! Look! Stop! Stop! Stop!'

The Bentley being the Bentley, it just was not possible for Robyn to pull up as suddenly as Caro was now begging her.

'Turn, you must turn, and go back!'

'Sorry, old thing, the Bentley is not a horse. We cannot rein in and turn on a sixpence.'

Robyn shoved the gear stick in and out of the appropriate settings, turning slowly, and then made her way back down the now rain-soaked road.

'What? What are we now stopping for?' she asked.

'We are stopping for – that!'

Caro leaped out of the car and started to run back.

'If this is another of your blessed fox cub rescue outings, I will wring your neck, young Caro,' Robyn muttered as she shut the Bentley door, and bending her head against the rising wind, she battled her way to where Caro was now standing, her arm around a stooped female figure who, in her turn, was leaning against a tree.

'It's Betty!' Caro said. 'I thought it was. It's Betty, and . . . and . . .' she nodded to Robyn, 'and she's you know!'

They both looked at Betty's baby bump, which, even to their unversed eyes, appeared as if it might be going to turn into a baby any time now.

Robyn swallowed hard, and pulled her cap further down on her nose. Babies were just not her.

'What are you doing here, Betty?' Caro demanded. 'Why are you walking alone in the rain?'

'No one at home. Everyone's out. No one in any of the cottages, no transport. I couldn't stay there alone, had to try to make it to the road and get a lift!'

'Well, I'm not surprised. Really, leave a bunch of men in charge of a pregnant woman, and *this* is what happens.'

Had it not been raining so hard Caro would have raised her eyes to heaven.

'We'd better put her on the back seat and drive like the clappers to the hospital,' Robyn told Caro quietly.

Caro extricated her arm from round the stooped and groaning figure, and walked Robyn a little way away from the tree and Betty.

'You can't drive too much like the clappers, Robyn,' Caro begged. 'I mean, one large crater in the road, and we could be left holding the baby. Don't worry,' she added, before turning back to Betty, 'if the worse comes to the worst I have some scissors in my handbag.'

'That has made me feel so much better about the whole situation, really it has,' Robyn said, rolling her eyes. She

390

raised her voice. 'Now come along, young Betty, let's get you to the hospital.'

They laid Betty across the back seat of the car, Caro bundling up her military coat for Betty to rest her feet on, keeping her legs higher than her head, in the hope that the baby would be induced to stay where he or she was, while Caro also found herself praying, possibly harder than she had ever prayed, that the main event would not start until they got poor Betty to the hospital.

'Oh dear, oh dear, oh dear!'

Each time Betty groaned, Robyn glanced at Caro, who glanced back at Betty.

'Oh dear, oh dear, oh dear!'

'Oh, for goodness' sake, Betty,' Robyn finally called to her. 'Have a good swear; we're all girls here!'

'Bloody bluebottles,' finally came from the back seat.

Robyn sighed with relief, not at Betty's more than feeble attempt at swearing, but because, bluebottles or no bluebottles, and after driving at what seemed like nought miles an hour, they had at long, long last reached the blasted hospital.

Afraid that they might damage the baby if they tried to carry Betty between them, and rather than wait for a stretcher, Caro and Robyn half carried, half dragged the luckless Betty through the cottage hospital doors, and slowly made their way to the sister's office.

Sister, still as large, bonny-faced and starchly pretty as the last time they had seen her, many years ago, smiled at them, looking from one anxious face to the other.

'Hello, Miss Harding, and you too, Miss Garland. Why, we haven't had the pleasure of seeing you since

Miss Garland pushed Miss Harding out of a tree, have we?'

'I didn't push her!' Caro protested. 'I fell on top of her, and then she fell, we both fell, at the same time.'

'Well, well, you were a couple of tomboys, at any rate, and so what have we here?' Sister went on. 'A young lady in the last throes of producing a lovely new life, is it?'

She pressed a bell, and two young nurses hurried to the office door. Sister beckoned them in.

'Wheelchair, and into a side ward with this young lady, please, Nurse Bennett and Nurse Collingwood.'

'Yes, Sister.'

'Don't keep a book on what time this baby arrives, will you, Nurse Collingwood? It does distress some mothers so if you keep shouting out one more push and I'll have won the jackpot.'

'But you won five shill—'

'Thank you, Nurse Collingwood, that will be all.'

'We are lucky here,' the sister said, with some satisfaction. 'We do have gas and air for our mothers for the end, and that is not always the case, at the moment, I'm afraid. Mind you, we have been very frugal. Country girls, taking plenty of exercise as they do, tend to deliver quite easily, which is how the maternity ward came to be nicknamed The Byre, but we don't tell them that. Gracious, not another mother, and another?' She raised her eyes to heaven. 'There must be something in the air this afternoon.' They all looked round as she stared past them into the car park beyond the little hospital. A charabanc had been parked, out of which were now streaming a host of pregnant women. 'Oh, not another influx from Westington on Sea,' Sister sighed. 'They will not keep pregnant evacuees there, just won't have anything to do with them. It's the old people, you know. They hate the sight of fecundity, I'm afraid. Can't take it, won't take it. Dear, oh dear, we can't have this. There must be forty of them. Some will have to go on to Brewham General, really they will.' Sister started to move with surprising agility. 'Stop the driver, stop the driver! He must take some on.'

As Betty was wheeled off, Caro and Robyn stared with some fascination as Sister placed herself firmly in front of the charabanc.

'Now that is a battle of the giants all right,' Robyn stated with some satisfaction. 'Sister versus a charabanc. The charabanc has no chance at all, but how long until the driver discovers as much?'

'I don't like the sound of that cough,' the medical officer said sharply.

Walter looked down, uncomfortably aware of the man's fierce look. The cough was only sporadic, but Caro too had noticed it getting worse.

'Where've you been lately, Mr Beresford?' The way he said 'Mister' was contemptuous, and Walter knew it. The MO obviously had little time for artists. 'I have to ask you – have you been down the Underground, or down the East End? Where? That cough is not good.'

Walter frowned. 'Well no, perhaps not. And yes, I have been here, there and everywhere, lately in a gun turret painting the men rehearsing the loading and reloading of those huge guns, and all that. Theirs is a tough regime,' he added, as if the medical officer would not know that.

The MO looked so unimpressed that Walter knew at once that as far as this medical johnny was concerned, painters were probably always on the wrong side of masculinity, and he couldn't care less if this one decided to strap himself to a mast in the North Sea to paint the work the men carried out on the convoys.

What he cared about was disease, and that cough sounded all too graveyard to him.

'I'm going to examine your chest, and if I find it wanting, you will be put on a back burner until it's cleared, you understand? Can't have you taking disease on board,' he jerked his head towards the port, 'giving God knows what to God knows who.'

Walter wished that he could relish the other man's contempt, but he couldn't. He knew that proper people, service people who were not artistic, despised types like himself as being unnecessary bits of fluff, as well they should.

The medical officer would be thinking, who needs people like this Beresford chap on the convoys? Who needs him under their feet? Haven't they trouble enough without having to take him along?

And yet in years to come, if people like Walter got it right, perhaps succeeding generations would stand back and say, 'So *that* was what it was like,' and be moved to pity at the sacrifice of it all, just as they stood in front of Sargent's vast painting of a line of blindfolded men gassed in the trenches of the Great War, hands on each other's shoulders, making their stilted, trembling, darkened way to who knew what. Through such work people realised the reality of the hell of war. So perhaps Walter, too, would, in the end, be proved to have had some sort of purpose, whatever the medical officer thought.

Walter started to strip, and as he did so he thought of Caro. She had left London on a thirty-six-hour pass. He wondered why. He was more concerned about that than about the outcome of this footling examination, which he felt sure would come to nothing.

Nurse Collingwood gave Caro and Robyn's uniforms a puzzled look.

'I don't recognise the uniform. You're from?'

'We're from the First Aid Nursing Yeomanry,' Robyn said in a crisp tone.

'First Aid Nursing Yeomanry? Ah, good, so you'll know how to deliver babies, won't you?'

'Of course,' Robyn replied, without batting an eyelid.

As Robyn gave the nurse the most accommodating smile, Caro's mouth dropped open, and with good reason. Until that moment the only thing either of them had ever delivered were officers to their destinations.

'Of course, nothing to it, we always say. What has to come down, has to come out, doesn't it?' Robyn went on blithely. 'Lots of hot water and tea, or, in time of war, just lots of hot water, and keep the tea for the nursing staff.'

Nurse Collingwood laughed.

'Very good, Officer. I always think lots of chin-up talk helps too. First babies can take a great deal of time to make their entrance, so if you don't mind, since we are looking like being short-staffed by times about forty, stay with your friend and let me know only when things get really interesting.'

Robyn nodded and, giving Caro a brisk 'follow me' look, she walked into the side ward, past a host of other pregnant women, to where Betty was now lying.

'Right, Betty,' she said in cheerful tones. 'We're going to stay with you until things get interesting.'

Betty gave a little gasp. 'Very well,' she said, and she put out a hand to Robyn, who despite wanting to drive off behind the now departing charabanc, took it.

Caro looked at the ceiling. She was not good with blood, so please God there was not going to be too much of it.

'You must have been coughing blood. You must have noticed?'

'Only a little, nothing to speak of.'

The medical officer sighed so heavily his nostrils flared.

'Can't let you join a ship in this condition. You'd infect the whole crew. No, it's curtains for your plans now, I'm afraid.'

He snapped his appointments book shut, as if he wanted to put an end to the whole boring business of giving Walter a medical.

Walter did up his jacket and sat down firmly in the chair opposite the MO.

'So what happens next?'

'You'll have to go to a sanatorium somewhere. There's one in Scotland, one in Haslemere, and one in Sussex beside the sea. Well, actually on the sea.'

'I'll take the seaside.'

'If they'll have you.'

'Yes, of course, if they'll have me. Is it crammed to the brim with TB patients?'

'I don't know. It's only just opened. There's less of your particular disease than in the last war, when it was rife in the trenches. I can telephone for you, if you like?'

The medical officer reached for the telephone on his desk, and as he did so Walter realised that he was in a great hurry to get rid of Walter, which was good, because Walter was in a great hurry to be shot of him.

'Bertie? Johnny here, Johnny Kirby, we were at St Nits together, remember . . . ?'

Walter stared in fascination as the medical officer changed from cold, despising medic to warm chummy old school friend.

'Got an artist chappy here with something just up your street, Bertie. You're not full yet, are you? Empty beds everywhere? Well, that does make a change to hear.' He lit a cigarette. 'Tell you what, I'll send him along. He can be your first victim, ha, ha.'

After a small burst of chummy public school laughter, and not much more than ten minutes later, Walter was handed a scrap of paper with the address of St Christopher's Sanatorium, Brewham on Sea.

When he reached his car he stared in some despondency at his neatly rolled-up luggage. It had been carefully sorted down to the last pencil and oilskin, all ready for joining a North Sea-bound convoy, not a sanatorium. He started to cough, holding on to the side of his car. Oh, for God's sake, or someone's sake, what a thing to contract. A poncy operatic disease that most people were convinced came from being dirty.

'Will I get better?' he had finally asked, before being turfed out of the medical officer's room.

'I dare say,' was all that came his way. 'Most people do nowadays. Treatments are more sophisticated, you know. A great deal more. Hot baths and cold air, and all sorts of fascinations.'

'Oh, well, that is something to which to look forward, then.'

Caro would have dearly liked to have lit another cigarette, and smoked it down to the stub, only that wasn't allowed in the hospital, so she thought about Walter instead. She imagined that he would be on his convoy, being thrown about the North Sea somewhere, perhaps feeling sick, which faced with the awful reality of Betty's hours and hours of painful labour was how she was now feeling.

She switched her mind to the last time she and Walter had seen each other. No tearful goodbyes, just love, and more love, and then he had left her sleeping, a note on her pillow that said 'I love you' and a drawing of her asleep underneath it. It was a scrap of paper she now carried everywhere with her in her top pocket.

'What's she saying?' Caro asked Robyn when she came back to reality.

Robyn was leaning over Betty, who had just been administered a nice dose of gas and air by Nurse Colling-wood.

'I don't know, how should I know? I just want the baby to arrive.'

'It's hours off yet, Sister says,' the nurse told them, before shooting out of the door again.

Robyn beckoned to Caro, who approached Betty with understandable caution.

'It's Miss Katherine, I know it is . . . Miss Katherine, Miss Katherine . . .'

Caro shrugged her shoulders and raised her eyebrows in Robyn's direction. It was hardly surprising that poor Betty was talking rubbish after what she'd been through.

'It's the gas and air, it must have made her delirious. People talk rot when they go under; I know, our dentist told me. Although actually, sometimes they talk more than rot, they talk truths that they don't want anyone to know so their dentist can blackmail them!'

'Shut up, Caro. Shut up and listen! This is all about your sister.'

Caro looked and felt crestfallen. Katherine, blasted Katherine, everywhere she went her sister seemed to be shadowing her now.

When Katherine was very young, she and David had played at death, at facing firing squads, at falling on their swords, along with the rest of the children on their estates. They had stalked each other, they had trapped each other, and now she herself was both stalked and trapped. She thought of how her mother had used to say, 'War games, darling, not always war games, surely?' And of how she used to reply, 'It comes with playing with boys, Mamma. Boys love war.'

Her mother . . . Faced with what she was going

through Katherine tried to imagine her mother, tried to think of what her mother would think of her. Please God, eventually she would know that her Katherine was not a traitor, but had died for her, for all of them, for Chevrons, for sunny days to come to them all again. That was what she and David had died for, and please, please, dear God, send her death quite soon, oh, soon, please soon!

Edwina was listening to Colonel Atkins, who had visited after what he called 'a polite interval'.

In true British fashion he did not mention the fact that it was his cottage in which Edwina was now staying, but Edwina, knowing that it was, had made a great effort to make it look as comfortable as possible – flowers, nice clean glasses for the gin and tonic, small snacks that she had fashioned out of pastry and a piece of cheese.

The colonel seemed pleased, looking round the cottage sitting room as if he hadn't seen it before, as if everything was quite new.

'This is nice,' he said in admiring tones.

'Yes, isn't it?' Edwina said, all innocence. 'I really love it here, do you know that, Colonel, dotey?'

Edwina handed him a drink.

'Now what's to do?'

'You're worried.' It was a statement.

'Not worried, just want to prepare myself for the future. Don't want to let anyone down. Now I'm rested I want to start tightening up again, preparing for the task ahead, you know? No good letting down too much, or I'll become useless to you. You know how it is, agents who are let off the hook too long never want to go back.'

The colonel looked surprised.

'How do you know that?'

'I read it in a cracker!'

She was to return to London, this side of soonish, perhaps in a few days. To return to social duties, disseminating false information.

'Yes, yes, of course, but this time it will be a bit different, won't it?'

The colonel nodded, and then went to close the cottage door, which, given the warmth of the day, had been left open. He shut out the beach, the sea, the sounds of the waves, and sat down.

'Here's how it will be,' he stated in his charmingly mellifluous voice.

It seemed that Edwina was to memorise two dates. One of them was the wrong date, and one of them was the right date. Only a handful of people knew those dates, and none of them, not one of them, knew which might be the right date.

'Oh God, Colonel, dotey,' Edwina started to laugh, 'this is a nightmare, truly it is. You'll have to get someone else.'

'For the reason of?' The colonel frowned.

'For the very good reason, Colonel, dotey, that I, Edwina O'Brien, am completely innumerate. You have only to tell me something with a number in it for me to completely forget it the next second. You'll have to get someone else.'

The colonel considered this for a moment.

'It will not be possible,' he said eventually. 'Just not possible because there is no one else we can trust in this matter, no one else who is in your position either. You are ideal. That is why we chose you.'

Edwina raised her eyes to heaven. 'Oh dear, oh dumpling, Colonel, dotey, then we may well be in the claggy!'

'I will find a way around this,' the colonel said after a short pause. 'I think, indeed, I know how we can overcome this problem. We will leave as small a space in time as is possible. Then we will whisk you up to London, you will give a party, disseminate the wrong information, and then make good your escape down here.'

'Will I need to do that?'

'No.' The Colonel lit a cigarette, looking thoughtful. 'But you might, just might want to enjoy another few days by the sea, that is all I am saying.'

Every night after that Edwina, while not exactly pacing the floor, did find difficulty in sleeping, wondering, always wondering what it was that was going to be expected of her, and wondering, always wondering if she would be capable of shouldering the responsibility. Supposing she failed? Supposing she let the side down? The consequences of her innumeracy might be unimaginable. These were thoughts that she found so difficult to keep away on her own in the evening when, after listening to the news on the wireless, she climbed the old oak stairs to bed.

It was all right during the day, when there were distractions, but in the dead of night the worries started.

A couple of days after Colonel Atkins's visit, Edwina's attention was caught by a man on the promenade painting. She knotted a scarf under her chin. It flapped furiously in the wind, making a noise that reminded her of sailing on the lake at home. She stared out to sea, wondering what the man was painting, and saw that it was a vast new arrival, something so strange that not just the painter, but everyone on the seafront was staring at what seemed like a harbour – either that or a sea of concrete – arriving.

'What on earth is that monstrosity, when it is at home?'

Walter turned at the sound of the lilting Irish tones and, seeing a beautiful young girl standing a few yards away from him, he beckoned her over.

'Don't I know you?' he asked above the sound of the waves, and the excited voices that were gathering around them.

'No – no, not at all. I am at present anonymous to all but my closest friends.'

Walter narrowed his eyes. 'Of course I know you! You're a friend of Caro Garland. We met at the flat—' He turned away discreetly, coughing briefly. 'I thought as soon as I heard your voice that it rang a bell.' He looked down at her, after putting away his handkerchief. 'You're looking very well and beautiful, if you don't mind me saying, Miss O'Brien.'

'Oh, I don't mind you saying at all. It's just that I wonder that you feel you have to say anything, so. I mean, there is a war on, and really, talk of beauty and such like matters is on the back burner until after it is over, surely?'

'Oh, I love the Irish. They can talk better nonsense than anyone else, and yet it is always nonsense grounded in a strange kind of reality.'

'And the Irish love you, just so long as you're not English.'

Walter started to laugh, and then coughed again, once more turning away, this time embarrassed.

'It's the sea air, it's too healthy!' he joked.

'Whenever yous laughs, yous coughs,' Edwina told him, but she was careful not to glance back up the road behind them, where she had seen an increasing number of nurses wheeling patients from the sanatorium. It would have taken an idiot not to recognise that Walter had an unnaturally high colour, and the almost ethereal look that always seemed to accompany tuberculosis, even in its earliest stages.

'You'll be painting the new arrival then, Mr Beresford?' she asked to distract him, nodding towards the sea.

'I am going to do a watercolour of it straight away. Somehow it seems to underline the strangeness of it all.'

They both stared ahead of them at the strange islands of concrete.

'I don't know what it is, but whatever it is, it looks formidably mysterious and important,' Walter said.

Edwina frowned. She knew the colonel would be calling her back to London soon, and she had a feeling that what was in front of them was part of the reason, but how, or what her part would be she had no idea.

Part of Operation Overlord, the plan codenamed Operation Neptune involved seven battleships, two monitors, twenty-three cruisers, three gunboats, 105 destroyers and over one thousand smaller vessels.

The navy's orders were quite simple.

First of all it was to minesweep the English Channel, making corridors of safety for the combined British and American invading force. Next it was to keep up offshore bombardment, while escorting and landing troops and keeping German destroyers, E-boats and U-boats away from the said landings and supplies.

Next it was to escort two million tons of concrete and steel – two floating harbours – that would put the necessity of capturing a major French port to open up the supply chain on the back burner until such time that it would prove necessary. The Mulberry harbours, as they were known, were made up of sunken blocks, and prefabricated piers and jetties.

But before troops could be sent or the harbours constructed, they needed to fool the enemy with proposed dates: put the German command on a first alert, let them relax when they found out it was wrong, then put them on another wrong alert, while all the time waiting, waiting, for that most elusive of moments in the English Channel – a fine day.

By the time Betty's baby finally decided to make his entrance into this world, an overworked sister and an exhausted midwife had arrived beside his mother to complete his entrance into life. To Caro's great relief, but Robyn's hurt pride, the Fanys were asked to leave before he took his first bow.

'What a shame to miss the last act,' Robyn said, as they staggered out of the cottage hospital and flung themselves into the Bentley, having waited and waited to see the baby, who was finally presented to them as a small red head wrapped in a blue towel.

'Betty will be pleased to have a boy,' Caro stated with some satisfaction.

'And why not a girl, pray?'

'Because he can help on the farm, that's why,' Caro said, yawning.

They both lay back in their car seats, heads lolling, caps forward.

'Who'd be a midwife? I've had more sleep in the Blitz than I had last night,' Caro grumbled.

It was Robyn's turn to yawn. 'It is not easy to deliver babies,' she agreed eventually. 'Much worse to have one, though. I think I might have been put off for ever. It all seems to take so long. It would be so much better if you just got a pain and it shot out.'

Caro looked appalled at this notion, then she too yawned.

'And I mean to say, have you ever seen so many pregnant women?' Robyn continued.

'Apparently nowadays pregnant women are more or less banned from cities, so they bus the poor creatures out to country areas and just offload them anywhere and everywhere. It seems no one wants to know about you if you're a pregnant evacuee.'

'Mmm, I know. Poor Sister. She doesn't flap easily, but she was flapping like a tent door in a desert storm last night.'

'Oh dear, what a thought, Sister as tent *and* door.'

They started to laugh.

'Oh, for heaven's sake, here we are talking tosh about

babies when we haven't even touched on *the* subject. I mean, what about what Betty was on about in her delirium?'

'How do you mean?'

'What do you mean, how do I mean?'

Caro looked mulish. Robyn knew the look. She turned the engine over, and put the car into gear.

'I understand. You need a bit of time to absorb what we heard.'

Caro put her feet up on the dashboard, and as a favour Robyn let her leave them there. It had been quite a night, and if what Betty had muttered in her delirium was true, then there was almost too much to think about, particularly for Caro – well, particularly for all the Garlands, and all the Astleys. She turned to say something to Caro, but she was fast asleep.

Betty's little boy was underweight, but she was able to feed him straight away.

'I expect you would like to call him after his father, wouldn't you?' Smith asked when he called at the cottage hospital a couple of days later.

Betty was still so tired, and so traumatised by the baby's arrival, she could only smile weakly. For the life of her, for a few seconds she couldn't even remember what her late husband's name was meant to be.

She nodded and smiled at Smith in a vague way.

'It was a dreadful shame that the baby should decide to arrive when there was no one else in the house,' Smith said in a shocked voice. It was as if protocol had been broken. 'No one at Chevrons to drive you here. I don't know who to blame, but it shouldn't have happened. It certainly wouldn't have happened in Mrs Garland's day, I know that. That's a woman's touch, you know. Remembering details, that's what women are so good at. Let's see the little chap.'

Betty pushed the small cot towards him. Smith stared in.

'He looks very like that photograph of your late husband in your cottage, I would say,' he said at last. 'Not at all like Winston Churchill,' he finished.

Betty nodded, pleased.

'I shall call him David, after the late— after the . . . Bible, and then his father's names, Mr Smith,' she told Smith. 'And I would be thrilled if you would stand as his godfather.'

Raymond frowned, and his cheeks reddened.

'That is a very nice thought, Betty, and although some might consider me too old for the responsibility, I accept, gladly, really I do.'

They both smiled, and then looked down at the baby.

'David can help on the farm, when he gets older, of course. But until then I'll make sure he always has a place at Chevrons, that I will, Betty. My godson will have the run of the place, of that you can be sure.'

They both looked pleased and shy at the same time, and were oddly glad when Nurse Collingwood came bustling into the room and removed the flowers that Smith had brought to put them in a vase, and Smith was able to take his leave without too much embarrassment on either side.

He walked back down the hospital corridor. There was nothing quite like a new life – nothing to beat it.

Aunt Cicely's face was grave. She had arranged for Robyn to come back on compassionate leave, not on her own account, not on account of her father, but because of their neighbour, David Astley Senior.

'He has just had confirmation that young David is as previously presumed – dead. The news came from a contact in the War Office, or was it the Foreign Office? At any rate they have heard that he is dead, although not killed in battle.' She paused. 'Apparently he was not a Nazi, he was just posing as a Nazi all this time, while acting on behalf of his country.'

Robyn tried to look amazed, and then realised she had failed, because Aunt Cicely said, 'You knew something of this, did you?'

Robyn shook her head. 'I didn't know about David, but we did hear, in a rather roundabout way, that Katherine might – well, that she might have been an agent, in France.'

'Yes. She was.'

Aunt Cicely looked away. She had known young Katherine since she was born. 'She too, you know, is no longer with us . . . so brave.'

Robyn dropped her eyes to the floor. She had never seen Aunt Cicely upset. It didn't seem fair that the old lady had had to live through so many wars, and that now she had to face yet more bad news, and such bad news too. Robyn put out a hand and touched her arm.

'Why don't we both sit down?'

'Why were you so late back on your leave?' Aunt Cicely asked suddenly, after a long silence during which Robyn saw her willing herself to take control of her feelings. 'I have been waiting and waiting.'

'Yes, I'm sorry, Aunt Cicely, but you know, it was Betty. Well, at least you don't know Betty. She was a maid at Chevrons, and she married and had a baby, and we found her in the woods, or rather beside the road, and we had to take her to hospital, and it all took rather a long time – having the baby, I mean – because we had to stay with her until the end, there was no one else, the hospital being so crowded.'

Aunt Cicely nodded, it was so difficult to know what to say, but her feelings were in such a tangle, she had to find a way. It was just not good enough to brush it all under the carpet. For once she would have her say.

'We have all been so hard on those two young people.' She stood up again, and started to walk up and down. 'So hard on them, and yet all the time they were being so brave, risking their lives in the most terrible way, risking everything so they could help the war, and long, long before it happened.'

'We weren't to know. None of us knew, how could we?'

'Yes, but now we do, we must make reparation in every way we can.'

Robyn nodded, and now she too stood up.

'I must go and talk to Caro. Really, the Astleys and the Garlands should meet. It is the only way.'

'You can only have a few more hours of your leave left.'

'Just enough to get a little done.'

Robyn's tone was sad and sober. She knew that neither David nor Katherine's names had been allowed to be mentioned in either household. Now they would probably still not be allowed to be mentioned, but for really very different reasons. The guilt of both households, the grief, the feelings of regret – they would all be so hard to bear, and yet that was war.

She turned back to say something to her aunt, but the old lady had left the room, wanting to be alone with her feelings, which was only understandable.

Robyn sighed. She would go and see her father and tell him that Bill wanted to speak to him. It would not be what he would want to hear, but there it was. Bill wanted to marry her. Now that they had heard that poor Eddie had died of pneumonia in one of those utterly wretched prisoner of war camps, Robyn wanted to be married to Bill as quickly as possible, before everything changed, as things had a habit of doing nowadays, before either one of them was taken, before something else happened.

'Father is going to write Katherine's name back in the Bible,' Caro announced, when they returned to London later that day.

It seemed that was all she had to say on the matter of her beloved sister, and really, for the moment, perhaps it was quite enough. The misery of what they had all said about Katherine, about what they had wished on her, had hit them both hard, almost more than the news of her death.

No point in saying to each other 'we weren't to know'

and all that kind of drivel. No point at all. But later, when they had had a bath, changed and opened a bottle of gin, Robyn noticed that Caro's face was more heavily made up than usual, her mascara too thickly applied, her nose heavily powdered, and that around her neck she was wearing Katherine's green scarf.

Chapter Thirteen

Mr Fleming was looking inscrutable.

'The bitter past, more welcome is the sweet,' he murmured.

'Shakespeare, Shakespeare, Shakespeare, was there anything he didn't say first?'

Mrs Cherry stubbed out her cigarette preparatory to getting up and starting to make the hors d'oeuvres for that evening. There was to be a large and grand dinner party, a party at which much had to be accomplished in a very few hours.

'I only hope our Edwina has got it right,' she murmured to Mr Fleming, who said nothing, only breathing on a glass and polishing it to glistening perfection.

He would not say, he could not say, that the two dates Mrs Cherry's old school friend from convent days had been given, were both wrong, as wrong as wrong could be, and that Colonel Atkins and he were counting on her to get both wrong, or to get both right, it really didn't matter, just so long as she made a good entrance to the dinner gathering – late and, most of all, reliably drunk.

Edwina now entered the kitchen, looking moody. She

surveyed its occupants with a resentful expression. She plucked one of Mrs Cherry's cigarettes from its packet and lit it without so much as a by-your-leave. They waited, watching her, as she smoked, too quickly and without any sign of enjoyment.

'Why is it so difficult to pretend to be drunk?' she asked no one in particular, after a short pause. 'It should be easy to pretend to be drunk, but I swear to goodness, it's more difficult than pretending to be sober when you're drunk, and that is a fact.'

'You could get drunk, if you wanted?' Mrs Cherry murmured, quickly hiding what was left of her cigarettes.

'No, I can't *get* drunk, I must *appear* drunk, those are my instructions,' Edwina replied.

'Oh, well, you know best, dear,' Mrs Cherry told her in a nannying tone.

'I don't know best. If I knew best, I wouldn't be here with you, then, would I?' Edwina stubbed out Mrs Cherry's cigarette halfway down, then left the kitchen as abruptly as she had entered it.

'She was always a bit nervy, even at school. As I remember it, she was one of those girls that used to swell up before exams,' Mrs Cherry stated, picking up the cigarette and straightening it out, before replacing it carefully in her packet.

'Let's hope she doesn't swell up until after the dinner party,' Mr Fleming stated, his cold grey eyes staring after her.

In the bathroom Edwina studied her reflection. Despite Trixie's really quite expert touch with the cosmetics, Edwina looked deathly pale, as if she had not spent most of the last weeks at the seaside. It was nerves, nerves, nerves. She leaned her head against the mirror. It was cool and calming. She straightened up, and stared at herself: still pale, but not looking quite so much like death warmed up. She pinched her cheeks hard, and watched with some interest as colour returned to them.

'I am in command of information, I disseminate it, in a drunken manner, while remaining sober. It is quite simple.'

And yet the simplest tasks always seemed to be the hardest. Her guest list, carefully chosen, was made up of at least two known double agents, and one suspect traitor. Never mind their nationality, Edwina was aware that they were in constant contact with the enemy. She sighed, before leaving the bathroom, and issuing forth to the drawing room where Mr Fleming would make sure that she was given water, not gin, and where she would begin acting out her role.

'Did you put any gin in this, Fleming?' she asked him, as the first guest was announced. 'I don't think you put any gin in this, really I don't. I think this is water, in fact I'm sure of it. What a thing,' she went on gaily, 'when one's butler mistakes one's poison and gives one water instead of gin.'

Edwina had always thought the world of the double agent was terrible, playing both sides against each other, never knowing quite who to trust, or quite who trusted you. Most particularly tonight, through narrowed and splendidly feigned drunken eyes, she watched the two suspects pretending to find her amusing while listening, always listening, to what she was saying. The date of the reinvasion of France, she had been told, unofficially of course, was to be . . .

'My dear we have so enjoyed ourselves!'

The first to leave, a balding civilian, was all too well known to Mr Fleming. Fleming had been watching him since long before the war; now he watched him with minute interest, silently saying to himself, 'Off you go, traitor. Off you go to your Nazi masters. Enjoy yourself while you can because, believe me, you are not long for this world.'

'Strangling's too good for their kind, wouldn't you say, Mr Fleming?' Mrs Cherry asked him, *sotto voce*, a few minutes later, as the party continued apace.

Mr Fleming held up a glass to the light. He liked a perfectly polished glass. In fact he liked everything what he called 'tidy'. He would make sure that the gentlemen in question would, quite soon, be 'tidied up'. He would see to it himself.

'What's now? I could swear I just heard Miss Edwina ring, Mr Fleming.'

'So you did, Mrs Cherry. The guests must be ready to leave.'

There had been another air raid while the dinner party was taking place, and now, as the all clear sounded, Mr Fleming hung his tea towel carefully, straightened his tie, removed his service apron, and put on his black jacket once more.

The last of the guests had to be seen out into the noisy night, the light of the fires from the bombs should be enough to see them all home. He held the door for them, his expression, once his two suspects had gone,

416

phlegmatic. Soon it would really be the beginning of the end of the war, and these people, whom it had been his job to use ruthlessly and heartlessly – sometimes for their own good, sometimes not – would be able to return to their own countries. But before then all that was on anyone's mind was this last great push across that narrow strip of water known as the English Channel.

'Well, thank God that is over!' Edwina rolled her eyes at Mr Fleming. 'I never ever want to have to do something like that again.'

'Bit of a strain, was it, Miss Edwina?' Mr Fleming managed to look both sanguine and polite at the same time.

'At least now I can have a drink! Bring me a whisky, for pity's sake, Mr Fleming. Half a vat of whisky in a large glass, for the love of everything.'

Mr Fleming handed her a double Scotch in a Waterford crystal glass. Edwina glanced up at him briefly, and it was then that a very strange thing happened, so strange indeed that if she hadn't been raising a glass to her lips, Edwina's mouth would have dropped open.

Mr Fleming smiled.

'Well done, Miss Edwina,' he said gravely. 'You acted drunk better than Sarah Bernhardt could have done, better than Duse, and certainly better than anyone on the West End stage of today, and that is my considered opinion.'

'That from you, Mr Fleming, dotey, is as good as a diamond bracelet, and that is for certain.'

Edwina took a very generous sip of her Scotch.

'Now I *can* get tight!' she said. 'I can get as tight as

several ticks. Sit down and have one with me, do, Mr Fleming.'

Mr Fleming removed his black jacket, went to the drinks tray and poured himself a generous whisky.

'Let's ask Trixie and Mrs C to join us. Let's all celebrate together just for a little. Since the all clear has sounded, both inside the flat and out, surely we should have some *craic*, as we say in Ireland.'

A party broke out as soon as the others arrived, and pretty soon the drawing room resounded to genuine gaiety and, as is so often the case with impromptu parties, it turned out to be a great deal better than anything of a more formal nature that had been held in that room before. The four of them clinked glasses, and laughed and talked all at once, and then clinked glasses again and drank some more. There was so much to drink to, most of all the hope of victory in Europe.

'I feel quite sober, so I must be tight!' Edwina joked, just as Mr Fleming raised his arm.

'Ssh.'

They listened.

'I'm very much afraid it was the doorbell.'

They all looked at one another with resigned expressions, and Trixie and Mrs Cherry immediately hurried off to the safety of the kitchen, clutching their drinks.

'It's probably someone who has left something behind, Miss Edwina,' Mr Fleming murmured. 'More than likely.'

'Well, tell them to go away. Miss O'Brien has had it,' Edwina muttered as she slid further down the sofa into the cushions.

Mr Fleming quickly put his jacket back on, checking the inner pocket for the reassuring feel of his gun.

'You stay there,' he said quietly to Edwina, who gave him a droll look.

'Feeling the way I do, I have no choice, Mr Fleming, dotey,' she returned. 'I can honestly . . . er . . . no, I don't think I can say anything honestly, as a matter of fact, but I can tell you, categorically, Mr Fleming, that should you require me to appear sober within the next half an hour, or even the next half a day, I doubt very much that I could oblige.'

'You stay just where you are, Miss Edwina. You have had quite enough to do tonight.'

After a minute or two Mr Fleming was back.

'It's a visitor for you, Miss Edwina,' he told her.

'Not Roberto at this time of night? No, no, no, please not Roberto,' Edwina murmured, groaning and holding a cushion over her face. 'Please, please not Roberto, please!'

Mr Fleming's expression was serious.

'Not Roberto, no, Miss Edwina. No, this person is maintaining he is a certain Robert . . .'

'Oh, so he's taken to anglicising himself now, has he?' Edwina groaned, throwing the cushion into another chair. 'Tell him I am sick and weary, and cannot receive anyone.'

Mr Fleming leaned forward and gave her a card.

'Captain Robert Plume is what it says on this card. He's waiting outside.'

Mr Fleming's face was an unusual picture of innocence as Edwina's expression changed from vaguely tight to utter incredulity as she stared at the card. She struggled up from her prone position and, shoeless, her hair streaming down her back, she ran out into the hall.

'Robert? Robert? Is it really you?'

Seconds later, as he closed the drawing-room door behind the two lovers, Mr Fleming smiled for a second time that night.

Everything was quite tidy in there. He liked that.

Walter stared at the watercolour he had done of the Mulberry harbour. It was an odd little painting because really, when you thought about it, painting floating concrete was a strange thing to do, but the truth was that the floating islands that he had painted before they started on their journey held a mystery, a menace, and he hoped he had managed to get the feeling that they were about something so important, it was almost unimaginable.

Now, despite terrible losses, they all knew that victory in Europe was imminent, that Hitler was defeated, that the Allied armies had advanced and crushed the mighty forces of Germany. And yet still there was no announcement.

It was as if the authorities, in their wondrous ability to get everything wrong, imagined that by cheering up the battered people of Britain who had fought on the home front, given their all, including their loved ones, to the war effort, and were now so exhausted that they were hardly able to switch on their wirelesses for the news; it was as if they were reluctant to admit that there was a victory to hand, because it would mean that their power might be lessened.

'You know they were all for suppressing poor old Vera Lynn singing the "White Cliffs of Dover", don't you?' one of Walter's old friends told him, when he was visiting Walter in the sanatorium.

He nodded towards an oil painting.

'Who's she when she's at home? Someone special? Very beautiful indeed, very beautiful.'

Walter smiled.

'Yes, she is beautiful, isn't she?' he agreed. 'And yes, she is special, although not to me. She was staying along the way for a few weeks, and she used to come to see me work, so I used her ruthlessly as a model.'

'Beautiful copper-coloured hair, beautiful colour, and that white skin – what a stunner.'

'Oh, yes, she is a beauty, all right, and quite a handful, but her heart lies in the hands of another.'

'Shame.'

Walter shook his head. 'No, no, she would be too much for either you or me to handle, old boy, but truly.'

His friend left him soon after, and Walter stared at the painting he had done of Edwina. It was good. Even he had to admit that. It captured her restless provocative spirit, as well as her beauty.

He looked at his watch. Any minute now his lucky charm would be arriving. He went to the mirror and stared at himself. They hadn't seen each other for so long, she thinking he was on convoys, he too afraid to tell her that he was holed up in a sanatorium, not wanting sympathy, not wanting to burden her either, only wanting to get better. And now, it seemed, he was. The sea air, the weeks spent outdoors, painting, had caught the bastard disease in its infancy, and whacked the life out of it, thank God.

He cleared his throat. No cough, not even a trace of it. He started to walk up and down. Perhaps she had met someone else? Perhaps that was why she was late? She had been to the wall and back waiting for him, thinking that he was on convoys, and now found that she was in love with someone else. It would not be surprising. Caro, after all, was an original. Maybe not a beauty like Edwina O'Brien, or Katherine Garland, but quite definitely not like anyone else. He would dearly have liked a cigarette. For the first time for months he could have smoked. He looked out at the gardens that ran down to the beach. Failing her arrival over the next five minutes, he would go for a walk to try to calm himself. He had written to her about everything, but it seemed she had been sent up North to sort out some personnel problems, and had, after many months, only just come back to London. She had written to him to say she would be down the following week, this afternoon. But she wasn't. She was very much not down, and he was very much waiting for her, and it was driving him mad.

He flung himself through the French windows of his large bedsitting room, and walked off down the lawn, just as Caro's car was drawing up outside the sanatorium.

She stepped out of it, and then stood looking about her. The house was a pleasant Edwardian country house of the sort that prosperous families would use for the summer holidays, and then shut up for the rest of the year. She walked up the steps, to find a nurse wheeling a patient out of the double doors.

'I'm looking for Walter Beresford, could you direct me to his room?'

The nurse indicated behind her. 'Ground floor, number seven. Just follow the smell of paint and turpentine!'

They both laughed, and Caro's pace quickened as she realised just how long it was since they had seen each other, just how long since they had kissed and held each other. Walter had said in his letter that he was better – but would he look the same?

She knocked on his door and called, but on not receiving an answer she pushed it gently open. No Walter, just paintings, lots of different paintings. She hurried past them, because in the distance she could see a familiar figure walking up the garden. She started to run towards it, as fast as you never run in a dream, although it might have been a dream, because coming towards her was Walter, not sick-looking or aged, but bronzed and well, and holding out his arms to her.

They kissed and kissed, and kissed some more, and then they walked up the lawn and into Walter's room and it was only then that Caro saw the painting that Walter's friend had so admired earlier.

Caro stared at it.

'What is this?' she asked tightly, turning back to him. 'How did you do this, and when?'

Walter attempted to put his arm around her, but she stepped away from him, determined on the truth.

'This is a painting I did of a young woman, one Edwina O'Brien, whom I happened to meet when the powers that be sent her down here on a sabbatical, to stay at Colonel Atkins's cottage.'

'Oh, really?'

'Yes, oh really.'

Caro stared up at the painting, and as she did so her anger subsided. It was brilliant. The painter, quite evidently not in love with his subject, had captured the wild waywardness, the look of defiance in the eyes, the free spirit that was Edwina.

'I seem to be doomed to be always seeing portraits of beautiful women by you,' she complained, turning to Walter.

Walter took her in his arms.

'I promise you that from now on I shall paint only you and the sea,' he told her.

Caro frowned. 'That would be quite dull.'

'Not to me.'

'No, maybe not, but to me. How come I never knew that you and Edwina were—'

She stopped suddenly stepping back and away from him as she remembered that there was so much that neither of them knew, so much to catch up on. Most of all Walter didn't know about Katherine.

'I'm afraid we have had bad news of Katherine, and David,' she confessed.

Walter's expression immediately changed from happy and expansive to grave, and by the time Caro had finished telling him her news there were tears in his eyes, and in hers too.

'We weren't to know, were we? We all keep saying "we weren't to know", although it doesn't seem to do much good.'

'No, of course we weren't to know, but it doesn't

424

stop the feelings of guilt, of wishing to God we had known.'

Walter turned away, but Caro followed him, walking round so that they faced each other. In the distance there was the sound of the sea, and of the gulls, of the wind getting up, gradually seeming to invade the seashore, just as other feelings, feelings of uncertainty, and yes, shamingly, of jealousy, started to flood Caro's mind.

'Is it worse for you? Because you loved her?' she asked, eventually. 'Because you were in love with her?'

'Good God, no. I wasn't in love with Katherine as I am with you,' Walter stated. 'I fell in love with your sister, as all men fall in love with a beautiful woman, but I never knew her, I never even got to know her. Only ever painted the shell, really. And the ladybird, of course . . . Strange thing to have wanted painted on her.'

'It was one of her code names that she had started to use, long before the war.'

'She said it was one of her nicknames. I know she didn't want Astley to see it.'

'No, just because it was a code name. Typical of Katherine, to dare to ask you.'

Walter took Caro in his arms, and held her against him.

'You're the girl I love, my lucky charm. No one else. I know you – I never knew Katherine, only the person she was pretending to be. And if I had I would still not have loved her as I love you, believe me.'

They both turned towards the windows, and because sometimes that is the only thing to do, they went out for a long walk to try to make sense of things.

To begin with, the Astley and the Garland families were at a loss as to how to deal with their grief, and the inevitable guilt attached to their treatment of their young.

Finally, it was Aunt Cicely's idea to bring the two families together and talk about a fitting memorial, although it was Caro who thought of the form it might take.

'They always used to love to play together, ever since they were small,' she told the assembled company, speaking hesitantly because all eyes were on her, and she was suddenly aware that she was the youngest. 'Well, you know how it is, Katherine and David always had their favourite haunts, so I was thinking, how about instead of an actual memorial, we make a walk in their memory?'

The heads of the two families stared at her, their faces grave.

'After all, our two family estates run so close to each other, we could make a beautiful walk, full of wild flowers on either side, and we could make quiet places with benches to sit upon where we could put quotations in both their memories, and there could be pieces of sculpture along the way – a nightingale, for instance, and a pair of swallows – which could be fashioned out of some of their favourite things. It could be beautiful, and different – like they were – beautiful, and different.'

And so it was decided that this was what they would do, and then both families knew that the feelings of guilt and sorrow would eventually be replaced by something more joyous. The idea came that the Garlands and the Astleys would make the walk together once a year in memory of their brave young, who had lived and died for freedom.

Certainly, hardly had the meeting finished than Jag and Francis, back from the war without a scratch – 'Well, isn't that the twins all over?' Mr Smith remarked to Betty – at once set about mowing and planting, felling and seeding, to make the necessary grass paths and flowered ways, while Anthony Garland and David Astley Senior commissioned Walter to make a sculpture of Katherine and David, walking hand in hand, as they had always used to do in the happy days before the war.

Once finished the sculpture which had the words 'Goodnight Sweetheart' engraved on the bottom, was placed at the end of the woodland walk, in the hope that everyone would carry away with them the lasting impression of a young couple moving towards the fields beyond, larks above them singing, the lush grass of their homeland beneath their feet.

Epilogue

After a suitable delay, during which, inevitably, Edwina called off her wedding several times, she and Robert were married in Ireland. The occasion kept its promise to be riotous, if only because there was food in Ireland – ice cream and butter, and yards of beef and lamb, and chickens and . . . well, food.

Once the little group of friends had returned and duly recovered from the week-long celebrations, Walter and Caro too were married on a sunny summer day at Chevrons. But for them there was not quite such plenty, because of rationing, except in affection, and lasting good wishes.

Not long after that Robyn and Bill too were married. Robyn was given in marriage from Brookefield House, by her father, while Aunt Cicely, to everyone's astonishment, rolled up her sleeves and made the wedding cake herself.

Trixie and Colonel Atkins married too, but very quietly, because, as Trixie said, 'He's a bit shy, you know.'

The colonel was fed up with London, so they settled happily in his cottage by the sea, which suited both of them admirably.

'Well, I think that's quite enough weddings for the moment, don't you?' Aunt Cicely remarked crisply to no one except the Cairn Ferriers, a few days after her niece had driven off in Bill's Austin for a very prolonged honeymoon. 'Any more festivities, and really this piece of borrowed veiling will have quite given out.'

She wrapped the old lace up in tissue paper and put it in an old and dusty trunk. She herself had never had any desire to be married, which was probably why she had kept her own mother's veil so carefully. It was the only wedding veil she would ever have, and a reminder of her mother.

Having completed this task, she and the dogs went out of the house and stood on the steps waiting for Mr Smith, who, after a short pause, arrived driving, of all things, Robyn's Bentley.

'Well, there we are, Miss Harding, all ready for you!'

They both smiled as Mr Smith handed first the dogs up, placing them on the back seat, and then, carefully, reverentially, he handed Aunt Cicely into the driver's seat.

'Now the great thing about driving, Miss Harding, is that you need to know how to . . .'

Half an hour later Aunt Cicely, her face beaming with the kind of contentment that it is impossible to quite capture, steered the Bentley out of the drive and on to the open road.

'Gracious heavens, Mr Smith, there's only one thing one can say at a moment like this – and that is "Poop, poop!"'

She rammed her hat further down on her head.

'What an adventure! Just you and I and the open road.

I'm sorry to tell you, but I have a mind to think that this is what life is all about!'

Mr Smith, one hand poised carefully over the handbrake, could only agree. And of one thing he was particularly certain, and that was when he got back to Chevrons, he would have a great story to tell Betty.

Back at Chevrons, only Betty ever went into the Long Room. Walter's painting still being a sad reminder of the happy days before the war, the family could not bear to go in. When Betty did go in, she was careful that it was when none of the family was around, and she would hold up her little son and go through the names of everyone there depicted.

'That's Mummy, and that's Aunt Trixie, and that's Uncle Raymond – and that's Mr Anthony, and that's Mr Jag and Mr Francis.'

She always left Miss Katherine until the last, always stopped in front of the beautiful dark-haired Katherine Garland, in her blue dress, and stared up at her in silent worship. For some reason, over the weeks and months it seemed to Betty that Miss Katherine's beauty appeared to have grown. Not just her face, and her lovely dark hair, but the expression of haunting sadness in her eyes, and the fact that she was holding out her left hand with the tiny ladybird painted on it, where in happier times, she would have had a wedding ring, meant so much to someone who had once decoded her increasingly desperate messages from France.

'*Ladybird*,' Betty would murmur for her little boy to repeat. '*Ladybird.*'

Eventually she did not have to repeat the word. The moment that he went into the room he would point up at it first because, in common with his mother, he appeared to think that it was the centrepiece of the painting. Finally, it seemed, the Ladybird had come home, and that perhaps, was her final message.

THE END

If you enjoyed *Goodnight Sweetheart*, look out for Charlotte Bingham's next novel, *The Enchanted*.

Charlotte Bingham would like to invite you to visit her website at www.charlottebingham.com

THE ENCHANTED
by Charlotte Bingham

Joint ownership of a small dark chestnut colt
from western Ireland brings together a
group of very different people . . .

When Kathleen finds a mare in foal, despite the fact that
she and her father can barely afford to feed her they
take her in. Tragically the mare dies, leaving an orphan
which they name The Enchanted. But even as he is
growing up among Ireland's lush pastures, Kathleen
knows that they will, eventually have to sell him, and
with him will go her heart . . .

The recently widowed Helena is encouraged by her
eccentric friend Millie to take the plunge and buy
a share in a horse. Suddenly, both women find
themselves involved not just in the fate of the little
horse, but of Rory James, his trainer, who has only
recently taken over the run-down racing yard.

Luck does not run Rory's way when The Enchanted
mysteriously sickens. It seems only Kathleen can help,
and so it is that under her care The Enchanted is able
to live up to his name and astonishing things start to
happen to all those around the little horse . . .

'Charlotte Bingham's devotees will recognise her
supreme skill as a storyteller'
Independent on Sunday

9780593055946

NOW AVAILABLE FROM BANTAM PRESS

BANTAM PRESS